Dead Moons
RISING

First book in the Honest Scrolls series

Jack Whitney

Bonus Scene Edition

For my sister.

For supporting and encouraging me always.
And for giving me the courage to burn the kingdom myself.

Thank you for the torch.

Warnings

The Honest Scrolls series
is classified as an adult, dark, high fantasy series.

It is therefore not intended for persons under the age of
eighteen.

Dead Moons Rising contains the following triggers and
subjects:
Graphic sex with one or more persons, graphic sex with
belts, explicit language, gore, battle scenes, abuse, death,
sexual assault, and mentions of rape, incest, and mental
manipulation.

This is a work of fiction.

Please keep these triggers in mind and proceed.

PROLOGUE: *History of Haerland*

The Chronicles say there was once a time, so very long ago, when the creatures of Haerland, both big and small, could roam free about the undisturbed and timeless lands without fear or restraint. A time when the curses of the current Age did not exist. A time when the term 'war' had no meaning.

This was the First Age.

During this Age, the earthen mother herself, which the land had been named, lived in complete harmony with her creatures. After centuries of solitude, however, Haerland found herself growing lonely. She turned to the Architects of the sky and earth in the hopes they would answer with a solution.

Three Architects answered her call.

The first was the Ghost of the Sea.

"In the southern waters," said the Sea, "you will find my gift. Take caution, dear Haerland. Treat this gift as you do your creatures. Only then will it serve you with respect and not disdain."

For a fortnight, Haerland searched up and down the southeastern coast. On the fifteenth sunrise, the Sea's gift showed itself.

A man had washed up on the beach, sand covering his olive skin. Haerland approached him, pulled him off the coast, and out of the way of the crashing surf.

He coughed seawater from his lungs and looked up at her. "Haerland?" he asked.

She nodded. "I am."

Once on his feet, he crossed his right arm over his chest and let his fist rest on his breast. "I am Lovi Piathos. The Sea sends me," he said. "This reef behind me is my home. If you will have me, it would be my honor to serve out my days here on your beautiful land."

Haerland reached out, placed her hand over his exposed breast, and replied, "Welcome home, Lovi Piathos."

Upon removing her hand, she revealed a symbol engraved into his chest: five tight lines, the second and fourth more prolonged than the others. It is the same symbol Lovi's children bear today.

The second Architect to answer her call appeared to her weeks later, eager to give Haerland his gift. This Architect was the Ghost of Fire.

"Haerland," he addressed her, "Tonight, I will awaken this mountain. You will know him as Mons Magnus. Treat him with respect, for he is a loyal being and has a hard-working and pleasing spirit. He is my favorite of the range, and now I give him to you."

The ground shook beneath her that night from dusk until dawn. Haerland woke from her slumber with the rising sun and strode to the foothill. There, she found a crack cut into the mountain that had not been there before. Inside this cave, she found a being.

The tall, bared male rose from his place on the ground and stepped directly in front of her. His body was streaked with soot and ash; his chest was plagued with red burns.

"Haerland?" he asked.

"Yes?"

He took her hands in his and knelt down before her. "My name Mons Magnus," said the ashen-faced and darkly bearded man, "and I am yours, my dear Haerland."

She smiled as he kissed the backs of her hands and then she said, "Rise, Mons Magnus. And welcome to my home."

The last Architect to find her was the Ghost of the Sun. She found Haerland on the first sunset of the new year at the highest cliff on the western coast.

"My dear Haerland," began the Sun, "I apologize for the time it has taken me to bring my gifts. Your patience is the greatest of your traits. As your reward, I come to you bearing not one but three gifts. Three seeds. I hope they will find their home in your land, and upon their maturing, I am sure you will never feel lonely again.

"The first is a creation of mine and mine alone. Plant it here, on this hill, so that I may look over its growth directly." The Sun placed a small cloth in Haerland's hands. Within it lay a single tiny seed, pearly-white in color.

"The second was created with the help of both the stars and my beloved eagle, the Aenean Orel. Plant this seed in the north of the

Preymoor." Again, the Sun gave Haerland a small cloth with a seed wrapped in it. This seed was mossy blue in color, speckled with flecks of white and gold on the outside.

"My last gift is one whose creation required the deepest and most tender care. During its inception, I enlisted both the help of the Dead Moons and the wind. This is an exceedingly special seed, Haerland. I cannot stress the amount of care and passion it will require to reach its full potential and growth. Nurture this seed with as much adulation as you give your own creatures. Plant it in the southern depths of the Forest of Darkness. The rich soil will give it the strength it needs." The Sun laid the last small cloth in Haerland's hands. This one was much different from the other two. It was black in color, lines of white scarring the outside.

"Remember, Haerland: use these gifts with caution. Treat them not as your equals but as lesser ones. This is your only warning."

Haerland took the seeds and did exactly as the Sun had instructed her.

The pearly white seed was the first of the Sun's three to grow into its maturity. Haerland discovered it on an extended summer evening. The adolescent tree's pearly bark notched in various places, the perfectly crooked limbs reaching high towards the clouds. However, the tree was not the only thing Haerland found that evening.

A small girl sat on the edge of the cliff, her feet dangling over the side. The billowing tendrils of the adolescent girl's white hair matched that of the tree's bark.

"Hello?" Haerland called out.

The young girl stood and faced her. "You are Haerland?" she asked.

The stark blue of the girl's eyes against her nearly translucent skin startled Haerland.

"I am," Haerland answered.

"She tells me my name is Arbina," the girl said. "Arbina Promregis Amaris. I believe you asked for me."

Years later, the Sun's second gift, the mossy green seed, also reached its adolescence.

Haerland discovered its growth on the dawn of an early spring morning. Just as the child 'Arbina' had accompanied the tree atop the hill, a young child also accompanied this tree.

The adolescent girl sat at the tree base between the uplifted roots with her knees pulled up to her chest. A pair of scared and severe white-blue eyes met Haerland beneath the girl's mousy brown hair.

This child introduced herself as Somniarb Crelib.

Both Arbina and Somniarb, as well as their trees, had matured into full adulthood by the time the Sun's third grew to full maturity.

He was found towards the end of the First Age. On the fourteenth night of the last Dead Moons cycle, Haerland found herself trapped in the middle of the Forest of Darkness during one of the worst thunderstorms she had ever experienced. She took shelter beneath the engrossed canopy of trees to wait out the storm. Just as she nodded off, a fully grown male figure appeared in a flash of lightning directly before her.

She backed herself closer to the trunk of the tree, but the male continued to approach her.

"Haerland?" he called out into the darkness.

"Yes?"

He came forward and proceeded to kneel in front of her. "The Noctuans tell me you are the one to which I owe my life."

"Who are you?"

In the cracks of lightning, she put together his appearance. His buff and vigorous body scarred to the point of mutilation; however, his once handsome and strong face had not been lost beneath the red scars.

"They tell me my name is Duarb," he answered. "And I want to thank you, Haerland."

Remorse filled her for him, and she knew he was of the Sun's third gift, the black seed. She gave him the smallest of smiles and said, "You are welcome, Duarb."

With the Sun's three maturing, Haerland knew the First Age was drawing to a close. She decided upon giving the Architect's five a collective name. Only one name fit, and it was how the Sun had told her to treat these gifts. Haerland would call them the Lesser Ones.

As the Second Age dawned, the Sun's three, along with Lovi Piathos and Mons Magnus, aided Haerland in making her lands better than before. But with five strong voices came quarrel and division. Something Haerland was not accustomed to.

She made a proposition to the Lesser Ones. She asked each one to give a child, a child possessing any and every quality they thought most important to the survival of a living race.

Seven children, each with distinguishing characteristics and abilities, came from this proposal.

Duarb's 'Venari' child, or 'Hunter,' was the first born. The child was created in the very bowels of the earth beneath Duarb's roots. Pulling his powers from the sun and the wind and the moons, Duarb created a child worthy of living in the Forest of Darkness. The child's most distinguishing abilities, and most vital to his survival, was hearing sounds carrying on the winds and the ability to see in the dark.

The 'Dreamer' child was the second. Somniarb Crelib's child reflected the free spirit she thought necessary for life with its pointed ears and flawless appearance. Wing marks were placed on its backs, representing the freedom she wished for them to carry. She swore her Dreamers would be masters of all trades and thus granted them the ability to quickly learn and pick up new skills.

Not to be outdone by the Sun's second and third, Arbina Promregis Amaris was quick to present Haerland with not only one but two children. She gave two: a son and a daughter. Her daughters would be given the ability to speak with creatures. Which creatures and how deeply they could connect with them would be determined by the practice of that daughter. Her sons would be given the power of fire and a form to hold that power upon their markings--when Arbina deemed them worthy of such an ability.

Lovi Piathos called his child 'a child of the Honest.' Along with the gift of eternal life, Lovi's child was born with slits on each side of his neck. They were gills, given so that he would be able to breathe upon his birth in the deepest parts of the reef in the southern Sea.

In the mountains, Mons Magnus presented Haerland with a child known as the 'Blackhand.' This child was gifted in that he could tell how far away or how close his enemies were by the vibrations deep within the dirt beneath his feet.

Haerland also produced a child. Born deep within the northern realm caves of the Forest of Darkness, Haerland gave her daughter's race the name of 'Martyr,' for they were the only ones she knew could save her if needed.

Towards the end of the Second Age, the Lesser Ones existed alongside their children. Tensions rose between the Sun's three. Haerland grew furious with Duarb's immature ways. She cursed him and the Noctuan creatures.

A new race rose from Duarb's roots. A cursed and unwanted race. The race of the Infi.

The Third Age began when the Lesser Ones took a step back and let their children take over. Over time, the races quarreled over the land, became allies, betrayed one another, and sometimes existed in complete harmony. By the end of that Age, Arbina's sons and daughters were no longer simply beings of Haerland. They had become Kings and Queens. The Dreamers called them the beings of Promise, praising them for their compassion and loyalty where they felt other races fell short.

In the caves beneath the rocky cliffs of the Dysis Highlands came a new race: 'the Belwark.' Haerland gifted this new race to Arbina specifically to protect the new Kings and Queens. The Belwarks, from that day on, guarded the walls of Magnice and became the throne's closest ally.

But the Chronicles are not always truth.

So we turn to the Honest Scrolls to find our answers.

It is here that we begin our journey.

1

The thief's head rolled off its body and into the crowd.

Shrieks echoed in the air as the crowd jumped back. Blood spewed onto the wood at Aydra's booted feet. She handed the bloodied axe she'd just used to behead the Infi creature back to the armored Belwark guard behind her. Her long ginger curls broke free as she pulled the executioner hood off her head and tossed it on the ground.

Her brother, King Rhaifian Sunfire, stood from his throne and addressed the crowd.

"Good people," he began. "Fear not. These cursed creatures will not roam our town again. Please return to your lives, and remember: your safety is the first priority of the crown. Allow us to take care of you."

He waved once more and turned on his heel, his purple cloak billowing behind him as he exited down the darkened hallway towards the bridge to the castle. His Belwark guards trailed behind him, the crash of their armor filling the stagnant air.

Aydra pulled the blood-stained gloves off her fingers one by one and glared at his retreating figure.

Coward, Aydra's raven said to her as he landed on the bloodied stockade.

Calm, raven, Aydra replied in a murmur incomprehensible to all those except her raven. *We will have our day.*

"My Queen," said the Belwark behind her. Aydra turned to find her brother's personal captain, Bard, standing behind her. "Your brother requests you join him for meeting before the Council's arrival tonight."

"You may tell my brother I will see him when I have returned," Aydra replied, throwing the gloves at his face. "The people have just witnessed a creature we thought to be vanquished from this world be

9

beheaded twice in a month. I'll be tending to the ones he hurt this afternoon. And after that, perhaps a dip in the ocean." She unclasped the royal black cloak on her shoulders and threw it too at his head.

"Your Majesty," Bard addressed her with a bow.

"Lady Ravenspeak!"

Willow, her lady-in-waiting, called out her name, and Aydra turned to find her pushing through the crowd in her direction.

"Yes, Willow?" Aydra asked the pointy-eared brunette Dreamer woman.

Willow pulled a handkerchief from her pocket and pressed it over her nose as she approached the stage, furrowing her brows in disgust at the smell of the dead man's body. "Disgusting," she muttered quietly before turning her attention up to Aydra. "My Lady, your day crown—" she said as she pulled the small, dark champagne, limbed crown from her side, "you should wear it if you will be mingling with the people today."

Aydra scowled, but she took it from her nonetheless. "Have my dress ready for my return before the Nobles arrive, please. And Willow—" Aydra stopped her before she could leave "—make it a dark one. I've just beheaded a man. Showing up in some brightly bejeweled sundress might give the wrong impression."

Willow gave her a quick bow and then retreated from the stage. Aydra placed the circular crown in her hair and then turned her attention back to the Belwarks who were waiting for her instruction.

"No large escort today, boys," she told them. "Go home. Get some rest. We have a long day of fracturing niceties tomorrow." She turned then to her Second, Hilexi Ashbourne. "What do you say to a stroll through town today, Lex?"

Hilexi pulled the silver winged helmet off her head and allowed her shaggy, pixie cut, tawny blonde hair to fall over her eyes. "Any day I am allowed to leave the armor behind and mingle with these beautiful people is a day I will take, my Lady," she said as she tossed the helmet back to one of the men. "Take my things back to my quarters, Jorna," she instructed. "I have no need of it until the Venari arrives tomorrow." She stripped herself free of the silver plates and revealed the matching long sleeve gambeson to Aydra's, the only difference being the golden weavings featured on the capped shoulders of Aydra's.

Aydra reached down and brushed the blood off her tall black boots. People were already starting to gather around the bottom of the stage.

She hopped off it without glancing back at her guard and made her way through the thinning crowd. People immediately gripped her, thanking her for ridding their kingdom of the Infi creature.

The sight of Aydra and Lex walking through the crowd usually made it part ways. Not only because Aydra was the Queen, but the mere presence of them would have made anyone think twice before cutting across the pair.

Aydra acknowledgéd the people she knew, stopping to speak with some for only a few moments. It was three miles down to the beach from the square they were on. Belwark guards on horses strode by every now and then, none of them in armor, only in their scarlet gambesons to mark their place in the kingdom. Dreamers passed, their always beautiful faces illuminated by the striking sun now well over the horizon.

"Your Majesty," said a petite blonde woman upon reaching Aydra in the street. Aydra paused, recognizing her favorite seamstress, Maye, coming up to her, a child in her arms. Aydra felt her gaze soften.

"Maye—*Sweet Arbina*, you were given a child?" she asked, wrapping an arm around Maye's shoulders. "I knew I hadn't seen you in a while."

Maye smiled widely at her. "The Orel found us three weeks ago. Wouldn't leave us alone, so we knew it was time. Packed up immediately and made for the Village."

Aydra stroked the sleeping child's cheek, her finger tracing up to its tiny pointed ears. "She's beautiful. How many were born on the crescents?"

"Three," Maye replied. "We were the only from Magnice. One went to the Village, the other to Scindo."

Aydra pulled back and reached out for Maye's cheek. "I can think of no greater two than to have received one of this cycle's children."

A glisten rose in the Dreamer's gaze. "Thank you, Your Majesty."

Aydra and Lex continued through the streets a bit later, greeting and speaking with Dreamers coming up to Aydra. Lex mostly stood back, as she usually did, saying little to add to the conversation but staying supportive of the Queen and patient with the people nonetheless.

"The birth of you Sun tree children always amazes me," Lex said over Aydra's shoulder. "Born beneath a great tree's roots as infants. An eagle Orel deciding who is to become parents of such children."

"That only applies to Dreamers," Aydra said. "The Dreamers' giver, Somniarb, is in the Village of Dreams. Infants are given year-round from her roots, not just in a cycle of ten years like Promised children. Promised children like myself are born in Arbina's waters and raised by the previous kings and queens before us. They are the ones who determine what we learn and do not learn."

"Nevertheless, infants are bewildering," Lex said. "To be born without being able to take care of yourself is... not very smart on the Lesser Ones' parts."

"So says the one born fully corporeal beneath this great cliff and made of earth," Aydra drawled in a mocking tone.

"Exactly. Grown. Spat from the earth beneath this kingdom a fully grown person with the instincts of an assassin," Lex said proudly. "Insides of fire and ash like our land, none of this blood nonsense."

"And all the urges of us Architect children," laughed Aydra.

"Mm... and what great urges they are—" Lex plucked an apple from a cart and tossed a gold coin to the farmer with a nod. Her teeth bit into the flesh of it, and a pleased noise came from her throat "—I love fruit."

Aydra chuckled under her breath at the comments. The breeze of the sea filled her nostrils, intermingling with the smell of fire and ash as they passed the row of smithing shops. Aydra's gaze caught on a table of jewelry. Lex laughed at Aydra upon her stopping to look at it.

"You never wear any of the jewels you have now," Lex teased.

Aydra spotted a crude, unpolished gold ring, three raw black stones sitting on the melted band. She picked it up between her fingers and allowed the sun the spark off the raw edges.

"Tourmaline," came a voice from inside the shop.

Aydra's eyes met those of a tall, slender man, long white-blonde hair pulled halfway upon his head above his pointed ears. His thick pepper-spiced beard sat on his angular jaw. He stepped slowly out of the shadows and wiped his large hands of the soot on them.

"Your Majesty," he acknowledged with a short bow, "to what do we owe the pleasure of your company through the smithing street?"

"Where did you get this stone?" she asked, holding up the ring.

"Traders from the south," he answered. He reached out and took the ring from her palm, then turned her hand over and slowly pressed it onto her ring finger. "If you're being attracted to such a stone, you need optimism, relief of stress—"

"Sounds like it was made for her," Lex muttered under her breath.

Aydra cut her eyes at her friend and then turned back to the handsome man standing in front of her. His wide grey eyes danced deliberately over her figure.

"It's beautiful…" she paused, unsure of if he'd given her his name.

"Many call me Grey, Your Majesty," he informed her with a smile.

"Grey. It has been a pleasure to meet you, Grey. Your work is beautiful." She pulled the ring off her finger, but he closed her fist around it.

"Keep it," he said. "It calls to you."

Aydra and Lex continued walking down the streets upon leaving the smithing shops. They paused only a moment for Lex to look at the decorative braces and helmets made by another shop owner. Lex treated herself to new armor pads for her shoulders that looked like sharp wings.

"Fearsome," Aydra had told her. Lex grinned and paid the man, and then they continued on. They were treated to small chats with a few more Dreamer families on the next level. The families spoke with her about the Infi creature and how they were scared since there had been two to walk among them after years of being rid of such filth. Aydra assured them of their safety, on her life.

They stopped in to see the woman who they had found in the street the morning before. Her screams continued to echo in Aydra's thoughts. She and Lex were welcomed into the woman's home with a joy that Aydra recognized as forced.

"What can we do?" Lex asked as the pair sat.

The girl's mother, Lyri, set tea down in front of them. "You have done enough," she answered. "We are grateful it was you two who found her. I don't… I don't know what would have happened if you hadn't."

"May I see her?" Aydra asked.

Lyri paused a moment and then gave her a quick nod.

The girl was still shaken when Aydra went into her room. She started to stand, but Aydra told her to remain. Aydra sat down at the end of the bed and grasped the girl's hand. She was no older than sixteen. A beautiful brunette girl with delicate features, apple cheeks, and hazel eyes that had once held the sun in them. Aydra knew this girl from before. Her name was Sonya, and she was a free-spirited girl, never known a stranger. She'd taken it upon herself to help the Infi when he'd claimed to be a traveler from the Village.

"How are you?" Aydra asked her.

Sonya tucked her hair behind her ear and avoided her gaze. "Okay, I guess," she admitted.

"You were very brave yesterday." Aydra squeezed her hand.

"Did you kill him?" Sonya asked, meeting her eyes.

Aydra nodded. "I did it myself."

"Will there be more?"

"I certainly hope not, but… we cannot be sure. It is on us to stay vigilant. I have stationed more Belwarks on the ground and at the gates. If any strangers come through, we will know about it."

Sonya nodded but didn't reply.

"The offer still stands, you know," Aydra told her. "You and your family could move up to one of the homes at the walls. You'll be—"

"Can you promise our safety there any more than you can promise our safety here?" Sonya interjected.

Aydra sat in silence a brief second, and then whispered, "Okay," in agreement with her.

The girl's sorrow sat heavily on Aydra's shoulders as she and Lex strode down the beach a while later. The echo of the crashing waves pounded in her ears, barely drowning out the thoughts in her mind.

"I think I will take my leave of you here, Lex," Aydra said as they reached the edge of the water.

"No company on your swim today?" Lex asked.

"My mind fills with a constipated ache I dare not press onto you," Aydra replied. "Besides, I think you've more pressing matters to attend," Aydra said with the rise of a brow. "Like that last baker. She gave you quite the once over, didn't she?"

Lex ran a hand through her hair and started walking backward. "What can I say? Power is an attractive thing."

"Have fun," Aydra called to her.

"I'll come back for you later—"

"No, that's okay," Aydra assured her. "I will see you at dinner."

Aydra made around the corner of the cliff out of sight and then stripped herself of the pants and gambeson, revealing her high black underwear and corseted bra. The sun baked her skin, allowing the golden freckles on her arms and face to emerge at its warmth.

She cracked her neck and stretched her arms above her head as her toes touched the water. Her eyes closed, her head laid on her shoulders. Her flesh quickly adjusted to the cold of the ocean water as it swallowed her and then she floated back to the surface.

The mock of her kingdom stared at her as she lay atop the clear water.

The castle stood high up on the cliffside, far behind her. Arbina Promiregis Amaris, the Sun's first tree, the tree from which she and her brother were born, roots wrapped into the edge of the cliff at nearly the top, its large limbs reaching high into the blue sky. They'd built their open Throne Room around it. Water from her never-ending poisoned pool spilled over the edge of the cliff and around the roots.

Higher up than that was the main of the castle built behind the tree. The castle grew and grew with more rooms than she could count before it wrapped around to three towers. The tallest tower was the dungeon tower. It curled around and sat high above the tree's tallest limbs. It sat so that the doorway to death was directly above the waterfall. Any persons who were sentenced to death by its fall would ultimately plunge themselves into Arbina's poisoned waterfall as they dove to their untimely end.

It hadn't been used since three Venari Kings ago when he'd tried to start a war with Magnice by unleashing Infi in their streets as a protest for their giver, Duarb, being banished into his tree.

She wondered if the current Venari King, Draven Greenwood, had a similar plan.

The water wrapped around her body, and she sank into its depths. It consumed her: mind, body, and core. Her eyes opened to the clear blue of the liquid. The noise of the girl's screams lingered as the water's weight held her.

She let it take her breath. Her lungs began to struggle after a few moments. She allowed it to pull at her. Pull her into the abyss until she could not take it any longer.

Her head burst to the surface. She wiped her face and inhaled an audible breath.

The sun danced on her skin once more.

To feel something.

Anything.

Her thoughts consumed her beneath the waters a few more times before she finally retreated to the sandy beach. She sat down in the wet sand to let the sun dry her body. Her eyes closed, and she wasn't sure if she actually dozed off or if the warmth of it simply drug her into the mindless abyss her body had craved for some time now.

Before she beheaded the first Infi creature, they'd not had a public execution in nearly twenty years. The last she remembered had been the previous king beheading the thief himself. Something her brother would not dare touch with the sword their giver mother had gifted him with.

It was some time before her raven circled over her head to inform her that one of her brother's Belwark guards was approaching.

"You know, I commanded my brother's men earlier not to follow me today," Aydra called as the Belwark arrived behind her. "I even gave my own Second the rest of the day off."

"Forgive me, Your Majesty," he said as he joined her. "The King—"

"Do you do everything my brother tells you to do?" she interjected.

The Belwark seemed to give it some thought. "Yes," he finally replied.

She took her shirt off her face that she'd been using to block the sunlight, and she looked over at him. His dark brown skin glistened with sweat in the orange hue of the waning sun beneath his gambeson. The long sleeves of it were snug against the taut of his muscled arms, and his short black curly hair was twisted atop his head, falling just above his ears. She deliberately let her eyes dance over his figure, feeling herself bite her lip out of habit.

"My brother outdid himself this time," she mused at the sight of him. "What is your name, Belwark?" she asked.

"Corbin, Your Majesty," he replied with a short nod. "Corbin Ashember."

She closed her eyes back to the sun again and relaxed. "If you're going to be stalking me the rest of the day, you may as well join," she told him. "No sense in sweating in that gambeson out here."

The Belwark didn't move.

"It's not really a request, Corbin," she said without moving. "If you are staying, you'll take your clothes off and join me. Otherwise, get on your way."

"Your brother asked me to retrieve you," Corbin told her. "The Bedrani Council is arriving in a few hours. He wishes you to be there when they arrive."

Aydra finally sat up as annoyance ran through her veins. "I am aware of when they are coming. I am aware of the time. I am also aware that you are new—" She stood from the ground and crossed the space between her and the Belwark. "And you have a look upon your face as though you have been struck."

His weight shifted, and he made a point to push his arms behind his back. "I don't know what you mean," he said.

She stopped in front of him, a curious brow on her bemused face.

"You look frightened, Corbin," she teased.

"Apologies, my lady," he said quickly, shifting his feet again. "I... I was told—"

A sly smile tugged at Aydra's lips. "Let me guess," she cut him off. "You were told not to get wrapped into me on fear of death. Is that why he sent you to me and not Mord or Bard? Worried of distractions along the way?"

Corbin's breath shortened as her fingers trailed up his arms. "I was not told the reason for my being sent," he managed. "Only to retrieve you."

"And how's that working out for you?" she asked with a tilt of her head.

"Ma'am, I—" his words stuck in his throat as her fingers mused down his chest. She grasped his hands and placed them around her waist, to which he hesitated at first, but then his fingers squeezed her hips, and she smiled inside.

She allowed her hands to continue to trail, and when she struck a finger below the belt on his hips, she heard an audible groan come from him.

"Tell me, Corbin... have you ever fucked a Queen?" she asked.

"I haven't."

She could already feel him hardening through the fabric. "Would you like to?"

His eyes darkened with smolder. Fingers gripping tighter on her hips, and he bent just slightly to make himself level with her. "If that's what she wants," he said in her ear.

She unbuckled the belt on his waist so swiftly that he nearly fell off balance. His length filled her hand, and she stroked it, watching his face as he groaned into the wind. She took his hand off her waist and pushed it between her legs.

"My Queen," he whispered into her hair.

She pushed him backward until his back hit the cliff wall, and just as quickly, he grabbed her and switched, pinning her against the rough rocks, his mouth sucking at her throat.

She pulled back and gasped at his boldness, to which he gave her a sultry smile. She rewarded him with a full kiss, her leg hooking around his waist. She allowed her hips to grind into his, feeling his length against her.

"On your knees," she commanded breathlessly in his ear.

He didn't hesitate. His knees hit the sand. He yanked her high waisted underwear off and threw them. Aydra didn't notice where they landed. He had pulled her leg over his shoulder, and she limped when he kissed between her thighs. Tongue deliberately raking the length of her clit.

She pushed her hands through his hair, eyes rolling as she relished the feeling of his mouth against her. Her hips bucked. The sunlight warmed her body, and she grasped her own hair upon her breath catching in her throat. He sucked her clit hard, and his tongue fluttered against her throbbing sex. Her thighs tightened around his face. It wasn't long before she could feel herself coming apart on his lips. He lapped at her wetness as she cried out in ecstasy, not caring if it bounced off the cliff behind her.

Corbin rose to his feet, her leg still hooked around him, his hand now grazing her sensitive vagina slowly.

Aydra willed her breaths even, and she kissed him hard. Teeth tugging at his bottom lip, she whispered, "Fuck me, Belwark," and Corbin grabbed her legs.

He obliged swifter than she expected. His length filled her, and he hugged her thighs against him as he pushed harshly in and out. Her fingertips dug into his body, nails scratching the surface of his skin to reveal the fiery ash of a Belwark's insides where there should have been blood. The rock behind her grazed her shoulder as he pushed harder and harder. Finally, he let himself go with an audible groan into her hair. Sweat had beaded on his forehead, and she smiled at the sight of it as he released her.

She pushed her hair off her face and smiled wickedly in his direction. "Exceeding expectations, Corbin. I think I'll keep you."

Aydra's smile lingered as she allowed the Belwark to escort her back through the town and up to the castle. Her skin was sticky with the salt of the beach beneath her blackened vest and leather pants. Her boots full of sand. She reminded herself to bring an extra set of clothes the next time she thought she might go to the beach after an execution.

"Where is he?" she asked Corbin as the great doors of the castle closed behind.

"His study," Corbin answered.

Sand danced on the black rug through the hallways of the castle as they walked through it. She was sure she would hear complaints from Willow about it later.

His study was in the eastern corner below the Council room, where he had his own secret staircase to the back of it. Two Belwarks stood guard at the door, and both gave her a nod upon reaching it.

"I will announce you," Corbin said, stepping in front of her.

She considered the handsome Belwark's eagerness, and then gestured for him to go first. "Very well, Belwark," she purred.

The doors opened, and Corbin stepped inside.

"Queen Aydra, as requested, Your Majesty," Corbin said with a bow.

Rhaif turned from the grand window he was staring out of, his curly black hair falling over his eyes as he gave Corbin a nod. "Thank you, Corbin," he said. "You'll stand guard and accompany her back to her room and then to the front to greet the Council after I've spoken with my sister."

"No," Aydra interjected as she strode into the room. "Corbin takes orders from me now." She turned and gave him a smile over her shoulder. "Thank you for the escort, Corbin. I can handle things from here. Take your leave for the night," she told him with a wink.

Her brother was glaring at her once she turned back around. Rhaif's knuckles turned white against the cup in his hands as the door closed.

"How many more of them will you take from me?" he growled.

"As many as want to come with me," she mused, throwing herself into the new taut leather armchair behind his desk. Her body practically purred at the feeling of the supple leather. "This is nice. Is it new?"

"Get out of my chair," he hissed.

She grinned but stood nonetheless and retired herself to the lounger on the other side of the desk. "What's up your ass? You're in a more anxious mood than usual."

Rhaif sighed and met her eyes. "It seems the Infi have infiltrated more than one of the Dreamer towns," he informed her. "Nobles from the other three sent word this morning of their having to deal with the infestation."

Aydra's mood shifted, and she sat up in the chair. "How many?"

"A total of six were discovered," he said.

"In addition to the two found here?" she asked.

Rhaif nodded. "So it would seem."

He paused and circled around the desk, leaning against the top of it as he faced her. "I thought with your being head of security, you should know. Also, I was hoping you would have some ideas as to how to vanish such a problem."

Aydra quieted as she thought about it. "We will speak

with the Venari King when he gets here tomorrow," she said. "Bring it up at the meeting. If he's allowing the Infi to walk out of his wood, what else is he up to?"

Rhaif met her gaze. "I am glad to know we are on the same page, sister." He paused and gave her a bold stare, eyes traveling over her body. She hugged her arms over her chest uncomfortably and then stood.

"Was there anything else before we go meet the Council's arrival?"

"These men you concern yourself with," he started. "Why not choose one of them instead of carrying a train of them in your wake."

Her head tilted at him, eyes narrowing. "Why should a King be allowed to have his fun with as many different Dreamer women as he likes, but a Queen not be?" she asked. "Do I not deserve the indulgence of a variety of pleasures myself?"

He considered her a moment as he leaned against the desk. "What about Ash? Is he not a favorite?"

"Ash is not always here," she said. "Not to mention Ash can be a bit… *safe*."

The first smile she'd seen in years on her brother's face rose onto his lips. "And the Belwarks aren't?"

She met his smile. "Belwarks are a different breed. Born of the earth. Strength of fire. I love the trail of ash and fire beneath their skin when I scratch it."

"You know—" he pushed off the desk and came to stand deliberately in front of her, his eyes only a couple inches above hers "—if you wanted fire, all you had to do was ask."

His hands ran the length of her wrists, up her arms, to her throat, and the amusement she'd been filled with only moments before evacuated. She started to step back, but he caught her. He seized her neck in his hands, and he crudely pressed his lips to hers.

She pushed his chest, breaking her lips free, and uttered a quick, "Rhaif, no—" but to no avail. He grasped her curly hair between his fingers and yanked her roots down. Before she could move, he whipped her around between himself and the desk as she fought against his grip.

"Rhaif—Rhaif, *stop!*"

She managed to shove him hard, and he tripped backward over the rug at his feet, almost falling into the couch. Her heart was pounding in her chest. He'd bit her lip harshly, and she could feel the faint trickle of the blood threatening to fall down her chin. His eyes were wild and narrow as he stared at her, obviously bewildered that she'd actually hit him.

She blinked and made herself move. "The Council will be here soon," she managed as she pushed off the desk. "I must be getting ready."

2

She was late.

Later than she'd anticipated.

But the sun basking on her skin had been precisely what she'd needed after her peace being taken away so abruptly the day before.

A moment to be herself. A moment of peace before the horror of the Council she knew she would have to endure that night. A break from the daily duties of being Queen of Promise.

The Belwark guard, Corbin, had accompanied her to the beach instead of Lex that morning. She'd allowed him the indulgence of continued pleasure from the day before. The water had glistened on his dark skin as he took her roughly against the cliff walls and then again when he'd splayed her legs open on the sand and devoured her. She could still feel the marks on her shoulder blades and on her ass from the rock defacing her skin as she strode through the halls back to her room.

"Queen Aydra!" Willow called out. "My Queen—you're late."

Aydra shoved her bracelet off her arm and began stripping in the hall as she walked with little care to who might be coming down it. "I am aware, Willow."

"Your brother sent for you—"

Aydra tossed her tunic over her head and into the Dreamer's outstretched arms. One of the Belwarks walked by then. She gave him a sultry smile as his gaze lingered and studied her figure. "I'm aware," she repeated, winking at the Belwark. "Please inform my brother I'll be a few minutes late. He can start without me." She pulled her linen pants off, nearly tripping on the legs, and tossed them into Willow's arms. "Is my dress ready?" she asked.

"I left it on your bed," Willow answered.

Aydra pulled the clip out of her hair as they ascended the last set of stairs, and she gave the mess of it a fluff, allowing it to wave in the air behind her. She wasn't surprised when she saw the Prince, Dorian Eaglefyre, coming down from his own bedroom.

"*Whoa*— No one told me we were streaking before the banquet," he said as she passed him, his widened, round, blue eyes searing through her. "Nice suit, sister," the dark-haired nineteen-year-old teased with a wink at Aydra.

Aydra attempted and failed a look of disgust and ended up biting back a knowing smile on her lips. "Grow up, Dorian," she said as she smacked the back of his head. "You're disgusting."

"Fearless and annoying would better suit me, I think," he grinned.

"The favored family traits," she called back to him.

She turned her attention back to Willow as they reached the top of the steps. "Please go to the Chamber and let my brother know I will be there momentarily."

Willow gave her a nod outside her bedroom door. "Yes, Your Majesty."

Her feet flapped on the floor as she crossed the grand stone room to her four-poster bed, the door to her bedroom slamming behind her. Black linens draped around the top and wound around the wide wooden posts. She paused at the end of the bed, and her lips pursed upon seeing the dress laid out on it.

Leave it to her brother to pick out the dress she hated the most for her to wear.

Powder blue. Frilly. Conservative.

Aydra flung it out of her window and went to her wardrobe.

Color. Color. Color.

No.

She was feeling confident that day. Her dark freckles were radiating on her skin--she could see them popping off her cheeks when she looked in the mirror. The pure steel color of her upward turned, wide eyes reminded her of the rocks the castle was made from.

Black.

A long black lace dress stared at her from the back of the wardrobe.

The dress that pissed her brother off the most and the one that she felt most confident in.

Her raven flew past her window.

She pulled the form-fitting black lace over her muscular thighs and the curvature of her hips. It fit around her waist, and she pushed her arms through before bringing it up and over her breasts. Sections of the black rose lace pattern draped over her breasts and up to her collarbone. The sleeves were off the shoulder and hugged her limbs. The beige underlay of the dress appeared nude on her pale skin. The bottom flared out just below her knees, and the train behind it extended a few feet. She reached for her heels under the bed and kicked the fabric out to put her feet in them. The tulle skirt she belted around her wrapped around the back of her waist like a cape. She gave it a fluff behind her.

She pushed the raw tourmaline ring on her ring finger and ran her fingers through her hair again, and the elbow-length curls cascaded down her back.

For a long moment, she stared at her grand golden twigged crown. Turning it over in her hands. Fingers dancing along the rough edges and points.

A crown made just for her by her own giver mother.

Her chin lifted as she looked into the vanity mirror and placed it on her head.

This should piss him off.

She left her room a moment later and was not surprised to find Lex waiting outside her door. Lex's expression faltered upon seeing her.

"Wow," she said, looking Aydra over deliberately. "Someone is looking to royally piss off the King."

Aydra fell in step with her down the hall. "He deserves it after yesterday."

"I told you we could make it clean," Lex said, arms pushed behind her back. "Very quiet. I doubt many would be upset."

Aydra almost laughed. "You sound like the raven."

"Knew there was something I liked about that creature," Lex grinned.

"Take a guess at which one he had Willow leave on the bed."

"The pink one?"

"Powder blue," Aydra told her.

"Oof," Lex scoffed. "I can't wait to see the look on his face when you walk in."

The white stone hallways mocked Aydra as they walked. She fumbled with the sleeves of her dress, trying to pull them down enough to wrap the string around her ring fingers. She twisted her ring upon seeing the great portrait of herself and her brother at the end of the hall. The painters had drawn it onto the white rock, just as they had the last three kings and queens.

Lex paused a moment in front of it. "They didn't do you justice, my Queen," she affirmed.

"They rarely do the Queens justice," Aydra agreed. "Makes me wonder if we were meant to only ever be an accessory on his arm."

"Perhaps Arbina should have thought about that before creating you," Lex countered.

Aydra smiled at the accuracy. "Come. We are later than usual, I think."

"I'm positive we are."

They finally reached the double doors of the Chamber a few flights of stairs later, and the pair paused in front of them. Aydra twisted the ring on her finger once more, a shiver running down her spine. The Belwarks on either side of the door waited patiently for her approval.

She cracked her neck and gave them a nod.

The doors opened, and the great room went silent. Corbin stepped inside before her and started to announce she and Lex, but Aydra pressed her hand on his chest and pushed him to the side.

"I think they know who to expect this many minutes past the hour." A stern brow raised on her face at the still sitting members around the table, and every person quickly rose to their feet—

All except one.

"Sister!" Rhaif announced upon rising from his own chair. She could see the annoyance written in his dark eyes as he crossed the room toward her, his cloak billowing behind him. He'd pushed his navy black hair back to one side, allowing his curly bangs the liberty to fall over his left hazel eye, the golden crown on his head standing out against the dark of his hair. One look at him, and she knew she was not the only one who had gone swimming that morning. His natural golden skin glistened in the firelight.

"My dear sister—" he clasped her face tightly in his hands and brought her to him, kissing her cheek in a manner that made her cringe "—*what are you wearing?*" he hissed in her ear. "I left you—"

"Did you have fun on the beach today, brother?" she asked, ignoring him as she acknowledged a few of the Nobles in the room with a smile and a small fluttering wave of her fingers. "Your skin is positively glowing."

He wrenched her arm down from her insistent waving and glared at her. "You *embarrass* us before our people," he scolded.

"Why? Because I choose to embrace who I am instead of hiding it?"

"And you—" he turned his attention to Lex as though Aydra had not spoken "—*you encourage it!*"

"You mean do I encourage my Queen to not shove her desires away and instead wear it as she should be allowed to? Yes. I do encourage it," Lex replied, her stature towering before the King's.

One of the men at the table cleared his throat, and Rhaif turned back around and gave the Council member a smile. "Ah. Back to where we were, of course." He linked his arm around Aydra's shoulder and squeezed it as he led her to the table. "Sister, join us," he said as he pulled out the chair beside him.

She took her seat, and without meaning to, met the eyes of the one person who had not stood up upon her arrival. The man sitting directly across from her at the other end of the twenty-person table.

Venari King and Alpha, Draven Greenwood.

King of Noctuans, born beneath the cursed fated tree: Duarb Fatum Infinari.

Ruler of the southern realms.

Her enemy King.

The Chronicles say this man's giver had once tried to ensnare Aydra's own giver into a slave relationship. The man whose only reason for being at that table and invited to their kingdom is because of a deal struck between previous kings, King Stephan of the Promised and the Venari King Bailnor, a hundred years earlier. A deal that said the Venari King would never have to kneel before the Promised throne so long as he kept to his own realm and swore to protect the south while the Promised kept to their own in the northwest.

Their races' trust in one another had never recovered even after such a deal was made, and the hatred between them boiled at the surface of every meeting.

Draven stared mockingly at her beneath the black and ivory-boned crown sitting over his thick shoulder-length walnut and light brown streaked hair. He leaned back in his chair, his leg thrown lazily up over the side of the arms as though he were lounging in his own home. His hooded sage eyes were cold as they stared at her, as though he were perturbed by the fact that she'd been late and thus extended the time it would take to get this meeting over with.

Aydra zoned out as her brother began discussing the crops coming in from the Village of Dreams, fingertips strumming on the tabletop.

Her gaze darted around the room, finally landing on the Prince and Princess standing at the back. She gave her sister a wink and a small smile, to which the Princess chuckled under her breath, but she didn't stop watching the people around the table.

"—of the precautions you're taking for the next Dead Moons," she heard her brother say.

Her attention averted to Draven as he moved his leg off the side of the chair and leaned forward, the snug black cotton tunic and leather vest he wore tightening around his rippled muscles. He cracked his neck and his gaze flickered around the faces in the room.

"Precautions?" he repeated in his low, raspy voice, a sharp brow raising.

"You remember what happened during the last," Rhaif continued. "Half the Village's sheep were taken."

"Then perhaps you'd better instruct your hunting parties to back down on how many deer they take in the next month," Draven said as his long hair fell over his shoulders.

"You'll learn to control the whereabouts of these creatures, Venari," Rhaif seethed.

Aydra snorted.

The entire room stared at her.

She huffed amusedly and shook her head, staring at her brother. "You cannot be serious," she laughed. "Venari control where the Noctuans hunt? They are wild animals, not pets."

"I cannot believe I am saying this, but…" an annoyed twinge in Draven's taut jaw "—your sister is right," he finally managed. "They are wild animals. To contain them to the Forest, you would have to ask the Nitesh to place one more curse on their heads."

"She is due to arrive at one of our near meetings," Rhaif said. "Perhaps we will."

"The only reason they leave the Forest to begin with is if they cannot find food," Draven said slowly. "They would not risk going so far from the darkness and chance being caught out in sunlight if their hunts were plentiful. Halt your parties from going inside the Forest until after this cycle. Give the Forest a chance to be inviting to them again."

He paused and looked around the table, head shaking in apparent disbelief. "I ride all over the Preymoor and Bitratus Hills to get here, and all I see are deer and rabbits. Yet you send your men into my realm to hunt, pushing the food out. They no longer fear the openness.

They fear the Forest."

"As they should," said one of the Dreamers. "It has taken us years to get these animals trained out of there."

Aydra heard Draven's knuckles crack above the table. "You admit you are trying to starve us and the Noctuans then."

The Dreamer, Ash, said nothing in response, and instead, his gaze wandered to Rhaif. Rhaif held a lazy hand up to Ash.

"No one is saying such, Venari," Rhaif said in a calm tone. "We merely ask that you—"

"How exactly do you expect me to control them?" Draven asked, his arms crossing over his chest.

"Send your men on hunts and ensnare their meals for them," Rhaif suggested, "Just take care of it."

A great bellow of a laugh emitted from Draven. "You want me to hand feed them?" he mocked. He leaned forward again, a sarcastic smirk playing on his lips as his amusement settled. "Perhaps I'd be better giving them the location of this castle. Let them have a taste of royal blood."

Rhaif lunged out of his seat, but Aydra shoved him back down.

"Not here," she hissed.

A pleased glint rose in Draven's dark gaze as if he'd achieved what he'd come there to do. He relaxed in his chair once more, fingers stretching over the armrests, and his eyes locked with Aydra's.

Challenging and maniacal, she wasn't sure what to make of the glaring stare.

Rhaif straightened his high collared black and gold long shirt. Aydra pressed a hand to his arm to calm him before leaning forward.

"Ash, Haut, can you not hunt in the Preymoor for the next few weeks? Or focus on fishing in our own backyard?" she asked them.

Ash and Haut exchanged an apprehensive look that she wasn't quite sure how to take. They looked down at the end of the table towards the Venari and then back to Aydra.

"We'll increase the fishing parties," Ash finally answered. "Give our men a shake up of their routine."

"Thank you," Aydra declared triumphantly. "Now, what else can I straighten out before my brother finds his voice again?"

A nervous chuckle radiated around the room. Her eyes found Draven's again, and he gave her a silent nod of appreciation.

A nod that had never happened before.

It wasn't that she had any sort of soft spot for him, but his creatures, the Noctuans, were another story. The Noctuans were creatures who were only able to hunt during the Dead Moons, or when the two moons vanished for a fortnight and complete darkness took over the land. A misunderstood group of creatures. They were feared by most not only because of their appearance but because most were bloodthirsty—which, who could blame them if they were only allowed out to hunt four times a year.

"And as a last matter," Rhaif said, "there is the need to discuss the pests running amuck in our streets."

Every person turned to look at Draven, and his head tilted just noticeably.

"I am here because I am requested, not to run amuck in your streets as you say," Draven stated, clearly confused as to why they were all staring at him.

"It was our understanding that you took care of the Infi upon their births," said a councilman. "Tell us why then we have had to behead two within the last month."

Draven stilled a moment, his surprise evident, and he sat up. "You've found Infi... here... in Magnice?"

"And in our towns," said one of the Nobles as he nodded towards the other three ambassadors.

"Would you like to see their heads?" asked Ash.

"Is this of your doing?" asked Councilwoman Reid. "Another ploy to take over this realm as many of your past Kings have done?"

"If you've Infi in your streets, it is by no doing of mine." Draven looked sternly between them, entire body seeming to tense. "I should hope you threw their entire bodies into the Bitratus Hills," he added.

"And why is that?"

"Because unless you did, they will come back."

The words staled in the room.

"I'm sorry," Aydra found her voice. "They what?"

"Their bodies must be taken by Duarb's roots," Draven said, his words sounding of daggers as they left him. "Until their bodies leave this realm for one that his roots can reach to and consume their bones back into the earth, they will keep coming back. You've probably killed the same one each time."

"I slid the axe across their necks both times myself," Aydra seethed. "And you're telling me I've only killed a ghost?"

"Since when does the Queen handle executions?"

"Since I am the one who discovered both of them raping Dreamer women no older than my sister in the streets," she argued.

"How is it you've let one escape long enough to live to such an age?" Rhaif asked.

"If they are alive, then they are not true Infis. They are Infinari, born with both fates and assumably marked with the cursed fate if I do not know of them. I cannot keep track of every Infinari after it has reached its age of marking anymore than you can keep up with every Belwark uncovered beneath your temple."

"My Belwarks do not steal and rape in the streets!" Rhaif hissed. "You will get your brethren under control, Venari."

"They are not—"

Rhaif's cup slammed on the table. "Get them under control or you'll find your beloved giver's tree guarded with Belwarks after the next Dead Moons. Do not force me to take care of this problem on my own."

The shadows in the glare on Draven's face settled into his features, almost as though they were darkening him with clouds. A gust of wind blew through the room from the open windows, and a chill ran down Aydra's spine.

Venari King wind.

"Is that a threat?" she heard Draven growl.

Rhaif's eyes flashed fire, the flicker of blue flames rising just noticeably beneath his collar. "A promise."

Her raven screeched overhead, letting her know he was there if she needed him. Her hair billowed back off her face as Draven's wind ensnared the room. Aydra could see her brother's fingertips turning black with his fire form as he nor Draven backed down.

Their powers were strong enough to take down the entire castle if they got in a fight, and Aydra was getting tired of their challenging one another at nearly every meeting.

"Enough," Aydra commanded into the paralyzed room. "Cease before you both kill everyone in this room except each other."

But neither moved.

"Now," she almost shouted.

The wind slowed. The blue flames receded from Rhaif's collar. Draven cracked his knuckles above the table, and she swore she heard a growl leave his throat.

As the wind died, Aydra's raven flew down to perch on the back of her chair.

"Where is the body of the one found here?" Draven finally asked once he'd calmed.

"Tossed over the cliffs," replied a Belwark captain.

"How long ago?" Draven asked.

"Yesterday morning," Aydra replied.

Draven scoffed, muttering, "Idiots," under his breath before declaring loudly, "He'll be walking your streets again by sunrise." Draven stared across the table at Rhaif. "Send a party to search for him. Quietly. The moment he learns his secret is discovered, he will head for the mountain town of the Bryn. Once he gets there, he'll become another one of their road thieves."

"You do not give orders here, Venari," Rhaif spat.

"If you want this man gone before he causes any more damage, you'll listen," Draven said firmly. "The Infi are master manipulators. Shifters. Whoever finds him at sunrise will probably take him in thinking he is a lost old man."

Rhaif looked up to his Second and gave him a nod. "Send a company out to the lower streets and beaches. Ask for any newcomers looking for food or shelter. Find the creature and kill it."

"No," Draven interjected. "You'll find him and bring him to me. Your men have wasted enough time not knowing what they're doing. I will show you how to properly dispose of its life."

"Finding him could take days," said Bard.

"You have until noon tomorrow, Second," Rhaif interjected to Bard. "Take as many men as you need."

"Discreetly," Aydra cut in. "We don't need him disappearing."

"And what about the ones in our streets?" asked Councilman Asherdoe.

"What did you do with the bodies?" Draven asked.

"Burned," answered one of the Nobles.

A quiet chuckle escaped Draven's lips.

"Do our troubles amuse you, Venari?" asked Ash.

"Do you people even read your own Chronicles?" Draven asked incredulously. "Or the Honest Scrolls?"

"The Honest Scrolls are nothing more than tales of—"

"Truth," Draven corrected. "The Honest Scrolls are truth. Unlike the biased nonsense your scribes take note of in the corners of quieted rooms and call Chronicles." He slumped back in his chair and gestured toward the scribe sitting in the corner of the room. "Do you think he is getting this conversation or just the bits of your King demanding orders?"

"Your point, Venari," Aydra interjected. "Make it."

Draven's eyes flickered to hers, and he tapped on the top of the table with his fingertips, clearly perturbed by the conversation. "I will show you proper disposal tomorrow and then travel to your towns to do the same. My suggestion is that you have them ready for me upon my arrival."

The councilmen and Nobles all looked to Rhaif then for confirmation.

"Nobles, send word to your Belwark captains to search the towns for any Infi. You'll heed the Venari's suggestion and have them ready for disposal upon his arrival."

Silence rested over the table for a moment. Aydra could feel her brother's anger at her side, but he didn't move.

"Are there any other demands for the meeting?" a councilman asked.

Everyone looked around the room, waiting for someone else to speak out. But no one did.

"Thank Arbina," Rhaif muttered as he pushed his chair back. "Let us feast," he announced.

Aydra didn't move from her chair. Her eyes nearly rolled as the men and women stood, all sighing in relief as though the meeting had been some great marathon. She grasped her drink in her hand and took a long swig of it, gulping it down with a glare over the rim. Her brother stood and shook hands with the man at his side. Aydra watched them all kiss one another's ass for another moment. Fake smiles. Taudry comments of war and snide remarks of grander.

For once, she wanted to hear someone say something that didn't go straight to the crown's head.

"I believe you're the only one in this room who wouldn't be beheaded at such an entrance."

She was reminded of her own fraudulent place in this kingdom. Her royal facade took over, and she raised a sly gaze up at her favorite Dreamer, Ash. His short sun-streaked light brown hair was cut clean over his pointed ears, and he gazed down at her with stark hazel, narrow eyes. The triangular set of his jaw matched the high collar on his white gambeson.

He extended his long hand down to her, and she allowed him to bring her to her feet. He pulled her close, his hand wrapping around her waist. "If I didn't know any better, I'd say you were trying to distract the entire council from some secret workings of yours," he said, his eyes darting down at her figure.

"And because you do know better?"

"I'd say you simply had a pleasant day on the beach." He lowered his head, his breath tickling her skin. "And were rested enough for an even more pleasant night." His lips pressed to her throat, and she cursed her body for its response.

She reached for his chin and lifted it. "Eat up, Dreamer. You'll need your strength later."

He smirked and nudged her nose with his, his long fingers clenching at her waist. His lips met hers, and she gave in to his musings, allowing his tongue to rake her own—but only for a moment. She pulled back and grazed his lip with her thumb.

"Sister!"

The noise of her sister's excited voice brought her back to the room. She gave Ash's chin a tug. "Find me later," she whispered.

Her sister's arm sank around her own as Ash stepped back. He gave her a short bow, his hair falling over his eyes. "My Queen," he acknowledged. His eyes averted to Nyssa, and he gave her a short bow as well. "Princess."

As he turned on his heel to leave her, Nyssa squeezed Aydra's arm. "One day, I'll make an entrance as you do," Nyssa said eagerly.

Aydra smirked, still watching Ash as he joined his company cohort, Haut. "One day, sister, you'll rule over all these men and not know the threat of a man underestimating you," she said as she turned to face her. "Of that, I am sure."

Nyssa's bright almond amber eyes sparkled at her above her freckled apple cheeks. Aydra smiled down at the beautiful nineteen-year-old standing in front of her. She'd braided three sections of her long dark cinnamon hair above her right ear, the rest of the silken waves flowing over the left side of her face, the side-swept bangs just hiding her eye. Aydra reached out and pushed the thick hair back, revealing the small blushed smile on her pouty lips, one of her dimples showing with the crook of her grin.

"You look beautiful, Nyssa," Aydra said, envious of the bright natural beauty her sister possessed. "Where did you get the dress?" she asked as her eyes darted over the navy velvet gown on her petite figure.

Nyssa held out her arms, showing off the long flared sleeves of it.

"Found it myself," she answered. "Dorian and I went out to the shores yesterday. We stopped at a few of the shops. He found a few items and bought me this."

"Your brother buying you clothes?" Aydra asked. "Careful. He'll think he can dress you next," she added with a wink.

Nyssa laughed. "Let me guess. Dear Rhafian left the blue dress out?"

"Mm… that he did."

"I assumed as much as soon as you walked in. You usually wear the lace ones when you want to piss him off."

Aydra took a long swig of her drink. "I think this time I exceeded expectations," she said, noticing her brother's glare from across the room.

"Drae," Nyssa said then, her voice taking a serious turn. "Why did you stand up for the Venari?"

Aydra looked around them and then pulled her sister over to the window. "What do you mean?" she asked her.

"I mean… you asked the Dreamer company to hunt elsewhere. Why?"

"I did not stand up for the Venari," Aydra argued. "After everything Duarb put Arbina through before him being forced into his tree. The greed of their ancestors, attempting to take over our kingdom, I dare not trust their kind. But… the Noctuans are different. The Venari have no control over the creatures that roam their Forest. Innocent creatures deserve to live, regardless of how misunderstood they might be."

"Innocent? The Noctuans?"

Aydra's stomach knotted at the confusion on her sister's face. "Oh." She realized she had not taken her to meet them yet. "Oh, I'm so sorry, Nyssa. I should have… We'll ride out together before the moons set. It is past time you learn of them. I'm sorry I have not taken you before."

Nyssa's weight shifted, nervousness taking over her features. "To… the Forest? Won't—"

"We'll be fine," Aydra assured her.

"If you'll not need me, my Lady, I will take my leave of the evening," Lex said upon reaching Aydra.

"Please do, Lex. Take a Noble with you," she teased. "Or perhaps my sister. She could use a night to lessen that frustration of hers."

Lex laughed. "That will be up to your princess to decide. In the meantime…" Her eyes trailed to one of the Dreamer women from the Village of Dreams in the corner. Aydra watched as Lex gave the woman a subtle wink.

"You always find the prettiest little thing in the room," Aydra cooed. Lex smiled, one arm pushing back behind her. "I take it Ash expects to warm your bed after this?" Lex asked.

"That he does," Aydra replied.

"Sure that's what you're thirsting for tonight?" Lex asked, brow lifting and gaze averting to the far corner.

Aydra frowned but followed her eyes and then nearly smacked her Second upon realizing whom she was referring to. "Please. I'd never give him the satisfaction."

"Oh, I'm sure he'd satisfy everything," Lex mocked against the rim of her cup.

"Perhaps you should invite him to your party."

"Perhaps I will. I'm sure he would love to join."

Aydra almost laughed at the smug glint in Lex's eyes. "Right. You have fun with that."

Lex swirled the last bit of wine in her goblet and then drank it, finishing with an audible "Ah," that Aydra smiled at.

"If you get bored of Ash, I'm sure we will have room enough for one more," Lex grinned at her.

"I will be sure to knock first."

Lex sat her cup down on the table. "Don't bother. Just join in," she added. "I'll see you tomorrow, my Queen."

Aydra raised her cup to her. "Yes. Tomorrow. We'll get to start our day with another beheading."

"Oh yes, that's right," Lex said delightedly. "Love a good beheading."

Aydra laughed as she watched her best friend wave and then stride over to the other side of the room.

Aydra found herself wandering absently around the room for some time, allowing her mind to wander as councilmen and women spoke with her about things she cared nothing about. The wine in her golden goblet swirled upon her walking. She chatted with her sister a few more times, but soon, she wandered into the darkened hall, itching to get away from the noises of the men and women fake laughing and discussing politics in the Chamber.

Almost immediately, the smell of Black herbal smoke filled her lungs, and she knew she was not the only one in the darkened hall.

"I believe I owe you an unfortunate thanks," said the voice she'd dreaded to hear since the meeting adjourned.

Aydra searched the darkness, only to find the Venari King, Draven, leaned against one of the tall open windows halfway down the hall, long pipe in his hand as his eyes met hers beneath the square of his brows.

"Lurking in the dark, Venari. How very… *you*," she drawled.

His muscled arm was silhouetted in the light of the torches and moons coming in through the windows. She noticed he'd taken his crown off and hung it on his belt as though it were an accessory. His long hair was now pulled up on his head in a thick bun, stray hairs falling out of it.

He struck a match against the stone, the amber light illuminating the most robust features of his handsome face, the pale of his sage eyes, and he lit the pipe. The short darkened beard around his mouth and along his jaw did not hide the bite of his lips around the pipe as he drew a long inhale. He allowed it to swim in his lungs, and then he extended the pipe to her. A great O of smoke emitted from his lips and fluttered out the window into the wind.

Enemy or not, black herb was black herb. After the day she'd had, she wanted nothing more than the swim of it through her veins.

She took the pipe from his callused hands and sat her wine goblet on the windowsill. The moment the wood touched her lips and she inhaled, she closed her eyes, allowing it to radiate through her muscles and send a chill down her spine. It was sweeter than she was used to, and her brows lifted as she opened her eyes to meet his.

"That is not from Dorian's garden," she managed as she handed the pipe back to him.

"No," he replied as he took it. "It's from mine."

She nodded quietly and picked her drink up once more, swirling the liquid in the goblet. The twinkling of the torches down in the village danced back at her, the lights looking like stars on the ground. Patterns emerged as the herb swam in her mind.

"I didn't do it for you, you know. The hunting agreement," she told him. "I did it for the Noctuans. As misunderstood as they are, they do not deserve to starve and die at the hands of those who fear them."

"Nevertheless, I appreciate it," he said as he puffed on the pipe once more.

She could feel his eyes on her, and she had to look twice upon finding his deep-set, green eyes deliberately traveling over her and then lingering at her hips.

"Eyes front, Venari," Aydra growled.

She hated him for his handsomeness and arrogant nature. The fact that they'd grown up opposite one another, always opposing the other, didn't help when he leered at her with his best lustful gaze.

The smirk she'd just thought about was staring at her when he lifted his eyes to her own.

A crooked smirk rested on his lips as he bit the end of the pipe in the corner of his mouth.

"Perhaps you should think about that before wearing something as distracting as this dress," he uttered.

"Your being distracted by body parts has more to do with you than me," she snapped back.

"You're not wrong," he agreed as he straightened. "A man's lust should be checked at the door and not allowed free roam on his features at the expense of a strong woman not in need of saving."

"Says the one who can't keep his gaze off something that isn't his," she mocked.

He held out the pipe to her again, tongue darting out over his mouth as he seemed to find her words both amusing and alluring.

She took the pipe with a perturbed twist of her lips.

"I think this dress says a lot about the both of us," he continued.

She pulled a deep inhale again and exhaled into the wind. "I am probably going to regret this, but do explain, Hunter."

He pushed off the wall and took a few slow steps around her. "You, in that you're confident enough to wear this for yourself and only yourself. It makes you feel empowered, in charge, like you could take on the world, which you certainly should. No other could pull this dress off. Your sister certainly couldn't... And me, in that—"

"You're a pig?" she interjected, handing him back the pipe.

He huffed amusedly and pushed the stray hairs that had fallen out of his ponytail back off his forehead. "Me in that I realize I've been in the woods far too long if I'm being distracted simply by the sight of a beautiful woman in a dress."

"What's wrong, Venari?" she teased. "Does the Hunter girls' attire not bring you to your knees?"

"I've not let a woman bring me to my knees in a long while."

"Don't—" she interjected before he could add anything more.

He met her eyes in a sideways stare off that she stood her ground on, knowing the both of them too stubborn to turn away. The challenge of ending the other too tempting.

Until Ash's voice caught their ears.

"Am I interrupting?" Ash called out.

A moment of silence stretched in the hall, Aydra nor Draven breaking their stares.

"Not at all," Draven said.

Aydra glared a final second, and then she averted her gaze over her shoulder to the Dreamer who was holding steady at the entrance of the hall.

"I was just telling the Venari King what a pig he is," Aydra informed Ash.

"Care to take a walk out of here, Venari?" Ash said.

Draven chuckled under his breath, blatant smug mockery settled in him from their staring, and he leaned his head down, nose brushing against Aydra's ear.

"You know where I'll be if you'd rather see a King on his knees before you than this lonely Captain." His words tickled her ear, and she nearly called her raven to maim him.

"I'll enjoy killing you one day," she uttered as her lashes lifted to his.

"And I'll enjoy watching you burn," he growled.

The fire blazed in his gaze once more as he left her side. He clapped Ash on his shoulder upon passing and pressed the pipe between his lips. "Enjoy your night, Ash," Draven mocked.

Aydra stared at Draven as his shadowed figure disappeared into the darkness, still fuming from his advances and the way he riled her up with simply a few words.

Ash crossed the space between them and reached for her hand. "My Queen," he said upon kissing her knuckles. "Shall we retire for the evening?"

Her lips twisted upwards just slightly, and she brought herself out of the exchange she'd just shared with Draven with an audible sigh.

"We shall," she agreed.

3

Aydra watched the torches on the beach for some of the night. Wherever this Infi creature was, it was hiding very well, or perhaps smart enough to make itself scarce at the sight of Belwarks patrolling the surf.

"Idiots," Aydra muttered about them.

The arms that wrapped around her a few moments later didn't startle her. Ash pressed his lips to her neck beneath her ear and nuzzled her skin. "Come back to bed," he urged her. "Your men can handle finding the creature."

The swim of the black herb she'd smoked continued to pulse through her veins. Her head sighed back into his embrace as his hands began to wander. She hadn't found her end with him so quickly in a very long time. Ash could be a blunder, treating her as though she would break at times. But that night, she didn't know if perhaps he'd learned new tricks or if it was the herb that made her so sensitive. Whatever the cause, she wouldn't deny herself the pleasure of it a few times more.

Ash left her bed a couple of hours before the sunrise. Aydra was more satisfied than she had in a long time, probably since the last time she and Lex had, together, enjoyed the company of one of the Honest trader men to come through.

The torches remained lit on the beach, and she saw the Belwarks had clustered together towards the entrance wall. Aydra scowled at the display and grabbed for her riding clothes.

Lex was still asleep when Aydra knocked on her door a half hour later. After a few knocks, Aydra simply burst in, finding Lex lying between Councilman Asherdoe's twin daughters. The two were most commonly known as the Scindo twins and had been known to frequent Dorian's bed as well.

"Well, well," Aydra said, arms crossing over her chest at the end of the bed. "I suppose one daughter wasn't enough?"

A small smile rose on Lex's face, and she stirred. "It is not sunrise, my Queen," she managed, sitting up and rubbing her face. "Did you —" she paused in her speech, and her brows narrowed at the sight of the clothing Aydra had on. "Did something happen?"

Aydra nodded towards the window. "Rhaif's men are useless. We're taking over the search."

A soft grin pressed to Lex's sleepy face. "Why we ever send them to do our job is beyond me," she said.

"Agreed." Aydra turned on her heel and started for the door. "I'll be on the first terrace. Put on clothes and get our horses ready."

"Oooo... So demanding so early," Lex mocked. "I like it."

The brunette in the bed stirred. "What's going— Your Majesty!" The girl nearly shrieked in surprise at seeing Aydra in the room and pulled the sheets up over her breasts. "My Queen—I—"

Aydra nearly laughed, and she held a hand up. "I've seen worse in more compromising positions, Aani," she told her. "Lex, I'll see you in a bit. Aani, clean yourself and your sister up. Your father will expect you innocent once more at breakfast."

Aydra exited Lex's room and went downstairs to the terrace below the Throne Room. It was a favorite place of hers to go whenever she woke so early.

The crisp night air welcomed her. Two crescent moons waved at her from over the ocean far below. She moved her hair off her neck and pulled it into a messy ponytail atop her head as she reached the stone edge wall. Stray curls fell out of the bun and tickled her face and neck.

She could see most of the kingdom from that terrace. The only people out in the streets far below were the bread makers, smells of honey and yeast filling the air. She closed her eyes and pressed her palms onto the stone, leaning over it as the wind circled around her.

"You know when I chose this spot, I had thought I would be alone to watch the sunrise," came a deep groggy voice she recognized all too well.

Her eyes opened, and she turned just slightly, finding Draven sitting on the ground in the darkness behind her, back leaned against the opposite facing wall. He was packing his pipe, the only glimpse of him being the strongest of his features silhouetted in the moons light. His hair was down, the thick, unkept waves pushed over to cover the left side of his face. She turned, leaned her own back against her wall, and crossed her arms over her chest.

"A bit early, isn't it?" she asked about the herb.

He didn't look up as he continued to pack the pipe with a pale looking herb she wasn't familiar with. "This is my morning herb. A different sort from that of yesterday evening." A match was pulled from his pocket, and he struck it against the stone as he'd done the night before. It illuminated his face, and he pressed his lips around the pipe, taking a long draw. His head leaned back against the stone as he held it in a moment, and then a long O of smoke exhaled from his mouth. She watched him take a long, deliberate look over her body once his eyes opened, and he pulled his knees into his chest.

"I take it you had a pleasant night," he said.

Aydra couldn't help her brows elevating at the memory of it, and then she noticed the smug look on Draven's face, and the entire pleasantry of her night nearly vanished.

"The herb?"

A gentle huff of amusement left his lips, and he glanced up to the stars, exhaling smoke. "No idea what you mean."

Her arms hugged tighter against her chest. "That would explain a few things," she mumbled. "I haven't come that quickly with Ash in ages."

He choked on the inhale he'd just taken and doubled over coughing, gripping to the stone floor. A triumphant smirk made its way to her lips.

"Did I say something?" she teased.

He clenched his chest, attempting to regain his composure. "No, I just—I wasn't sure you knew how to joke."

"Who says it was a joke?" she asked, finally meeting his eyes.

He watched her a moment, an unfamiliar play in his gaze, and then he stood from the ground. He stretched the space between them in only a few steps. As he leaned over the wall as she was doing, he extended his hand with the pipe towards her, and she eyed the green herb in it. She didn't entirely trust that this was a weaker brand as he'd claimed. Especially as Draven's tolerance was sure to be more than hers with his grand stature.

"I smoke that now and I won't be able to manage the rest of the day," she told him.

He puffed on it again and nodded towards the east. "I think we have a bit of time we could take care of any... *urges*... you might have."

Her lips pursed in his direction, and she almost rolled her eyes at his suggestive brow. "You're disgusting."

A smile briefly quirked on his lips, but it was gone in a flash, and she was left wondering if perhaps she'd imagined it.

"Have you any word if they found the Infi?" he asked.

"Nothing. But I was watching the guards some during the night. Rhaif's men are completely useless," she answered. "You'll show me proper disposal when it is found, not the others."

"Why are you the one beheading criminals?"

"I refuse to give orders which I am not comfortable taking care of on my own," she answered. "I am in charge of the security within this kingdom. I will be the one to serve up any punishments as decided by our Council. Whether that is by torture or death. Their lives are mine."

Draven's eyes fluttered, teeth clenching, and she swore she heard a low growl emit from his throat, but she didn't have a moment to ponder it. He inhaled the herb deeply, fist clenching and unclenching at his side as his eyes opened once more and met hers.

"What?" she asked, wary of the weight of his gaze.

"Nothing," he said quietly. He straightened and leaned over the banister again. "This title... it's new, is it not?" he asked.

"It was given to me upon my discovering the Infi the first time. I brought him before Council and then took care of his execution myself."

"And exactly how many of these punishments have you had to fulfill?"

"The inner workings of our kingdom is not your concern."

"So two, then?" he dared to say.

Aydra glared and opened her mouth to retort, but she was cut off by Lex's voice coming from the doorway.

"My Lady, your horse is ready," Lex said.

"Going somewhere?" Draven asked.

Aydra pulled her riding gloves from her belt and began pushing them on her fingers. "Would you like to stand here getting high and gazing at the fog on the beach, or would you like to join us on hunting the beast this morning?"

"Beast..." Draven's amused voice trailed, and he deliberately puffed on his pipe again. "The Infi is but a Lesser being. Not a beast," he said with the exhale.

"A wretched being that should never have been allowed to walk this land on two feet," she argued.

"You're joining the hunt?"

"We're relieving them. Myself and Lex," she said. "Taking over for the night party. My brother's guards think they can have all the fun. They're wrong." She pulled the hood of her cloak up over her head as Lex handed her her bow, and then she turned back to him.

"Are you coming?"

Draven considered her a moment before stuffing his pipe down his vest. "Do you have a horse?"

"I think we can help with that," Lex replied.

The gallop of the horses' hooves on the stone echoed in the still morning air. The fog licked at their feet and entwined through the streets. The sun was just peeking over the horizon in the east when they reached the beach, and Rhaif's men met them at the bottom.

"To what do we owe the pleasure of the Queen on this morning?" Bard asked her.

"You may take rest, Bard. My Second and I will take it from here," Aydra told him.

"I'm afraid I cannot do that, Your Majesty," Bard argued. "The King —"

"Is she not your Queen?" Lex interjected.

"Well… Yes, but we have orders specifically from the King to find the beast—"

The deep chuckle from beneath Draven's hood ceased Bard's words.

"Beast… again with that word," he muttered. "If you're looking for some great beast, you will not find it. Infis are methodic, manipulative, secretive, and stealthy. You are hunting a ghost, Belwarks. Not a beast."

"Then perhaps you should have been out here all night," called one of the other Belwarks.

Draven eyed the guard a moment. "Go home, little soldier. The grown ups will take it from here." He clicked his tongue twice, and his horse started forward down the beach.

"Taking orders from the Venari King now, Your Majesty?" Bard asked her once Draven was out of earshot.

"You've lived here long enough to know by now that something as rash as this plan is one of mine, Bard. Not his. He's here because he's stupid enough to follow me." Her horse shifted under her. "Did you find anything last night? Anything odd?"

"Nothing out of the ordinary to report," Bard said.

"You're sure he couldn't have snuck past you and into town?" she asked.

"As I said, Your Majesty, there was nothing to report. Nothing at all. Makes me wonder what we are even doing out here," he replied with a look back at Draven's disappearing figure.

"You don't believe him?" she asked.

"I'll believe him when you've got the Infi's head in your hand."

Aydra exchanged a glance with Lex and then gave Bard a nod. "Go home, Belwarks. Get some rest. I will call when we find him."

Bard called for his men then, and the throng of thirty men on horses passed them by, each giving Aydra a nod upon their passing. As they left, Lex and Aydra urged their horses forward. Draven was already well ahead of them, scanning the beach in the faint purple light of the sunrise behind the cliffs to their right.

"Do you think Bard has a point?" Lex asked after a while.

"I'm aware of the Chronicles' stories of their betrayal." Aydra paused a moment and considered the Venari King once more. "But I think if this Venari wanted our kingdom, he would have a better plan than sending the Belwarks on a chase through the darkness for a creature that doesn't exist."

A yawn slipped on her face then, and she let go of the reins to stretch her arms over her head.

"Assuming Ash finally learned where things are?" Lex mused.

"I can honestly say, I'm not sure," Aydra answered.

"Not sure?" Lex frowned. "How can you not be sure?"

"Because I'm not sure whether he actually found it or if the herb I smoked with the Venari had something to do with it," Aydra said. "Judging by the way he—"

"Whoa—" Lex pulled on her horse. "Hang on, you smoked with the Venari last night? How drunk were you?"

"Oh, shut up," Aydra muttered.

Lex snorted and started forward on the horse again. "Queen of Promise getting high with her enemy King," she mocked. "What will the Chronicles say about that?"

"The Chronicles will never know," Aydra said fast. "And you'll keep your mouth shut about it."

"Yes, ma'am," Lex grinned.

They trotted in silence for a bit, both of them staring at the back of Draven's figure up the beach. She could not deny the curiosity of his shadowed facade… Wondering what he hid so well beneath his hardened and dangerous exterior.

Aydra's eyes fluttered close a moment as the memory of the herb came to mind. She only remembered flashes of feeling, of ecstasy and desire pulsing through her as it had not done with Ash in the past. The brown-haired Dreamer was always desperate to please her, even if he did go a bit sideways at times, trying perhaps too hard or treating her more gentle than she liked to be handled.

Then again, she was the Queen.

She was sure Ash didn't want to be beheaded if he pressed too far.

"I can't believe you smoked Venari herb without me," Lex said after a few minutes.

"Would have made quite the crowded bed," Aydra bantered.

"Maybe I could have finally shown Ash what he's doing wrong," Lex said with a wink.

"This is true," Aydra couldn't help but agree.

Lex sighed audibly, and they watched as Draven stretched his own arms up over his head, pulling and stretching those taut muscles behind his back. Aydra allowed her gaze to wander, to take in the ripple of his stretch, feeling her head tilt despite herself at his movements.

"Imagine if you'd smoked it and went to bed with him," Lex muttered. "I told you he'd satisfy everything."

"Maybe you should try it after the next meeting," Aydra said. "Give yourself a change of pace."

"If that man cornered me in one of the servants' tunnels, I daresay I'd get on my knees and do whatever he wanted," Lex admitted.

An audible chortle exhaled from Aydra's mouth. "*Hilexi Ashborne,*" she drawled, "Who knew you would get on your knees for such a man?"

"Do you know which other man I'd get on my knees for?" Lex asked, raising her brow.

Aydra eyed her sideways, a knowing smile on her lips.

"Grey," they said together.

"That man…" Aydra's voice drifted as she remembered the salt and pepper bearded, smith's face and arms. "How is it we've not noticed him before?"

"Surprised you didn't go back to see him after the beach the other day," Lex said.

"I was pre-occupied."

"Ah... the greenhorn Belwark, Corbin," Lex remembered. "Do tell. How was he?"

"Bold," Aydra said. "It was quite enjoyable. Actually have a scratch from where he pushed me against the cliffside."

"Good on him," Lex said. "I'm impressed."

"You know, he did this thing with his tongue, almost like a flicking —"

The sudden flash of fire before them made their horses balk.

Draven stood in the sand a few feet ahead, flaming torchlight in his hand. He stared between them, nostrils flared in an annoyed manner. His jaw twitched upon meeting her eyes.

"If you two are quite done talking about your conquests, I'd like to get on searching for the Infi," came Draven's low bark.

"What's wrong, Venari?" Lex asked as she reached down and calmed her horse. "Jealous you weren't a part of it?"

"Had I been a part of it, neither of you would be able to sit on your horses this morning," he said in a voice that so resembled a purr that a chill ran down Aydra's spine.

He looked between them again as they dismounted their steeds.

"Your voices carry," he continued. "We'll be lucky if you haven't driven the Infi further up the beach."

Aydra left her cloak on the steed and hooked her quiver of arrows over her, along with her bow. "Very well, Venari," she said once Lex was ready too. "Lead the way."

Draven's stern gaze darted between them, obviously unsure of how to take the women standing before him. "Are there any caves or hides around here that you are aware of?"

"Behind Arbina's pool," Aydra replied. "We threw the creature's body off the tower into her waters."

"We'll start there," Draven said.

Silence surrounded them as the three set off down the beach, Draven leading the way towards the waterfall. The air chilled around them, soft waves crashing in the ocean to their left. Aydra heard the squawk of the seagulls fighting over food all around, and she tried to shut their voices out. Her raven must have heard her, for she heard him cut through the sky a few moments later, cackling at the annoying ocean birds and shooing them away.

"What exactly are we looking for?" Lex asked.

"Infis are shiftlings," he said in a low tone.

"Duarb was cursed with giving children of both fates, the Infi and the Venari, after he did what he did to my giver mother," Aydra cut in.

"Lies of your Chronicles," he growled.

"How else would you say your giver came to bear them and your own kind—"

"Do not speak of my kind as if you know anything of it," he hissed, rounding on her.

She balked. "You—"

"Neither of you has answered my question," Lex interjected lazily.

Draven paused. The glare he stared at her with should have struck fear into her, for she was sure that's what he was accustomed to. But her lips pursed, and she raised her chin, daring him to blink or back down from her as they'd done the night before. The severe beating of her heart slowed, almost as though the adrenaline were calming her.

The wind whipped around once, and then Draven turned away from her. He started walking again, a conviction in his deliberate strides, one hand on the handle of his sword. She could see the flex in the back of his bicep when his hand tightened around it, and he scanned the shadows with his night-piercing gaze.

"When Infis are born beneath Duarb's roots, they are in their true form. Skin near translucent, red boils on their flesh. If this one is still shifting back from death, he will look like this. If he has already mutated, he will look like a normal being, possibly either old and frail or tall and handsome, appealing to what they think would manipulate you most."

"Do they ever change to women?" Lex asked.

"I've never seen a woman Infi," Draven answered. "But I suppose it wouldn't be out of the question."

It wasn't long before the sound of the waterfall began to block out all others. Aydra could smell the poison of Arbina's pool at the bottom of it, the clear liquid looking so inviting that any who did not know better would have succumbed to its depths.

"Careful," Aydra said as Draven neared the water. "It is poison to anyone not of her own."

"Of course it is," he muttered. "I'm sure that bitch has a special poison for Venari as well."

"What is that?" Lex asked.

The noise of the waterfall was so loud, Aydra barely heard her. "What is what?" she called loudly.

Lex leaned over and pointed in front of Aydra's face towards a light coming from behind the water. "That."

Draven tensed at Aydra's side, and he stepped in front of them. "That... is an Infi," he said quietly.

Faintly behind the water was the sight of a small fire going. A being was bent over it, a blanket covering its mangled body. Aydra could not make out much of it, but what she could tell looked like a skeleton child, flesh milky white and balding. So different from the ones whom she'd beheaded that she almost began to argue with the Venari.

But when it turned its head and stared at them through the water with bulging yellow eyes, her stomach dropped, and she knew she'd seen the creature before.

"If he runs, shoot him in the neck," Draven said.

Aydra didn't get a chance to respond. Draven was already creeping around the fall towards the creature. She gave Lex a nod, and Lex moved around the opposite way. Aydra stood her ground and slowly pulled an arrow from the quiver on her back.

The creature spotted her. She noticed it crouching down, inch by inch, as though trying to hide in the shadows of the fall.

A sudden wind wrapped around her, and a chill struck her skin. She wobbled on the spot, blinking as her breath shortened. Incomprehensible whispers filled her ears. The beach began to spin around her.

The creature ran.

Draven shouted something. Aydra shook the nauseating rush and blinked back to reality. She realized then that the creature was running straight at her. It thrust itself through the water, not seeming to give thought to the liquid blistering its flesh.

It was fast. Faster than any creature Aydra had ever seen. The creature's wild yellow eyes paralyzed her on the spot.

"SHOOT IT!"

Its mouth opened. Nubs of teeth lined its gums. The blanket flew off its shoulders. It seemed to be growing taller as it ran, faster and faster towards her.

"AYDRA! SHOOT IT!"

Aydra finally moved. She pulled the arrow through her bow and let it fly through the air. It hit the creature in the shoulder. But the Infi barely slowed, still running at her. She didn't have time to pull another arrow.

—Her sword caught the creature's throat as it jumped in the air at her.

A spray of thick black blood shattered over her, and the creature landed in the sand at her back.

"What the fuck was that?" came Draven's angered voice. "You see an Infi running toward you, and you paralyze?"

Aydra spat out the Infi's blood that had landed on her lips and glared at him. "I—"

His sword thrust into the head of the Infi behind her, and he picked it up like he had stabbed dinner. "I said shoot it in the neck," he snapped. "Do they not teach archery in this fucking shit of a kingdom?"

"It is dead," she argued. "What is the problem?"

"I'll have them put that in the Chronicles where it asks for your last words," he growled as he knelt beside it. His knife ripped through the creature's grey flesh. His hand plunged inside it, emerging to the surface again with its heart in his hand.

"Catch."

He tossed the heart towards her without a glance. She nearly dropped it when she realized it was still beating.

"Oh, Architects," Lex mumbled upon reaching them. "It's still—"

Draven stood then and pressed the hilt of his knife into Aydra's palm. "To kill an Infi outside of Duarb's territory, you have to remove its heart and keep it separate from its bones. Otherwise, it will merge back together before you can reach the Hills for Duarb to take it back. The body and heart must be taken to the Hills, which means we've two days ride ahead of us."

"Two?" Aydra repeated.

"Your territory stops at the Bedrani pass," Draven explained. "Duarb's roots cannot reach past there. It's why so many Infi travel to the mountains and now, I suppose, to this realm to hide."

"I'll get the horses," Lex said as she took off in a run.

Draven gave an upwards nod to the knife in Aydra's hand. "Knife into the heart, and it must stay there until we reach Bedrani," Draven told Aydra. "The only way to stop its beating is for Duarb to take it back."

"Is it this hard to kill a Venari as well?" Aydra asked.

"The Infi are an immortal curse," he glared. "The Venari are not."

4

Aydra tossed the impaled heart and knife into one of her saddlebags once Lex had returned with the horses. They helped Draven roll the Infi creature into a blanket and tie it to the back of his horse. Aydra washed herself of the blood in the surf before they headed back to the castle.

"My Queen—"

Aydra held a hand up to Bard as he met them on the castle steps. "Wake my brother," she commanded him. "We do not have time to waste."

Lex jumped from her horse and began barking orders to the guards standing around, telling them to pack up water and food for their journey east.

Prince Dorian was first to arrive on the scene, his blue robe tucked around him, his fluffy black hair still disheveled.

"Morning, sister," he said with a yawn. "What's this about your bloodlust taking over before dawn?"

Aydra eyed him, reaching up to lift his chin. He was a couple of inches taller than her and growing by the day. "You know for someone of nineteen—" she raised a brow at the hickey marks on his neck "—you are certainly getting around."

He gave her a sleepy wink and smiled. "Reputation to maintain," he yawned. "You understand." His eyes traveled back, and he met the gaze of the Venari King. "Morning, King," he said with an upward nod. "What trouble did my bloodthirsty sister find for you on this morning?"

Aydra shoved his arm, and Dorian laughed softly. Draven looked between them before gesturing toward the dead creature on the back of his horse. "Infi creature behind your mother's pool," Draven told him.

"He's showing me proper disposal, should we ever need it again," Aydra informed Dorian.

"Can I come?" Dorian asked.

Aydra met Draven's eyes. Draven shrugged, and Aydra turned back to her younger brother. "I suppose you are the next King..." she thought aloud as she started petting her horse. "Can't imagine it would be up to Nyssa to behead criminals," she mumbled under her breath. "Fine," she finally agreed. "Change clothes. Quickly."

Dorian beamed. He ran up the steps to the castle again, nearly running over Rhaif on his way through the doors. Rhaif said something to Dorian about it, but neither stopped walking. Aydra stopped stroking her horse as Rhaif approached. He was still in his nightclothes, and for a moment, he looked like the old Rhaif that she had once adored and played sticks with on the beach.

He reached out for her wet hair upon reaching her, a look of confusion on his features as he twirled the curl between his fingers. "Why are you wet?" he asked, releasing the strand.

"Good morning, brother," she almost snapped.

His eyes locked on hers, having apparently heard the annoyance in her tone. "What?" he asked.

"You're welcome."

"Welcome for what?"

She pulled open the bag on the saddle and revealed the heart inside. "Finding the Infi creature," she told him. Her gaze cut to her brother's Second standing behind Rhaif. "No thanks to you, Bard," she practically snarled. She turned again to Rhaif. "Lex and I will accompany the Venari to Bedrani where he will show us proper disposal of the creature's body."

"I do not want you going alone," Rhaif said. "You will take my company with you."

"Your company is a near embarrassment to this kingdom," Aydra countered. "They had all night to find the creature, and there he was, in the exact spot we threw him to." She waited for him to say something, but when he didn't, she continued. "My Second and I are leaving, and we are taking Dorian with us. We will return in a few days, finally rid of the filth in our streets."

Rhaif's jaw set. "And the Dreamer towns? Will you be traveling to those to dispose of those bodies as well?"

"I will accompany the Venari King to the Villages," came Dorian's voice as he rejoined them.

Rhaif's stern stare flickered between the pair and then back to Draven. "Very well," he finally agreed.

The first day and night were a blur. Not many words were spoken between the four as they traveled and then rested overnight on a hill. Aydra's butt was numb from the horse, and she could feel the exhaustion of each one of the beasts pouring through her, making her more tired than she would have been were it only her own exhaustion.

Aydra's abilities allowed her core to connect with all creatures. She was well practiced in feeling their emotions just as she felt her own and could even transport her consciousness into her raven if she wanted. Different from Nyssa, who could only hear the creatures, and different from previous Queens, who may not have even heard all animals.

Aydra fell asleep in the grass curled next to her own horse before they ate supper.

She dreamt of running, of fire chasing her, and only when it caught up with her did she jolt awake. Cold sweat beaded on her forehead, but the soft coo of her raven and dewy fog around her calmed her heartbeat.

Draven was already awake, putting out the fire and checking the straps on his horse. Aydra didn't speak to him, but she did the same, too sleepy still to get into any sort of argument with him so early in the morning. She woke Lex and Dorian. Within the hour, they were riding across the Hills once more.

The path they were on was beat of grass and full of mud. It had been a few years since Aydra had ridden so far south. After her predecessor, Zoria, died from sickness, she'd not ventured far from the castle except to the cliffside an hour out.

How she missed the fresh smells and wind in her hair.

It took them the rest of the day to reach Bedrani, having only stopped a few times during the day for water, food, and to give the horses a small break.

Bedrani was a cluster of three great stones on a high hill, which sat stark in the middle of the Haerland flats, south of the Blackhand Mountains. It marked the fork in the road from the south. If you took the path due northeast, you would find yourself the path of the Knotted Caves to the Blackhand Mountains. A treacherous journey as the caves were not easy to navigate and could easily consume you if you did not know the way.

The path northwest, the path they'd taken from Magnice, was the path most used as it was the path every Ambassador and Bedrani Council member took from their southern Dreamer towns to reach the kingdom of Magnice.

Aydra hadn't seen the Bedrani boulders since she was a child, so when it rose on the horizon, she had to pause. Her raven circled overhead, and she took a moment to take in the sights around her.

Dorian and his horse came up beside her, pausing for a minute as well. "We should do this more often," he said.

"Yeah," she agreed without taking her eyes off the horizon. "We should."

They stopped and rested on the hill with the boulders. Because of the darkness, Draven insisted they start a fire and get some rest first, determined to not send the creature back to Duarb's roots until the morning.

Once more, the exhaustion of the horses filled Aydra, and she hardly stayed awake past dinner. Darkness consumed her as she leaned back against the cold stone.

The next thing she knew, she was running again, the fire tickling her feet on the floor of the castle. Every turn was wrong. It was an endless maze of fire and chills.

She bolted upright once more, the fog on the ground filling her vision.

A violet hue settled across the landscape as the sun threatened to rise. Aydra cracked her neck and stood. The wet grass curled beneath her bare toes, and she inhaled the scent of the dirt she so rarely got to enjoy.

Dorian and Lex appeared to still be asleep around her.
What time is it? she asked her raven as he landed on the top of one of the boulders.

An hour to sunrise, he told her.

She wrapped her cloak over her arms and stepped around the boulder. A sudden chill ran over her, almost nauseating. She blinked and looked around her for any explanation. It felt as though she'd stepped through some invisible gateway to a world not her own.

"Interesting," came Draven's unexpected voice.

Aydra nearly jumped, and she looked down to find him sitting against the rock just to her right, opposite side of the same rock she'd curled up against for the night.

"What is with you and sneaking up on people?" she snapped.

He looked as though he would laugh. "You live in darkness long enough, you learn to become one with it," he replied cryptically.

She pulled her cloak tighter as she gave him a once over, noticing him whittling something with his knife, a new long pipe it looked like. "What is interesting?" she asked, referring to what he'd said.

"The shiver you felt upon entering my realm," he answered without looking up. "Not everyone feels it."

"Perhaps it is a warning from your giver for me to stay out."

"Perhaps." He blew on the end of the pipe, blowing away any stray shavings that were left.

"Other pipe not working very well?" she asked.

"Not really your concern," he said as he turned it over to inspect it. "Tell me, Sun Queen, are you ready to dispose of your beast, or should I let you sing to the hills this morning?" he asked, finally making eye contact with her.

Her arms tightened over her chest, and she knew he was mocking her. "Just show me how to get rid of it, Venari."

She woke Dorian and Lex soon after their exchange. Draven pulled the body of the Infi off the horse and unfurled it from the blanket, letting its rotting corpse roll onto the grass at the bottom of the Bedrani hill. Aydra pulled the heart from her bag and tossed it to Draven's open palms.

The moment he took the knife from it, it began to beat once more.

"The Chronicles do not speak of this part of the curse," Aydra muttered.

"The Chronicles are lies," Draven replied.

He shoved the heart back into the gaping wound of the creature's chest and stood. Its chest rose off the ground, and its bones began to crack. Aydra took a step back and put a protective hand across Dorian's chest. Draven went back to the horses, and a moment later, he shoved Aydra's bow and an arrow into her chest.

"Try not to miss this time," Draven warned.

Aydra glared at him as he and the others moved back from the creature.

Bones continued to crack, and the creature started to lift off the ground as though it were putting itself back together. It hovered between creature and being for a moment before it found itself doubled over on its hands and knees on the ground.

Not a creature, but a male looked up at her as it lowered its mangled hands.

One yellow eye. One blue eye. Nose crooked but slowly straightening as the flesh twisted on its face, morphing from burned and disfigured to smooth and handsome. Its wide eyes pleaded with her from the ground.

"My Queen," she heard it say. "My Queen, please. I mean you no harm."

Aydra stared down her nose at it, chin raised, weary of the begging it was doing before her. The memory of it running at her across the beach reminded her of what it indeed was.

A monster manipulator.

It reached up towards the bow in her hands. "Please, I—"

It must have seen Draven, for its face flashed the foul creature once more, and it hissed in Draven's direction.

The creature bolted to its feet and took off running in the opposite direction.

Aydra pulled the arrow through her bow, aiming for the neck, and—

The arrow landed with a thud in its throat. Its feet dragging on the grass before it fell flat on its face.

"Look at that," Draven muttered behind her. "The Queen does know how to use a weapon not made of her body."

She glared back at him. "What now?"

"Just wait," he told her.

"For what? For it to get back up and run away again?"

Draven wrapped his arms over his chest, that confident Venari aura exuding from the prominent stance he stood in. He gave an upwards nod back at the body once more when he caught her stare.

The ground began to tremble.

The earth snapped.

A gaping crack moved fast towards them. Fissures opened up around the Infi's body. A violent tremor shook her to the point that she nearly lost her balance, and Lex grabbed her arm as she, too, almost fell.

The wind wrapped around them. Aydra looked bewilderedly back at Draven and started to speak, but he was watching the Infi, utterly unfazed by what was happening around them.

Tree roots shot up from beneath the fissures. Her eyes widened back at the scene as the roots' finger-like ends paused above the Infi as though it were waiting to pounce. The wind whipped past them once

more, and then—

The roots dove inside the creature's body.

"I think I'm going to hurl," she heard Dorian say.

She could see the roots wrapping inside the creature's mouth, ears, and wounds. The wind began to slow, and she noticed something white inside the roots' grips as they reemerged into the open air.

Bones.

The ground trembled again, and the fissures slowly closed. The last root to retract back into the earth carried the Infi's heart in its grasp. And then—

The hills were silent once more.

Aydra couldn't move.

She'd just watch a creature's insides get pulled into the ground by its giver.

"You wanted to know how to kill an Infi," came Draven's voice. "I assume you are satisfied?"

"That was disgusting," Aydra said as he walked around her towards the creature.

"I never claimed it to be pretty," he said, crouching down beside it. He pushed on the rubber-like skin left behind. "The rain will take care of the shell." He stood once more and brushed his hands on his pants as he turned back to them.

"Who's hungry?"

Draven left them to hunt for rabbits a few minutes later. Aydra sat with Dorian against the boulders, and neither could stop staring at the empty skin lying at the bottom of the hill.

"We should tell the Scribe of this when we get back," Aydra said.

"I volunteered to help him get rid of the others," Dorian said in an almost trance-like voice. "Tell me again why I volunteered for that."

"Because you're the bravest of us," she replied in a sing-song voice.

Dorian leaned back against the boulder, eyes still staring into the distance. Aydra curled her knees into her chest, and movement caught her gaze across the field. She squinted, and she could see Draven lying in the grass on his stomach. She couldn't see the weapon he had in his hand, but she felt the thud of the rabbit's life leave its body a moment later.

A grunt behind them made Aydra smirk. Lex was trying to get a fire started, but the wind kept putting it out. She heard her curse Duarb's winds and then throw something forcefully into the open field.

Aydra exchanged a look with Dorian, and he laughed as he stood. "Looks like your Second could use some help," he said as he offered a hand to Aydra.

"I believe this is your chance to show off," she said, taking his hand.

Dorian had grown more in the last year. He was a few inches taller than her now, which was honestly saying something as Aydra herself was nearly six feet tall. But Dorian was still as gangly as ever. As though his muscles seemed to be struggling to keep up with the stretching of his bones. His shoulders were trying their hardest to grow with all the training he had begun doing with Lex. His deep-set, widely rounded stark blue eyes tore through her beneath his bold brows. His fluffy black was unruly, sticking out in every direction and curling at the top when he would push it back off his forehead, which he usually did.

She was glad he was finally growing into his stature. At one point when he was younger, she remembered his eyes being all she would see when she looked upon his young face, and while that still rang somewhat true, at least he was growing into the sarcastic smirk he wore on his features all the time.

Aydra reached out and fluffed his hair playfully. "I can't decide if you always look as though you're up to no good or if you're sad with those eyes," she said fondly.

He huffed amusedly under his breath. "Ah. Secrets, sister," he said.

The noise of Lex throwing something else, frustratedly, into the air diverted their attentions. Dorian grinned at Aydra, and she knew he was excited about the chance to show off his own fire powers.

Dorian practically ran down the hill.

"Calm down, Second Sun," Dorian called out. "I'll help."

Lex's hands sat haughtily on her hips. "You can't. This damned wind of the Venari is debilitating. I can't—"

Dorian put his hand beneath the pieces of wood she'd piled up, and a navy flame grew in his blackening palm. Similar to the way Rhaif's fire grew on his skin, Dorian's looked like lightning streaks spreading up his flesh instead of intricate spiderwebs like Rhaif's.

It started in his nail beds and stretched until it turned his whole hands black.

Aydra saw his eyes flash black—the true form of the Fire Prince coming to the surface—but the form receded quickly, and the smirking teen turned back to his usual self.

Aydra crossed her arms over her chest and smiled proudly at her brother.

"Oh." Lex's gaze met Aydra's. "I forgot he could do that."

"You can thank me when I get back from the villages," he said with a wink.

"Bold," Lex laughed, exchanging a look with Aydra. "But you're not really my type."

"Didn't know you had a type, Second," came Draven's voice as he rejoined them. "It was my impression you merely took your Queen's leftovers."

Lex snorted and quickly clapped a hand over her mouth, and Dorian chortled aloud. Aydra felt her nostrils flare as she attempted to keep her amusement inside at the snarky crook of a smirk on Draven's face.

"Funny, Venari," she finally said. "Lex, I'll finish packing the horses if you want to get a move on with breakfast. We have a long journey back to Magnice."

The deliberate once over Draven gave her made her hug her arms around her chest. She returned it with a raised brow and then turned on her heel to pack their things.

Damn Venari.

5

Two days passed before Aydra and Lex returned to the ever bright kingdom they called home. Aydra paused her horse upon seeing its glory a few miles out, and she allowed herself a moment to take in the sight of its white facade built into the cliffside. Soldiers walked along the top of the great walls surrounding the bottom of the hill: the gates to the kingdom.

The wrought iron gate was open, as it always was. Farmers and traders flooded in and out, the busy day coming to an end. Colorful tarps sat stark against the white rock over some of the winding streets to block the bright sun.

The road was busy as they continued on at a leisurely pace. Every Dreamer to pass gave a nod and moved off the path, allowing Aydra and Lex to push through. Aydra knew a few, and she paused to speak with them. They told her how their goods were moving, if they were having any troubles with securing items, and how their families were doing.

Bard and his men were waiting for them at the castle gates.

"My Queen," he acknowledged upon her dismounting her horse.

She handed the reins to him and gave him a full once over, noticing him wearing his best gambeson and that he had brushed his long hair.

"Bard," she managed as she started removing her riding gloves. "You're looking delectable today. What's the occasion?" she asked.

"Your brother asked that we attend the banquet he is holding in your honor tonight," he replied.

"And where is my brother? Could he not be bothered to welcome his favorite sister back to the safety of our home?"

"He waits for you in the Throne Room, ma'am," Bard replied.

Aydra frowned. "The Throne Room? Why there?"

"I do not question my King," Bard said. "I only heed his orders."

Aydra heard Lex snort at the sentence, and she looked around her horse to see her Second laughing. "Perhaps you should take pointers from Bard here, my Second," Aydra bantered.

Lex grinned at her. "What would be the fun in that?"

Aydra chuckled and turned back to Bard. "My horse is tired, Bard. Have her fed, watered, and thoroughly washed. I will go to my brother after I've bathed myself of this riding stench." She turned and gave Lex a nod. "Get some rest before the banquet. Perhaps we'll have an eventful night."

"I look forward to it," Lex said.

Aydra pushed her way into the castle, stripping herself of her riding clothes with little care, as usual, to those passing her. She'd hardly reached the steps leading up to the level her room was on when she heard Willow calling behind her.

She paused and waited on the brunette to join her. "My Lady, your brother—"

"Yes, I'm aware he is waiting on me," Aydra said as she began walking once more. "I doubt he would want to see me with four days stench attached to my body. Whatever he wants can wait until after I've bathed."

"He had me lay a dress out for the banquet tonight," Willow informed her as she caught the clothes Aydra was tearing off herself.

"You'd think he would have learned by now not to bother," Aydra replied. "What is the color?"

"Blue."

"He's an idiot," Aydra muttered. They reached her room, and Willow followed her in to start the bath.

She unpacked her bag on her bed while she waited for the water. Her clothes, she tossed into a bin to be washed, and she threw away the scraps of food left inside. But something dumped out that she didn't recognize at first glance. She frowned at the trinket and baggie that didn't belong to her.

Draven's pipe. And a small amount of the herb from his garden.

What was written on the note, inside the bag, made her nearly throw it out the window.

In case your favorite needs help bringing you to your end again.

"Asshole," she muttered.

Willow told her the bath was ready soon after. Aydra excused

Willow from the room and then sank herself deep into the warm water. The pipe twirled in her hand as she thought about whether she wanted it that night. There wasn't much of the herb. She would have to be selective.

Finally, she sat it on the table by the tub and simply sank herself beneath the water.

The dress her brother had chosen stared at her from the bed. The navy blue color she didn't mind. But it was heavy, bejeweled, and she didn't much care for such things.

So she grabbed one of her own navy dresses from her closet and put it on instead, hoping he was stupid enough to only remember the color. Her dress tonight was form-fitting, long sleeved, and totally open on the back, V-ing at the dip in her hips and hugging her curves. She took her hair out of the plait she'd put it in for the bath and fluffed the curls before grabbing her crown from the vanity.

The note Draven had left caught her eye from the bedside table. She grunted in frustration and left the room, only to find Lex leaning against the opposite wall waiting on her.

Lex frowned upon seeing the look on Aydra's face. "What's wrong?"

"Fucking Venari," Aydra cursed as they descended the hallway.

"Letting him get your panties in a twist without even being in the room," Lex mused. "Interesting."

Aydra glared. "Not like that. He gave me his pipe and a small amount of the herb we smoked the other night."

"And he's an asshole for doing that because…"

"Because he also left a note with it. Said 'in case your favorite needs help bringing you to your end again.'"

Lex snorted. "He has a point."

Aydra shoved her sideways. "He has no business in my sex life. Period."

Lex continued to chuckle as she pushed her hands behind her back. "Have you seen your brother yet?" she asked, changing the subject.

"I haven't. I'm sure he is not happy about my not going directly to him."

"Suppose we'll find out."

They reached the Throne Room a few minutes later, and Aydra had Lex wait at the bottom of the stair.

Rhaif was pacing in front of their chairs when she reached the threshold. He paused, eyes narrowing beneath the hoods of his thick brows, upon her approach.

"Do you enjoy disobeying me?" he said in a low tone, and she could tell he was holding back an attitude.

"I don't know what you mean," she countered as she reached him.

"I asked that you come here after your arrival," he snapped. "It has been over an hour."

"We traveled for nearly five days without having the opportunity to bathe. I thought you'd not want to smell my stench or have it cling to your best capes," she replied, crossing her arms over her chest. "What did you want? Why here?"

"I wanted a report for how the mission went," Rhaif replied. "Did you rid this land of the creature?"

"We did," she answered. "The Venari was helpful for once. His instruction on how to kill the creature was thorough."

"And our brother? Where is he?"

"On his way with the Venari to the villages. I told him I would send an escort to come back with him in a few days so that he was not riding across the Hills alone."

Rhaif was silent a moment before he started her way. She considered his sudden calmness, the rise of his chin as he straightened his high-collared black and gold gambeson.

"You know, my men were hurt by your words before you left," he said.

"Which words?"

"When you called them useless." He paused, his fiery eyes searing through her. "I think you should apologize."

"Apologize?" she balked. "For what? For doing their job for them?"

"Why should they have thought the Venari was telling the truth after years of not being helpful and betraying this crown?"

"If they cannot heed the orders of our three crowns, then what good are they?" she snapped. "There are plenty of Belwarks out in our streets that would love to be part of the royal guard. I will not apologize to them because they are ignorant."

Rhaif made like he would retort but instead took in a long look at what she was wearing, and his brows knitted together once more. "Is that what you're wearing to the banquet?"

"It is."

Rhaif's hand ran the back of his neck, fingers tightening on his skin. "I will have Willow's head," he cursed. "This is the second time this week she has failed."

"Willow has only ever done as you've ordered. Just because I refuse to wear the dresses you have her put out for me does not mean she has not done her job."

He looked deliberately over her again, as though he were holding back, and she pushed her chin higher, waiting on his comment.

"Spit it out, brother."

But he huffed, and whatever was on his mind was forgotten as he extended an arm to her and said, "Come. We will be late."

6

The banquet was grander than she'd expected.

Something didn't feel right in her bones. She was wary of the extravagance, cautious of whatever it was her brother was up to. She felt him watching her most of the night, and she only began to forget about his gaze when she was rescued by one of the Ambassador of Scindo Creek's daughters.

Aydra found herself immersed in conversation with this woman as she told tales of her own village, of the journeys she'd taken with her father to the Village of Dreams and to the Hill towns. It seemed she had had a life of travel that Aydra found herself envious of. Aydra invited her and the Belwark who had accompanied her back to her room later that night.

Aydra retreated to bed not long after the exchange, eager to have a few moments to herself before the true festivities of the night. Willow had drawn her another hot bath, this time with salts and lavender flower, for which she was grateful. Her muscles ached from the long journey on horseback. She sank into the water and allowed the scent of the purple flowers to fill her nostrils, relaxing her stresses and willing herself into a trance.

She tried to think of better things than the Infi being pulled back into the ground and whatever her brother was up to. Even going as far as to pull herself beneath the water and letting her breath catch and struggle before emerging back into the cool room. The pipe stared at her from beside the tub, but she didn't reach for it. She wanted to be sober when her new conquests found their way into her bed later that night.

The moons' light cascaded through her open window. It was

raining, but the clouds did not hinder the moons in the far distance. It was an odd sight to see, the light reflecting off the droplets as they poured outside. Her raven sat on the windowsill just out of the rain, merely keeping her company as he usually did.

She wondered what Dorian and Draven were doing, if Draven was getting her younger into trouble or if he was actually taking care of him. Dorian was as free-spirited as herself, and she knew he could look after himself. But she would feel better about it when the Belwark escorts journeyed to retrieve him in the morning.

Only when her fingers began to wrinkle did she emerge from the bath and wrap a black silk robe around her body. She'd just started moving the pillows off the bed that Willow insisted she keep up there when she heard her door open. She didn't bother looking up from the bed to see if it was indeed the Belwark and Dreamer from Scindo.

"Someone is eager to please tonight," she muttered, pulling the sheet back.

The person, or persons, didn't speak, and she almost frowned at the shadowed being standing against her door. "Are you going to stand there in the dark, or should you like to come join me?" she asked.

She heard a boot step forward, and she looked up, only for her stomach to drop.

Lightning cracked outside.

Rhaif stood in front of the door, half of his face lit up by the moons, the other half still shadowed by the curtains of her bed.

Her face went pale, her heart began to throb, but she stood her ground as she walked around the bed. "Brother," she managed. "I thought you would have been pre-occupied with the dancers," she said, voice cracking nervously despite herself.

Thunder shook her room.

He didn't answer. Instead, he began to roll up the sleeves of his shirt. He'd removed his royal garb and was wearing a loose white night tunic. Aydra's jaw tensed.

I am here, her raven called to her from the window. *If you need me. Wait for me.*

Rhaif's eyes darted from the raven to her upon hearing the noise, and he huffed amusedly under his breath. Though Aydra wasn't sure what was so funny about her having to tell her raven to wait in case she needed an escape.

"What do you want, Rhaif?" Aydra asked in a soft voice she didn't recognize.

He finished turning his sleeves and shoved his hands in his pockets, shrugging slightly and allowing his fluffy black curls to fall over his eyes. "Simply answering your cry for attention," he told her.

Her ears began to ring.

"My cry for attention?" she repeated. "If I ever cry for attention, it is not meant for you."

He almost looked upset at her words, and his bottom lip pouted just so. "That hurts, sister," he said. "You know I would never do anything that you didn't want."

"And what exactly is it you think I want?"

A cruel smile curled on his lips, and he walked over to her fireplace. He took the poker out and taunted the fire in its depths. "This new title is going to your head, I think," Rhaif said. "My men are beginning to question me."

She watched the fire poker glow red hot in his hand, breaths shortening. "Your men were useless this week," she countered firmly, trying to regain some of the sternness in her voice.

"Are you saying they disobeyed me?"

"I am saying they did not believe the Venari simply because of who he is and thus had no regard for his warnings. They did not search that beach. I watched them half the night."

Rhaif turned back to face her. "And here I was under the impression by your screams that you were otherwise pre-occupied that night."

Aydra's heart grew cold and still at his mockery. "Something you'd like to get off your chest, *brother dear?*" she sneered.

—His arm snatched around her throat.

He'd moved so quickly, she hadn't seen his shadow cross behind her. She choked on her own breath as his forearm pressed against her trachea, his body firmly flush against her back. He grabbed her other arm before she could move and yanked it back, nearly popping it out of joint.

She grappled at his firm forearm, struggling for breath.

"Rhaif—"

Lightning flashed again.

"Did you think you would get away with the stunts you've pulled this week?" Rhaif hissed in her ear. "Did you think you could mock me and undermine my authority without punishment?"

Thunder rumbled.

Her raven cried out for her.

She wriggled against Rhaif's grasp, but his skin was heating beneath her flesh, and her insides convulsed at what she knew would come next. She closed her eyes and felt for her raven at the window, willing her subconscious out of her body—something she had learned to do over the years. She allowed the raven to consume her thoughts and mind, for her entire being to flow into him and push her core out of this horror.

If only for a few moments—

Smack!

Rhaif's hand seared across her face. She blinked back into herself, realizing she was somehow on the floor, robe disheveled. His feet came into view, and she looked up through her messy curls to see him standing over her, shirt removed to reveal the taut skin against his trimmed torso. His hands blackened, and the color grew up his skin like spiderwebs embedded in his golden flesh. His eyes blazed literal fire, and the pale blue flame curled into life on his muscles.

This was the true form of the Promised King.

The Fire King.

"I know you've figured out how to escape your body to one of your pets," he said in a low tone. "Not tonight. Tonight, you will remain here when I punish you for what you've done."

Angered tears rose in her eyes, and she began to shake. "You're just like him—"

Smack!

Aydra shook off the sting of his slap and pushed up on her hands again. "We promised we would be different from them—*Better*—"

"We are better—"

"Then explain how your threatening me with fire is any different from what Vasilis did to Zoria? *To me?*"

Rhaif stopped his advance. His head tilted, and he crouched down slowly in front of her.

"Because Zoria never asked to be punished," he said slowly. "And you have done everything you can so that you will be."

She balked. "You think I ask to be punished—"

"You have begged every day this past fortnight for this," he cut in. "Embarrassing me in front of the Council. Calling my men useless and galavanting off with the Venari of all people. Blatantly disregarding my requests and taking our brother on quests you should have left up to Belwarks to begin with. Do you know the Council actually asked for you to be subdued?"

"Their fear is not my problem."

"Admit it, sister. You have craved for this moment. You *want* this."

"*No one wants this!*" she cried.

He reached out towards her, his gaze softening as his thumb brushed her cheek. "And you were doing so well, too."

She flinched at his touch and spat in his face. "You're vile," she managed shakily. "Despicable—"

He wiped the spit from his eye. She pushed herself backward, trying to back into the shadows away from him. Struggling against gravity as her body ached with whatever it was he had already done to her while she'd escaped to her raven.

The right corner of his lips quirked upwards, and his eyes traveled deliberately over her body.

"Scream for me."

He seized her ankles. The pain of his fire seared into her flesh and caused an unwanted shriek to emit from her lungs. She grabbed for anything—the bed, the ground, the rug— but to no avail. Fingernails digging into the floor and threatening to bleed.

He pulled her backward and hoisted her body up over his shoulder. His flamed skin burned her, and it was all she could do to will herself not to scream. Wholly paralyzed by his flesh burning hers as he carried her off towards the servants' tunnel.

The comfort of her raven slowly drifted away, replaced with a numbness she couldn't shudder out.

Lies.

7

Aydra's skin was stiff and raw.

Burns plagued her entire figure. The worst of it was across her stomach where he'd thrown her over his shoulder and carried her to his room. She'd vomited more times than once since he'd left her back on her own bed.

Exhausted and subdued.

Empty and numb.

He hadn't burned her since the day he'd been marked by their mother and given his fire powers. Since the day their older, Vasilis, had died.

But she'd never forgotten the pain of that day. And the night she'd just had had been worse.

The only good thing to have come from the night before was that once Rhaif had released her body and thrown her onto his bed, she'd managed to clear her mind enough to send her raven after him. Her raven had cut Rhaif's cheek deep with one of his talons.

Her punishment for that was the heated iron cuffs Rhaif had crudely placed around her extremities.

She'd had the raven take a pail to Arbina's pool to get water from it — the only thing that would heal the burns on her body. Despite her giver's waters being poison to others, it was healing to her children, and Aydra knew she would need it.

The red marks around her wrists and the rawness of her skin stared back at her as she poured the last bucket of the water into the tub. She hadn't stopped shaking. Every move she made was precarious, subdued... Flashes of blue continued to flash in her mind. Her only relief being when her raven would reach out to her and try to pull away some of the pain.

Once the tub was full, she clenched her teeth and made her legs move, one after the other, into the water's depths.

An audible scream evacuated her lips as she stepped in. A debilitating shake grasped her straining muscles. The pain of the liquid wrapping around her skin was nearly as paralyzing as his fire had been.

"Morning, my—*fuck*—Aydra!"

The noise of Lex's voice made her nearly fall into the water. Aydra grabbed the sides of the tub and steadied herself just as Lex came running to her. She couldn't hold back the shriek from her lips when Lex put her hands on her dry shoulder.

"Don't—" Aydra could hardly form words as the agony swept her bones. She stilled a moment to gather her wit, vomit pushing up from her stomach and into her throat.

"What the—*who did this to you?!*" Lex demanded in a voice Aydra had never heard.

Aydra's eyes closed as she forced herself into the water. "Don't touch the water," she said quickly as Lex started to reach for her again. "It is Arbina's."

"Aydra—Did..." Lex's voice trailed, and Aydra knew she was figuring it out. "Did Rhaif do this to you?"

The water wrapped around Aydra's body, and she surrendered to the paralyzing pain. She couldn't speak. The agony of her flesh mending itself beneath the liquid making her shudder. A nauseating chill rose up her spine, and she pulled herself quickly to the side of the tub, where her insides evacuated onto the floor.

Lex started to reach for her hair, but Aydra muttered a quick "No, don't—" and grabbed her hand before she could—

The water on her fingertips burned Lex's wrist.

Lex flinched backward.

"Shit," Aydra realized. "Lex, I'm sorry—I didn't mean—"

Fire glowed beneath Lex's flesh, and she picked at the ash formed from a water droplet that had sat on her skin. "It's fine," Lex assured her. "I'm fine."

Aydra leaned back and closed her eyes. She heard Lex leave her side and then felt the plop of a chair beside the tub.

"What happened?" Lex asked softly.

"It doesn't matter—"

"Yes, it—" Aydra's eyes opened just in time to see Lex squeeze and un-squeeze her fist, as though she were wrapping it around someone's throat and wringing the life from their body. "It does matter," she continued deliberately. "You are my Queen. I cannot sit back and let you tell me that this is nothing."

The darkness of Lex's ordinarily bright green eyes made a lump form in Aydra's throat. She said nothing in response and instead started rubbing the water over her back.

"Aydra, speak to me," Lex begged.

"What do you want me to say?" Aydra whispered.

"How did he do this to you? Did you not fight back?"

"Of course I did," Aydra said fast.

But then she thought about it, and she surrendered to the truth. "I mean... not really. No," she admitted. "My raven managed to get him once, but..." Aydra sighed and brought her knees to her chest, the shame of it spreading through her shaking body. Her stomach knotted at the admission of her loss, and her ears reddened beneath Lex's stare.

"Once his body is of fire, it is paralyzing. You cannot move," Aydra breathed. "You don't understand."

"No, I don't," Lex almost shouted. "I don't understand how the most fearless woman I know was pushed to submission in the middle of the night, burned, and then raped by her own brother."

"Because I did not know it would be this bad," Aydra argued. "He hasn't burned me in years," she whispered. "Not since the night Vasilis died."

"And the rape? Are you going to condone that?" Lex balked.

"I am not condoning anything," Aydra spat. "My brother loves me. He promised a long time ago, his pleasure would be all he would ever take from me, and only on occasion... He has been true to his word since. I learned quickly how to rip my consciousness from my body and into the raven's so that I did not have to endure his nights." She paused and started rubbing the burns on her wrists, watching the red wash into the liquid as though it were painted on her skin.

"It's my fault he's like this," she whispered. "Our mother and Vasilis were always so hard on him. Arbina never treated him as her son until he was marked, and Vasilis... Vasilis pushed him to be crude, to lose the sweetness he'd long clung to, just to speak down to Zoria and me. But... we swore to be better than Vasilis and Zoria. That our youngers would never know the hurt of it. And they haven't. I've made sure to keep them in the dark about this."

"You're making excuses for him."

"I'm not—"

"Yes. You. Are," Lex seethed. "You may think he loves you, but this is not what love is. Love is not this pain. It is not the excuses and promises he's made to you." Tears were in Lex's eyes, and she started to reach out for Aydra's hand but stopped short upon remembering the water.

"I have always supported you, whatever decisions you make, whatever you needed or wanted... But I will not stand here and watch him do this to you as though you are nothing more than a servant for him to throw around. You are the Queen. Not a decoration on his arm. Not just a pretty face wearing a crown. Whatever problems he has faced in his past, they are not your fault. You have never been anything less than the strongest woman I know. Do not let his words get in your head and make you feel inferior."

Aydra inhaled the deepest breath she'd taken in a long while. She nodded slowly and sat her chin on her knee. A moment passed, and Aydra continued rubbing at the red marks on her skin, burying the pain of it washing away deep inside her.

"You cannot breathe a word of this, Lex," Aydra managed after a few minutes. "And you cannot harm him."

Lex sighed audibly, and Aydra knew the look she would have on her face without looking up. "I know," Lex finally said.

"I will be ready next time," Aydra promised.

"Next time?" Lex repeated. "I—"

Aydra held up a hand. "He is on edge. Something is wrong, and I'm not sure what."

"And that is an excuse to hurt you?"

"I am not saying it is an excuse. I am simply telling you the truth of it," Aydra almost snapped. "I will not pretend to think this is over."

"What can I do?" Lex asked.

Aydra thought about it a moment, "I want you to stick closer to Bard. Find out if anything is going on that he's not telling me. I want to know everything and everyone he speaks with. Employ Corbin or any of our women if you need to."

Lex nodded. "Yes, ma'am."

"And I've told Nyssa that we will be traveling to the Forest for the Dead Moons. She's yet to meet any of the Noctuans. I have failed her training."

"You haven't failed anything," Lex argued. "But I think a break from here would do you both well," she agreed. "Our trip to rid the Infi was short-lived. Now that the streets are safe once more, I believe a month away would do you a great favor."

"I'm not sure a month away would be wise," Aydra said. "A couple of weeks, sure. But not a month."

"Why not? Your brothers can take care of things in your place. You need a break, Aydra. A real break. Not just one of your trips off to the cliffs."

"Where would you like to go?" Aydra asked her.

"We'll go to the Forest and then travel back through the mountains on our way back to Magnice. Visit these Blackhand people that I've so long heard stories about," Lex said with a wink.

A small smile rose on Aydra's lips. She looked down at her wrists then, noticing the redness had turned to pink, and the rawness of the burns on her stomach now resembled yellow bruising.

"In the meantime, we need to find out what is going on. They are hiding something from us," Aydra said.

Lex stood from the chair and grabbed the thickest robe from across the top of the three-pane divider. "We'll find out. But today, we go see if Maye can make you a dress befitting of pissing your brother off again. "

A swell of gratitude filled Aydra's chest at her Second's affirmations. She nodded again and forced herself to stand from the tub. "I'd like that."

8

Dorian returned one morning the next week, and Aydra swore he'd grown an inch and filled out more in the time that she'd missed him. She and Nyssa met him at the gates, and Aydra watched him hug his sister, swinging her around in a circle as the joy of seeing one another exuded on both their faces.

The sight of it brought tears to Aydra's eyes. She remembered when her own brother had been so happy to see her once. Whenever she and Zoria would return from the Forest, he would hug her as Dorian had Nyssa. The smile he would meet her with, the fill of happiness in his eyes... Her heart ached for that feeling again. For the butterflies and swell of her chest, for the skipping of her heartbeat and jagged breaths that came with the joy of seeing someone you could not explain a love for...

Dorian sat Nyssa back on the ground, and his eyes found Aydra's a few feet behind her. A slight frown slipped on his face, and he eyed her. "What's this? Did you actually miss me?" he mocked.

Aydra couldn't help her smile. "Funnily enough, I did," she answered. Her arms opened to him, and he hugged her tightly.

"Are you okay?" he whispered in her hair.

She pulled back and pressed her hands to his cheeks. "I'm fine," she assured him. "But tell me, how much trouble did the Venari get you into while on the road? Shall I skin him when he arrives for meetings next month?"

Dorian laughed. "No skinning needed. He stuck around until Scindo Creek and then left me to deal with the other two towns on my own. I think I'm beginning to understand your thirst for blood, my sister," he added with a wink.

Aydra grinned and then gave his hair a fluff. "Come. I've had the cooks prepare your favorites for breakfast. You can tell Nyssa and I all about your journey. I'm sure she's eager to hear how exactly you vanquished the Infi."

Nyssa came up beside Dorian then, and he wrapped an arm around her shoulders. "Oh yes. I'm sure she wants to hear exactly how much they bleed when the roots are taking them back to Duarb."

Nyssa's face paled. "I'm sorry, what?"

Aydra and Dorian exchanged a knowing grin, and Dorian started walking with his sister in tow beside him. Aydra heard him telling her an exaggerated story of how the Infi was killed, and she couldn't help her laughter.

Lex joined her. "Good thing he hasn't remembered the deal he tried to make with me," she muttered in Aydra's ear.

"I remember it well, Second Sun," Dorian called back to her. He turned and gave Lex a wink over his shoulder.

Aydra snorted and covered her mouth with her hand. Lex attempted a glare at her, but it quickly turned to a smile.

"What am I going to do with you Promised children?" Lex wondered aloud.

Breakfast consisted of all of Dorian's favorites, from venison sausage to the sweet danishes he had once snuck out of the kitchens at night before bedtime. They took their breakfast in the kitchen at the small intimate table as they used to when Dorian and Nyssa were younger. It was much more comfortable than the stuffiness of the grand table where Rhaif liked to take dinner with them now.

"Will Rhaif be joining us?" Dorian asked as they sat.

Aydra exchanged a look with Lex. Truthfully, she hadn't seen much of him since the burning. He'd avoided her on most days, taking his dinner alone in his study, leaving Aydra and Nyssa to eat at the large table by themselves.

Nyssa's gaze met Aydra's then, and Aydra gave a forced smile to the pair.

"You know your older," Aydra forced, "always dramatic. He's likely to show up as we're finishing and insist we take our food to the big table."

"I quite like this table," Nyssa said. "I miss taking our meals here."

"As do I," Aydra agreed.

The swell of warmth Aydra felt sitting there with them as they laughed and picked at their food made her heart hurt once more. Dorian told stories of Draven and how fond he was of him now, which totally bewildered Aydra and Nyssa, for they'd not known anything else of the Venari except to be wary of them. Dorian exaggerated his tales from ridding the Infi at Nyssa's expense, and by the time they wrapped up their meal, Aydra's cheeks were hurting from laughter.

9

In the week that followed, Aydra tried to stick close to her youngers. When Dorian found out Aydra was taking Nyssa to the Forest, he argued, wanting to go with them, but Aydra insisted he stay with Rhaif so he could help in case another Infi infiltrated their streets.

"He will be useless if another finds its way here," she told him. "He wouldn't know what to do with it."

"Then perhaps he should learn," Dorian argued.

"That's why you're staying," Aydra insisted. "Let Rhaif deal with the inner workings and small things. You deal with the criminals and punishments. Nyssa will be the one to take over what Rhaif does eventually. But she needs to learn these creatures. You never know when you might need them as allies."

"Wouldn't we have to go through the Venari for that?" Dorian asked.

"It's a good thing you're friends with him then, isn't it?" she teased.

Dorian huffed. "I suppose."

As for the information Aydra had hoped to find out about what was happening with her brother, she never did. Rhaif had become more held up in his study than usual. Reports came to Aydra every night from Corbin and Lex, but neither heard anything out of the ordinary. Nothing that would have prompted his attitude as of late.

The first she truly spoke to him was the morning of her departure.

"Do you think you've packed enough?" Lex mocked as she hoisted Aydra's bag on her shoulder.

"You told me a month on the road," Aydra argued. "What did you expect?"

"I expected you to wash clothes, not bring all of them," Lex said as they exited Aydra's room.

Aydra paused and threw one of the bags back into her room before shutting the door. "Very well. Have you checked on my younger this morning?" Aydra asked her.

"I did. She and Dorian are meeting us out at the gates."

"Did she have on actual riding clothes or—"

"Where are you going?"

The sound of Rhaif's voice made them stop in their tracks. Aydra tightened her hand around the knife on her belt. Lex tensed at her side, and the pair turned.

"My Queen—"

Aydra held a soft hand up to stop Lex from stepping in front of her.

"Lex and I are taking Nyssa out to the Forest for training. She is behind," Aydra told him shortly.

Rhaif apparently considered her words and then gave Lex a nod, muttering a quick, "Leave us, Second," to her.

Lex didn't move.

Aydra didn't drop her stare with her brother. "Lex, wait for me at the gates. Make sure Nyssa is ready."

Lex turned away from Rhaif to stand at Aydra's shoulder. "Are you —"

"The gates, Lex," Aydra demanded.

Lex looked like she might argue but didn't, and she turned on her heel.

As Lex's footsteps grew quieter and quieter down the hall, the siblings didn't move. The sound of the waves outside turned to white noise in Aydra's ears, and she almost didn't find her voice.

Rhaif began to fumble with his hands, and Aydra became suspicious of the movement. She'd not seen him fumble in years.

"You have avoided me for two weeks," Aydra said, eyeing his nervous figure. "What is it you suddenly want?"

"I wanted to apologize."

Aydra stiffened. "Excuse me?" she managed.

As he looked up at her, his eyes softened with the shame that had spread over his features. "My behavior two weeks ago... I realize I should not have hurt you as I did. You did not deserve it," he apologized. "You were right. We did promise to be better than them."

She didn't say anything. He abruptly took three long strides to stand directly in front of her. She saw his hand move up towards her face, and she flinched backward out of instinct.

"You burned me," she managed. "I had to sit in our mother's waters for an hour—"

"I know, I know." He pushed his hands through his hair. "I know, and I'm sorry."

The thick air made her breath quicken. "Rhaif, you cannot think I will simply forgive you so quickly for what you did."

"My temper can get the best of me," he said, a glisten rising in his eyes that she almost fell for. "You know this."

She hugged her chest, staring at the ground a moment before muttering, "I do," in a whisper, her heart breaking. "But that doesn't make it okay."

A deep exhale left him, along with a single tear.

She cursed the day she was born beside him in the waters as her heart fell for his apology.

He reached out for her again, and her skin became rigid against his touch.

"I am so sorry, Aydra," he whispered.

She didn't speak. She couldn't.

He leaned forward then and kissed her deeply, to which she pushed away after a brief moment. His throat bobbed as he took a step back, still holding on to the tips of her fingers.

"How long will you be gone?" he asked.

"Two weeks," she answered. "Perhaps longer. I need a break, Rhaif. I need time to think about things."

"Don't leave because of me," he begged.

"I would be leaving with her whether you had done what you did or not," she affirmed. "Nyssa does not know the Noctuans. She is behind on her training. She deserves better than what I've done for her."

"The Dead Moons rise in three days. Come back in ten days. Do not stay longer."

"I will stay as long as we need to," she argued. "I am not asking for your permission."

"Why can you not—" A loud grunt of frustration left his throat, and his hands shot up as though he would grasp her face. She flinched back so quickly that she nearly fell.

His now black fists clenched and unclenched in the air as an angered strain of breath left him. A flash of his blue fire showed beneath the blackened streaks on his wrists. And her eyes widened at the display of him nearly going off again.

"Did you just—"

Her raven landed on her shoulder. Rhaif placed his hands on his hips and turned in a circle, eyes staring at the ceiling as his jaw tensed and the blackened webs receded into him.

She nearly laughed at how quickly his apology had turned to anger.

"Wow," she managed. "Just wow, Rhaif… To think I almost fell for your *bullshit*—"

"Please, Aydra—"

She swatted his hand away this time. "No," she cut him off. "No. You are out of control. Whatever is wrong with you, fix it. I cannot stand to see you reduced to this person you haven't been in *years*."

She turned on her heel as he grabbed her arm, whirling her back around. She snatched her arm back just before the flames of his grasp reached her skin.

Terror filled his eyes. He took a step back, cowering at her gaze and raising his hands.

"I'm sorry," he managed. "I'm sorry, I didn't mean—"

"*Sorry?*"

She couldn't breathe.

"Three times—that's *three fucking times* in a matter of a minute, Rhaif!" Her body began to shake uncontrollably, her words barely coherent in the high-pitched voice she had used.

"Sorry is not good enough. We are *done*," she managed. "I hope you can work out whatever is wrong with you while I'm gone. I expect my brother to be waiting on me when I return. Not this… *this monster.*"

He didn't reach for her again when she turned to leave. The thick air followed her, and her raven didn't speak as they walked through the castle down to the gates. Her insides were fuming. She willed her breath to catch, feeling herself on the verge of panicking at any moment. Silent tears jerking down her cheeks. The grip the raven had on her shoulder tightened, and its calming energy filled her, bringing her breaths back to normal just as she reached the doors.

She quickly wiped the tears from her face and held her head high upon seeing her youngers and Lex waiting on her.

Lex's gaze widened. "Are you—"

"I'm fine," Aydra said quickly. "Let's go."

10

The women traveled east for three days and finally reached the edge of the Forest just as the sun began to set. Aydra insisted they set up camp near, but not too near, the Forest's edge so that they would hear the Noctuans upon their waking.

It was the first night of the Dead Moons.

Aydra knew their thirst and hunger would be plentiful. She also knew they would likely not be so bold as to leave the Forest on this first night, so she felt comfortable being so close without fear of being eaten alive.

Lex caught rabbits in the clearing and prepared them as Aydra sat watching Nyssa struggle with her bow. Her raven squawked at Nyssa's golden eagle sitting beside her, and the eagle's piercing cry echoed around them. Aydra laughed at her bird's frustration.

"I'm still trying to work out how a golden eagle found you," Aydra said as she eyed the beast.

Nyssa didn't look away. Instead she gritted her teeth before releasing the arrow toward their makeshift target. The thud of it landing off center made Nyssa grunt.

"I think your target is off," Nyssa argued.

"Exhale the fire," Aydra said sternly.

Nyssa huffed at the mantra but gripped her bow tighter in her hands. "Breathe in the smoke," she muttered.

Aydra's gaze traveled over her sister's defiant facade, and a smirk slipped onto her lips.

"Hey, Lex—"

"Yes, my Queen," Lex replied.

Aydra took the day crown off her head and tossed it in the air towards her Second. "Hold my crown." Stepping up to the spot her sister was on, Aydra pulled her own arrow through and let it fly.

It landed with a thud in the middle of its target.

"I think you're giving excuses," Aydra said with a raised brow.

Nyssa glared at her. "Show off."

A huff of amusement left Aydra's lips. "Says the one with the *eagle*."

The sharp hiss of a blade cut through the air, startling them. It sheared Aydra's arrowhead and thunked into the target.

A knife had landed in the same spot as the arrow, and the noise of someone crunching on an apple averted the Promised daughters' attentions behind them.

Lex chewed her apple and gave Nyssa a wink. "Aim for the middle next time."

Aydra snorted and clapped her hand over her mouth quickly.

Nyssa glared at Lex and crossed her arms over her chest. "You two —"

"You'll learn nothing with those temper tantrums," Lex cut in as she took a seat on a fallen log. "Shut up and pull another arrow. You're a daughter of Promise. It should be instinct."

The eagle flapped his wings in protest, and Nyssa quickly shook her head at him. She spoke with him in a different dialect that Aydra didn't understand, but Aydra heard the eagle telling Nyssa she could take one of Lex's eyes. The thought amused Aydra.

Wind swept past them so forcefully that they were almost knocked off their feet. The fire Lex had worked so hard on blew out. The sun all but disappeared as though a shadow had swept over it. Purple engulfed the landscape. Trees cracked and bent.

A lone howl pierced the quiet wood.

Aydra's chest swelled, and a smile rose on her lips as she looked fondly towards the Forest of Darkness.

"There she is."

The Ulfram wolf's howl was joined by the rest of her pack. It echoed through the air, and Aydra closed her eyes as the wind circled them.

"Only you would look so happy at the noise of a deadly creature waking for the first time in seventy-two days," Lex said as she tried to light the fire once more.

"No creature deserves to have to sit and wait for moon cycles to align to be released from their curse," Aydra argued. "Besides, her howl is beautiful."

Nyssa was staring at the darkening wood, her mouth slightly agape, as the Ulframs continued to howl into the wind. Aydra wrapped an arm around her sister's shoulders and pulled her out of her daze.

"Come sit. We can hear their songs together," Aydra told her.

A shriek so high-pitched that Aydra's eardrums pulsed, cut through the air. Nyssa jumped at her side.

"What was that?"

"Aviteth," Aydra answered. "Noctuan brother of the Aenean Orel. Looks much like your eagle except black and also taller than you."

"They say that screech you just heard pierces the ears when you are near it and causes your eardrums to bleed. You are still alive when they begin to consume your flesh," Lex chimed in.

Aydra sat down at the now lit fire, expecting Nyssa to sit as well, but her younger simply stood and stared between them. "Okay, now I just feel like you two are making this up."

"I honestly wish we were," Lex assured her.

"I'm not sure I understand," Nyssa managed, shifting uncomfortably. "Why are we here?"

"Because learning these beasts might be the difference between life and death one day," Aydra argued. "The Noctuans are beautiful, powerful creatures. They deserve the utmost respect for their way of life. Yes, they are different and born in darkness, but their ruthless bloodthirst is not their fault. There are Noctuans who do not hunt for sport as well as those that do."

"Name one that doesn't," Nyssa asked incredulously.

"Noirdiem," Aydra said. "Berdijay. The Bygon. The Bullhorn. Wyverdraki—"

"You're telling me the great Wyverdraki dragons are not bloodthirsty?" Nyssa interjected.

"I am saying they would not eat you if you would just respect their realm and authority," Aydra said.

"They're not pets, Drae," Nyssa argued. "They're wild animals."

"Wild animals that you are going to get to know tomorrow night. Period."

11

The sun was just beginning to set.

They'd entered the Forest earlier in the day, intent on learning some of the landscape before night fell so that they would be familiar with where they were. They'd helped Nyssa more with her bow, and for some of the day, simply relaxed while Lex told stories that made Nyssa eye her in a wild way.

But they'd overstayed their welcome and were now caught deep inside it with the sun setting. As much as Aydra wanted Nyssa to meet the creatures, she did not want to do it so deep inside with no easy way out were something to go wrong. They quickly retraced their steps back to the edge of it.

The sharp cry of the Ulfram wolf startled Aydra's horse. It shifted, rearing up violently on its hind legs, causing Aydra's hands to slip from the reins. Aydra flew backward into the air. Her back hit the ground, head thrown against the trunk of a tree. She could hear Nyssa speaking to her horse as it continued to whinny and buck against the sound of the Noctuan creatures' calls.

Which was when she felt something wrap around her ankles.

A shadow latched onto her core. She gasped for air and opened her eyes to nothing but black and silence around her. Trapped. Her voice cried out. She searched around her, but there was nothing. Not her sister. Not her Second. Not their horses.

Just black.

She closed her eyes and listened for the creature that was consuming her.

Let me out, she told it.

The tense silence that filled her told her the creature did not expect to be heard. Her eyes opened once more, and in front of her was a mirror. She was standing in front of it, naked. Her own grief-stricken eyes stared back at her.

You cannot scare me, she continued. *Let me go.*

The mirror vanished into smoke. Everything spun around her. And then—

She gasped for air, thrown back into reality.

Hands were on her cheeks. Nyssa's shouting in her face made her ears hurt.

"Shut up," she groaned. "I'm fine."

"Drae!" Nyssa's arms wrapped around her desperately. "Drae, I thought you were dying—"

"I'm fine, I—" a sudden pain shot through her ankles, and she pushed Nyssa back so that she could see her feet. Red handprint welts and bubbled blisters stared back at her. Searing pain rippled through her to her bones, and she grunted under her breath.

"Come," Lex said, wrapping an arm around Aydra, "We need to leave before they come back."

Aydra grabbed Lex's body, and her ankles nearly gave out as soon as she tried to stand. Her knees buckled at the agonizing pain, and she shook her head quickly. "Nope, put me down. Down!"

Lex sat her down and hovered over her. "We have to leave. You'll need to get on my back."

Help.

The noise of her horse's voice made her heart stop. She looked up and saw it lying down between two trees ahead, and she could see the same reddened welt around the steed's ankle.

"No—" Aydra started to crawl towards her, ignoring the protests of Lex and Nyssa. She sat down beside her and rubbed her cheek.

It's okay. I've got you, she promised the horse.

"My Queen, there is nothing we can do," Lex said. "The Noctuans are waking. We have to leave."

Aydra didn't look away from her steed. "Go get help," she told them. "Go. Now."

"We cannot leave you—"

"And I will not leave her," Aydra interjected.

"But the Noctuans—"

"Are friends. Now go," Aydra cut Nyssa off. She glared up at them over her shoulder, jaw tensing at the sight of their bewildered faces. "I will be fine. But I will not risk both of your safety. I made a mistake coming this far, so late. I am injured. It will call to the ones that may not heed my words. You have to get out of here. Now."

The pair did not move.

Aydra was quickly losing her patience.

"Go! Now!" Aydra nearly shouted.

"My Lady, I cannot leave you," Lex told her.

"Yes, you will," Aydra insisted. "Your orders are to take care of my sister. Go to the Village of Dreams and see to it that she is safe. Find someone there with a cart that can help you come back to retrieve us. I am not leaving her here to die."

"But…" Nyssa crouched down in front of her. "What if the Venari find you?" she said with widened eyes. "What if the Noctuans—"

"My orders are to take care of you," Lex interjected to Aydra.

"And I am giving you new orders. As your Queen, I demand it," Aydra said sternly.

Aydra thought she might argue, but Lex didn't. She grasped Nyssa's shoulders and pulled her to her feet. "Come, Princess. We must go quickly."

"No! No, I'm not leaving her—"

"Nyssa, we must go!" Lex nearly shouted. "You will see her again —"

"By any means necessary," Aydra called to Lex.

Lex's hand struck Nyssa's cheek. Nyssa gasped and stared at her with wilding eyes.

"*You*—"

"If you think I am going to give my life for your kicking and screaming, you are wrong," Lex hissed. "Your sister is hurt, but she can take care of herself. If we stay here much longer, we will be eaten or worse. You will listen to me, Princess. Now get on your horse and shut up."

Nyssa's mouth ceased movement, and she looked toward Aydra.

"Listen to her," Aydra demanded. "It could mean your life."

Lex was still staring sternly down at the Princess when she turned again, but Aydra didn't miss the smirk and wink Lex gave her when she met her gaze. Aydra bit her lips to keep from smiling.

The noise of their horses' hooves on the dirt quickly vanished just as the sun set around her. Aydra was torn between starting a fire or keeping herself in the dark so as to not attract more Noctuans than she would already.

But as the chill of the Forest surrounded her, she decided she would rather die swiftly in the teeth of a Noctuan than slowly in the cold.

She'd just got the fire started with what she could crawl around and find when she felt familiar creatures coming up on every side. Her horse began to shift hysterically, but she placed a hand on her neck and tried to calm her.

A low growl cut through the rustling winds. And slowly, from the darkness, emerged one of the most beautifully menacing wolf creatures she'd ever seen.

Sharp yellow-green eyes pierced the wood. The slender of its elongated narrow wolf-nose rose into the light of the fire. It was crouched down as it came into the light, teeth bared.

The alpha female.

The Ulfram.

The sheen of her dark silver fur vibrated in the firelight. Five feet tall at the tops of its tall pointed ears. Black lines like shadows lined beneath her eyes and down the sides of her nose. She inched closer, and Aydra saw one of the breast's great paws press into the dirt.

She felt the breath of another standing directly to her right. Her head twisted just slightly to see it towering above her, white fangs flashing. The rest of the pack was black in color, opposite from the female, with silver shadows beneath their eyes and down their noses.

Aydra allowed their cores to consume her, and when she opened her eyes, she was filled with the voices of its kind.

Hello, alpha, she acknowledged the one standing in front of her.

The alpha gave her a slow blink. ***Queen Aydra,*** she knew. ***It has been a long time since your last visit.***

How do the moons treat you on this round?

Enough with the small talk, Sun Queen, she said, sitting back on her haunches. ***Tell me why I should not eat your filly.***

Because I know the truth of you. I know you have more pride than to hunt and eat something that was not worthy of preying upon.

The alpha stared at her for a long while, long enough that Aydra heard the tree canopy rustling over her head. The number of creatures swarming and reaching out to her consumed her to the point of nausea. Voices, all questioning her presence, filled her ears. She shut her eyes tight.

Who is she?

Why is she here?

Why is she not dead?

Can we kill her?
The horse is a good meal.
Who dares come into our realm?
What stranger is this?

Aydra's hands pressed to the sides of her head, and she doubled over as she tried to push them out. Their voices overwhelmed her. Asking the same questions over and over. Her breath was short. She didn't know the creatures in her head. There were too many. She couldn't shake them. Hungry. Bloodthirsty. Alone. Scared.

Who is she?
Who is she?
Who is she?

SHUT UP! she finally shouted into the darkness.

Silence.

Chest heaving, she tried to catch her breath. Her eyes widened, and although she could not see the creatures in the trees and sitting in the darkness, she felt them heed her words and listen at once.

My name is Aydra Ravenspeak. I can hear all of you. I feel your pains. I mean you no harm or intrusion. I am hurt. My horse is injured. I am simply waiting on my companions to return.

The alpha settled down on the ground in front of her, its paws crossing over each other.

Then we will wait with you, she told her. **Our darkest brothers will not harm you.**

The black Ulfram beside her laid down and sat its great head in her lap. Her chest swelled with gratitude for the beasts surrounding her. She poured that gratitude into the cores of each in an attempt to show her thanks for not only their sparing her life but also for protecting her from the Noctuans who would not have such mercy on her.

An hour passed in silence. Aydra's eyes began to droop with exhaustion, but she dared not sleep. Despite the promises of the creatures surrounding her, she did not know what might consume her if she let her guard down. So she stroked the head of the Ulfram lying in her lap and let the smells of the Forest fill her.

Until she heard the noise of hooves pounding the dirt once more.

Venari, the Ulfram told her.

It didn't surprise her. She'd assumed they would find her. She only hoped she knew who it was.

"Well, well…" came the mockingly deep voice of the one she had least wanted to find her that way. "If it isn't the Sun Queen."

Aydra looked past the Ulfram to the left to see three men on horses, and she cringed.

"Venari King," she said through clenched teeth as he dismounted his horse.

Draven's smug smile was the first thing she saw illuminated in the light from the fire she'd made. Faint curly scruff danced along his long, angular jaw and above his lips, and his green eyes were hooded beneath his dark brows.

He continued to smirk as he pulled his long walnut hair into a thick bun atop his head, his taut muscles flexing as he moved them. Two other Hunters dropped to the ground from their own steeds, and before she could move, Draven crouched in front of her.

"What happened? Monthly patrols gone wrong?" he teased.

"It's not your business."

A laugh emitted from the two Hunters still standing. Aydra glared at their annoyingly handsome faces. She didn't recognize the one to her left, with his mop of tight brown curls fluffed on his head, the dark tan tone of his skin glistening in the fire's light.

"You're hurt," Draven noted.

A flash of green showed behind his already emerald irises, and she remembered he could see in the dark.

"Her horse is hurt as well," called one of the men. "Looks like trees had a bit of fun at her expense."

"Shadow thieves," Draven muttered as he looked at the welts wrapped around her ankles.

"Don't look so happy," she snapped. "Your glee for my being harmed might come across as macabre to your men."

"My men know of the darkness themselves," Draven said. "Your lying in it makes the pain dance in their eyes."

The curly-haired Hunter grinned and lifted his sword behind his head, stretching his limbs. "She looks frightened," he mocked.

"Fear has no place in my core," Aydra spat.

"It should," Draven said. "Where is your Second?"

"Taking care of my sister. Back to the Village for help," she admitted. "You can leave me. I will be fine waiting for them here."

"What bewitchment have you placed on my Ulframs?" Draven asked, ignoring her other words.

"Your Ulframs?" she repeated. "And here I thought these creatures were free."

A low guttural noise came from Draven's throat, and he muttered a quick "Dammit" under his breath. "Dunthorne, Bael, go back to the kingdom and get a cart. I'll wait with the Sun Queen and her horse. We'll need one to get it out of here."

"I don't need your help," she argued. "Lex will—"

"You're hurt. Your Dreamer friends won't make it back inside this Forest without certain death. And they'll be four days away. You come with us, or you can die of thirst."

She hated that he was right.

"You don't have to wait with me," she told him.

He ignored her and sat down in front of one of the trees, leaning his back against it. "Don't think this is out of pity. I'll not watch one of these Noctuans rob me of what is mine."

"Excuse me?" she balked.

"Your death," he informed her. "Being the one to kill you. It's been promised to me since we were children."

"Perfect chance, Venari," she said, opening her arms. "I'm hurt. Alone in your realm. Strike me down."

He stared at her a moment, apparently considering it. "Too easy," he decided. "It'd be my luck that you were faking this whole thing."

"Oh yes. Faking my horse being hurt during the Dead Moons, surrounded by Noctuans just so I can ambush you."

"Sounds about right."

"No, it *sounds* like you're scared of me."

"I'll not pretend to know the secrets you keep. Especially with you so cozily sitting there with an Ulfram in your lap."

Aydra eyed his deliberate gaze a moment, and she turned back to the alpha. *Is he always like this?* she asked it.

My life is his. I dare not speak ill of him.

I didn't realize Noctuans were so loyal.

"What was that?" Draven called to her.

"I did not say anything to you," she replied. "You're hearing things."

12

They waited in the dark for Draven's men. Draven fell asleep against a tree, faint snores evacuating his body. Aydra could just see him from the firelight. Leaned back against the trunk, legs crossed in front of him, muscular arms crossed over his chest… The peace on his features was something she'd not seen on him before.

Every now and then, she would hear the crunch of leaves beneath feet that she couldn't see, and the alpha Ulfram would growl in its direction. Whatever creature it was did not come any closer. And when she asked the Ulfram about it, she would tell her it was not her concern.

Her raven stood guard in the canopy above. Aydra's eyes were threatening to close when she finally heard him tell her the Venari guard was coming.

Aydra turned to tell Draven his men were back, but he was no longer sitting against the tree when she turned. She frowned into the darkness and turned around, only to find him crouched down behind her horse.

She jumped at the sight of him.

"*Sweet Arbina, Venari,*" she breathed, grasping at her chest. "Can you not do that?"

"Do what?" he asked as he continued to look at her horse's injured hoof.

She glared in his direction. "That thing you do, sneaking up on people."

"It's really not my fault you don't listen properly."

His men backed up a cart next to the horse. Aydra reached out and stroked her horse, telling her it was okay. The men loaded her up gently, and Aydra felt a swell of gratitude for them.

Draven brushed his hands on his pants after and then reached a hand down to her. "Come along, Sun Queen. The darker ones will be out soon. We should get a move on."

She swatted his hand away, and the Ulfram rose from her lap. "I can get up myself," she spat. She pushed off the ground, ignoring the searing pain in her ankles, and then—

—fell straight into Draven's arms.

He swooped her off her feet and into his arms before she could protest.

"Put me down, Venari!" she argued.

"Shut up before I shut you up," he growled as he crossed the space to his great black horse.

She winced at the pain now clamoring through her and resisted the urge to punch him in the throat. He clicked his tongue twice, and the horse kneeled so he could place her on the saddle.

If she hadn't been so angry, she would have been impressed.

The horse's golden eyes radiated into her own, and she placed a hand on its neck.

What is your name? she asked it.

The horse's weight fidgeted, and it whinnied once. ***You hear me?*** it asked.

I do.

Faryn, it answered.

Draven was staring at her with squinted eyes when she started to respond to Faryn. She straightened, and the horse rose to its feet again. Draven grabbed the back of the saddle and hoisted himself onto the beast behind her.

"What are you—If you think I want you anywhere near me after the musings of the last council meeting—"

"If I am not mistaken," he cut her off, "It was you who came to me, and you who smoked my herb."

Architects, she hated him.

A slow smile rose on his lips, and she heard him chuckle under his breath. "You and the Prince are one and the same. Never one to turn down the release of your own reality."

"You've smoked with Dorian?" she wondered.

"It's not a matter you should bother yourself with."

"Dorian is my younger brother. It is my business."

"Funny how you Promised children call each other brothers and sisters when you've literally no more blood relation than any other two Lesser beings born of the Sun. Tell me, queen, how many of your previous so-called brothers and sisters have fucked one another as you do the Dreamer you like so much?"

Her heart constricted. If she could have slapped him, she would have, but her only choice was to elbow his stomach hard behind her. He grunted in response, and she heard his breath catch.

"What the Promised have done before me is none of your concern, nor is it any of my own business," she hissed. "And as for who I choose to share a bed with—"

"Let me guess," he interjected. "Not my business either?"

"It is the very last thing you should ever concern yourself with."

The silence of the wood consumed them as they rode back to the Venari home. She ignored the heat of his body behind hers and tried to listen for any creatures around them. The Ulfram pack had not followed, and neither had the others that had stayed with her earlier.

It surprised her how at ease she felt surrounded by the darkness. Stark darkness. She couldn't see anything. The Venari could see enough in the dark that they could move without the use of the firelight, but she was blinded by the black of the night.

A chill suddenly ran down Aydra's spine. She couldn't hear a voice. But what she felt shuddered her. Emptiness. As though her insides had been ripped clean from her body.

"There's something around us," she managed, her hand gripping Draven's thigh to steady herself.

"What?"

"Something—" her balance wavered on the horse, and she gripped the saddlehorn in her other hand as her breath shortened.

"You don't feel it?" she breathed. "It feels as though an emptiness is crawling in my mind."

The wind brushed through the forest. Draven's body tensed behind her. He reached around and grabbed the reins, pulling back on his horse.

"Off the horses," Draven said. "Into the canopy."

Draven dismounted in one swift movement, boots colliding with the earth. She was startled by the sudden feeling of his hands pulling her from the saddle. "Get on my back."

"I'm not—"

"I don't have time for your protests," he growled. "If you wish to live and have your broken filly be spared, you'll obey my orders.

Now."

The cold shudder latched onto her again, and he turned his back to her. She leaned down and wrapped her arms around his neck, hooking her legs around his waist. They walked a short distance to what she assumed was a tree.

"Hang on tight," he told her. "We're going up."

Her horse screamed out for her.

Quiet, she told her. *Do not make a sound. All of you.*

"What was that?" Draven asked her as he pulled them up the branches.

"Nothing. Just relishing being so near you, Venari," she said sarcastically.

"You can relish it another day. For now, you'll not utter another word."

He pulled them up into the canopy quickly and took one of his men's hands to make it up to the final branch.

Aydra closed her eyes as they reached a sizeable steady branch. She couldn't see the creature, but she could feel it moving in the darkness. Four legs. Stalking the ground as a whisper. The shudder of night bled through her muscles. She'd never felt such darkness. As though black were as bright a color as the sun.

She tried to shake the consuming feeling. Her stomach turned. The creature's purr vibrated her insides, and her eyes rolled into the back of her head.

"Aydra—"

The noise of his voice was a distant echo. She hardly felt him squeeze her hand as her grip slipped. Darkness spun around her.

She fell.

13

Wet dirt met her body. She winced at the pain of the root hitting her hip. But she didn't have time to register any more than that.

Vomit evacuated her insides. Her head began to spin. She rose to her hands and knees and her eyes closed.

The ground froze beneath her.

A fog surrounded her, the tiny droplets of moisture pressing into her skin. Her heart pounded loudly in her chest. A primordial purr vibrated her bones. It wasn't fear that rippled through her body--it was unfamiliarity. She pulled for the noise of the creature's voice, attempting to connect with it.

But she felt no core.

Only an empty void.

It pulled her in. She was a moth to its flame of obscurity.

A huff of breath hit her face. Her hair blew back off her shoulders. She tried to shake the dizziness of her head as it clawed its way into her mind, filling her with its shadows of death and necrosis.

I… I see you… she managed to cry out into the void. I am not your enemy.

I know no enemies.

Its deafeningly low growl made her feel as though she was being pulled inside out. Her stomach lurched into her throat, and she puked nothingness. She gripped the dirt beneath her fingernails.

I know nothing but the dark.

The overwhelming growl of its voice leeched into her consciousness. A jagged breath left her lungs. Her eyes rolled, almost slipping, but she forced herself to her knees.

The dark is your home.

Vomit left her again. Searing pain tore through her abdomen as though the chasm of the creature's being were consuming her.

Come home... Aydra Ravenspeak.

—Fire.

Feet hit the dirt behind her.

The beast's face illuminated in the orange glow.

A skeleton head of a horse with wide horns stared at her. Its head was as large as her own steed was tall. No eyes. Fangs where nothing should have been in its mouth. She knew this creature.

This was the Spy.

A creature born to live in the shadows of darkness. Not a Noctuan, but rather a beast allowed to live in Duarb's realm to feed on the soft-minded.

The fire above her moved, and a horn bellow echoed into the air.

The beast's mouth opened, and it emitted such a shriek that the entire forest shook. The wind of it nearly blew her off balance.

Once more, it sank into the darkness, and her corporeal insides slowly began to return. Her breath heaved in her chest as though her lungs hadn't received air in minutes.

Something moved beside her, and she jumped, eyes wide at the fire torch in her face.

She froze at the look on Draven's face as he appeared kneeling beside her.

His jaw was taut, thin lips pressed into a line. The fire illuminated his dark eyes. Every vein in his neck and the one on his forehead puckered as though they were straining for freedom. His sharp cheekbones looked like razors on his face. His features held the shadows in them as though his face were their home. She stilled at the fearsome sight of him.

This was the Venari King she'd been warned about.

"Are you okay?" he asked in a lower voice than she was used to.

She couldn't move. Her voice remained stuck in her throat.

Draven reached for her, but she flinched at his touch and backed away. He held up his hands and sat the torch slowly on the ground.

"Are you real?" she managed in a voice so hoarse she barely heard it.

His face softened just noticeably, and he held out his hand. "Why wouldn't I be?"

Wary of the man standing before her, she hesitated.

She remembered the stories of the Spy. Of the void that would plague your mind with tricks and consume your thoughts of what you wanted to hear, not the reality of it. Of how people would get stuck there in a realm that wasn't their own, leaving their corporeal bodies to shrivel and die of hunger and thirst as your mind remained behind.

This wasn't real.

She stared at his figure, willing her eyes to look past the blatant mirage.

I told you, Spy, she spoke to him. *I. See. You.*

A smile rose on Draven's face, and his eyes flashed solid black.

Darkness filled the forest once more.

Actual breath returned to her lungs, entering her almost as an attack on her body. She willed herself to calm, feeling her raven push comfort through her bones. Her muscles as water against the ground.

Feet hit the dirt. She jerked so quickly at the noise that she hit another root with her wrist.

The orange glow of fire lit up the dark as it had moments before. The real Draven stood over her, the same stern look she'd just seen on him in her vision plastered on his face.

She swatted his hand away and glared up at him as he reached for her. "Get your hands away from me," she spat. "You left me on this floor to be taken."

"Would you have preferred for us to have interfered?" Draven asked.

Aydra huffed, hating that he was right. "No," she grunted.

"Look at that. A Queen not in need of saving," Draven mumbled, eyes flickering to his men behind her as a ghost of a smile rose on his lips.

She wanted to slap his stupid face.

The men chuckled quietly, and Draven looked back at her. "We were right here. Above you the entire time," he swore.

"And if I had been consumed by the Spy?"

"Actually would have saved me a bit of grief if you had."

A low growl emitted from her own throat. He smirked and stretched his hand out once more.

"I'm impressed you knew him," Draven mused as she reluctantly took his arm. "How did you get out?"

She was forced to put her arm around his shoulders so that she didn't stumble, teeth clamped so tight together she thought her jaw might break.

She hated herself for falling in his Forest.

"It's—"

"Not my business," Draven interjected upon wrapping his hand around her waist. "Got it."

It was the last she saw of his face before he plunged the fire into the wet dirt at her side.

"Come along, Spybreaker. We'll all be consumed if we do not get moving."

14

Aydra passed out halfway through the night on Draven's horse. Draven assumed she would after her being nearly consumed by the Spy. He wasn't sure how she'd gotten herself out of its void. In all honestly, he thought he was going to have to carry her coreless body back to Magnice, have to somehow explain it to her brother and the people of their kingdoms that he'd let the Queen be drained of her insides.

They arrived back at his home in the trees before dawn. He took her sleeping body into his own quarters and left her in his bed. She never even stirred as he moved her.

"How do you think she did it?" one of his men, Dunthorne, asked as Draven laid her down.

Draven glanced questionably back at his curly-haired friend leaning in the doorway, arms crossed over his chest. "Did what?"

"Pulled herself out of the Spy's void," Dunthorne answered. "We've nearly lost men to it before. How would someone not of our kind figure it out?"

Draven looked back down at Aydra's sleeping figure. "I don't know."

Draven only went to check on her once during the day.

He'd napped for only an hour on the small extra bed on his roof before awakening to his people's protests in the clearing below his treehouse home. Word had spread that they'd rescued the Sun Queen from the darkness and that she was now held up in their own King's home, injured. They voiced their fear of her brother invading their realm, asked Draven to send her back immediately or even just to kill her and say she was taken by the wrath of the Noctuans or the Infi.

Draven refused.

He squashed their doubts the best he could, assuring them if Magnice did, in fact, send an army, that they would be ready to fight but that he would happily give back the Queen at the first word of it.

"She would not have done the same had you been injured in her realm," argued Balandria, Draven's Second.

"And what have I told you about our people?" Draven snapped.

Balandria's weight shifted, and she crossed her arms over her chest. "That we have to be better."

"Right," he affirmed, clapping her shoulder. "Besides, I may have a way she can help return the favor."

"I don't like it," she argued. "She's as likely to tell her brother you kidnapped her as she is to help you with whatever plan you've come up with."

Draven nodded knowingly. "We'll see."

His people's doubts stayed in the back of his mind throughout the day.

He spent the daylight sorting out the things they would be using for trade in two days. The Bullhorn would be coming through that night, as he always did on the third night of the Dead Moons cycle, and it never failed that his nerves shook him.

Around mid-afternoon, he went upstairs to change into something warmer for the night and to check in on Aydra.

When he checked on her, he made a mental note to remember the look on her softened face. This would be what he would force himself to think of when he would inevitably want to kill her upon her waking in a few hours.

Her hair splayed out on the brown linens. He could tell she was dreaming by the darting of her eyes beneath their lids. It had been a long time since he'd looked upon her face and not seen her teeth clenched, her bow-shaped lips not pulled into a taut sour purse, or her biting the inside of her cheek.

The thought of her made his fists tighten. Her brother had been the bane of his existence since their childhood. And she... she'd hated him since their first fight, even though she'd won.

Despite her gangliness as a teen, Aydra had fashioned herself into a woman, by all standards, by the age of twenty. And now, nine years later, she'd grown into the attitude she wore on her sleeve on a daily. Tall. Fearless. Passionate. He dared to think he could have cut his hand on her sharp jawline or entangled himself within the confines of her fiery gaze. He found himself thinking about her curves in that dress from that last banquet on more nights than he dared admit.

She stirred just slightly and rolled over onto her side, grasping the linen blanket in her hands as she curled into a ball.

He squinted at the bruise on the back of her neck, barely visible beneath the raven silhouetted triad tattoo marked on her throat that signed her place as Arbina's Promised daughter.

He placed the cup of water he'd brought up with him on the table at the bedside and turned on his heel to change his clothes. He didn't want to be the first thing she saw when she woke up.

15

Aydra woke in an unfamiliar bed. The smells of dirt and trees filled her nostrils. Her first instinct was to balk at the smell, but as she lay there, unable to move from the pain shooting through her ankles, she allowed the smells to swell in her lungs. An unfamiliar warmth settled in her bones at the comfort.

Around her was wood. A tree sat at the edge of the room, and the walls were built around it. She squinted at the wide opening across the room on the other side of the tree. It almost looked like a doorway into the forest. She could see trees outside past an expansive deck.

The noise of men outside perked her ears. A tall wooden staff with a small post on the side, a crutch she realized, was leaned against the bed. She turned towards the edge of the mattress and tried to stand but almost fell as her weak ankles gave out. She cursed herself as she looked down and saw the purple welts around her ankles and the red scratches on her feet.

A few moments passed, and she surrendered to the crutch to help herself out of bed. Taking one step at a time, falling twice, and finally crawling out to the deck. It was sunset, which told her she'd slept at least one day. A stench radiated through the air as she reached the outdoors. Like a wet dog or bear.

One look down into the clearing told her exactly what it was.

The Bullhorn was standing in front of Draven.

The Bullhorn was one of the most well-known Noctuans. He was the only one of his kind. A great beast no less than eight feet tall. It towered over Draven by just over a foot, a double-headed axe in its elongated sausage fingers, long pointed nails like daggers digging into the wood of its hilt. The Bullhorn had the head of the Ulfram, the lengthy tree-limb like magnificent grey horns of the bull, and the torso of a man. Its lower body was more like a bull's haunches, but it stood on its wheel-sized hooves upright. The thick black fur that covered its entire body was thick around its hips and splayed out like a mane around his head, and down his back, in a V. His darkened purple eyes stared at Draven, and Aydra could feel the pull of the great beast's core in her own.

She closed her eyes and listened for his voice, for the groan and ripple of its vibration. And then she heard him.

—idiot like Parkyr before him, the beast was saying.

Aydra snorted and quickly clapped her hand over her mouth. She couldn't tell what Draven was doing or what he was instructing his people to do around the Bullhorn, but she heard the Bullhorn continue to insult Draven.

Why do you follow if you think him such? she called out to him.

The Bullhorn's head rose slowly, and she was met with his penetrating gaze. He blinked slowly at her. *Daughter of Arbina*, he acknowledged.

You have met us before? she asked.

Only such could converse with me.

What is your name?

Cees.

I am Aydra Ravenspeak. Why do you follow these men if you think they are idiots?

On my life will theirs be taken.

Draven was staring at the Bullhorn, apparently bewildered at the low grunts emitting from his throat. Aydra pulled herself between the slats beneath the deck rail and allowed her legs to dangle off the side.

"He says you are an idiot," she called down.

Draven whirled around. "Excuse me?" he spat.

"Cees. The Bullhorn. He says you are an idiot," she repeated.

The ivory horn Draven was holding clenched in his fist. "And you would know this how?"

"Because I can hear them," she said with a tired shrug. "I would have thought someone who thinks he is as smart as he is would have figured that out by now. Especially after last night."

"What are you doing out of bed?" he glared.

"I can manage just fine," she argued. "Do you have an extra horse? I expect one ready to ride within the hour. My sister and Second will be looking for me. I need to meet them on the Preymoor."

A deep chuckled radiated from Draven's lips, and he turned to face her, arms crossing over his chest. "Who exactly do you think you're speaking to? Your steward?" he mocked with a shake of his head. "I take no orders from you, little Princess."

Aydra fumed. "I am your Queen. And if not—"

"I have no queen," Draven interjected. "So before you get all mighty and start giving out orders, remember who's realm you're injured in."

A rustling came from the wood, and ten more Hunters emerged on tree branches, all with their weapons in hand, daring her to speak another word.

Aydra looked to Cees.

Are you sure you would give your life for his? she asked him.

Idiots. But my life remains his should he need it.

"Stop putting words in their heads," Draven snarled. "They are not yours to lead."

"Believe me when I say this, Hunter: I would not call on them were it the day of my death," she countered.

She stayed outside and watched them a bit longer before retiring to the bedroom. She had to crawl back. She dared not reveal this to the Venari King below, for she did not want to hear the mocking words from his lips when he saw her crawling on her hands and knees.

The crutch helped her rise to the bed. With a huff, she surrendered to the middle of it, cursing that she had let herself get hurt.

Draven's room was cool. The breeze of the tree canopy continuously swept through it. She wondered how the Venari ever heard anything on the wind if it was constantly blowing as she felt.

Or perhaps it was that Duarb knew she was there, and he disapproved.

Her boredom quickly set in. The only thing interesting in the room was the great desk that he had by the door. Stacks of papers and maps piled atop it. There was shelving behind the chair, rolled parchment in the boxes stacked as tall as the ceiling. She wanted to snoop, allow her curiosity to get the best of her.

But when her feet gave out from under her, she cursed the day and simply surrendered to the bed once more.

The howls of the Ulfram echoed off the trees. And then she heard something she'd not heard before. The great song of the Wyverdraki family.

A smile rose on her lips as it filled her ears.

She'd just sank back onto the bedspread to listen when she heard footsteps coming up the staircase.

Draven appeared on the deck, and he paused in the grand opening, a tray of what she assumed was food, in his hand. "Good. You're awake," he noted, stepping inside. "Are you hungry?" he asked as he sat the tray of food on the small eating table to the right of the door.

Her stomach growled, and he raised his brows at her in response. "I suppose," she managed.

Draven didn't comment. He crossed the room to his dresser, where he started changing clothes.

She wished she could say that she looked away as he changed clothes. But she didn't.

His back muscles rippled as he moved his arms to take the shirt off and search for a new one. She hated her body's response to seeing the dimples at his hips, the chisel of his broad shoulders. It was her favorite thing on a man, and Draven's exceeded expectations. She squinted at the crude black marks on his shoulder blades, like lightning streaks on his skin. They stretched from the phoenix marks on his hands to the back of his forearms and up over his collarbones.

"Would you like me to turn around or is this how you usually seduce your women?" she asked in a low voice.

"I should think we're both old enough to have more tricks up our sleeves for wooing prey into bed than just the lure of body parts," he replied as he turned towards her. His sage eyes danced in her direction as he pushed his arms through the snug long sleeve tunic and then stuck his head through the top.

"Why? Were you seduced?" he mocked.

All the leer she'd felt a second before vanished at his smugness. "You're insufferable," she declared.

He chuckled under his breath, amused by her retort, but he didn't comment more. "Do you think you can make it over to the table, or shall I have to carry you over?"

"Can you not bring it to me?" she grunted.

"Food is not served in my bed," he told her. "That is reserved for a different spread." He paused a moment, slowly taking a step towards her as he said, voice deepening, "So my question, Sun Queen, is can you walk to the table."

She looked down at the swelling in her ankles and cursed herself for the word she knew was about to come from her mouth. "No," she said in such a voice she barely heard herself.

"What was that?"

"I said no, okay?" she nearly yelled. "I can't walk."

She dared to look up, but what she saw on his face was not amusement or mockery but rather a softened expression she didn't understand. He finished crossing the space between them and bent beside her. His arm tucked around her waist, and he brought her arms around his neck. Her breath stilled as he lifted her off the bed, waist in his hand. Her toes never touching the ground as he walked across the room to the table as though she were simply a bag on his shoulder.

Her pride fell as he sat her in the chair and poured her a cup of wine.

She hugged her arms across her chest and sank herself as far back as she could into the seat. "Why are you doing this?" she asked.

"What?"

"Being nice," she replied. "Helping me."

He paused a moment before placing the cup in front of her. He didn't speak and instead simply took the seat opposite her and took a long sip of his wine.

"You hear them," he said as more of a statement than a question.

"Who?"

He pushed the tray of food in front of her, and she reached for the baguette.

"Creatures."

She met his curious gaze, and she swallowed the bread in her mouth. "I do."

"All creatures?" he asked.

She nodded just as the raven squawked outside, and a smile curled on her lips.

"I take it she's yours?" Draven asked.

"Why would you think that?"

"Because she showed up here this morning."

He paused and swirled the wine in his cup a few times. "Can you communicate with them?" he asked after a few moments.

"Why are you so interested?"

"Because I have a lot of creatures in my realm who cannot converse with me. It might be nice on occasion to have someone who can."

"I'm not your servant, Venari," she argued. "You cannot summon me to do your bidding."

"Perhaps we can come up with some sort of trade. Your help for mine."

"I have no need for your help."

107

"Really? So you and your horse are both better now? A miraculous recovery after only one night. I did not know it was possible."

She glared at his sarcasm. "Fine," she mumbled before taking a long swig of her wine. "What do you need?"

A long sigh emitted from his lips, and he tapped his cup on the table a few times, avoiding her eyes. She watched him as he stood and hovered over her for a brief moment. "Get some rest," he said. "We'll talk more tomorrow."

16

The only thing Aydra remembered about her second day in the Forest of Darkness was Draven bringing her breakfast.

He'd brought up a tray of roasted potatoes at sunrise, and he'd urged her to eat it all before drinking the thick liquid he'd brought up as well.

"Trying to poison me, Venari?" she asked him.

"Poison is not how I would kill you," he promised. "I would have thought you'd know that by now."

She eyed him but trusted his words nonetheless. "So, what is it?"

"Potion the Nitesh taught us to make," he said as he rummaged through some of the papers on his desk.

She brought the cup to her lips, sniffed it, and immediately regretted the decision. "This is disgusting."

"You'll drink it unless you'd like to stay here longer than the Dead Moons cycle," he told her.

A great annoyed huff emerged from her nostrils, and she started to pick at the potatoes. He left her without another word after finding whatever map or letter it was he'd been looking for.

Her raven flew inside and perched himself on the chair across from her. She looked at him as he stared at her and the food she wasn't sure she wanted.

Is it poison? she asked him.

Drink the potion, he told her.

She was standing in the street.

Children came running up behind her, nearly knocking her off her feet.

But the sight of the bright red ringlets on the girl's head made her look twice at the children.

"Aydra!"

A little boy's voice filled her ears, and she watched as a black-haired boy ran beside her and engulfed the small red-headed girl in his arms. Their giggles echoed as he lifted her off the ground in a sideways hug.

"You left me!" the young Rhaif declared.

"Bina told me to run," she had said, referring to their mother, Arbina. "She said you wouldn't catch me."

"I will skin the both of you!" came the sound of Willow's voice. Aydra turned, remembering the way Willow had run after her and her brother when they were children.

Rhaif leaned over and whispered something in young Aydra's ear that Aydra didn't remember. But her younger self grabbed Rhaif's hand, and they fled off down the street giggling, ignoring Willow's shouts.

She was sitting on the edge of a cliff past the castle.

She looked down at her hands, noticing the blisters on her knees and on her palms. Rhaif sat beside her, his fourteen-year-old self staring at her with a glisten in his eyes. He reached for her hand and wrapped his own around it.

"Are you okay?" he asked softly.

Aydra pushed the tears from her face. "I'm okay," she lied.

"If I had my fire, he would not touch you again," he promised.

"I don't want you to worry," Aydra whispered. "Zoria said—"

"I know what she said," Rhaif argued. "I was in the room. But… he hurt you."

"It's okay," she told him.

"Drae, it's not—" His words ceased, and she winced at the grip he took on her hand. He must have felt it, for he softened and pushed her hair off her face.

"Our youngers will never know of it," he declared. "Nyssari and

Dorian. We can be better than our elders have been."

Aydra met his eyes. "Do you promise?" she'd asked him.

Rhaif leaned over, and he took her face in his hand. "I swear it."

Aydra awoke groggily on the third day and sat up in the bed. Her head throbbed. She realized the noon sun was staring at her, which meant she'd been asleep for at least a day. The memory of the dreams she'd been cursed with made her heart constrict. Her stomach growled. She pushed herself to her feet with the crutches beneath her arms and limped out onto the balcony.

Her feet did not sting as badly as they had the day before. On this day, she could actually put some weight on them. The easy healing made her chest swell with gratitude. She wasn't used to dealing with prolonged healing methods before. Were she in her own kingdom, she would simply go to her mother's waters and sit, but as she was stuck in her enemy's territory, she would have to heal the 'normal' way.

Below was a line of wagons full of goods settled between the trees and around the clearing. Hunters were in lines, moving bags and goods from the trailers to their own storage carts. She stared at Draven's figure, who was speaking with-- who she assumed--was the trader. The light olive-toned man had his blonde and brown dreaded hair pulled up high on his head, the thickness of it stark against the dark forest. Draven handed him something, and the man shook his hand and clapped his shoulder.

"Morning, Sun Queen."

The woman's voice caused Aydra to jump and fall onto the floor as her ankles gave out from under her. Her head snapped up to the one who had spooked her—a Venari woman. She was smirking down at her, dark skin glistening in the light from the sun. Her thick black curls were pulled up onto her head in three buns down the middle. Aydra eyed the tight brown pants and white tunic she wore, the leather vest fitted against her slim torso.

The woman huffed amusedly and shook her head as a grin spread across her beautiful face. "He said you were jumpy," she muttered. "Didn't realize he meant this jumpy."

Aydra exhaled boldly, cursing herself for falling over her feet. "Who?"

"My King," she informed her. The woman held out her hand, and Aydra reluctantly took it.

The strength of her pull made Aydra's breath catch. Aydra found herself within a few inches of the woman's body, and the woman huffed again.

"Balandria," she said.

Aydra gripped to the crutch beneath her arm. The name was familiar. Her eyes squinted as Balandria's dark gaze twinkled at her.

"You're the Venari King's Second, aren't you?" Aydra asked.

"I am," Balandria answered. "He asked that I bring you something to eat. If you'll excuse me, Spybreaker, my king needs me."

Balandria turned and made her way down the steps without another word. Aydra stared after her, confused as to what had just happened.

You're staring, her raven said.

Aydra pulled her cloak around her and looked down at the field of Venari men and women. *I need to leave. Soon*, she told him.

You are not healed.

If I stay here much longer, I'll be seduced by all of them.

The squawk of her raven echoed in her ears. She glared at his cackle and made herself go inside to where Balandria had left her food.

The fill of her belly brought energy to her muscles. There was a rope out in front of the balcony that Draven had used the morning before to let himself down. It was more helpful than her trying to get down the stairs without ultimately making a fool of herself, so she reached out for it and gripped it in her hands.

Her crutches landed in the grass, causing a few of the men to stop and frown up at her as she descended the rope. She thought she was doing well until she got to the bottom and realized she had no way to stand on her own with her crutches lying on the ground.

And she refused to ask for help.

So she used her foot to pick up the handle of one and brought it carefully to her hand. She was pretty sure she flashed a few of the men, but it was better than her admitting defeat.

"I see you made it out of the tree," came Draven's voice behind her.

She poised herself on the crutches and blew her frustrated hair out of her face. "I did," she managed, chin lifting.

He didn't speak any further as he took a large bag of some sort from one of his men, and then he passed it to Balandria beside him. This continued for a few minutes until the point that Aydra huffed impatiently.

"Where are my things? My crown? Bow? Sword?" Aydra asked, leaning on the crutches.

"Do not fret," Draven said with an annoyed sigh. "They are safe."

"I need them. I must take my leave."

Draven straightened and dusted his hands off. He gave her a deliberate once over then and said, "All right. Walk to me," using his hands to gesture.

"Excuse me?" she balked.

"You say you're well enough to leave. Walk to me. Without the crutch."

Aydra's teeth set. She hated the smug look on his face, the arrogance in his eyes. Not only that, but the snickering of the other Venari around the clearing made her blood boil.

She gripped the crutches and glared at Draven. She knew she couldn't. And she didn't need more mocking from the entire Venari race when she would inevitably fall.

A slow twist rose on Draven's lips. He crossed his arms over his chest, hair falling out of its ponytail and over his eyes. "You'll leave when we say you can leave," he told her.

"This is kidnapping," she hissed.

"No," he snapped, crossing the space between them. "This is saving my ass and yours. If you were to go back right now, your brother would send an army of Belwarks into my home, attack all the Noctuans, and he would do it without bothering to hear yours or my side of what really happened. He would think I hurt you, and he and your little minis would start a war we do not need." He paused to tower over her, and she could hear her pulse beating in her ears.

"Do not think for a moment that I want you here any more than you want to be here," he hissed. "Do you think I relish argument at every waking moment? Hearing your voice doubting and making me question everything I do? We were building at peace before you got here. And now—" He made like his hands would grasp the sides of her head, and he instead gripped the back of his neck. "The faster you heal and get out of here, the better."

He turned and walked away from her then, leaving her words stuck in her throat. She hated that he was right.

"Then I must send word to my sister and Second. Let them know I am okay," she called to him. "It would have been Lex's responsibility to make sure I came home. And my sister… She is likely terrified. I do not know where she is."

"We do," came Balandria's voice. "She's in the Village of Dreams."

Aydra eyed Balandria's smirk, and if she could have crossed her arms over her chest, she would have.

"What's wrong, Sun Queen? Didn't think women Hunters would speak such to you?" came Draven's voice as he started helping again with bags of food. "Balandria is my Second and also our fiercest fighter. Be glad it was Dunthorne who was with me on patrol the other night and not her. Your Princess would now be Queen."

17

"What exactly is it you trade with?" Aydra asked Draven later when he brought her dinner.

"Why? Planning on telling your brother our secrets?" he asked, his fingers strumming on his cup.

"Despite what you think, Venari King, I do not tell my brother everything."

A daring smile rose on his lips, and he sat up, elbows sitting on the table. "Do I sense a feud between Haerland's most loved brother and sister? Squabbles between the perfect pair?"

Aydra gripped the cup in her hands.

"Do tell, Sun. I'd love to hear it," he said with a smug wink.

A flash of blue flames poured through her memory, and she blinked to push it from her mind. "It's not your concern," she managed.

His smirk widened. "I knew there was something not perfect about those banquets. Not everything can be that grand all the time."

"And here?" she asked. "Is everything always so 'family first' as you like to put it?"

Draven took a long swig of his drink, his eyebrows elevating. "Generally yes," he said. "We usually settle arguments with challenges. Duels. But, if you must know, those that have problems with our ways are usually of the Infi. And we do not let them walk among us."

"Are the Infi not your brethren?"

Draven's cup slammed into the table. A wild look of anger flashed in his green eyes. "They are not my brothers," he snarled.

She slowly sipped her wine, almost amused that she had riled him up with such a minor accusation. "And here I thought Venari King meant the leader of all Duarb's cursed," she teased.

"The Infi are nothing more than savages, only living for themselves —"

"And that is different from Hunters how?"

He stared at her for a long enough moment that she felt her weight shift.

"You know nothing of my people, Sun Queen," he said in a hauntingly quiet voice. "Nothing of the sacrifices we have made defending your own kingdom. Did you even know about the ship that arrived on Lovi's shores almost three weeks past?"

Aydra froze. "What?"

"Exactly."

"What kind of ship?"

"The enemy kind," he replied shortly. "The kind carrying strangers and disease. With beings not of our own, not of Haerland, suited up in armor and carrying weapons made from minerals not of our land. Beings who were not created or sprung from the land but rather from each other. The kind of ship that only means there will be more, and if we are not vigilant, the kind that will take over our land without question."

This made her sit up. "What happened?" she asked.

"We took care of it. With the Honest," he answered. "Fighting alongside those not of our own is something we do here in the southern realms."

"Do you speak ill of your beloved mountain friends?" she asked, referring to the Blackhands.

"The Blackhands have nothing to fear, no reason to fret any such war coming to their homes. They stay to themselves and secure their own. I cannot fault them for that."

She crossed her arms over her chest. "We would have sent aid," she told him. "Had you asked for it."

A laugh emitted from Draven's lips, one that mocked her and told her nearly all she needed to know about what exactly had been wrong with her brother before her leaving.

"Oh, you poor thing," he mocked. "You really knew nothing of it, did you?"

She eyed him from across the table, and he shook his head.

"Your brother knew all about the ship," he informed her. "He knew everything. We asked for a Belwark patrol to be sent to take one of these men back to Magnice alive so that your brother could question them. We offered that. We offered for him to take the lead on the charge. He refused to send aid. Refused to even acknowledge an enemy arriving on our shore. Simply told us to take care of it as though it were a hunting party. And this isn't the first time."

Aydra couldn't believe what she was hearing. "That's not... he wouldn't. I am head of security. Anything threatening our borders should have gone through me. He would have told me."

Draven scoffed. "A title given to make you feel as though he trusts you, as though you have a place in his court. Nothing more."

"I was not given such a title to simply execute wandering thieves," she seethed.

"No. I'm sure you chose to do that on your own," he said. "I think you crave getting your hands dirty."

"I refuse to sit back and bark orders when I can take care of a problem myself."

He stared at her another moment before pushing off the top of the table where he'd rested himself. He walked across the room to the desk where she'd seen letters upon letters strewn over the top of it, and he plucked one from the top of the pile.

"You want evidence of your brother's cowardice? Here it is."

He flung the letter into her lap before turning his back on her and striding onto the deck.

She recognized her brother's handwriting at once.

What lands on Lovi's shore is your problem, Venari. Take care of it.

Aydra nearly crumpled the letter between her tightened fists. She never felt so betrayed in her life. That her own brother, who had put her in charge of security and told her such would be her contribution to their kingdom while he dealt with the rest of it. He'd *lied*. He'd kept her in the dark, and for what? Her own safety or because he thought the Venari to be lying?

She struggled to her feet and grasped the crutch in her hands, forcing herself out on the deck. The cool wind wrapped around her body. Draven's back was to her. She could just see the outline of his figure from the great bonfire going down below them in the clearing.

"I am sorry, Draven," she said softly. "I didn't know."

His gaze flickered surprise at her over his shoulder. Or so she thought. He sighed heavily, and the surprise she thought she'd glimpsed vanished. "I know you didn't."

"How many men did you lose?" she asked.

"Five. The Honest lost thirteen," he answered. "It sounds like a small number to you, I am sure, but for us… when our children are born from Duarb's roots with one of two fates, and the Infi claims a majority, every person counts."

"I would have been here," she assured him.

"Somehow, I doubt your brother would have allowed you to bring a guard of your own."

"My brother doesn't dictate everything I do. Nor does he own every single Belwark."

He looked her over deliberately. "No. I'm told you have a special way of luring them into your own company."

"How I choose my pleasures is not your concern, Venari."

He smirked and held his hands up. "I've no judgment for how you live your life. Every king has taken the liberty of multiple persons in their bed. Why should you not enjoy life's pleasures simply because you are a woman?"

"And are you such a King?" she heard herself ask.

A pause washed over the air as they dared one another to blink.

"What do you think?" he asked.

"I think you're hard to figure out," she admitted. "But what I am sure of is that you've never found yourself wanting or bereft of pleasure."

A huff of agreement left him, and he turned back to the bonfire. "Infinari persons rarely do."

She squinted questionably at his use of the word. She gripped the railing at the edge of the deck and used it as a prop, lowering herself down to the wood floor to sit. "You chose that word at the banquet to speak of the Infi in our streets," she said as she laid the crutch on the floor beside her. "Why that instead of calling it what it was?"

"Because it wasn't always Infi," he said simply.

"What do you mean?"

He met her eyes, and she swore she saw a shadow of darkness fall over his features. "Are you genuinely interested?"

"I am," she answered. "I never understood how you are born with two fates. Can you tell as infants what fate they are of?"

He sat down on the deck a few feet away, his legs dangling over the edge of the wood. His eyes danced with the flames of the fire in the clearing, and she could see his hands fidgeting in his lap.

"It's in their wailing," he said softly. "By the Dead Moons. Venari children do not wail upon hearing the Aviteth scream. They grow quiet. Her cry calms them, a comforting lullaby. Infi children scream as though the screech is piercing their ears and shutting them down. They turn red. Their skin burns.... And then there are those with both fates, also known as the Infinari."

"Are not all of them born with such?"

"We used to be," he said quietly. "Infinari children laugh. As though the sound of the Aviteth is a joke. It's easy to tell the three different ones as we are only born during the Dead Moons."

Something dark rested in his orbs, and she could see his mind working behind his gaze, a battle to admit something to her that she wouldn't expect.

"Which were you?" she asked.

"Every Venari King has been Infinari at birth," he said. "We grow up with an inkling of the fate Duarb would choose for us, but it is not always certain. Previous kings decided that by the age of ten, we would have our fates chosen. We are taken to Duarb, and he marks such a fate in our hands and arms—" He stopped and held up his forearms, revealing the phoenix marks of the Hunter etched crudely into his skin on the backs of his hands and his forearms. "Once chosen, the current Venari King takes those marked Hunter under his wing."

"May I see your mark again?" she asked.

He hesitated at first but then lifted his arms in front of him once more. He pushed his forearms together, and then she saw it, the whole of the phoenix bird, half etched into his left and half etched into his right. The wings wrapped around his muscles on either arm and the tail flailed out and continued to wrap up his arms, all the way to his shoulder blades and collarbones.

"The other Hunters... You and Balandria are the only ones with the marks up to your shoulders," she noted.

"Fair observation," he muttered, resting his arms once more. "Only those of Kings are marked so crudely. A symbol of the pressures and trials we would have to face as leaders of our kind."

"And those marked Infi?" Aydra asked.

He fumbled with the ring on his finger. "Most disappear before their markings. They escape into the darkness. But if we do find them..." His voice trailed, and her heart constricted.

"And the infants?"

He slowly raised his eyes to meet hers. "If you were to find an Infi child in Duarb's roots... if you knew what it would become, that its very presence on this land would mean death and betrayal to all of Haerland... what would you do?"

The unimaginable decision repeated in her mind, and she considered the options.

"I would make sure it did not get that chance," she finally whispered.

He turned his gaze to the fire again. "My people have lived as long as they have because the Kings of this Age have had to do what they must to keep us safe. But Duarb's curses do not simply lie with our births."

"What do you mean?"

He rubbed his arm and met her eyes again, this time giving her a small smile. "Enough for tonight," he said then. "I'll have your dreams filled with nightmares if you learn all our secrets." He stood from the ground and offered her a hand.

She swatted his hand away. "I can rise myself, Venari," she said, grabbing onto the pole. Her hand slipped, and his strong arms caught her.

She cursed herself as she came face to face with him, near an inch between.

"Sure about that?" he said, voice low.

But she didn't respond as he helped her rise to her feet. She grabbed the crutch and smacked his shin with it, to which he winced, but laughed nonetheless.

"Glad to know you've not lost your fight while being entrapped here," he mocked.

"I am not entrapped here."

His hair fell over his face as he looked down at her, and the smile on his lips met his eyes. She found herself stunned at the sight of it. How the anger had faded, and playfulness had replaced it. She had never denied his handsomeness, the stern angered facade he always wore being one that piqued her interest but not one she'd ever allowed herself to think more of. He was the enemy King of the southern realms. Born of a cursed race she'd been taught to think less of throughout her years.

"Goodnight, Aydra," he said to her.

Her name coming from his lips made her eyes squint just briefly. He turned away and started down the steps from the deck. The noise of his brothers and sisters welcoming him to their fire chats filled her ears. One of them clapped him on his shoulder and rattled him, laughing as they told some joke at his expense.

The Venari are beneath you, she'd been told, *No matter what these people say, no matter this 'equality' previous kings swore to them. Never turn your back on a Venari.*

Lies.

There stood a man, a race of people, who bled for their own, for Haerland. A race of misunderstood beings whom the Chronicles had betrayed because of the wrongdoings of their giver and the curses on their heads. There stood a man worthy of the crown he dared not wear except at the banquet, a man who walked and fought equally with his people, not above them or watching on the sidelines as they died.

She allowed the flames to dance in her eyes a few moments longer, and as he gazed up at her again, she watched a tiny smile rise on his lips, and then he turned away once more.

18

On the fourth day, Draven gave her more tonic so that she would stay in bed instead of trying to walk. He told her she was stubborn and that he would be forced to strap her into it if she didn't stay in bed that day.

So she took the tonic and surrendered to the weight of it as it forced her to sleep.

A dreamless slumber met her, and the next thing she knew, the warmth of the darkness swallowed her whole. She only awoke when shouting somewhere in the distance broke her out of it so harshly that she bolted upright.

The shrill noise calmed outside, but it rang in her ears for moments after. It was dark out, but the fireplace behind the tub was lit, its last embers emitting a warm glow as it died, along with a couple of flame-filled lanterns on various surfaces scattered about the room.

The high-pitched wailing vibrated the wood once more, and she realized what had awoken her.

Infi children had been born beneath Duarb's roots.

The next wail sent a shiver down her spine. It reminded her of an animal dying slowly, crying out in agony as its insides were ripped away. The screech of the Aviteth poured through the air, and she reminded herself that was probably what was happening to the Infi children.

She hugged her knees into her chest, and the cold wind surrounded her body.

The wailing only lasted a few minutes more, but it made her feel as empty as the Spy's void had. Her nose burned with emotion as she thought of what the Venari needed to do since at least one had been born. She could not imagine the torture of having to end such a life would have on a person.

An hour later, she heard boots hit the wood of the steps. When Draven's figure turned the corner and he strode through the door, her eyes widened at the bewildering sight of him.

He was covered in dark, nearly black, blood. It was much darker than she was used to seeing beneath her own skin. His hair fell out of the bun he had it in, and the stains of the sticky substance covered parts of his hairline. He didn't acknowledge her as he strode over to the dresser.

His fist punched into the vase sitting atop it, and the glass shattered to the floor.

"Draven?" she said into the still air.

His head jerked in her direction, apparent he'd forgotten she was there. "Shit," she heard him mutter. He pulled a shirt out of the dresser and slammed the drawer shut. A low guttural noise emitted from his throat resembling a growl, and he said, "Go back to sleep."

"I heard the wailing," Aydra said as she hugged the blanket around her.

Draven stopped moving, but he didn't respond. She could see the hurt reflecting in his eyes from the lantern on the dresser.

"How many were born?" she dared ask.

"Go back to sleep, Sun Queen," he growled as he continued to the wash, "don't bother worrying about us cursed ones."

He turned the tap for the clawed bathtub. On the other side of the room, the three-sectioned screen was pulled around the tub, but she could still see him behind it, and she couldn't stop herself from watching from the darkened bed.

His shirt thudded on the wooden floor, red staining and running on the lumber. His pants did the same, and her brow raised on her face at the sight of the Hunter's entire body she'd long sworn to hate silhouetted in the firelight. She could just see parts of his stained chest reflecting. The blood dripped down his long torso, curling in the blackened hair that stretched over his pecs and thinned between his abs to below his belly button. He turned, and the ripple of his shoulders made her mouth dry, just as it had in the days before. He didn't bother wiping himself off before getting in the tub and sinking himself into the hot water, steam rising off the surface as his body disappeared beneath it.

"If you're going to stare, you may as well join," he muttered as he leaned his head against the edge of the tub and shut his eyes.

She forgot he could see in the dark.

"Don't flatter yourself," she snapped, pulling the cover up to her face. "I couldn't walk over if I wanted to," she heard herself add.

"Your hands and knees still work."

An annoyed huff exited her lips, and she forced herself to turn away from him. "Goodnight, Venari."

The noise of him pushing himself under the water echoed in the still room. She tried closing her eyes to drift back to sleep, ignoring the movements of the water as he began to wash the blood from his body a few moments later. But it wasn't much use.

Morning light drifted through the tree canopy a few hours later. A fog settled on the land, creeping its way into the treehouse and hovering on the floor around the bed. The damp mist kissed her skin. She sat up and forced her feet over the side of the bed. As much as she hoped her ankles would allow her to stand upon them, she could tell by the ache in them that she would not be able to. Her left ankle seemed to be healing a bit quicker than the right. She could actually wiggle it in a circle without her wanting to just cut it off and spare herself of the pain.

She was quickly growing tired of not being able to do anything.

She gripped the crutch Draven had left by the bed in her hand and made herself stand on her left ankle. It almost wilted beneath her, but she moved her weight into her fists and maneuvered just a small step at a time. Eventually, she made it out onto the porch, where the warmth of the just rising sun greeted her. A sizeable wooden lounge chair sat in the right corner by the banister, a blanket laid across the back of it. She forced herself over to it and practically fell into its grasp.

Draven brought her more of the potion a bit later, but he didn't say much. In fact, she didn't see much of him throughout the day. An air of sadness rested in the forest as though the night before had been taxing for all of them. Every Hunter had the same darkened expression upon their face.

Aydra stayed on the balcony for the entire day, allowing the sun to bask on her skin and help aid her ankles back to health. She napped for most of it, and only when darkness fell did she see Draven again.

"Everyone was quiet today," she said as he sat down across from her at the table.

He lit the pipe in his hands and took a long inhale of the herb—a different one than the two she now knew him to have. His head leaned back against the tree at his back, and the smoke filled the air with his exhale.

"The eighth day of the Deads is always the hardest," he admitted softly.

"How many were born?" she dared to ask.

Draven avoided her, his hand gripping and releasing above the table, as though he were remembering clenching something in his fist. Perhaps his knife.

"Five," he told her.

"And how many did you bring back?"

"Are you always so interested in the dealings of other races' givers?" he growled.

She didn't lose his gaze and instead raised an impatient brow. Draven sighed heavily and tapped a finger on the table. "None," he finally said. "We brought none back."

"What do you do with them?"

"What do you think?"

She could see the sadness flickering in his pupils.

Her weight shifted in her seat. "And after?"

He ran his hands through his downed hair. "Duarb takes them back from where they came," he whispered.

Aydra ate the rest of her food in silence, her gaze simply watching him puff on his pipe in a daze as though she were not even in the room with him. It was only when she finally finished and downed her final bit of wine that he packed another herb in the pipe and extended it to her.

"What will this one do to me?" she asked.

His eyes shaded over. "Let the worries of your days fall into the darkest corner of your core."

She gave him a full once over, and then she took the pipe from his hand. One inhale, and her mind swirled. Her head leaned back onto the wood at her back, and she closed her eyes as the deep sweetness took over and radiated warmth over her muscles.

"Send me back with this one," she muttered.

Draven huffed amusedly under his breath and stood from the table. She started to hand the pipe back to him, but he held up a finger. "I'll let that one take you on your own tonight," he told her.

"Leaving me to smoke by my lonesome, Venari?" she asked.

"I'll not pretend to think I am the one you want in the room when that herb finally hits you," he replied in a low tone.

Something happened when he looked at her then—an unfamiliar

warmth and ache radiated between her thighs, one that made her mouth open slightly. He apparently saw it, for his tongue darted out over his lips, now smirking.

"What did you give me?" she asked slowly.

Another scoffing chuckle emitted from him. He picked up the plates from the table and backed out of the room. "Goodnight, Sun Queen."

19

She was starting to believe the potion was actually poisoned with how much he was giving her.

On the following day, she awoke to find him standing in front of the tub, his muscular back to her and cheeks glistening in the light from the fire. Her mouth dried at the sight of it. She cursed her aching body as she surrendered to the pillows once more.

He left the room without a word after getting dressed, only giving her a quick glance as he strode past the bed. She gathered her wits after he exited and made herself stand, pushing herself to hobble out onto the deck so she could see below.

The fog wrapped through the forest floor, bending and breaking along the great roots of trees thicker than she'd ever thought possible. She curled herself onto the lounge chair and wrapped the warm blanket around her shoulders as she watched the men and women down below chat with each other, a few showing off weapons to the others. One couple was knocking wooden swords beneath a tree to her right.

Footsteps coming up the stairs averted her attention. The person was taking them two at a time, so she knew it was Draven. He slowed upon seeing her, taking the last few steps deliberately.

"I thought perhaps you were awake," he said upon reaching the top.

"Hard to sleep with all that splashing," she lied.

A quiet huff of amusement left him, and he then held out a cup to her. She eyed the smoke rising from the liquid inside. "What is it?" she asked cautiously.

"You don't want it?" he asked, pulling it back.

"No, I do—"

She wanted to slap the smirk off his face.

He held it out for her again, and this time she took it from his fingers. The warm smell of tea filled her nostrils, and she inhaled it deeply with a close of her eyes.

"Thought you could use a bit of home," he told her.

She considered his gesture as she took a sip, silently wondering why he'd taken the time to bring her something comforting. The familiar spiced warmth of the tea consumed her chest as she drank, and she nearly melted into the chair, forgetting about the words he had just spoken.

"Thank you," she managed.

He gave her a slow nod, then leaned over the railing, watching his men as he sipped his own drink.

"I have a proposition for you," he said after a few minutes.

Her eyes narrowed. "Go on."

He turned slightly, left elbow resting on the rail, and he took a long sip of his drink. "I am taking a few men with me into the forest tonight. One of my men heard something unfamiliar last night on his patrols—"

"The strangers?" she interjected.

He shook his head. "One of the Noctuans. He thinks perhaps it is injured. I will go tonight to find the animal and assess." He paused and gave her a deliberate, yet nervous, once over. "If what I find is a beast that can be saved, I may need your help."

She settled back in the chair, letting her eyes linger into the woods for a moment as she contemplated her answer. "Okay."

"Okay?" he repeated, obviously taken aback by her quick agreement.

She shrugged and sipped on her tea. "For the beast. Not for you," she told him. "With any luck, it will take care of you and I'll not have to do any of this."

He looked as though he might laugh. "Is that—"

"My King—"

The sound of Balandria's voice as she bounded up the stairs averted both their attentions. She slowed her bounce at the top step, grinning, as she pressed a bowl into Draven's arm.

"Second batch," she said proudly.

Draven looked as though he would laugh, and he set his cup on the banister so that he could reach inside the bowl. He pulled a yellow circle from the inside and popped it in his mouth, and she could hear the crunch of it as he chewed. He made a pleasing noise and clapped Balandria on her shoulder.

"Like that. Every time," he told her proudly.

Balandria beamed. She turned quickly and ran back down the steps, leaving Draven to munch on whatever food it was she had brought. Draven caught Aydra's stare and proceeded to hold out the bowl to her.

"What is it?" she asked cautiously.

"When someone offers you food, the polite thing to do is eat it," he argued playfully.

She hesitantly reached into the bowl and took out one of the circles. One sniff and all she could smell was fat and salt. "Are these potatoes?" she asked before popping it in her mouth.

He watched her a moment as she fought the pleasing look her face wanted to make upon her savoring the taste of it on her tongue.

"Chips," he answered. "Bala's been working out temperatures for years now."

Aydra hated that she enjoyed it so much.

She pressed her cup back into her hands and leaned back in the chair. "How exactly is it you people look as..." her eyes traveled up and down his husky body and then back to the fried potatoes in his hands "...well, as you do," she managed, "when you are all always eating?"

Draven's gaze danced. "Climbing trees," he said with a shrug. "Battling each other. Constant training. Gifts of Duarb. Take your pick." His eyes traveled down her own sitting body, and he raised a brow when his gaze landed on her hips. "Am I to think Arbina simply gave you that weapon, or did you find the secret to a man's lust on your own?"

"Wouldn't you like to know?" she mocked with a small smile.

Draven huffed amusedly, and she hated the way he stared at her. As though he could see straight through her. As though he'd figured out what she held beneath the facade and was determined to break it. Mocking and eager all at once.

"You know that wall is going to shatter one day," he said then, popping another chip in his mouth. "I can't wait to be there when you're trying to pick up the pieces."

She watched him chew smugly for a moment, contemplating whether to throw the rest of her tea in his face. "Is it not you who tells your men constant vigilance?" she finally decided to ask. "To never trust words, only instinct?"

His chewing slowed, and she knew she'd hit a nerve.

"My kind have been persecuted over the years for simply being what we are... for the mistakes of our giver," he said in a low voice. "Would you expect me to tell them to live as though they could trust every being to walk this land?"

"There are good people in this land," she said. "Not everyone has ulterior motives."

"And are you one of these... good people?" he asked.

She pondered his question, the life she lived echoing in her mind.

"I may not have alternative motives... but I don't know that I would call myself a good person," she finally determined.

He slowly grabbed for another chip and crunched it in his mouth. "Look at that," he mocked. "A crack."

She glared at his words, but it didn't seem to bother him. The smirk on his lips returned. He went inside, sat the bowl of chips on the table, and returned with a cup of the familiar potion he'd been feeding her. He set it down on the ground beside the chair and then turned towards the staircase again.

"Drink the potion, Sun Queen," he called back to her.

Aydra grumbled as she switched from tea to the thick liquid, and she shot it back into her system before she could hurl at the smell.

20

Draven was not the one to bring her breakfast the following day. He sent Balandria up to her with food and more of the potion around midday. When Aydra asked Balandria where he was, she insisted Aydra not be concerned with her king's whereabouts.

Aydra sipped the potion instead of gulping it as she usually did, allowing her curiosity to get the better of her as she sat down at Draven's desk to pour over some of the maps he had spread across it.

Maps of the southern shores, of the Forest dwellings. She paused at this one, staring at the vastness of the forest home she realized she'd only seen a fraction of. Another set of drawings caught her eyes, and she pulled one page to the top of the pile, finding an illustration of one of the Noctuans— the Rhamocour.

The dragon-like beast was sketched deliberately into the parchment. Long neck raised, great wings spread out, each the same length as its body. The drawing made the beast look like it was black as smoke with whisps drawn around it to signify shadows. But what stood out was the great horns on its head and the apple-green color its eyes had been filled with.

"You know—"

Aydra jumped so quickly at the sound of Draven's voice that she nearly fell to the floor.

"—The last time someone snooped in my things, they found themselves in the middle of Berdijay territory on the last night of the Deads."

Draven was leaning against the frame of the door, shadows over his features as he stared pointedly at her.

"Sweet Arbina, Draven," she managed, willing her heart to an even

131

pace. "Can you—" But her words ceased at the sight of him. A large slash ripped through his shirt, his forearm bleeding from what looked like a scrape.

"What happened to you?" she asked breathlessly.

He pushed off the wall to go to the tub. "I'll show you," he said. "Tomorrow night. In the meantime, drink your potion and get back in bed. I need you well enough to not have to worry about your safety in the Forest tomorrow night."

Aydra rose to her feet, and she hobbled around to the front of the desk. "So demanding, Venari," she mocked. "Should I look forward to this kind of dominating leer on our journey?" she attempted to banter.

The rate at which he stepped before her made her gasp. Papers flew onto the floor. He grasped her hips and pushed her to the top of the desk. His hands pressing her wrists into the wood as his torso came flush with hers. Her breath caught, and she found herself frozen to the spot. His hair tickled her shoulders as he stared down at her, his face only inches from hers.

"Careful what you ask for, *Sun Queen.*"

Her heartbeat throbbed in her ears at the noise of his growl. In that moment, she decided to play his game. Her head tilted up at him, exposing her neck. Her thighs squeezed around his hips, pointed toes and heels digging into the backs of his thighs, and her mouth opened just slightly as her eyes darted from his sage eyes to his lips. His chest rose and fell against her own. She swore she heard a low groan emit from his throat as her thighs tightened around him.

"Remember who you're playing with, *Forest King.*"

His eyes fluttered, and then a tiny smirk rose on his lips. For a moment, he didn't move. And the longer he stayed, the quicker her heart began to beat. His nose grazed her cheek. His touch burning on her skin and making those muscles restless. He smelled of the forest and blood. Of dirt and leather and whiskey. Of pure loathing and danger.

She cursed her body for its response to him.

Until finally, he glanced down at her lips one last time and then stepped back, gaze traveling predatorily over her. "Right," he muttered.

Aydra's breath returned, and she stared after him as he finished crossing to the tub.

The raven flew inside and landed on the desk, where he tapped his beak on the potion cup. Aydra snapped out of her daze and grasped the cup in her hands.

She shot the rest of it into her mouth and pushed herself to the bed before her feet carried her to the tub with him.

It was much past dark when Aydra awoke to the noise of a lullaby echoing through the forest. She recognized it immediately and welcomed the one whom it belonged to. She hobbled out to the deck and sat on the lounge chair so that she could better hear it. She'd heard it once before, a very long time ago, when she'd been taken to the Forest with Zoria.

It was the sweet melody of the Bygon, Samar. The only one left of her kind. She lived in creeks and waters, taking form during the Deads to lure wandering men into her grasp. Her lullaby would rock them into a slumber they didn't want to be parted from, and then she would devour their blood while they slept.

Her voice grew louder as Aydra snuggled further into the blanket around her on the chair. And when a brisk wind swept through the balcony, Aydra looked towards the misting fog in front of her.

"Hello, Samar," Aydra called.

Samar's womanly figure appeared from within the fog. She rose out of it not as smoke appearing to form but as bone first, followed by muscle and blood, until the skin wrapped around her, creating the corporal being that came to sit on the railing.

Samar smiled dreamily and twirled her stark straight black hair in her fingers.

"Queen Aydra," Samar purred with a bow. "It has been a long time."

"Your lullaby is even more beautiful than I remember," Aydra said.

Samar smiled. "To what do we owe the pleasure of your company on this turn of the Deads?"

"Shadow thieves." Aydra pointed to the welts around her ankles. "What about you? I did not think you to venture inside their homes when you've so few nights to hunt."

"I come on occasion of the King's call," Samar replied.

"I did not hear the horn."

"That's because he does not have to bellow or blow the horn for my attention," Samar said. "The horn carries many different songs. One simply has to learn them. Draven has near mastered them all."

"And why does the King call you?" Aydra asked.

"He asks for my lullaby when he cannot sleep. I oblige any way I can."

"What exactly would he be having nightmares about?" she

wondered aloud.

Samar's lips twisted smugly. "Who said anything about nightmares?" she asked with a tilt of her head. "And what of you, Queen? Why do you not sleep? Has my lullaby not worked for you on this night?"

"You know as well as I that even your strongest of songs cannot put me to sleep."

Samar jumped off the railing and knelt in front of Aydra, her breath an inch from the Queen's. "You know I have other ways to help in such times," Samar whispered, her hand pressing to Aydra's cheek. She moved her hair off her shoulder, revealing the pale skin of her neck. Aydra's body shuddered as she felt Samar's mouth on her skin. Feeling the Bygon's flesh was different from sharing with a Lesser being. Samar's touch was of fog on your flesh, whispers on your body. She could shift into that which you wanted the most.

So when Aydra found herself lying on the bed a few moments later, legs splayed open as she almost reached her climax, and she looked down to see Draven's face between her thighs, she nearly jumped out of her skin.

"Sweet Arbina— *Samar!*" Aydra hissed, grabbing her hair.

The Bygon shifted into herself again and wiped her lips of Aydra's wetness as she grinned over the startled Queen. "Something wrong?" Samar asked innocently.

Aydra drew the knife from the bedside table and pushed it to Samar's throat. "What are you playing at, Bygon?" she hissed.

Samar's eyes danced. "Not what you were expecting?"

Aydra pushed her off and sat up, chest heaving at the thought of Draven being in bed with her.

"Get out."

"But I have not completed my task," Samar argued.

Aydra grunted at the creature's pouting face. She wouldn't deny she was still in want of an end, for her body to give in to the fatigue her mind felt. "No more tricks. Find someone else in my subconscious to mimic," she warned the shifter. "I want nothing of his face near me."

Samar gave her a nod, and in a whisper, the Dreamer Ash appeared before her, and Aydra settled back into the bed again.

"That's better," Aydra muttered.

21

The noise of the birds woke Aydra from the deepest slumber she'd had in weeks. She rose up from the sheets and stretched her arms overhead, relishing the feeling of her muscles waking and pulling with the glow of her mother Sun coming in through the opening.

"You should really learn some manners, Sun Queen," came Draven's voice.

She was getting used to him appearing from nowhere by then, but the sound of his voice brought back the memory of the night before, and it caused the flash of his face between her legs to come to mind.

As he leaned against the frame of the door, smiling smugly at her, she felt the color drain from her face.

Perhaps she hadn't been as quiet as she thought.

"Manners?" she made herself repeat. "This coming from the Hunter who pushed me on a desk yesterday without my asking for it."

Lips twisting crookedly, he glanced towards said desk. "I take it Samar paid you a visit last night?" he asked, ignoring her words and instead changing the subject. "I'm guessing her lullaby didn't work for you either."

And she heard the mockery in his tone.

Aydra pushed herself to the edge of the bed. "How I fall asleep is no business of yours, Venari," she made herself argue.

"It's not. Except when your moans are what kept me up for near an hour. Tell me, who was it she mimicked that took so long to bring you to your end?"

She almost fell onto the floor at his question, and she glared up at him, but she didn't reply. He smirked triumphantly and pushed off the

135

doorframe.

"My men brought back deer two days ago. We have hash and potatoes for breakfast if you'd like to come downstairs today to eat."

"What, eat with your people?"

"Unless you'd like to continue eating alone…"

She paused to consider him. "I could eat," she decided.

"Perhaps later, you can accompany me deeper into the forest. Help me with the creature that tried to kill me yesterday."

"Shame it missed," she bantered, to which he truly smiled. She eyed him again, nothing that smile and pondering his being nice to her. "Remind me again why I am helping you?"

"Because we made a deal," he said, shoving his hands in his pockets. "And because your little princess rode in here this morning like a bat spat out of Duarb's roots, and I am the only reason she is not dead."

Her eyes widened. "Nyssa is here?"

Draven gave an upwards nod towards the staircase.

"—off of me!" she heard her younger sister complaining.

"Shut up, Nyssa, and come here," Aydra called out.

Rushed footsteps made way up the stairs and met Draven's annoyed gaze as Nyssa reached the deck. The young girl didn't hesitate before bounding into the bedroom.

"Drae!"

Nyssa jumped into Aydra's arms and nearly knocked her off balance. Aydra grasped the poster of the bed. "Nyssa, please. You're—you're hurting me—"

The strength of the girl's grip around her made her wince. Nyssa pulled back and placed her hands on Aydra's cheeks.

"Are you okay? You—" Nyssa's face furled, and she took a quiet step back from Aydra. "Has he not let you bathe?" she whispered.

Aydra's lips pursed, and she could see Draven smirking at her from the balcony. She pushed it from her mind and gave Nyssa her full attention.

"What are you doing here? I told the Orel to tell you I was fine—"

"Rhaif thought it was a trap devised by the Venari," Nyssa whispered, glancing around them as though to make sure Draven was not near. "He thought they'd kidnapped you and forced you to say you were okay. The only reason he is not here with an army is because I convinced him to let me come to you and find out for myself."

"He thought I was coerced?"

Nyssa leaned forward. "He thinks they are taking turns raping you."

"Taking turns—WHAT?" Aydra nearly shouted. She shook at the thought that her brother thought such of her... that he would even suggest it. Especially after...

Aydra shut her eyes tight and pushed the memory out.

"None of them have touched me. They have helped me. Draven has been nothing but hospitable, aiding me, helping me heal. Did you tell my brother I could not walk?"

"I did. But he did not believe me."

"And will he believe you when you go back without me and tell him I am okay?"

Nyssa balked. "But you're coming back with me."

"I am not finished here," Aydra argued. "I will stay the remainder of the Dead Moons. Draven needs my help with some things."

"But—"

"Nyssa, did you know about the boats?" Aydra demanded.

Color faded from Nyssa's face. Her weight shifted on her feet as she stepped back from Aydra. "What... what boats?"

The fear in the girl's eyes made Aydra's blood boil.

"The boats on Lovi's shore," Aydra snapped. "The boats my brother refused to help the Venari and Honest defeat. The boats of strangers who Draven asked for help defending the realm from. The boats whose strangers killed some of Draven's and the Honest people. *The boats*, Nyssa."

"What?" Nyssa managed breathlessly. "What—what are you talking about?" Her gaze darted between Aydra and back to Draven's stiffened facade leaning on the railing. Nyssa took another step back and shook her head voraciously. "I... I... I didn't—"

"Nyssa..."

"I didn't know that would happen," Nyssa promised. "I swear, I had no inclination that these people were dangerous, that a battle would be fought. I thought... Rhaif... I happened to be in the Chamber when the letter came, and he threw such a fit. He made me promise not to tell—"

"How could you not tell me?" Aydra asked softly, her heart breaking.

"I'm sorry. I didn't think it was serious—"

"My men died on that beach," Draven interjected from the balcony. "Do you call that not serious?"

"Not now, Draven," Aydra cut in.

Draven settled back against the railing, arms crossing over his chest. Aydra turned back to Nyssa's panic-stricken face, and she realized Nyssa was shaking.

"Drae, please," Nyssa begged. "I didn't realize."

A heavy sigh left Aydra as she saw the genuine regret in Nyssa's bewildering features.

"Don't ever lie to me again," Aydra said. "I know you think he is righteous, and he has the kingdom's best interests in mind, but… " She paused, her hand clutching the pole at the end of the bed to steady herself. "If you hear anything that he tries to stifle down, you have to tell me. You cannot believe any promises he makes you."

Nyssa's brows narrowed just slightly at her words, but she didn't argue. Aydra sighed again, and then she hugged her sister. Nyssa clutched hard around her.

"I'm sorry," Nyssa whispered against her. "I'm so sorry. I won't—"

"Did you eat yet?" Aydra interjected.

"We didn't. We rode through the night."

Aydra glanced back at Draven's annoyed figure still leaned against the railing. "Draven, do you mind if my sister joins us for breakfast?" she asked him.

"What— join the Venari?" Nyssa frowned. "But what about—"

"Not so long as she remembers who's table she's sitting at," he answered, eyes traveling deliberately over Nyssa's embarrassed figure.

"But—"

"The Chronicles lie," Aydra interjected. "These are good people. If you value the crown you'll one day carry on your head, I suggest you learn respect for them." She straightened up, looking at Draven again and then back to Nyssa. "You will join us for breakfast," she said sternly. "You will speak nothing out of turn. You will treat the Venari with as much respect as you show the Bedrani. You will not mock, jest, or talk down to them. And when we are done, you will ride back to Magnice with a message for my brother. Do you understand?"

Nyssa didn't move, apparent confusion written on her face. She glanced nervously back to Draven and then up to her sister once more. "Okay," she finally whispered.

Draven pushed off the railing and started towards them. He looked down the steps and nodded once to whomever it was down there. "Balandria, see to it our little Princess has a seat beside me. And remind the men to be at their best. We'll have Promised company at our table this morning."

Balandria came up the steps then and stood smiling in the doorway. "Come, Princess," she beckoned. "I'll take good care of you," she added with a wink to Draven.

Nyssa flinched at Balandria's grasp. "I can walk by myself," she snapped.

Balandria grinned and placed her hands on the Princess's shoulders, nudging them back and forth as she followed her down the steps. "Oh, Princess. Don't think about it. You stumble into the wrong hall here, and you'll be eaten."

What the rest of their conversation became, Aydra didn't hear. Draven was staring at her from the deck, the contagious amusement making her shake her head. "What a lovely bunch the four of you are," he mocked.

Aydra sighed and turned back to the bed, Nyssa's denial about the ships still ringing in her ears. She hugged her chest and stared at the ground. Draven slowly entered the room again.

"Do you think your prince knew as well?" he asked.

"I'm not sure," she admitted. "I would hope Dorian would have told me. Nyssa is scared of everything. I understand why she was scared to go against him. But Rhaif... he kept it from me because he knew I would want to send help."

"Would you have?" he asked.

She met his eyes. "I would have ridden out myself. With my own company," she promised.

His chest swelled then, and she couldn't figure out the look he gave her. He looked as though he would reach out to her, but instead, he pulled something from the back of his pants. She frowned at the black fabric.

"What is this?" she asked, sitting down on the bed then so she could hold it in her hands.

"It occurred to me you'd been wearing the same two dresses for a week now. The men were beginning to complain about the smell. Bala was nice enough to offer one of hers."

She didn't know what to go off about first.

"Okay, first, I do not smell. Second, if I do smell, it is because you have not offered to allow me to wash my clothes. And third, I'm surprised Balandria had a dress to offer. What could she have to do that would require one?"

Draven smiled the sardonic smile that she had come to know all too well in the last week. "Perhaps you should take a closer look at that dress, and you'll figure it out."

She held it up again. And her mouth almost dropped at the sight of it. It was lace—sheer lace— and was of a slim-fitting nature with long sleeves and such a high slit that Aydra was sure her privates would have shown.

"You cannot be—Venari!"

Draven's low chuckle vibrated the air as he backed out of the room. "I would have thought it to suit you after the dress you wore at the banquet," he said with a wink. "Make sure you wear that to breakfast."

"Venari! *You*—Draven! *Come back here!*"

She cursed the day as she glared at the dress in her hands once more.

"Fine, Venari," she muttered. "I'll play your games."

"My Queen—"

The sound of Lex's voice coming up the stairs calmed Aydra's nerves. Lex bounded into the room, wide-eyed.

"Oh, thank goodness," Aydra said at the sight of her Second. "I thought my sister had been stupid enough to come on her own."

"I tried to stop her," Lex said as she crossed the room and hugged her. "How are you? Are you okay? You—" her face furled in disgust, and she took a step back. "Ugh. Sweet Arbina. Has he not let you bathe since your being here?" Lex held her hand up to her nose. "And look at the state of your hair—" She began quickly looking around the room then for the wash.

"Haven't exactly been able to help myself to the bath," Aydra admitted.

"You would think the Venari would be able to contain himself long enough to help you at least get to it. How long?"

"Only a few days…"

Lex raised an expectant brow.

"Okay, so I've just been bird bathing since I arrived," Aydra finally admitted.

"Disgusting. If this is how he treats wounded guests, he and I will have to have a chat." Lex found the tub and began drawing the water. "Come on. You can't go down to breakfast like that."

Aydra held up the lace dress Draven had given her. Lex stared.

"What the Infi is that?" she asked.

"It's what he expects me to wear to breakfast," Aydra answered. "Said it was the only dress Balandria had."

Lex took it from her hands and then looked around the room. Her eyes fell on the black sheets on the bed, and a small smile grew on her face. "We can work with this."

When Aydra and Lex made down the rope a half hour later for breakfast, she was met with staring gazes from the other Hunters in the clearing. Raised brows and crooked smiles followed her hobbling figure until finally, she reached Draven standing a few yards away, his back turned to her.

Balandria was the first to notice her. A slow smile rose on her lips.

"Hm... Looks like someone's winning your game," she mused, grinning at Draven.

They'd taken his black bedsheets off and fashioned it into strips, making Aydra a sheeted bodysuit that stretched from her crotch over her left shoulder and then wrapped around the rest of her hips and torso. She had taken the lace dress he'd given her and merely pulled it around her hips, ripping the top part and then tying the sleeves behind her, fashioning her signature waist cape that she favored so much.

"Are those my sheets?" he asked upon seeing her.

"You literally gave me nude lace to wear," she mocked. "What did you think I would do?"

"You tore my sheets," he stated.

Her chin rose, and she fought the smile that threatened her lips. "I'm practiced in ripping things, as I'm sure you are," she said in a low tone.

His surprise turned to smolder, and he chuckled under his breath, eyes darting to the ground and then back up to her gaze. "All right, Sun Queen," he muttered, the vibration radiating over her skin. "I see you."

Aydra averted her stare to the widened eyes of her sister sitting down at the long table in the middle of the treeline. "I see you tamed her," she said with an upwards nod.

He turned fleetingly back to Nyssa and then said, "Leave it to the charms of Balandria," with a smile in his Second's direction.

Balandria raised her glass to him. "All in a day's work."

141

Breakfast proved to be more fun than she thought it would be.

Nyssa sat between Balandria and Draven, and she sat quietly between them, eyes darting around the table nervously as she was the smallest one there. After a while, Nyssa seemed to relax, allowing herself to laugh at some of Balandria's jokes and speak with her. Aydra caught her eye after a time and smiled back at Nyssa, giving her a quiet wink at the surprise of happiness apparent in her sister's features.

The Hunters told tales of what awaited them that day and what they'd found in their nightly patrols. Aydra laughed as Dunthorne told her his own stories of beasts he'd fought with in his past. Another Hunter joined in to tell her how Dunthorne was not as masculine as he thought he was.

Once, Aydra leaned back in the chair and looked around her, staring at the laughing faces of the free men and women around her, telling jokes at one another's expense, eating equally with their king. She'd never known such a family of equal people existed. Having been taught her entire life that she was somehow better than the Dreamers in her streets simply because of the Tree she'd been born beneath.

And when Draven attempted to keep quiet, she was told stories at his own expense, to which she couldn't help but try and memorize so she could use them on him later.

"Don't think you're getting out of this, sir King of the southern realm," Dunthorne mocked. "You haven't always been so strong and mighty as you think you are."

Draven's amused glare tightened at his Third, mouth twisting in annoyance.

"Please tell me more," Aydra begged, turning to Dunthorne at her side.

"Lies," Draven interjected, voice nearly a growl.

Dunthorne grinned. "What about the time we went to the mountains and you were caught in Dahrkenhill's square with your pants down?"

Aydra's eyes widened, and the amusement faded from Draven's gaze.

"I need to hear this," Aydra begged.

"You really don't," Draven argued.

Dunthorne began to tell the story in great detail. Draven bit his cheek and tapped his cup on the table as Dunthorne spoke. Dunthorne paused and grinned at Draven when he was done, taking a swig of his drink. Draven launched over the table and tipped it into Dunthorne's face, causing the water to spill all on Dunthorne's front. Laughter enveloped the table, and Aydra caught Draven's pleased gaze. She crossed her arms over her chest and shook her head at him, watching him shift in his seat as he then turned to Nyssa.

"Tell me, Princess, are there any embarrassing stories about your sister I should know about?" he asked.

Nyssa nearly choked on the drink she'd just sipped on. "Ah... no. Not really," she answered. "My sister rarely embarrasses."

Nyssa caught Aydra's gaze, and Aydra settled back in the chair, lips smirking at the Venari King before her. She shrugged mockingly at him —

Until Lex snorted.

Aydra sat up in the chair and glared at her over her shoulder. "Don't," she warned.

Draven's smile widened, and he settled into the seat, arms crossing over his chest. "Do tell, Second Sun."

Lex stifled her voice against the cup she pressed to her lips. "I said nothing," she muttered.

Breakfast continued like that, with laughter and stories all around. Until finally, they started to leave the table a few at a time, starting with their duties for the day. Dunthorne needed Draven's attention on some of the new weapon designs he'd come up with, and Draven delightedly agreed to look at them.

"I take it you can manage to get yourself back upstairs?" Draven asked Aydra as he stood from the table.

"Of course I can," she affirmed.

He paused, the corner of his lips daring to rise as he tapped his cup twice on the table. His eyes traveled to Nyssa beside him. "Princess. Safe travels back."

"Venari King," Nyssa addressed him formally.

Draven considered her a moment and then gave Lex an upwards nod. "Second Sun," he acknowledged

"You'll send my Queen back in one piece, Venari King," Lex affirmed sternly as she stood from her chair.

His eyes flickered between Aydra and Lex. "So long as she behaves herself," he mocked.

Aydra escorted Lex and Nyssa back out to where their horses were soon after the exchange. She told Nyssa to behave, to tell their brothers she was okay. Nyssa hugged her and got on her horse, leaving Lex waiting on the ground.

"You'll take my sister back to the Village. Keep her safe," Aydra told Lex. "Please insist to Ash and the rest of the company that I am fine. I am being well taken care of. Draven needs my help with a few things before I can leave."

"Oh, he's Draven now? Interesting," Lex said.

"What's interesting?"

"That a week ago, he was Venari King only," Lex smirked at her. "If I didn't know any better, I'd say you were growing a soft spot for him."

"It's a good thing you do know better then, isn't it?"

22

"Where are you taking me, Venari?" Aydra asked as she and Draven set off later that afternoon. "What creature is it I should thank for nearly slicing you in half?"

Draven huffed under his breath, his hands tightening on the reins of the horse as he walked on the ground beside them. "You'll see soon enough," he told her.

Night fell a few hours into their journey. The noises of the Noctuans entered their ears, and Draven continued to lead them on foot through the forest. Aydra couldn't see a thing, but she could feel the creatures moving around them.

But it was when an agonizing pain tore through her entire body that she couldn't stop herself from crying out into the darkness.

"Whoa—what is it? What's wrong?" Draven asked, his hand grasping her leg.

Aydra doubled over and clutched her chest, feeling the pain of the creature radiate through her body. "The creature—what is it? What's wrong with it?" she asked. "It's close."

"I don't know what's wrong, that's the point—"

The loudest roaring cry she'd ever heard bellowed through the forest, and her eyes widened toward the darkness.

"The Rhamocour?!" she hissed. "You brought me to the Rhamocour?"

"She's hurt and scared," Draven argued. "I cannot get close enough to help her."

"Get me down," she begged as the pain continued to stretch to her bones.

Draven's hands grasped hers, and he helped her onto the ground.

She doubled over on her hands and knees, and vomit evacuated her insides.

"What's wrong—"

"It's not me," she told him. "It's her. I can feel her pain. It's—" she fell to her back and allowed her eyes to roll into the back of her head as she felt into the darkness for the beast's voice.

I feel your pain, she cried out to it. *Where are you?*

Who are you? came its bellow.

Aydra winced as another sharp pain pulsed through her.

I am Aydra Ravenspeak. I can help. Please. Tell me what is wrong.

Not me. My child.

"—speak to me!" she heard Draven shout.

"Something is wrong with her child. It is the child I am feeling, not her."

A cold sweat broke on Draven's palm. "How... How do I help?"

Aydra inhaled a deep breath and felt for the Rhamocour again. *The Venari King is here to help. Can you flame something so I can see you?*

Purple flames ignited the tree thirty yards ahead of them. And as the light reflected into the darkness, she saw the apple green slitted eyes from the drawing.

The Rhamocour's long neck rose deliberately, and her horns grew until she was as tall as the tree she stood beside.

Draven stood from Aydra's side and stepped closer to the beast, his hands up. He took the sword off his belt and laid it to the ground. The beast's great talons gripped into the earth, and Aydra heard the deep purr emit from its throat.

A warmth wrapped her entire body as though the pain of the great dragon had washed away upon seeing Draven. An ache replaced it that made her heart constrict.

The Rhamocour's love for the Venari King poured through her.

—But another sting of whatever was wrong with the baby cut deep, and the Rhamocour cried out once more. Its great tail slashed the air, nearly hitting Draven. He crouched to the ground.

"Tell her I want to help," he called back to Aydra.

Tell him how to help you, Aydra begged.

The egg was damaged by the Ulfram pack. I cannot get him out without crushing him. My King will need to cut him from the egg.

"What?"

Aydra didn't realize she'd spoken the word aloud. Her body froze at what the beast had just told her. *Cut him from it?*

The Rhamocour moved, exposing the shaking damaged egg.

Draven turned wide-eyed at her. "What's she doing?"

"She says you have to cut her child from its egg."

The remaining color left his face. "What?"

"Exactly what I said. But it's the only way."

Aydra made herself get to her feet, ignoring the pain, and she picked Draven's sword up from the ground to take to him, using the weapon as a crutch. She fell to her knees as she reached the dragon's head, and Draven took the sword from her.

His hands were shaking.

Aydra reached a cautious hand out to feel the large black scales along the dragon's face.

Where does he cut?

The Rhamocour explained it to her, and Aydra told Draven. Draven listened to her instructions for the egg and then paused and met her gaze.

"If I do something wrong, and she eats me, make sure Balandria is crowned King," he told her.

"Get the baby out, Draven," she snapped impatiently.

Draven slowly stepped up to the moving egg, the top of it coming to his waist. The pain of the trapped child poured through Aydra once more, and she laid her head against the Rhamocour's nose.

The pommel of Draven's sword crushed into the egg. Aydra closed her eyes as she heard him ripping and removing the shell delicately from around the beast.

It was only a few moments before a radiance filled her, a freedom she had never felt before. She opened her eyes just in time to see it rip itself of the sac, and it flapped its great wings to shake the fluid from around its body.

Draven tried to move backward, but he tripped on a rock as the dragon child, taller than he, leaned over him.

And then it nuzzled his face.

The dragons were purring behind them as they sat in front of the fire. Aydra couldn't shake the pride that had filled the beast upon her being released of her pain.

But it was the feeling that had taken her over upon the dragon's seeing Draven that made her most curious. So curious that she couldn't stop staring at him.

"Come now, Sun Queen," he said after a while. "Keep staring at me like that and I'll think I've somehow broken you."

"You don't know how much they love you," she blurted out.

He stopped stoking the fire and looked at her. "What?"

"I mean…" She fumbled with the cup in her hands, choosing her words. "You have to understand, my abilities… they are stronger than my sister's and my sister's before me. They don't just allow me to hear the creatures. I feel them… Their pains. Their darkness. Their happiness. It swims through my core as it would my own emotions. The Rhamocour today… the pain of her child's agony tore through me, but when the mother saw you… it vanished, if only for a moment." She looked up and met his eyes. "They revere you. Anything you ask of them, they would do. They would die for you at a moment's notice. If what they feel for you is love, then what I have felt has been nothing more than lust and the child-like vision of love our Chronicles portray."

He watched her for a moment. "I envy you," he admitted.

"What?"

"The bond you share with them. Your ability to communicate as freely as you do with them. I would give anything to hear that."

The screech of the great Aviteth bird burned through the forest then, and the sound of its call made Aydra's chest swell.

"What?" Draven asked.

Aydra stared at the sky, feeling a genuine smile rise on her face. The Wyverdraki family's song rang through her ears as the grand dragon beasts also flew overhead.

She looked at him with a sudden realization.

"You've never heard it," she realized.

"Heard what?"

"The Wyverdraki song."

"They have a song?" he asked.

She smiled wider and then wrapped her arm in his. He stiffened but did not move as she closed her eyes and felt for their song as they flew above the canopy.

It started off as a melodic hum that she allowed radiate from her throat and into the still air, and when the chorus came from above her, she sang the words aloud to him.

From once a wind
And brisk of leaves.
There came a night.
Across the sea.
And in its shadows
There was a memory.
Of what once was
Our land of free.

From once a wind
And brisk of leaves
There came a night
So dark it seemed
No more light
The curse it brings
And so the dying moons said to the sun
Set me free

As the last of the song left her, she paused, feeling Draven's body jump slightly, as though he'd inhaled a sharp breath. She opened her eyes and started to speak, but he let go of her and turned away.

"Draven?" she whispered into the air.

He cleared his throat, continuing to avoid her gaze. She swore she heard a sniff emit from his lips, but she didn't push it.

"Thank you," he managed after a moment.

She started to reach out for him, but nerves washed over her, and she pulled back. "No Venari King deserves to have to live without ever hearing the song of its blood."

His head turned just slightly in her direction. "I wish my men could hear it," he whispered.

"Perhaps I'll sing it for them," she suggested. "Tomorrow night.

After supper."

He smiled back at her over his shoulder. "They would love that."

The look he gave her then made her heart skip and her face redden. Something she was not accustomed to. She pushed her hair back behind her ear as he turned back towards her.

"What?" she asked warily.

"You're... you're not what I expected," he admitted.

"Let me guess: you thought I was a female version of my brother," she knew.

"You never proved any different growing up," he replied.

Her memory flashed to the times when Draven had visited with the Venari King before him, Parkyr. How she'd been so high on her own horse, so arrogant even as a child.

The noise of Draven's chuckle brought her back to the present, and he laid back on the log behind them.

"Do you remember when you kicked my ass during our battle round at eight?" he asked.

"You swore to me that day you'd be the one to end me," she remembered. "That one day it would be your sword to slice my throat and rid me of my royal life." She paused and gave him a full once over as he smirked at her. "Makes me wonder if you're just keeping me alive so you can challenge me at the end of it when I'm well. The final battle."

"I am glad you know I would not kill you while you were wounded."

"There would not be enough fun or glory in that for the Venari King," she mocked.

He grinned up at her, his hand coming up under his head to support it against the log. She smiled and fumbled slightly with her hands, the memory of the day they'd fought as children coming to mind.

Her raven landed on her knee.

"You know, I earned my mark after our battle," she informed him, stroking the bird's head.

"Really?"

She nodded. "Arbina marked me first. My brother was furious. Zoria and Vasilis were so proud. I remember Zoria taking me to the cliffs, introducing me to the Orel. My abilities were just coming in. It was the second voice I heard in the creature world, the first being my raven. And then when the moons died, she took me out across the

Preymoor to the forest."

"I remember that," Draven said. "Parkyr was livid at her taking you in without protection."

"We could handle ourselves," Aydra said.

"I know that now, but at the time… he'd no idea. He simply thought the two daughters of Promise thought themselves invincible, and he was angry at your being so careless."

"Sounds like us," she mused.

He gave her a crooked smirk. "Looks like nothing has changed."

"Shut up," she muttered.

Within moments, Aydra found herself completely immersed in conversation that she'd not allowed herself to have in years. No talk of their kingdoms. No mention of the ships at their doors. They spoke of foods, their travels… Draven told her stories of the Honest traders that would come through every few weeks, of the times members of the Blackhand race from the mountains had ventured into their realm… how he'd had to save one such Blackhand from the grasp of the Ulfram pack after the man had attempted to challenge the pack during their graduating trials.

"Idiot," Draven laughed. "Blackhands have this power trip they send their children on when they come of age. Call it graduating trials. They're to venture into the northern Forest during the Deads and come back with a kill," he started to explain. "Most come back with Noirdiem or Aberd. This one, he challenged the entire Ulfram pack. Got a bit too south and lost his way. Dunthorne and I found him swinging his sword in the air at nothing. The Ulframs were taunting him, waiting for him to tire so they could feast."

"I'm surprised you didn't let them have the idiot," she bantered.

"Tempting," he agreed. "But he was no older than your youngers. We did have a bit of fun at his expense."

"I'm sure you did," she teased.

Draven chuckled under his breath, and for a moment, he simply stared at her, the smile on his face fading deliberately into his features. An unfamiliar swell settled in her chest, and she stared at the fire as the soft silence encompassed them, avoiding his gaze.

As the flames danced before them, her eyelids grew heavy. Instinctually, she sank herself back onto the log beside him, not realizing she was practically cuddling with him until he wrapped an arm around her shoulders.

It was the first time she'd ever felt small in a man's arms, as though her body fit into his instead of simply against it. His fingertips on her shoulder. The dance of the stars above them. The breath of the fire against her toes. Her stomach knotted, and warmth radiated from her bones into her every muscle, settling in her abdomen. It was a feeling she'd never felt before, and she found herself feeling stronger than she had in years.

And she wasn't sure how to process it.

23

Singing the song of the Wyverdraki in front of the Venari people was one of the more nerve-wracking things Aydra had ever done. She sang it at the head of the table after supper the following day, and she was sure she would hear mockery come from the men when she was done. But the response she received was the same as had happened with Draven.

Silent tears.

They all stood after she was done to retire to the fire as they did every night, and each one stopped to either give her a hug, kiss her hand, or clap her shoulder. The hug she didn't expect came from Balandria.

She found herself immersed in their chats later by the fire, feeling welcome and part of their group more than she ever had with her own people. She was laughing at a constructed jig a few of them made around the flames, arms linked together as they danced when someone dropped down in a crouch beside her.

She jumped at the appearance of Draven coming from the shadows and nearly hit his smirking face. "Can you stop doing that?" she hissed at him.

He chuckled under his breath. "Would you like to go back out tonight?" he asked.

The jagged breath she inhaled was unrecognizable. A smile rose on her mouth, her eyes darting from his gaze to his lips. "I'm starting to think you like traveling in the dark with me."

He huffed, and she watched a snarky grin fill his features. "I'll take that as a yes then." He rose from the ground and grabbed the crutches for her before reaching out his hand.

The touch of his skin was warm against hers, and her stomach knotted upon her coming flush with him. For a moment, they stilled. His staring down at her, his hands on hers. But she quickly grabbed for the crutches and cleared her throat. Snapping herself out of her apparent daze.

"I'll grab some things," he said softly, and she wondered if he had felt the warmth too.

"Dunthorne is getting a couple of horses ready," he continued.

"Will he be joining us?"

A single brow elevated over his left eye. "Would you like him to?"

Her lips pursed. "One of you is quite enough company."

"Now you know how I felt on the road to kill the Infi," he bantered.

She resisted the urge to shake her head or smile. "How long will we be gone?" she asked.

"Depends on if the Rhamocour still likes you."

And the wink he gave her made her heart jump. An excitement grew in her bones that she hadn't felt since the first time she had ventured into the Forest with Zoria and met the Noirdiem.

Dunthorne was strapping her bow and sword to the horse when she made her way over to him.

"My bow and sword? Should I be worried?" she asked him.

"Never know what you might find in the forest, especially as the Dead Moons draw to a close," Dunthorne answered.

"Don't worry," Draven said as he joined them. "I'm sure your aim will be true this time."

The baby Rhamocour curled itself beneath Aydra's arm, begging her to pet it. The laughter that Aydra heard from her lips was near unrecognizable as she sat there in the dark, alone with Draven with only the light of the fire and the purrs of the Rhamocour dragons around them. She couldn't remember the last time she'd genuinely laughed at something without a nagging in the back of her mind.

Draven was staring at her from across the fire when she looked up, and she glimpsed the first genuine smile she'd ever seen on his face.

Not sarcastic. Not smoldering. Not smirking.

A true smile that lit up his features and rose to his eyes.

"Look at that," she mused as she stroked the dragon's head in her lap.

"What?"

"You do know how to smile without being an arrogant ass."

He laughed softly, head slightly moving side to side as he considered her words. "I could say the same about you."

For a moment, she didn't break his gaze, feeling almost unable to even blink as she sat there. But Draven cleared his throat and laid back on to the ground, where he began to play the horn.

She recognized the song.

"It's the Wyverdraki song," she noted.

"I knew as soon as you started singing the other night that it was the same."

"Can I see the horn?" she asked him.

He stopped playing and stood from the ground, stepping over the fire to join her on the ground once more. He held the horn out to her, and she took it in her hands. Her fingers traced the Noctuan creature carvings on the ivory bone.

The huff of the mother Rhamocour's breath rattled their fire. Her purr sounded, and she nudged Draven's head with the tip of her great nose. Her teeth flashed, and Draven reached up to push back her top lip.

"It is made of a Rhamocour fang," Draven said, revealing the great tooth on the beast.

The dragon huffed annoyingly and shook its head, making Draven chuckle. The words the beast spoke made Aydra smile.

"What did she say?" he asked.

"She said you risk death doing that," she informed him.

He grinned and stood to face the beast. The dragon backed up, its wings flaring out, and she gave a great bellow as Draven puffed his arms out. He shouted a great cry in her face, and she bellowed louder back.

Draven ran at the beast.

Seeing him attempt and fail spectacularly at battling such a beast made her laugh aloud. He climbed on her back, to which she shivered him off. The baby joined in quickly, an adversary he stood equal to, and he wrestled it to the ground. The baby wrapped its wings around him, tumbling them to the floor. Aydra shook her head at them and turned back to the mother.

Do these fights happen often? she asked her.

A slow blink came from the beast, and happiness filled her. She shivered at the spread of it and allowed her eyes to close.

Draven appeared beside her a few moments later, dusting his pants of the dirt that had collected from his wrestling. Aydra laughed at him and then turned back to the horn, still admiring it in her hands.

"Samar said something the other night that puzzled me," she said as he sat at her side once more.

"Surprised you had time to talk with all the moaning going on," he mocked.

She glared at him but chose not to respond to his musing. "She said you know all the calls of the Noctuans."

"I do."

"I didn't know there were such."

He took the horn from her hands again. "There is the main call, which is simply blowing into it," he began explaining. "The great war bellow, which requires blood and your feet to be in the water of the forest."

"What if you are not near the forest and you need them?" she asked.

"Then I would call Samar," he said simply. "She can turn any water into the forest waters."

"How did you learn them?"

Draven stared at the fire and pushed his hair that had fallen behind his ear. "Duarb," he said softly.

Her gaze narrowed. "But... how..."

"After I received the horn, I didn't know what I was doing with it. I had no idea why it had been given to me. Nadir, one of the traders, came through town, saw what I had. I was chatting with him and happened to mention my questions. Two days later, the Nitesh showed up—"

"The Nitesh?" Aydra interjected. "You've met her?"

"Just the once," he replied. "She took me to Duarb's roots and had me sit in front of her. She channeled him. Before I knew it, it was he sitting in front of me instead of her. We didn't have long. He showed each of them to me only twice. I was left to master them on my own."

"Will you play one for me?" she asked.

He relaxed back on the log and crossed his legs out in front of him. "Who would you like to meet?" he asked, fingers strumming on the ivory.

She thought about it a moment. "Noirdiem," she finally answered.

A shadow passed over his face. "How do you know about the Diem?"

"They were the first creatures Zoria and I came upon when she took me into the Forest. I remember how elegant and beautiful they were."

"The Diem rarely show themselves," Draven said. "If they found the two of you..." His words faded as he considered her, his fingers continuing to strum on the horn. "All right, Sun Queen—"

"And the Berdijay after," she interjected.

"No."

"No?"

Some of the color had faded from his cheeks. "The Berdijay is not to be called upon. He comes when he sees fit."

"Sounds like you're afraid, Venari King," she mocked.

The look on his face did not fade. "Terrified," he told her.

"I can speak with him," she countered.

"You do not want to hear anything the Berdijay has to say."

"Have you ever seen him?"

Draven became quiet as he stared at the flames. She could see his breaths shortening, the haze of a memory flickering in his eyes.

"I was thirteen," he managed. "Parkyr took me out for training, and he left me there, three days ride from home. I had nothing to defend myself with. I was asleep on my second night, in the canopy. I heard large footsteps, and at first, I thought it was the Bullhorn. I knew Cees, so the familiarity made me jump down from my spot with glee, happy to see a familiar face. But when I looked down the trail and saw nothing more than red eyes staring back at me, I panicked. Whispers filled my ears. The words he spoke in them were the ones I had pushed to the back of my mind. The doubts and fears I'd had growing up as an Infinari, wondering if I would be strong enough to be named a Venari, much less a Venari King." Draven paused and looked up at Aydra.

"He is shadow and swamp. A giant of rotting melted flesh burned and braided like hair on his body. He is twenty feet tall and smells of your worst fears. Do you not remember the Spy the other night? The abyss you felt as it tried to consume you?"

She nodded as a chill ran down her spine.

"The Berdijay is much worse. Spyes merely pour their void into you. They rob you of your core, and then when you beg for the void, they consume you as water. The Berdijay... He feeds on fear. He will get in your head. He plays riddles, mind games; he manipulates... He makes you see things, all your worst fears brought to the surface. People can be consumed by their fears, driving them mad. There is no guarantee you will make it out alive."

"I am not afraid of him," she affirmed.

"You should be."

24

Draven was quiet when she woke the next morning.

They were surrounded by the fog penetrating through the trees, wrapping itself into the forest floor and roots. He'd already started a fire and was poking it, gaze staring into it as though he were deep in thought.

She watched him a few moments, noticing the unblinking of his eyes, the trance-like state he sat in. The fire danced on his features and settled in the shadows of his face, illuminating his eyes as his hair swept over to one side away from her.

"Reverie," she said finally. "I've not seen it ever rest so well in someone's features before."

His gaze didn't move from the fire, nor did he act as though he'd even heard her. She was not accustomed to this side of him, and whatever it was, it made her chest feel heavy.

"Is something wrong?" she asked as she sat up.

"How are your ankles this morning?" he asked without looking at her.

She shifted uncomfortably and moved the blanket off her ankles to look at them. The sting of pain did not alarm her that morning, and the welts were receding into her skin enough that she was sure she could at least stand on her own some. "Your poison seems to be helping," she replied. "Even if it is disgusting."

His eyes finally flickered to her, and he prodded the fire a few more times. "Do you think you'd be up for a longer journey today?"

There was something he was not telling her. It made her nervous, so nervous that she wrapped the blanket tighter over her shoulders. "What are you not telling me?" she asked.

The gaze he gave her confused her. He looked her up and down with a caution and hesitation she wasn't sure how to take.

"I need you to tell me something," he said. "And I need you to tell me the truth."

"Okay."

"Why do you want to meet the Berdijay?"

The question startled her, and she found herself fumbling with the hem of the blanket in her hand.

"You know the stories," he continued. "You know what he is capable of."

"Perhaps I wish to—"

Draven held a hand up. "No. No politics. No bullshit. Tell me the truth."

She stared at the flames as she gathered her words. "Fear is something I dare not allow on the surface of my core." She paused and met his eyes. "I'd like to know what its depths are hiding from me."

He stared at her a moment, and then he began to fidget nervously, his heel tapping on the ground. "You realize what I risk by calling it?" he asked.

"I do."

His eyes flickered back to the fire again, and then he stood. "We'll need to travel several more hours northeast from my home and into its territory. I will not risk it following us back."

His boots squashed the fire in an instant.

She wasn't sure what to expect from him in the hours that they traveled. But they traveled in silence for most of the hours it took them to reach a place where he was comfortable calling it.

Each time she would look over to him, he was staring into the trees, a blank expression of nothingness on his face.

"I did not know you knew how to stay so quiet," she muttered once she could stand it no longer.

His hand tightened and then relaxed on the reins, and he continued to stare straight ahead of them. "There is a lot you do not know about me," he replied. "For instance, my favorite food is--"

"Women?" she interjected.

She swore she saw a smile rise on his lips. "I was going to say potatoes."

"I wasn't aware we were on the 'favorite foods' level of our friendship," she bantered.

"Is that what this is?" he asked, looking towards her with a grin.

"And here I thought I was leading you to your certain death."

"Allowing the Noctuans to do your dirty work... All this time, you've promised my death would be privileged enough to have it done by your own sword."

"The Berdijay will only rob you of your mind," he assured her. "My sword will certainly be what ends your life."

She almost laughed. "I am glad to know the fantasy of my death is what you dream of at night."

"I'm surprised you were able to sleep without the aid of the tonic or Samar last night," he bantered. "All that moaning—"

"You know, you keep talking about my moaning as though you cannot get it out of your head," she mocked, raising her brow at him. "Something you'd like to share?"

Draven chuckled under his breath. "If I decide I should like to hear your moans again, you'll know it."

She didn't recognize the flutter in her stomach as she met his gaze then, his eyes dancing over her figure... She quickly pushed it to the back of her mind and looked out ahead of them.

Circumstance, Aydra, she told herself. *Pure circumstance.*

A chill grew through the forest before she could utter another word. Draven pulled on the reins of his horse, and she followed suit.

"What—"

He held his hand up, and she stopped talking. Leaves crunched to their right. Draven squinted into the treeline and then moved slowly off his horse, pulling his sword from its scabbard. Aydra quickly pulled her bow and an arrow.

Draven crouched as he walked around the horses, his feet making no noise on the dirt.

Infi, the raven called down to her. **He crawls into the canopy. Left tree.**

Aydra squinted into the shadows, searching for any movement. The white of its hands grasping onto the trunk caught her eye. She pulled the arrow through and sent it soaring through the air.

The arrowhead landed with a thud in the creature's neck, and it fell back to the ground.

Draven straightened and stared at the dead Infi now lying in front of him. "If you can land that shot in the shadows of this forest, do tell what happened that day on the beach," he said as he turned back towards her.

"You were shouting at me," she argued.

He kicked the foot of the creature just as the ground began to shake. "Must be nice to have never had to use your weapon under such pressure," he mumbled.

The horse beneath her began to waver at the ground shaking. She reached down and rubbed its neck, assuring it it would be okay.

"No one shouts at me if they want to continue breathing," she continued.

The roots began to take the Infi creature back into the dirt, and she had to avert her eyes, wishing she could close her ears at the noise of its bones being ripped from its insides and taken back to Duarb.

"I suppose that means my days are numbered then," he muttered.

She watched the Infi creature's bones disappear into the forest floor. Something he'd said days before continued to bug her, and she allowed her curiosity to get the better of her.

"There are no children in your home younger than thirteen," she said.

"Fair observation," he bantered as he pulled himself back onto his horse. "What else have you noticed that you'll be taking back to your kingdom?"

She wanted to throw something at him.

"I'm not taking back anything," she argued. "It was a simple statement."

"And where are you going with such a statement?" he said upon their starting to walk once more.

"I was going to ask if Duarb had given another Infinari child," she admitted. "You've no children under Balandria's wing, and…" she paused a moment, considering the words she was about to tell him. "Arbina has not given another since Nyssa and Dorian, who are now nineteen. She regularly gave children every ten years. I was curious if the same was happening to your kind."

Draven glanced solemnly in her direction. "Duarb has not given another Infinari child since Balandria," he admitted. "I fear he knows something is coming. What, I do not know. But something has stopped the line of Kings."

"What do you mean?"

He sighed heavily, his hand running through his hair. "It is written in the Honest Scrolls that if a Lesser One believes a threat great enough to our land is coming, they will cease breeding of the fated children. They will go into remission and await the right time for another to be brought forth to save the land." Draven paused for a brief moment, and he looked at her. "The birth of an Infinari child after such a time is the First Sign."

"First sign of what?" she asked.

"Haerland's true freedom."

"I'm not sure I follow."

"Freedom," he repeated. "As in the whole of the land free. No more curses or chains for my people or the Noctuans. No more Lesser Ones being bound to their trees or realms. No more fighting between the races. An entire united Haerland. The whole of the Echelon. Arbina's children.... They are the Second and Third Signs. Which is why the birth of an Infinari child is so important. Even if she gives two before he, without the First Sign, they mean nothing to the Scrolls."

"These stories... they are not written in the Chronicles. We have no record of such."

"No," Draven agreed. "The Chronicles only follow the way of the Dreamers and the Promised. They are not the truth."

"Have you always had such hatred for Dreamers?"

"I could carry no hatred for such a loyal group of people. I can only fault them for believing everything spoken by the Lesser Ones."

"Lovi Piathos is a Lesser One," Aydra argued. "Are the Scrolls not his writings?"

"Lovi is merely the keeper of the Scrolls. The Scrolls are memory. Not record."

"Who's memory?"

He stared at her a moment. "Haerland's."

25

They didn't speak much more in their travels. The sun was about to begin its set, and she could see Draven start to shift nervously on his horse the closer they got to their destination.

The forest opened up to a great stream. Rocks lined the bottom of it, the clear waters radiating over the smooth surface. Draven leaped off the back of his horse and then held his hands out to her.

"The horses stay. We need to travel a half-mile up the stream. Get on my back," he told her.

"Half mile seems excessive," she argued.

"I will not take the horses into its territory in the darkness," he said as he turned around for her to latch onto him. "Get on my back or crawl."

The forest became thicker on either side of the great stream. She could feel Draven's tense body against hers, squeezing her thighs once in a while as they walked along its bank. The air grew colder, the wind picking up as they stretched the length of the path. Birds no longer chirped above them. She searched into the wilderness for the cores of any creatures around them.

There were none.

The eerie silence rang in her ears.

"What's the plan?" she asked after a few moments.

His heartbeat quickened beneath the hand she had on his neck. He slowed and then stepped into the water. When they reached the middle, he crouched down, and her feet hit the cool stream. It was the look he had on his face when he turned back to her that made a lump rise in her throat.

"I will ask you only once more," he said softly. "Are you sure about this?"

The beat in his pulse throbbed beneath the fingers she had on his wrist. His breaths were labored as he looked down at her, eyes darkened, and a look of fear rested in his features that she did not know he possessed.

"I am," she affirmed.

The wind whipped around them, causing a chill to pour over her bones.

"You will be on your own," he told her. "I will go into the trees and call it." He paused and shifted on his feet again. "You will be consumed into darkness. Its fog is thicker than the ocean water. He will bring your darkest fears to wrap you up and manipulate you—"

"If I am taken, make sure Nyssa gets my crown," she cut in, her heartbeat starting to pick up. She turned away from him, forcing her feet to move in the water so she could face the end of the stream she knew he would be coming from.

She didn't feel Draven leave her side as she stared ahead of her. She dropped to her knees then as a pain shot through her ankle, and the cold water met her skin beneath the dress. The sky was slowly turning a darkened shadow. She reached out again for any other creatures around but was met with no response.

The sudden sound of the horn bellowing through the still air made her heart pause. It was a bone-tingling tremble that stretched over her entire being. Her stomach turned sour, and she held in the turn, determined to keep herself together as the rotting of her bones narrowed through her.

The water stopped moving and evaporated into the earth.

Wet dirt wrapped between her fingernails. The wind blew her hair off her neck.

The ground shook.

And then the reality of what she'd asked for set in with a sink of her chest.

A dense black fog wrapped around her hands and knees. It tickled her skin, whispering in her ear as the moisture of it hugged her flesh.

The sunset she'd been able to see a moment earlier was suffocated.

Rupture and rapture

The surface breaks

Who dares ask for their escape?

The nauseating curl of his rasp repeated in her head. The void felt like a hole tearing through her insides. She didn't have to close her eyes to see into the core of this creature.

Rotten. Black. Necrosis. Disease. Pain.

Red eyes appeared out of the darkness.

And Aydra stood.

This was how she knew she was in the Berdijay's grasp.

Her ankles felt not of weakness and brokenness but of strength, as though she could run for miles and miles without tiring. She inhaled deeply, feeling the fog enter her airways and dive into her organs, filling her with ice and fire all at once.

It's not real, she told herself.

The ground vibrated, his deliberate steps coming towards her, seconds between each. She stood her ground as it began to speak again.

Rupture and rapture
The little red raven sleeps
Tell me, dear, of your greatest griefs,

—She was in the Throne Room.

Her gaze narrowed around her at the throng of people scattered around the room. A hand covered hers on her side, and she looked up to see Rhaif's hand. Her immediate reaction was to flinch away from his grasp, but he clenched his fist around hers.

Men spoke around her. She opened her mouth to retaliate, but it wouldn't move. Her free hand reached to her lips.

Her sewn together lips.

The rate at which her heart beat made her shake. She ripped at the seams, pushing the pain tearing her flesh to the back of her mind. But each time she cut the stitching, it would grow back.

Her brother stood over her, his hands pushed behind his back. His head tilted mockingly at her, and a quirk of a smile rose on his lips.

"Silence," he mused.

Her blood boiled. She lunged out of the chair.

Rhaif's image disappeared in a cloud of smoke.

The screech of her raven sounded overhead. Belwark hands grabbed her body. She was shoved backward.

Her body fell into a free fall of black.

—A foot kicked her in the back.

She fell face first into the wet dirt, realizing she was once more in the forest and not in his shadow dimension.

Her hands pushed to the ground, and she rose her chest to see into the abyss before her. The smell of decaying flesh filled her nostrils. She flinched at the reek of it, her stomach turning over. The ground vibrated again.

And when she blinked, her eyes opened to the red pupils of the Berdijay kneeling before her.

Antlers rose out of his head, its body reflecting in the shadows and golden fire pulsing through the make of its body as though its nerves were on the surface of its body, and the golden glow was its energy surge. Its great flattened head, no more than black swamp-like hair covering everything about it except its eyes, tilted at her.

Rupture and rapture
Your raven calls
Tell me, queen
How will you fall?

It knew who she was.

—Its enormous hand wrapped around her body. She let him take her off the ground, lifting her foot after foot as it stood. She pushed herself up in its palm and grasped onto his fingers. A deep purr echoed from its insides. She didn't blink as she pushed her core outwards into his. She felt him shudder as though he were allowing her to fill him.

Speak, Queen Ravenspeak.

Fear evacuated her body. Power filled her. She straightened in its grasp.

Show me the secrets my insides hide.

Her chest launched forward. Breath departed her lungs.

She was sitting in the Throne Room again.

Nyssa and Dorian were on their knees at her feet, hands behind their backs, gags over their mouths.

Aydra tried to speak. She launched herself out of her chair. But the chains wrapped around her body cut against her torso. She looked down and realized her feet were locked to the floor. She tried to move, to speak, but the strings were sewn through her lips again.

And then Rhaif appeared behind her youngers, twirling his sword in his hand.

"You are the reason for this," he hissed, pointing his sword at her. "Because of your betrayal, they will die before you. You did this to them."

Aydra struggled against the chains, pleading and shaking her head. Her youngers. On their knees. Her chained to silence on her own throne.

Rhaif raised his sword over Nyssa's head.

ENOUGH, she shouted into the darkness.

The scene dissipated around her. Her chest heaved as she felt the wet swamp hair of the Berdijay beneath her once more.

Rupture and rapture—

Stop speaking to me in code, she ordered it. *Is that all you have? My brother and sister dying before me? They told me you were swamp and ash. Necrosis and angst.*

She rose to her feet and met its raging red eyes, feeling her heartbeat throb in the ringing silence of the forest around them.

Strike fear into my core, Berdijay.

His palm disappeared beneath her. She sank into the depths of its shadows, cold mist swarming around her body.

She was standing in the Council Chamber.

Wearing the frilly blue dress her brother liked to force upon her. A plastered smile she could not erase was stamped upon her lips. The council members laughed around her.

She was standing at her locked window.

The raven tapped on it desperately. She felt no connection to him, only an emptiness where her creature had once filled her. Her door opened, and Willow came into the room, carrying a great white dress.

She was standing in the Throne Room.

Ash stood by her side. The Temple maiden stood before them. A white veil shrouded over her head. She was turned towards Ash, the same plastered smile forced upon her lips.

"You'll no longer need to worry for your kingdom," he told her. "You can live out your days in peace with me. No more of the travels to take care of criminals or ships coming to our shores. No more worrying about people beneath you." Ash took her hands. She looked down and realized her fingers were burned, wrinkled, and damaged.

Her brother was staring at her from behind Ash, his eyes flickering fire.

Aydra ripped her hands from Ash's grasp. She reached for the veil on her head and threw it off. The noise of her crown hitting the floor echoed in her ears.

"No."

Rhaif pushed Ash aside, his fingertips darkening. He grasped her throat in his hand and rose her off the ground.

"Do as you're told, sister," he hissed. "Take your rightful role in this kingdom."

Her lashes lifted to his. "I'd rather die," she seethed against the heat of his fingertips.

She was thrown backward out of his grasp. Fog wrapped around her body beneath her. She fell into darkness and the void of it.

Her eyes closed, and she accepted the consumption of death surrounding her.

—Her back hit the dirt. She winced at the pain of a rock hitting her rib.

Stand.

Stand.

Stand.

Slowly, Aydra pushed to her feet again. The adrenaline coursing through her made her breaths short. The Berdijay paused before her. And then it did something she did not expect.

—It bowed.

The shadows evacuated the clearing in a split second, as though time were rewinding around itself.

Aydra dizzied on the spot.

Breath returned to her lungs.

She collapsed onto the ground.

The wet of the stream wrapped itself around her again. Water babbled in her ears. And then she heard the splash of someone coming towards her.

Arms grasped beneath her shoulders. They pulled her out of the water and onto the bank. She was sitting up against someone, and palms were pressed to either side of her face.

"Aydra—*Aydra*, come back—"

Draven's hands were on her cheeks, pushing her hair back off her face as he squeezed her. "Can you hear me?"

When she didn't speak, she heard him curse under his breath.

"Dammit, Aydra, *answer me!*" he finally shouted.

"Stop begging, Venari. It's unbecoming of a King," she managed.

His body relaxed, and he muttered another curse under his breath. The strength she'd felt standing up in front of the Berdijay flowed through her veins.

She'd survived the mind games of the Berdijay.

Sitting there. With his arms around her. Her heart began to pick up pace again at the warmth of his grasp.

"You're *crazy!*" he declared, palms pressed to her cheeks. "Have you no fear for anything?"

A jagged huff of amusement left her as she continued to try and catch her breath. Draven's fingers softened on her face. She could hear his shortened breaths, feel the wind of it on her lips. Her own breaths slowly evened, and she reached up to touch his cheek, wishing she could see his eyes upon hers. See the desperation that she heard in his words on his features. Her thumb stroked his lip, and she felt his nose touch hers. Her heart thudded in her chest as she felt an intense pull in his direction.

And when he pressed his lips to hers, she swore the wind stopped whirling around them.

Perhaps it was the adrenaline. Maybe it was the darkness.

She wasn't sure if she cared.

All that existed at that moment was the pair of them.

Fucking curses, *what was this?*

Their chests pulled flush together. He kissed her hard, his hands not knowing where to explore her first, but the need swelling between them did not give much time. She threw her leg over his waist and groaned into his mouth upon feeling him already hardening beneath her. His fingers tugged in her hair, quickly followed by the grasp of his digits on her hips. The moment he ripped her undergarments away and touched her wetness between her legs, he groaned into her neck, and she nearly came apart at the way he teased her clit.

She wanted him. Right then.

She found her way into his pants then and gasped at the girth of him in her hands. Her hips bucked, and she captured his mouth with hers once more, distracting him long enough that she could move onto his length.

Her heart stopped. She had to pull back from his face and pause a moment as he filled her. A warm tickle radiated over her every muscle. He grasped her hips and pushed himself deeper inside her, curse words emitting from his lips against her collarbone. The feeling washing over her body was of fire and ice all at once. An addiction, affliction, she never wanted to rid herself of. Every muscle in her body relaxed, and her entire being surrendered to him. She felt his thumb on her lip, and his forehead rested against hers once more.

"What are you?" she heard him breathe, apparent that he felt the same bewilderment as she.

"Yours," she whispered back.

He paused, and she wished she could see his face. She pressed her hands against his cheeks, and he pulled her flush against him as she started moving her hips, slowly up and down, savoring the feeling of him inside her as no other had ever filled her before. She didn't understand what sorcery or bewitchment it was radiating between them, but she knew she wanted to savor it, to feel it linger and radiate through her bones and muscles. She knew she would never feel it with another. And when she felt herself coming to her end just moments later, her hips digging deeper and faster with his, his mouth open on her neck, the stars danced above her with her final gasp, and she came apart with him beneath the forest canopy.

26

The flare of the sun washed over her face. She felt herself moving as though she were lying atop something breathing. A warmth she was unfamiliar with surrounded her. She nuzzled herself into its depths, not sure she cared who it was she was so comfortable against, but when she heard the grunt of him beneath her, she remembered the night before, and a small smile grew on her lips as she opened her eyes.

Draven's thick hair was splayed out over his shoulders and the ground. She couldn't help herself from reaching up to his neck and entangling her fingers in the luscious locks.

The sudden seizure of her hand in his made her eyes widen.

"No one touches my hair," he growled, one eye opening. "Not even the Sun Queen."

She smirked at him. "You Hunters and your precious hair," she muttered.

The brow over his open eye elevated. "How many Hunters' hair have you tried touching?"

Her lips pursed, and she shoved him as she sat up. "Hair is just hair, Venari. It is not as though it is some great crown."

"A Venari's hair is a symbol of triumph," he said. "It helps mark those who have shown their worth. The only persons allowed to touch said hair is persons of our own kind. We cut it for failures."

"And when is the last time your hair was cut?" she dared to ask.

He considered her a moment as he sat up, and she watched as his expression softened. As for what his response was, she never heard.

His great black horse met her then, and she grasped its reins in her hand, hoisting herself up to stand. The strength had nearly returned to her ankles, and the pain of it was a mere twinge that morning.

"Look at that," Draven mused as he dusted off his pants. "She stands on her own."

"Almost," she agreed. "Maybe I'll be ready to go home before you think."

A flash of something settled in his gaze... sadness? No. Something that made his weight shift, and his hand rub the back of his neck.

"What's wrong? No telling me I'm not ready—"

The feeling of his hands grasping her face made her words cease in her throat, and when she felt his lips press to hers, she had to grab onto his shirt to keep herself from falling to the ground.

Her muscles turned to water, and her chest swelled with the same warmth from the night before. A chill down her spine, a honey-like glow trickled down her arms. She let go of the reins and grasped the back of his head and waist in her hands, allowing him to deepen their embrace.

A great sigh left him as he rested his forehead against hers. She steadied herself in his arms, allowing him to hold her against him.

"What are you doing to me, Venari?" she heard herself whisper.

He pulled back to look at her, his palm resting on her cheek. "Last night... I wanted to tell you. I've wanted to do that since you sang their song," he managed. "I wanted to know what that was like before you left... before things went back to the way they were."

"I don't know that things will ever be as they were."

His eyes fluttered, and he kissed her once more. She relished his hands wrapped around her, squeezing her body against his. She could feel the need growing between them, his hands raking her sides and then squeezing her backside in his palms. Her thighs tensed at the desperation of his body, her hair raising on her skin. But after a few moments, she pushed slightly on his chest, knowing that if she let it continue that she would find herself against the trunk of a tree within seconds.

"I believe we have an eight-hour journey back today," she managed. "We should get going."

He growled into her ear, and her eyes rolled as he nipped her throat. "Leave it to the Queen to spoil the fun."

The horse met her then, and he let her go so she could hoist herself up. "The faster we make it back, the more time we have for fun later," she told him.

Draven considered this a moment, working out what she meant, and then he smiled slyly up at her.

"Then by all means."

Draven kept sneaking sideways smiles at her the entire journey, so many that halfway through their journey, she shook her head at him and said, "Keep smiling at me like that and your people will wonder what kind of bewitchment I worked on you these last two nights."

Draven chuckled and packed his pipe. "And what a bewitchment it was," he muttered as his eyes flickered to hers.

It was an hour out from his kingdom that a slew of birds flew over their heads and burst into the sky from the canopy.

Aydra's heart skipped, and she pulled back on the horse's reins.

Here. Here. Here.

"Fucking curses—"

A gust of wind blew fiercely through the trees.

Draven stopped his horse, his face paling.

GO! Aydra told the horses.

The horses reared, and both started down the path at such a pace, she nearly lost her balance.

"I thought you told your sister you were okay," he called over the wind.

"And when have you ever known my brother to listen to anything?" she argued.

"If he's touched any—"

"I'll handle it," she promised.

The birds continued to chirp over her head. Her heart pounded in the half hour it took them to reach his home. The raven flew past her shoulder.

Who is it? Aydra asked him.

Your brother's company.

Aydra cursed the day she was ever born in the waters beside him.

The noise of people shouting filled their ears as they approached.

The scene before them made Aydra fume. Rhaif's company was spread out over the clearing, a few of the Hunters on their knees. Every Venari in the trees had their arrows pulled on their bows. Swords were drawn. Belwarks in full armor as though they'd been marched five days from home for war. Rhaif stood in the middle, Balandria on her knees before him with a knife threatening her throat.

Draven bounded off his still running horse upon reaching the edge of the clearing.

"You're a long way from your beach, Sun boy," Draven growled as he crossed the space between them. "Unhand my people and get out of my realm."

Rhaif's lips twisted upwards as he met Draven's fury over his shoulder. "Your realm? No. Your realm will be forfeit. You've taken the Queen as a prisoner and thus declared war on all of Haerland."

"I am not his prisoner," Aydra called as she walked the horse forward.

Draven shoved Rhaif so hard that Rhaif was launched off the ground. "Unhand my people," Draven demanded.

Bard caught Rhaif's falling figure. Three Belwarks pulled their swords at Draven's throat.

"Put your swords down," Aydra almost shouted. "Now!"

Rhaif gave an upwards nod to his men, who lowered their swords halfway. His eyes met Aydra's then, and he straightened his cloak. "My sister—" he started to reach for her, but she bucked the horse dominantly over him. Rhaif glanced around them, and she saw him fumble once with the sleeve of his tunic.

"I have not heard from you in over a week," Rhaif said up to her. "Why have you been here near ten days now with no word if not for his kidnapping you? And where were you just now? Are you hurt? Did he hurt you?"

Aydra stared at him so intensely from the back of the horse that Rhaif's weight shifted.

"Draven... please point me in the direction of somewhere I can speak with my brother privately," she said through clenched teeth.

"As soon as your lackeys unhand my people."

"Unhand these people," she commanded. "That's an order. They are good people. They've done nothing wrong."

The slow rate at which the Belwarks released the Venari people made Aydra fume. Draven helped a few of them from the ground, including Balandria, before turning back to her.

"You can speak privately in my home," he told her.

Aydra winced as she stepped down from the kneeling horse. Rhaif started to reach for her, but she swatted his hand away. "Don't touch me," she warned.

Draven came forward with the makeshift crutches, and she took them from his hands. "I'll help you up the stairs," he said softly.

"I can carry her—"

"No," Aydra said as Rhaif started to reach out for her again.

Draven tensed at her side, but she put an arm around his shoulders nonetheless. The three said nothing until they were at the top of the stairs, and Draven let Aydra go by the bed so she could hold on to the post.

"I have to check on my people," he said to her upon letting her go.

Aydra didn't say anything, she simply gave him a nod, and she could tell by the look in his eyes that he knew something was wrong.

Draven made a point to bump into Rhaif's shoulder as he passed him.

"My horses could use water, Venari," Rhaif called back. "You'll see to it that they get it."

A low chuckle emitted from Draven, and the crude smirk on his lips when he turned made a chill run down Aydra's spine. Draven shook his head mockingly.

"Your horses…"

Draven seized the collar of Rhaif's shirt in his fists and lifted him up off the floor. Wind whipped the room, billowing a few of the papers off the desk and cutting around Rhaif and Draven's figures. Aydra didn't speak. She could see the strain in Draven's neck and arms not to crush her brother in his bare fists.

"If you ever come into my realm threatening my people again, I'll make sure your younger is crowned King before the sunrise," Draven growled.

"You dare threaten me—"

"It's no threat," Draven uttered. "It's a promise. On your sister's life and the sanctity of your kingdom."

Draven almost threw Rhaif upon letting him go. Rhaif stumbled on his feet but caught himself on the desk. Draven towered over the Sun King's bent figure, his fists clenching and unclenching at his side as the veins pulsed in his neck.

"Do not push me, Sun boy."

Draven gave Aydra a short glance over his shoulder and then retreated down the steps. She heard him shouting at the Belwarks upon reaching the bottom, telling them where they could get water for their own horses and daring them to pull another blade on any of his people.

Rhaif rubbed his throat and turned to Aydra. "He is—"

"You *dare* come in here as though you are concerned for my safety after what you did to me?" Aydra cut him off. "I told you when I left that I needed time. Alone. Away from you."

"Yes, with your Second and your sister, neither of which are here in this Forest," he argued. "You are injured. You should have sent for me as soon as it happened."

"Why? So you could come in here and act as though you are some great hero?" She crossed an arm over her chest. "Leave. *Now*. Take your men before they find themselves at the end of a canopy ambush."

"Drae, you are hurt," he argued. "Let me help—"

He began to reach for her again, but she flinched backward so quickly, she fell onto the bed.

"You do *not* get to call me that," Aydra managed, her body shaking. "And do *not* touch me."

Fire flashed in his eyes. "You refuse my touching you, and yet, you allowed the Venari to escort you up the stairs."

"The Venari has never put his hands on me with intentions to punish me simply because I wore a revealing dress to the banquet," she spat. "I will send word to Lex for her to meet me in the Preymoor in the morning."

He paused and stared down at her, fists clenching and unclenching at his side. He looked as though he would say something, but she flinched back.

"Get. *Out*."

His black riding cape billowed in the wind as he left.

Aydra forced her body to slow its shake. The memory of his fire flooded her, and the pain of it pushed itself to the surface. Simply seeing him there again after this week, of what felt like being in another universe, caused her heart to shatter. A tear dripped down her face, and she pulled her knees into her chest, allowing the pillows on the head of the bed to wrap around her as she willed her hyper breaths to even, forcing air into her lungs to keep herself from collapsing.

She heard him shouting, and then the unmistakable noise of the slew of horses they'd brought started. After a few moments, she could hear nothing more than the noise of the wind through the trees.

They are gone, the raven told her upon his flying in. *The Venari King is coming.*

Aydra wiped her face fast and sat up on the edge of the bed as Draven's feet hit the top deck. He slowed upon seeing her, and she pushed the encounter with her brother to the back of her mind.

He paused and wrapped his arms around his chest, leaning against the door frame. "Did you call for him?" he asked.

She stared at him, unsure of if she'd heard him correctly. "Excuse me?" she managed.

"I asked... if you called for him," he repeated.

She almost laughed sadistically at his words, and she shook her head, unable to even comprehend what he was accusing her of.

"You men in power... you're all the same. Always thinking someone is after your throne. Believe me when I say this, Venari, no one wants your crown, nor do they want your realm. And if you still think I am the kind of person that would want your people harmed, then you have learned nothing about me this past week."

"I don't," he said, pushing off the doorframe. "But I had to ask."

"No, you didn't."

"You're crying," he noticed.

Her teeth clenched, and she stared past him at the trees. "I am fine."

He didn't push her. Instead, he simply went over to the dresser and pulled a couple of shirts from the top drawer. Aydra watched helplessly from the bed. Her thoughts kept flickering to the forest, to the first moment of real happiness she'd felt in years.

"I expect you're leaving soon?" he asked.

"I have to send word to Lex to meet me at the edge of the Forest in the morning."

"Your horse is not healed," he told her. "You can take one of ours. I'll bring yours to the next meeting."

"Thank you," she managed. "For everything."

"It's what any decent person would do," he replied without looking at her.

"Somehow, I doubt you would have been treated the same had we found you wounded," she said.

"I said decent person," he countered, now meeting her gaze.

She gave him a slow nod. "Right."

He fumbled with the shirt in his hands. "Here," he said, handing her the long tunic. "Your clothes are filthy. You can wear one of mine. Do you need help with the bath?"

"I can manage," she assured him.

He gave her a solemn nod then and ran his hand through his hair. "I'll escort you in the morning," he told her. "To the Preymoor. It's much too late for you to set off now, especially after our being gone most of the day."

"You don't have to do that. I know my way through. Your people need you here, not looking after me." She hugged her chest once more. "I think... I think I'm just going to bathe and get some rest."

He nodded, and she watched as he ran a hand through his hair again, pushing it over to one side. "I'll bring food up later in case you're hungry."

27

She dreamed of running again. Of the fire licking at her heels. But halfway through her nap, the most soothing touch she'd ever felt came over her, and she found herself wrapped in the grass beneath the stars in her dreams.

There were arms wrapped around her, one over her waist that would occasionally squeeze her elbow or grip the tunic she wore, the other entwined beneath the space between her neck and her pillow. Not arms of fire or territorial ones. Arms of comfort that made her breath even and her heart settle. Arms that her body fit into and not upon. Arms that she nuzzled and sank herself into without opening her eyes for fear of it just being a blanket around her.

But she could feel the chest rising and falling at her back, the soft lips that pressed to the back of her neck and then her shoulder, causing a deliberate chill to run down her spine... And as much as she wanted to turn around and see his face, she fell deeply back asleep before she could.

The most peaceful slumber she'd ever experienced wrapped around her consciousness, and she fell into a darkness she didn't want to pull herself out of.

He was not in her bed when she woke up.

The sun had not yet risen.

But she smelled the smoke of his herb in the air.

She pulled herself out of bed and grasped one of the crutches in her hand. Draven was sitting on the lounge chair on the deck, one leg bent into his chest, the other laying lazily flopped down at the side. His back was leaned against the wood of it, pipe between his fingers as he exhaled the smoke into the air.

She sat herself down on the floor of the deck and leaned her back against the doorframe. The noises of crickets filled her ears along with the final noises of the Noctuans as they relished their last night of hunting. She sighed, feeling a smile rise on her lips, as she heard the sound of the Wyverdraki song echoing in the still air.

"You should come back during another," Draven said without looking at her.

She watched him puff on the pipe and exhale again. "I think it'd be hard to keep me away," she heard herself say.

The look he gave her beneath his brows made her heart warm in her chest. "The sun will rise soon. We should get you packed."

He rose from the chair and set his pipe on the table.

He helped her pack her things with few words, making sure she had all her dresses and shirts, making fun of the smell of her dirty clothes upon gathering them from the floor.

"I didn't realize Queens were capable of smelling so... *ripe*," he mocked, picking up one of her dresses.

She resisted the urge to throw something at his face. "The stench, if there is one, is your fault—"

"You were crippled. Did you think I would have my people wash your pretty dresses for you?" he asked, brow raised at her. "What if they'd ruined the lace on one?"

She felt a smile on her face at his banter. "You could have shown me where the wash was. I would have washed them."

A great laugh left him. "That I would have liked to see. A Promised Queen doing her own laundry. Next time you're here, I'll show you."

The smile spread fully across her lips then, and she folded the shirt neatly in her hands. "I'd like that."

It wasn't long before she was all packed, and Draven sat her bags on the lounge chair outside before he turned to face her. His hands were shoved in his pockets, hair falling over his arms as his shoulders rounded at her.

She watched him as he rubbed his neck, words sitting on his tongue but not flowing out of his mouth. Her heart was in her throat. She didn't know what to say, how to act...

"You'll let me know if something arrives on the shores, not my brother. I am in charge of the security of our kingdom. Not him," she finally decided to say.

He nodded. "Of course."

She shifted, unsure of what to say next. Whether to tell him what this time in the forest had meant to her. But she knew, whatever this was… it couldn't work.

They could never work.

"Draven, I—"

He started to lean down, and she knew he meant to kiss her, but she pushed on his chest, pulling back before he could reach her.

"I'm not sure we should… whatever this is… I don't know that it's a good idea," she managed.

"Since when do you care what others think?" he asked in a low voice.

"Since it is you, and I'd rather you not be beheaded by someone that isn't me."

Though the sentence was the worst lie she'd ever told.

His eyes flickered something she didn't expect - a sadness she did not ever think she would see expressed on him. But it was gone within the second that he blinked, and the stern, arrogant stare she was accustomed to covered his features once more.

"Your brother will be expecting you with your Second before lunch," he said coldly, avoiding her eyes. "Keep him waiting and he'll think I've kidnapped you again."

She took a deep breath and nodded. She paused at the rope, her hand resting on the threads as she faced him again. "Goodbye, Draven."

He met her gaze once more, and the look in his eyes made her stomach knot.

"Aydra."

28

Aydra and Lex were welcomed back to Magnice with a doting party that Aydra had not expected. Her ankles were not fully healed, and so she allowed Lex to help her through the halls to her room.

She was interrupted most of the day with people going in and out, bringing her gifts, wishing her well. Nyssa stayed at her side most of the day. Dorian brought the pair food twice. She was happy to see their faces and hear their voices, but she missed the independence of being in the forest.

At least there, no one treated her as though she were broken.

The one person who didn't come to see her was Rhaif.

After Nyssa and Dorian left her side, Aydra made herself get out of bed, using the crutch to make her way through the halls and up to her brother's study. She didn't know if he was in there, but she knew she needed to find out what had happened with the boats.

Not only had the thoughts of Draven's lips kept her awake in the days they'd traveled, but the letter her brother had written the Venari refusing to help them dug a hole in her. She felt betrayed, as though Rhaif did not trust her, which she reminded herself he didn't, but... Enemy or not, the Venari and Honest were Haerland's people. And Haerland was their home.

They should have sent aid.

She made a promise to herself upon reaching his door that if he came at her with fire, she would be ready.

The fireplace was blazing upon her entering, but Rhaif was not there. Her raven squawked in through the open window and landed on the edge of his desk. Aydra hobbled to his new leather chair and sank herself inside it, propping her feet up onto the desk.

It was an hour before the door opened. Aydra placed the papers she'd been reading back onto the desk and waited for him to see her sitting in his chair.

He jumped backward upon noticing her.

"*Curses of our mother*, Aydra—" his hand clutched to his chest, and he gathered his balance. "What are you—"

"We have to talk," Aydra interjected.

He considered her in that chair, and he straightened his shirt. "What about?"

"When were you going to tell me about the ship?"

Rhaif eyed her. Evident that he knew what she was talking about but that he would hide it by any means necessary.

"What ship?" he asked plainly.

"What.... *What ship?*" she repeated incredulously. "Do you think me stupid? That I wouldn't find out about it? I am in charge of the safety of this kingdom. I should have been told first about them."

He started towards her, calmly holding up his hands. "Sister, you don't understand—"

"What don't I understand?" she balked, rising from the chair and balancing herself against it. "The fact that you allowed two Haerlandian races to go into battle alone when they so very clearly asked for our aid? The fact that you basically spat in their faces when they even offered for you to lead the charge, even take one of the strangers back to get information from where they hailed? Tell me, brother. What do I *not* understand?"

"That Hunter is a liar," Rhaif snapped. "He has filled your head with lies this last fortnight. You know you cannot trust him or any of his kind."

"I saw your letter."

"What letter?"

"The letter you wrote back to Draven—"

"Oh, so he is Draven now? Not Venari scum—"

"What I call him makes no difference," Aydra nearly screeched. "How dare you not tell me about it. How dare you deprive me of my own duties—"

"Have you gone soft on me, sister?" he interjected. "What other lies did he tell you?"

Aydra was so frustrated, she felt on the verge of tears. "He told me no lies," she said through clenched teeth.

"Look at you," he snarled. "Weeping over the fate of a few deceased men not of your own kingdom." He paused crossed his arms over his chest. "Did you see this said boat?"

She almost balked at his question. The fact he was blatantly calling her stupid and a liar. That he thought her gullible enough to fall for any tricks the Venari might be capable of. That the Venari had lied to her.

She had seen the look in Draven's eyes. She had recognized that pain.

He couldn't have lied... could he?

She blinked twice. "No," she managed, heat rising on her chest at the thought of her being taken advantage of.

"Did he show you the graves of the men he lost?"

"No."

"Did he have any evidence of such a ship? Prisoners? Information? Perhaps even... oh, *a boat?*"

Her knuckles whitened around the edge of the desk.

"That's because there was no such ship," he spat, now walking around her. "The Venari lie, my sister. Had I sent aid, had I told you about it, we would have walked into an ambush. The Honest and Venari have been after this kingdom for a century. He told you of this boat to get you on his side and turn you against your own kingdom. The Venari are relentless. They are poison. Cursed. The only reason he is invited to any banquet or Council meeting is because they are born of the Sun as we are. We merely keep them here so that they continue thinking they are in charge of the southern realm."

"Are they not?"

Her brother let loose a loud cackle, one that would have rivaled their own mother's had he been in competition with her. "My dear, sweet, *sweet*, sister," he mocked, cupping her face in his hands. "So naive to the darkness you spent so much time in this last fortnight... Tell me..."

—He seized her throat in his fingers.

"Did you fuck him, too?"

Breath arrested in her throat. Her hand shot to his wrist, widened eyes pleading.

"Rhaif—" she nearly choked on his name "Put me down," she managed as she felt her feet leave the ground.

"Did you wrap your legs around him as you do every other man to walk our halls?"

Aydra stopped fighting him and allowed her eyes to roll in the back of her head.

"Did you let the wolf taste you—"

She felt for the creatures out his open window.

"—Allow him to fill your mind with his lies—"

Help, she called out.

"—fall submissively into his trap—"

The noise of wings filled her ears.

"—live up to the stupid girl you've been your entire life—"

Squawks of crows pierced her hearing.

"You are—*Ah!*"

Aydra's knees hit the ground.

Rhaif screamed out, his arms flailing wildly in the air, and he stumbled backward. The air filled with black wings, diving and pecking at his figure. Aydra coughed and rubbed her throat. Adrenaline swelled in her at the sight of her brother being attacked, swatting away at the birds he'd not thought she would call. He fell to the floor, hands thrown up over his face, blood pouring from the slashes on his hands. Aydra grabbed the corner of the desk and pulled herself up to lean on its surface. Her own raven paused on her shoulder, and they stared at the scene before them.

Wait, she told them.

The birds ceased and came to a rest on perches around the room.

Shall we kill him? her raven asked.

Rhaif removed his hands from in front of him, revealing the slashes he'd received on his face. One had slashed across his brow and cheekbone, barely missing his eye.

"You'll pay for this," he promised.

"Do you think that frightens me any longer?" she hissed. "Threats of fire and rape? You have done what you will to me to the point I am numb to it. You cannot hurt me."

He managed to pick himself up to his knees then, wiping his face of the blood trickling down his cheek. "No. But I can sedate you."

She couldn't believe what she was hearing. "*Sedate* me?"

"You want to no longer be in charge of this kingdom's security?" he grunted, getting to his feet. "I tire of your games, sister. I have done nothing but try and protect you from yourself. If you would just... *behave*. Your duties to this throne can be stripped to nothing more than the hand of the king at banquet. I implore you. Sit in your dresses and keep your mouth shut."

"Or what?" she almost mocked. "What will you do? I just told you. You cannot hurt me."

"No," he agreed, eyes flickering over her figure again. "But if you'd like your sister to remain oblivious—"

The raven shrieked off her shoulder as she lunged at him.

Her hands curled around his throat, and she shoved him onto the floor. Her knees sat on his hands over his waist. "If you *dare* touch her —"

Blue flames engulfed her hands. She made herself stay there for as long as she could stand it, willing him to burn and burn her to the point that she could not feel her hands any longer. But the flames wrapped themselves down his body and curled around her legs, and she was forced backward.

She fell on her back but pushed herself up to a seat immediately, shaking the agony of the blisters on her hands and thighs. Her eyes pricked tears, but they did not fall as the chills ran down her spine. She noted the look of satisfaction on his face.

"What happened to you?" she whispered. "What wronged you? You were not like this. We used to love one another, play, fight, laugh... And now... now you're nothing more than a *monster* undeserving of his crown. You promised me. You promised to be better than them."

He straightened the collar on his shirt and shifted his weight before beginning to tug at his sleeves. "It is your choice, sister," he said in a level tone.

She trembled so voraciously her teeth began to chatter. "Don't touch her," she pleaded, saliva sticking in her throat. "Don't you dare."

"Then I suggest—" he took two steps forward, and his hand wrapped around her jaw "—you get on your knees."

The single tear dripped down her cheek as she looked up at him. She noticed as the room silenced to a ringing. Her pull on the birds let go, and they flew out the window... all but her raven, who sat on the windowsill with his back to her as she was forced onto her knees.

She'd have rather been burned.

29

It was twice more in the month before the next Council meeting that she was forced into his study and given the choice of he taking her on her knees or he taking Nyssa.

She would protect her sister at any cost.

Both mornings on which Lex found her lying atop her covers, she argued with her about what he was doing.

"Lex, please. There is nothing we can do," Aydra said to her on the second morning.

"There is," Lex argued. "Do you think the people would stand it if they knew what he was doing to you—"

"The people love him," Aydra interjected. "They think he is fair, that he takes care of them, merciful… they think him to be perfect. The greatest of the Promised Kings so far."

"Do you believe Dorian and Nyssa would stand for this?"

"I will not drag them into it," Aydra argued. "This is my fight. They cannot know anything about it."

"And Draven?"

Aydra almost balked. "What about him?"

"You two—"

"Had sex?" Aydra said incredulously. "I have sex with a lot of people. Draven is no different from any other."

She knew it was a lie. But she wasn't sure why it was a lie or what made it any different from her other conquests.

Aydra's ankles healed within a few days of her going and dangling them in her mother's waters. She would stare at the tree she'd been born beneath in silence, its vast white limbs pouring out into the sky high above her. She didn't typically adorn the Throne Room where their mother's tree was unless they were receiving formal guests. They'd only truly used it once since Aydra's being crowned six years earlier. It was a sacred place, not to be taken as just another room in the castle.

As she sat there, she would daydream about all the times she'd visited her mother in the past. Like the time she'd walked into the Throne Room at the age of ten and found her mother sitting at the base of her tree. And in her arms were two infants. Arbina was singing a song to them, a song Aydra had never been taught the words to.

The infants had barely stirred, and Arbina had smiled up at Aydra, the beauty of her features lighting up in the sunlight glittering off her skin.

"Hello, my daughter," she'd cooed at Aydra. "Would you like to meet your brother and sister?"

Being ten and having not ever seen an infant before, Aydra was wary of the small beings in Arbina's arms. But Arbina stood from the roots of her tree and took the small marble walkway to cross the space between them.

"Sit down in the chair," Arbina told her with a nod towards what was then Zoria's throne.

Aydra sat, and Arbina stepped forward and placed one of the infants in her arms. Dark red hair stood stark against the child's pale skin. Aydra cradled the child against her, careful with its head.

"This is Nyssari," Arbina informed her. "Your sister."

Aydra looked up at the other child against Arbina's chest. Its thick black hair was wavy on its head. "Is that my brother?" Aydra asked.

"Dorian is his name," Arbina answered.

"What are their surnames?" Aydra had wondered.

Arbina sighed and bounced Dorian in her arms a moment. "I'm not yet sure. Such will be determined upon their markings."

"Will she be marked like me?" Aydra asked.

"Her mark will be determined by her actions. As your mark was determined by the raven who chose you, hers will be by the creature that chooses her."

Aydra stared down at the redheaded infant in her arms. The child yawned, and Aydra felt herself smiling at her dear sister, chest swelling with a pride she was unfamiliar with. "I'll protect her," she promised.

Arbina had smiled at her and then reached out to stroke Aydra's cheek. "You will."

Her raven landed on her arm.

Aydra snapped back to the reality of the present with a shake of her head.

The sheen on the white tree caught her eye from the sun, and she smiled as the great Aenean Orel circled the room above her. The hairs on Aydra's arm stood, and she felt another energy appear behind her. She sighed into the familiar energy but didn't move from the spot she sat on.

"Hello, mother."

The wind of someone walking around her rippled through her hair. A soft touch grazed her arm, and she looked up over her shoulder to see her mother's corporeal form: Arbina Promregis Amaris.

She was the most beautiful woman Aydra swore she would ever see. As tall as Aydra, but thinner, less shapely. She always wore a delicate white dress over her pale skin, belted with golden rope at her waist. Her white-blonde hair was usually pulled back away from her face, but today, loose curls laid long to her waist. Widened blue-green eyes stared down her thin nose at Aydra's sitting figure, her high, sharp cheeks intimidating on her long narrow face. Her full lips rose upwards at the corners, and she gave Aydra a short nod.

"Hello, my daughter," she said in her sing-song voice.

The appearance of her made Aydra's breath shorten, emotion bubbling to the surface as she felt so small beside her. Arbina sat down at Aydra's side and began playing with Aydra's hair.

"What bothers you, my child?" Arbina asked.

Aydra didn't know where to start. She stared out at the golden sun over the ocean, contemplating the stresses on her mind. "I think I am failing my sister," she chose. "I have been so consumed with trying to be a protector and guardian of this realm, I've neglected my first duty. I have not taught her as much as she needs to know. Not a fraction of what Zoria had taught me by the time she—"

"Zoria was an overachiever," Arbina interjected. "Her idea of fun was riding out and dining in the Village."

"What's so wrong with that?"

"You can't tell me such would bring you joy, my dear. I know you better. You crave adventure. Danger. Not sitting on a throne and dealing with petty crimes and Dreamer squabbles." She paused and looked her daughter up and down. "This kingdom flourishes. Your people do not know famine or any more danger than a single Infi walking among them for only a few weeks. The most danger to ever come to them is when the Venari show. These people have grown weak living in such peace."

"What is wrong with living in peace?"

"Nothing," Arbina said as she turned back to playing in Aydra's hair. "It is about time, after so many years of squabbles, that the people take rest."

Aydra paused a moment and stared out at the beach. A chill grew on her skin as Arbina played in her hair, and her eyes began to drift. But Draven's face came to the front of her mind, imagining him playing with her hair instead of Arbina, and she began to fumble with her hands.

"Why did you and Duarb become enemies?" she finally asked.

Arbina paused and stared at her. "Why do you ask?"

"No particular reason..." Aydra lied. "I just... I was hurt in their realm a few weeks ago. They took me in. Helped me heal. I knew no terror or felt no hostility from them. After everything I was taught growing up—"

"Duarb is a liar," Arbina cut in, yanking at Aydra's hair. "He tried to seduce me. Enslave me and tell me his children were so much more superior to my own. His children are no different. They are manipulative. Cursed. Treacherous. They'll say and do anything to get you to think they are anything more than a group of rebel mercenaries. The ones they call Venari are full of such vile miscreants, even more so than their shifting brothers they've entitled the Infi." A huff of amusement left her lips. "Venari King," she muttered with a roll of her eyes. "Such a title was given to them simply to appease their aggression. Make them think they have a say here in this world."

Aydra's eyes narrowed back at her mother. "I don't think that's true," she argued.

Arbina balked. "Are you calling your mother a liar?"

"I am not. But... I think these people have grown from what you knew them as what they used to be. What Duarb used to be."

Arbina reached out and pushed Aydra's hair from her face, cupping her cheek in her hand. "My dear, sweet, daughter... how do you think you came by those injuries in the first place? Did you think it was by chance?"

Aydra's stomach knotted at the way her mother looked at her, and she started to back her way out of the pool. "I think you're wrong."

Arbina rose to tower over Aydra, eyes blazing with a fury Aydra had not seen before. Just as Aydra thought her mother would snap at her, the rage in her gaze relaxed, and Arbina leaned down to give her a kiss on her forehead.

"Vigilance, my daughter," she told her. "Do not turn your back on them."

30

The next time the Council came to Magnice made Aydra's body nauseous. She met the Council with her siblings the night before as she always did. Ash had come early this time, and he'd joined her in her bed that night, but she never found her end.

Every time he would kiss her, all she could see was Draven's face.

And she hated him for it.

Lex met her in her room that morning as Aydra got dressed, kicking Ash out to his own room. Aydra was throwing clothes from her closet to the bed when Lex threw a grape at her back.

"What's your problem?" Lex grunted.

Aydra glared at her over her shoulder. "I'm fine," she insisted.

"Something tells me you should have used the Venari King's gift last night," Lex mumbled.

"I want nothing to remind me of him," Aydra spat.

Lex frowned and sat up in the bed. "Weeks ago, you told me he made you feel things you didn't know how to take. Now he's arriving on our doorstep this morning and you want nothing to do with him?"

Aydra pulled out one of her less formal dresses and held it against her. "It's not like that."

"Explain it to me," Lex said.

"My brother has Belwarks watching my every move. Whatever is between the Venari and I... it is too new to risk him being thrown in chains over."

"So you would allow him to think you feel nothing? That you hate him more than usual?"

"I would."

Lex paused and gave her a once over. "Is that why you've been wearing his shirt to sleep every night?" she teased, and Aydra nearly threw her hairbrush at her.

"It smells like the forest, and it's comfortable. Shut up," Aydra grunted.

Aydra had Lex meet Draven instead of her to retrieve her horse upon his arrival. Aydra filled her day as she usually did before meetings— on the beach. Only this time, she invited the Scindo Creek Ambassador's daughter and personal Belwark guard to join her.

The Dreamer, Jannah, told Aydra stories of her people, of the traders that came through who Aydra now knew were of the Honest people. Jannah's touch radiated on her skin when she would laugh with her. Her blonde hair fell over her pointed ears, and when the sun decided to begin its setting journey, Aydra found herself between Jannah's Belwark and Jannah herself.

But the images she'd been plagued with the night before entered her mind as she was graced between them. And this time, she didn't push him out.

She allowed the fantasy of Draven being with her to live in her head, allowing herself to find her end no matter how much it hurt her chest that it was not actually he between her legs.

Jannah was dripping with her finish when she kissed Aydra again, and Aydra slipped from between her and the Belwark, urging Jannah atop his extended length. She watched as he filled her, and then she stood to put her dress back on.

"I have to go," she told them softly, crouching down at their side once more. She kissed Jannah hard, followed by the Belwark. As she pulled back, her eyes met his, and she whispered, "Finish her grandly, Belwark," to him.

She cursed Draven's stupid face under her breath as she made her way back to the castle.

It wasn't a dress that Aydra chose for the meeting that day. It was a long black jumpsuit that hung off her shoulders. A wide belt hugged her waist, thick black tulle flaring out over her backside beneath it. She gave her hair a fluff and placed the crown on her head just as Lex entered the room.

"Oh, this is my favorite," Lex mused as she watched Aydra push her ring on her finger.

Aydra smiled at her over her shoulder. "Are we late yet?"

"Early, actually," Lex told her.

The apprehensive look Lex gave her then made Aydra's stomach knot. She picked her shoes off the floor and glared at her friend.

"Don't," Aydra warned.

"I said nothing."

"You were thinking it."

Lex huffed amusedly under her breath and leaned against the poster of the bed. "Watching you torture yourself is more amusing than I thought it would be."

Aydra threw a shoe at her face.

The Council had yet to sit upon Aydra's entering the room. She was met by a startled silence, followed by the low bows of the people around the room. Dorian swept to her side upon seeing her, and he escorted her to her chair.

"I cannot believe how early you are," he muttered to her. "Thought you would have still been cleaning yourself up after the beach."

Aydra's eyes flickered to the guests that had accompanied her earlier in the day, and she gave Jannah a nod. "It was a good day—"

Words ceased in her throat upon finding the darkened eyes of the one she'd been avoiding all day. She drew a ragged breath and allowed her eyes only a moment to take in his figure leaning against the stone, the sage green of his low cut tunic and tight of the pants he wore searing into her memory for later. His crown of thick hair splayed over his shoulders as he pretended to be interested in whatever it was the Ambassador was saying to him.

"—Drae?"

The sound of Dorian's voice made her blink out of her stare. "Hm?"

"I asked if you were okay," Dorian continued.

"I'm fine," she said quickly. "Of course, I'm fine. Why wouldn't I be?"

The doors opened once more, and Rhaif filed into the room, causing every person standing to bow upon his passing. Dorian squeezed her arm and excused himself to his usual place, standing at the back of the room, when Rhaif came around the corner.

Aydra felt her lips purse upon his coming up to her. Rhaif paused just beside her and gave her a full once over.

"Something you'd like to say before we get started?" she mumbled.

His gaze met hers, and he whispered, "This one I like," in her ear.

Insides trembling, she took her seat without another glance at him.

She was thankful the meeting was a short one.

They spoke of the Infi being banished in the streets, the expected crop of the wool for the winter— one of the Ambassadors had brought a sample of it for them to approve of. Rhaif declared the wool scratchy, not as soft as in previous years. Aydra rolled her eyes and insisted the wool was perfect, not wanting the Ambassador to feel as though his hard work had been for nothing.

But it was the way that Draven's eyes kept looking at her that made her chest red, her face heated. The confusion in his gaze caused her heart to constrict. She wanted to tell him what was going on, why she was avoiding him…

The moment the meeting was adjourned, she slipped from the Chamber through the servants' tunnels.

She watched from her window when he left the castle on horseback around midnight and rode into the darkness back to his realm.

And she cursed herself for avoiding him.

31

The letter came the week after the next Dead Moons cycle.

Willow delivered it to Aydra at the breakfast she shared with her siblings on that morn. Aydra nearly ripped it open sitting at her seat, and it fell from her hands into her egg scramble.

The boats are here.

—was all it said.

Her heart skipped. The boats. *Draven…*

She hadn't expected him to fulfill his promise to inform her after she'd treated him so terribly after the last meeting. But her chest constricted at the thought of him, and she could hardly contain herself.

Aydra wiped her mouth and stood from the table with such haste that she nearly knocked her food onto the ground.

"Everything all right?" Dorian asked from across the table.

Aydra nodded quickly. "Yes. Yes, everything is fine. I have to… *fucking Infi…* I have to go."

She exited the Great Hall without a second look back at her siblings and immediately went to her room to pack. Lex fell in behind her the moment she caught up with her.

"Where are we going?" Lex asked.

Aydra handed the letter back to her. "We leave in an hour."

"Boats… oh, the boats! *Fucking Infi—* And we're going where?"

"The Forest."

Aydra didn't need to see Lex's face to know she was smirking at her.

"Shut up," Aydra cut before Lex could coo at her. "Diplomatic mission. Nothing more."

"Yeah, you keep telling yourself that," Lex mumbled.

197

Dorian and Nyssa bid them goodbye from the gates. Aydra didn't go into detail about where they were going, only telling them she would send word in a few days of what she'd found and whether she needed help from the Village.

On the morning of the fifth day of their journey, they finally ventured inside the Forest of Darkness. Aydra could feel the morning creatures stirring through the wood, waking rabbits and deer stretching and welcoming the day as it wrapped around them.

They traveled an hour inside the wood before Aydra's raven swooped down and called out, *Archers!*

Aydra pulled on the reins of her horse and looked into the trees. Lex's horse stamped impatiently.

"Why have we stopped?" Lex asked.

Aydra didn't have a chance to respond. From within the darkness, she saw a figure appear, hood pulled over their head.

"Your business, Lady Ravenspeak," the man said without removing his hood.

"I was summoned," she replied. "Take me to your King."

A quirk of a smile rose on the man's face. "I'm beginning to think you like it here," he muttered.

"Take us to your King, Hunter," Lex spoke up. "Else watch your kneecaps be shattered."

The man pulled his hood off his head, and Aydra smiled at Dunthorne's smirking face.

"Calm, Lex," Aydra said. "Dunthorne means us no harm."

Dunthorne's dark eyes danced at her, and he gave her a quick nod. "This way, Sun Queen."

Aydra could hear the men moving in the canopy of the trees as they followed herself and Lex back to their home. It was another hour into the wood, the trees growing grander and grander until finally, a clearing swept open beneath great branches, and Aydra had to pause to take in their forest kingdom in the daylight.

Men walked on the thick branches above them, climbing down on ropes to reach the ground as they approached. Aydra exchanged a glance with Lex, and then they continued forward. Hunters gathered around, all whispering amongst themselves. Aydra noticed a few people she did not recognize, and she knew by the dreads in their hair that they were not, in fact, of the Venari.

And then she saw Draven standing by the armory shelter with Balandria, a large piece of parchment in his hands. The sun basked down on his walnut hair and made her stomach knot at the sight of him in his battle leathers.

A frown spread over Draven's face upon seeing them, and he twisted the map tightly in his hands, the grip of his fingers apparent against the parchment. She couldn't figure out the look on his face as he pressed the map into the chest of the man behind him.

"I see you found trespassers, Dunthorne," Draven called as he crossed the space between them.

"She says she was summoned," Dunthorne answered.

Aydra and Lex made their way down from their horses without a word. Draven paused over her, staring down his nose at her figure. She raised an expectant brow, unsure of the apparent annoyed twinge pulsing through him.

"You can escort yourselves to my home and wait there," he said shortly with a glance at Lex. "Second Sun," he acknowledged her with a short nod.

"Forest King," Lex replied with the same nod.

Aydra wasn't sure why she'd expected anything more than a cold shoulder from him, but it hurt nonetheless, and she reminded herself this was the freezing temperature she'd treated him with the last he was in her realm. Just as she opened her mouth to speak, Draven turned away from her.

"Bael, take their horses to the stables and give them food and water. The rest of you get back to your duties. We don't have time to waste."

Aydra stared after his retreating figure, and then she caught eyes with Balandria's flaring facade. Balandria said something upon his reaching her, but Draven grasped her arm and pulled her backward with him.

"Something tells me he wasn't expecting us," Lex muttered at her side.

"Something tells me you're right," Aydra mumbled back. "Come on. We'll wait for him upstairs."

They didn't have to wait long.

Aydra put the kettle on to make tea, yearning for something warm after their long journey. She'd just poured herself and Lex a cup when she heard footsteps coming up the staircase.

Draven met her eyes when he reached the entrance. His fists curled and uncurled at his sides as he stood there.

"Making yourself at home, I see."

"It's tea. Would you like some?" she asked coldly.

He stared at her, and she shifted uncomfortably under his gaze.

"Go ahead, Venari," she uttered. "Spit it out—"

"What are you doing here?"

Aydra's eyes met Lex's, and her friend raised a concerned brow.

"You—"

"Oi, Venari," came a voice with skipping steps up the stairs. "What's the plan, why—"

An unfamiliar man no older than they paused in the doorway at Draven's side. He stood nearly as tall as Draven, only a few inches shorter. His elbow-length blonde and caramel tightly wound corkscrew curls, most of which had been dreaded, were half pulled back away from his face. They not only made him look more of a darker, muted, olive tan than he was but much more handsome than Aydra wanted to admit. Dark blonde spiced stubble danced along his jaw, almost as though he had simply forgotten to shave it away that morning. His almond eyes darted between the three standing in the room.

She felt as though she were gazing into the ocean as his stare found her, for his eyes were the clearest cerulean color of the same sea she'd awoken to every morning of her life.

"Who's the stiff?" asked the unfamiliar man.

Aydra balked as his words brought her back to reality. She nearly slammed the cup in her hands down on the table. "The stiff? Who do you—"

"Whoa—" Draven stepped in front of her and grabbed her arms. "Do not forget you are not in your kingdom any longer," he said in a low tone. He let her go and turned to the stranger.

"Nadir, this is Aydra Ravenspeak."

Nadir's arms crossed over his toned chest, the vein in his taut forearms splintering around his elbow. The lean build of his swimmer-like body reminded her once more of the ocean, and she started to have an inkling of what he was.

"Ravenspeak?" he repeated.

"The surname my giver gave upon my marking," Aydra informed him as she pushed her hair off her neck to reveal the raven silhouetted triad marking on the side of her throat.

Nadir's gaze traveled over her once more. A scrutinizing gaze. One that told her he was determining her worth for battle. Whether she was who Draven said she was or worthy of the title.

"Where is your crown, Sun Queen?" he finally asked.

"I dare not wear it in a realm I do not command," she replied coldly. "And who are you?"

The right corner of Nadir's lip twisted just slightly, and he looked in Draven's direction. "I didn't know you kept the company of the Promised."

"It's new," Draven replied as he straightened some of the papers on his desk, eyes darting towards Aydra.

Nadir turned back to Aydra, and she watched as the gills on his neck flickered, just for a second, as though he were flexing them to prove he was what he claimed.

"Nadir Storn, Commander of the Honest army."

"The Honest have an army?"

"Who do you think has been protecting our shores for the last hundred years?" Nadir snapped. His weight shifted, and he looked to Draven again. "What's she doing here?" he asked him.

"Good question." Draven straightened and leaned his weight against the table, his butt just sitting on the surface as he pressed his palms into the wood on either side of him. "What are you doing here?"

Aydra eyed the way he looked at her then. "Did you think I would ignore you?" she spat.

"You wrote me back a letter with only one word. One. *Single*. Word. One word that told me you'd fallen for your brother's and the Chronicles' lies once more."

"I didn't write any letter."

Draven reached back and snatched a piece of parchment off the top pile of his desk. It landed in her hands, and he stood haughtily over her as she read.

Lies.

Her heart skipped at the writing on the page. "I didn't write this," she protested. "Draven, I swear—"

"Did the Orel go straight to you, or did your lady deliver it?" Draven asked.

Aydra's stomach plummeted, and she avoided his gaze, staring into nothing as she remembered the morning on which she'd received it. "My lady, Willow. She gave it to me."

"Just perfect," Nadir mumbled.

"You're under more of a watch than I previously thought," Draven said.

"My brother has had Belwarks escorting me, but he has no spies—"

"Really?" Draven cut in, disbelief on his features. He strode determinedly through the wide opening and onto the deck, where he leaned over the edge. "Then how do you explain the company of riders coming in from our west."

Color drained from her face, and she stumbled hastily to the deck. The wind wrapped around her, and she knew he'd heard the noise of the company carrying on the wind. Lex launched herself out of the chair and went to stand at her side.

"They must be from the Village," Lex said.

Aydra squeezed the railing in her hand. "Fucking *Rhaif*," she hissed under her breath. "But if they're from the Village, that means…"

Lex met her gaze, and at the same time, they said, "Fucking Ash."

A murmur of whispers and concerned voices had started in the yard below. Hunters were beginning to gather, all looking up to Draven for their next move. Nadir cursed under his breath, his long fingers gripping the banister as though he could ring water out of the wood. "How far out?" he asked Draven.

"They'll be here in an hour," Draven answered. He pushed off the banister and started down the steps faster than Aydra could muster a protest.

"Everyone in the trees!" he bellowed out.

Echoes of his orders sounded in the crowd. Nadir shouted something to his own men, and they bounded off the barrels and tree stumps they'd been sitting on. Aydra stared at the quickness of the men and women moving around her, arrows and bows being thrown in the air to their persons. Men took spears from the walls, knives slid into their boots. Then the Hunters began ascending to the canopies, clamoring up the trunks of the great trees and climbing the ropes hanging down.

Nadir ran down the stairs behind Draven, Aydra shortly following.

"There will be no shooting unless they shoot first," Draven called out. "Be prepared for anything. If it is a war Magnice wants, we shall be ready for it."

Aydra grabbed Draven's arm and whirled him around to face her. *"What are you doing?"* she hissed.

"Preparing my men," he said simply.

"Do you truly think—"

"I know you are a long way from home," he cut in, towering over her. "The last time you were in my realm, your brother accused me of kidnapping you. I will assume he thinks the same this time."

"I left of my own accord," she argued.

"Did you tell him where you were going?" he asked. "Did you tell him you were coming to help me? Did you tell him of the boats?"

"I didn't."

"And did you tell him about us?"

A pause washed over her, and she felt her weight shift just noticeably before straightening up, allowing her cold facade to possess the feeling in her heart. "What about us?" she spat.

Draven gave her a deliberate once over, an obvious stifle of anger in his taut jaw. "You've barely been home but a few months, and now you ride out again to a realm which your people have declared a resting enemy. Did you think he would not send his own company to follow after you?"

He turned briskly on his heel, and she quickly followed.

"Even if he did send his company, you've no reason to think they would be here for any reason except to ensure my safety," she argued. "He probably thinks—"

Draven stopped so suddenly that she nearly ran into him.

"He thinks I've lured you here under false pretenses. He thinks I mean to ambush you, take you as prisoner and as ransom. He thinks I want his crown. He always has," he said, now a little calmer than he'd spoken before. "I should never have involved you in this."

"But you did," she countered. "I am here. I want to help."

A great exhale left him, and she could see his firm chest resting in submission as he looked over her head to his men, the vein in his neck straining under his frustration.

"Help us by making sure your Belwarks do not attack first," he said, looking down at her again. "If they do... they will have started something neither of us will be able to finish."

He started to walk away, but she called after him, "It's not Belwarks."

Draven stopped in his tracks and turned around. "What?"

"No men followed us from Magnice. This is probably a Dreamer company from the Village. Which means—"

"Your fucking boyfriend is coming," he cringed, turning and cursing at the sky.

"Ash is not my boyfriend."

"Boyfriend. Lover. Indentured servant— I don't care," he whipped. "The fact remains that he will come in here threatening my men worse than any company of Belwarks would." He paused and met her eyes. "Get rid of them before I have their heads put on stakes and sent back to your kingdom."

32

Aydra was furious.

She had the raven fly out and escort the Dreamer company through the woods so they did not get lost. She and Lex walked out past the edge of the Forest kingdom to meet them so as to not provoke a fight.

It was the smile on Ash's face when they arrived that made her wish she'd had her brother's fire.

"My Queen—" Ash dismounted the horse and strode straight to her, his arms outstretched as though he expected to be welcomed into her arms.

Smack!

Her hand seared across his cheek the moment he reached her. Ash stumbled backward, obviously bewildered by her greeting.

"What—"

"How dare you follow me into a realm not of your own with weapons and threaten these people?!" she hissed at him. "Who sent you?"

Ash straightened and rubbed his cheek, his eyes darkening at her. "Your brother thought you'd been taken advantage of. He sent us to follow in case you found yourself in an ambush."

"Well, as you can see, I am perfectly fine. Your new orders are to leave this place before you find yourselves on the wrong end of the Venari fury. And I can promise you, Captain, you'll not see it coming before your life becomes theirs."

One of Ash's men leaned down from his horse, asking if they should leave. Ash held his fist up to silence them and looked over his shoulder. "Haut, take our company back to the Village," he instructed him.

"And you, Captain?" Haut asked.

"I'm going to make sure our Queen stays safe in this realm," Ash replied. "I don't trust these Venari people."

"It does not matter who you trust," Lex butted in. "I am her Second. I will look after her. Take your men and leave as your Queen instructed you to."

Ash didn't move from the spot. "I will leave after I've seen these boats my King told me you'd come to find."

"Rhaif told you about the boats?" Aydra asked.

Ash began taking his gloves off, one finger at a time. "He asked that I personally report back to him with the reality of the situation… if there was, in fact, such a situation."

Aydra's fists clenched at her side, and she was sure she could have broken her jaw at the weight of her clenching teeth. The fact that her brother had sent out men to escort and protect her as though she and Lex were incapable of looking after themselves.

She nearly sent all the crows to Magnice.

"Fucking curses," she muttered, knowing she had no choice but to surrender to his being there. "Fine. You stay. The rest of your men are to leave."

Aydra was not looking forward to having to explain things to Draven.

He was standing at the edge of the clearing, his arms crossed over his chest, when the three appeared through the trees. She could see the veins in his arms and his neck bulging.

"I thought you were taking care of this," he said in a low voice, eyes never leaving Ash's.

"Is that how you treat a guest in your home?" Ash asked in a mocking tone.

Aydra grasped his arm and twisted it backward, causing Ash to double-over. "Speak out of turn again, and I'll make sure he feeds you to the sea serpent when we reach the reef."

She released him with force, causing him to stumble backward and trip over a root. He landed with a thud and cursed the air. "Here I thought you'd be happy to see a familiar face," he muttered. "Didn't realize I was meeting with the royal bitch instead of the usual—"

He didn't get a chance to finish his sentence. Lex stepped forward and kicked him square in the face. Ash cried out, holding his bleeding nose as his eyes darted between them.

Aydra almost laughed. "The royal bitch…" she huffed sadistically, head moving side to side as she let the anger still over her. "No, I am PISSED, Ash," she finally shouted. "You come riding into the realm of your enemy as though you are welcome here, as though you are some great salvation to myself and my Second. Rhaif had no business sending you. If I treat you with hostility, it is because you are not wanted here."

Ash pushed himself to his elbows and then stood, dusting the dirt off himself.

A quiet smirk rose on Draven's lips, and he gave Ash a once over. "You can stay in the building with Nadir's men," Draven told him.

The crooked smile that placed itself on Nadir's face made a chill run down Aydra's spine. "Now that's an idea." He stepped forward and held out a hand to Ash, pulling him up from the ground. "Come on, savior. Meet the other bastards you'll be rooming with this night."

"What's wrong, Sun Queen?" asked Nadir as he joined Aydra on Draven's balcony soon after their encounter with Ash. "Not used to your brother—"

"Who does he think he is?" she heard herself spit out. "Ordering them to follow me, obey his orders instead of mine… I am their Queen. I am their security commander." A wild terror ran through her. "I have just as much right to command them as he does. I am Queen—"

"Yes, we've established that," Nadir mumbled lazily.

"I am—"

"She can be quite adorable when she gets like this," Lex mused with a delighted smile, leaning beside Nadir on the deck.

"—as much in charge as he. It is my birthright—"

Nadir snorted.

Aydra's feet stopped moving. "Something you'd like to add, *Commander?*" she drawled, noting his mockery.

Nadir considered her. "You've been handed everything your entire life. You've known no more terror or fight than the Infi who infiltrated your towns only a few months back.—"

"I wouldn't—" interjected Lex.

"What makes you think you'll stand any chance with us against these strangers coming on our shore?" Nadir finished.

"I—"

"Because if she dies, then we'll have done her brother a great deal of services she dare not gift him herself," came Draven's voice as he joined them. "A reason to go to war with us. Ridding him of the pest that annoys him on a daily basis. Shall I keep going?"

"What did you do with the Captain?" Aydra snapped.

"Killed him," Draven replied nonchalantly. "That's what you wanted, wasn't it?"

"Where have you been my entire life?" Lex said dreamily.

"Be serious, Draven," Aydra said, ignoring her Second. "What did you do with him?"

"He's fine. Balandria will take care of him," he said with a wink towards Nadir.

Aydra stepped onto the balcony once more, taking a moment to gather her wits. Her eyes darted around the camp, watching as the Hunters all gathered and sharpened their weapons.

"What is the plan?" she asked after a few minutes.

"Someone is anxious to die," Nadir muttered.

"You sent word about a ship. I assumed it was nearly here," she said.

"They are," Nadir said.

"*They*... are?" Aydra blinked.

"Set up camp a week ago. Three more ships have arrived since."

"So why are we sitting here?" she asked.

Nadir's eyes flickered towards Draven. "Because someone wanted to wait for the backup we weren't sure was even coming," he said, and Aydra didn't miss the annoyance in his tone.

"We leave at midnight for the shores," Draven said, ignoring him. "On foot. No horses. I don't want to give any inclination of our coming."

"How did you attack last time?" Lex asked.

"Last time, we didn't know what we were up against. I lost a great deal more men than I'd have liked to," said Nadir. He hugged his arms against his chest. "We have the element of surprise on our side. My company is preparing arrows. We'll take them before dawn."

Nadir only stayed in the tree a few minutes after the last of their exchange. He told them he needed to make sure his people were prepared for battle, and so he left them upstairs, but not before Lex insisted she would join him to learn more about his people.

Aydra felt herself fumbling with the hem of her dress as she sat in the chair across from Draven at the familiar table, sipping on the wine he'd given her.

"You should get some sleep," he said shortly, tapping his cup on the table. "We'll be leaving soon."

Aydra knew he was right, but something continued to bug her. "You saw the letter you thought I wrote, and yet you made him wait on me anyway," Aydra said. "Why?"

He paused in tapping the cup and stared at the table. "Because you know protecting your own means more than just the people of your kingdom," he said softly. "And you're the only one of your kind to have ever thought it."

She stared at him as the words repeated in her head.

"And—" he stood from the table and finally looked at her, "—I didn't want to think you'd abandoned your promise."

"You knew I didn't write the letter?" she asked.

"I said I didn't want to think," he corrected. He took their cups from the table and started out of the room again. "Take my bed. Get some sleep. The sun has nearly set. I'll tell Lex where you are and find her somewhere she can stay as well."

33

No matter how many times Draven told her she needed to rest before they set out, she couldn't. She paced around his room by the candlelight. After a while, she decided she would get dressed. She pulled her leather pants, black long sleeve tunic, and leather vest from her bags. She was just strapping on her sword belt when she heard footsteps coming up the stairs again.

"Don't worry, I'm up. I'm ready, I'm—" her words ceased at the sight of Draven's face standing there.

Black paints were smeared around his eyes, making the sage color stand stark against the darkness. It was as if they'd painted the color in every shadow of his face—his cheekbones, beneath his jaw, making his features stand stark and fearsome in the light of the candles. His walnut-streaked hair was down. Someone had woven two small braids in it over his left ear. It was displayed as his own battle armor was, the mane of the Forest King. The black leather vest he wore pressed against his torso, two belts wrapped criss-cross over his chest, and she could see the two blades sticking out from over his shoulders. She felt a brow raise slightly on her face.

"The true form of the Venari King… I wondered where you'd been hiding him," she mused.

The echo of his black boots hitting the wood sounded in the quiet room as he crossed the space to his dresser. He grabbed his leather wrist braces and avoided her gaze. "Do something with that mane of yours," he said in a low voice. "You'll have us found in the darkness by the sight of it."

She said nothing as she pulled it up messily and tied it up with a fabric she tore from his sheet. He stopped moving and stared at her.

"Did you just rip my bedsheets?" he asked.

"You told me to tame my mane," she said. "It was the first stray fabric I saw."

"I can still see it," he said. "You look like fire against the moons light."

"What do you suggest I do?" she asked haughtily.

He grabbed a black scarf from inside the top drawer and tossed the fabric at her face. "Wrap that around you."

She balked. "You wish me to fight, covered up like—"

"I wish you to do nothing," he argued. "You'll have no one there to save you tonight if you get yourself in trouble."

"Promise?" she muttered beneath her breath.

"On my life," he answered.

She pushed the anger swelling through her to the back of her mind. He turned and left the room then, leaving her to deal with the long black fabric. She took her hair down and tied it in a braid at her neck instead, then reluctantly wrapped the scarf around her.

The breeze from Lovi's waters blasted her face the closer they came to his shores.

Nadir's people met them at the edge of the forest. They paused at the perimeter, waiting on their scouts to return. Aydra had sent the raven off earlier in the day to look ahead at what was waiting on them.

Draven and Nadir were pouring over a map when she caught up with them at the front. Aydra stepped up to them, her eyes flickering and narrowing to the bag dangling on Draven's side, horns sticking out of the top of it. She pushed it from her mind and focused her mind on the task at hand.

"My raven says there are ten ships now," Aydra interjected into their conversation. "She says—"

"Your raven?" Nadir repeated, a frown across his face.

"She speaks to creatures," Draven said without looking away from the map.

"Like…" Nadir crossed his arms over his chest and gazed wearily down at her. "Like you talk to animals?"

"Yes," Aydra replied firmly.

"As in…. All animals? Like you speak rabbit?" he continued to ask.

"You make me sound like some fated Princess, Storn," she dared.

"But aren't you?" Nadir asked mockingly.

"Actually—" Draven straightened and looked to Nadir "—did you know about this? About Arbina's daughters being able to speak with creatures?"

Nadir's gaze stroked over Aydra, and he contemplated his answer a moment. "I've heard stories of them able to speak to certain ones. Not all of them."

"She can connect with their cores," Draven further explained.

Brows elevated on Nadir's face. "Really? That is—"

"Okay, we can talk more about the enigmatic freak that I am on another date," Aydra cut in. "I believe we have ships to take care of?"

Nadir scoffed, delighted eyes dancing at her frustrations. "What else did your precious raven say?" he mocked, voice lowering.

She told them about the shelters and tents the strangers had erected, as well as the large sharpened wooden spikes they'd planted in the sand.

"Fire," said one of the Honest women behind Nadir. "The darkness continues to surround us. We should wake them with fire."

"Why wake them when we could slip in their tents and slit their throats?" Balandria asked.

"They have sentries patrolling the dunes," Aydra cut in.

Nadir's gaze met one of his men's. "How many did you see when you scouted?" he asked him.

"Easily twenty," the man answered.

"We are stealth," came Dunthorne's voice. "We can take care of the sentries without a problem."

"You'll be taken down again," the Honest woman argued.

Aydra stared between them. "How exactly is it you two came up with a cohesive battle plan the last time? Was there this much division?"

"Last time, it was daylight," Nadir said. "We relied on our weapons to do the fighting."

"And how did that work out for you?" she dared to tease.

Nadir sucked in his cheeks, obviously annoyed, and exchanged a glance with Draven.

"All right, Sun Queen," Draven began in a low voice. "What do you suggest?"

She felt a soft smile rise on her lips as her mind began to work. "Using what you were born with instead of relying on the same weapons they will be using."

Draven and Nadir exchanged another look, their fingers tightening on their arms. Draven's weight shifted, and he gave her a full once over.

"Explain."

"—It's all right! I'm here! I found my way!"

The noise of Ash's voice cutting through the silent crowd made Aydra cringe. She'd hoped to leave him behind so that she would not have to deal with him that day. Aydra met Lex's eyes over her shoulder and raised a short brow.

Lex nodded. "Yes, ma'am."

Ash pushed his way through the people. As soon as his feet hit the edge of the crowd, Lex grabbed his throat.

"—what—" Ash's hands grabbed hers, and he struggled for air.

"Does the darkness around us mean nothing to you?" Lex hissed. "Do you think we walked all this way beneath moons so that we could be given away by some idiot Dreamer captain?"

His feet lifted off the ground.

"You will keep your mouth shut unless spoken to today," Lex continued. "Do you understand?"

Ash's head nodded vigorously. Lex released him.

His knees hit the dirt. He started coughing and holding his throat, recovering from the ordeal. Lex straightened her shirt and turned back to the others.

"Your plan, my Queen," she said to Aydra.

Aydra wrapped her arms around her chest and turned back to the raised brows of Nadir and Draven. She stepped closer to them and began pointing at the map as she spoke.

"Nadir, your people will go around this side beneath the waters, ambushing them from the ships' side. You'll take their boats first. They've weapons on them. You'll need to make sure they are not manned by the time the Venari ambush on shore. Balandria, you'll lead a stealth company to take out the sentries. Draven, your wind can confuse the guards, throw them off so that they are unawares about what is happening—"

"And what will you do?" Balandria said, cutting her off.

Aydra met her eyes, and the raven landed on her shoulder.

"The sun breaks in less than an hour," Aydra continued. "We should get going."

Nadir took two slow steps towards her. "If my men die because of your plan, I'm taking your castle."

"If your men die, it is because they do not know how to handle their weapons, not because of my plan," she replied. "And you don't have to threaten me to take the castle. It's not mine."

A quirk of a smile rose on his lips, and he clapped her shoulder upon passing her. "All right, you heard the Sun Queen," he called to his people. "Take your side of the dunes. Come in from the reef. Pluck the bastards out of our waters one at a time—" he paused and leaned back down to her. "Are we keeping the ships?" he asked in her ear.

"Yes, let's keep the ships—"

"Why would you keep the ships?" interjected Ash.

Aydra couldn't believe she'd ever been attracted to this idiot.

"Weapons. Supplies," she said. "We need to know what these people are capable of."

Ash shifted the weight on his feet but said nothing more. Nadir said something else to his people that Aydra didn't catch. They started to move out all around them. The Venari people remained, still awaiting orders from their King.

Draven hadn't stopped watching her. Balandria leaned in and whispered in his ear, to which Draven gave her a nod.

"My company comes with me," Balandria said to them. "The rest of you stay with your king."

The Venari people all moved then, embracing each other as they separated into their companies. Aydra gave Draven's silent figure a once over and then turned away from him. "We will meet you on the hill," she muttered before walking away from them.

Lex and Ash followed Aydra through the forest to the hill at the edge of the tree line. The moons light was bright enough to see the forest floor, but she had the raven fly in front of them anyway. She could just see fires down below on the beach, the silhouettes of men walking up and across the high dunes.

"Wait for my signal," Aydra told Lex as she stared down at their true enemy. "Charge with the Venari company."

"What will you do?" asked Ash.

"Don't bother yourself with what I will do, Captain," she said with a sigh. "I can take care of myself."

Ash's hand touched her arm gently. "I will not allow my Queen to be without a guard. I will stay here with you. Fight for you."

Aydra looked past him at Lex. "Do you see my Second Sun behind you? Turn around. Look at her," she asked Ash. "She is the only person on this land capable of taking care of me. So when I tell her to wait and charge with the Venari and not behind me, I mean you as well."

"But—"

"Wait with Lex for my signal," Aydra demanded again. "That's an order from your Queen."

Ash looked like he would argue again, but finally, he gave her a slow nod. "Yes, ma'am."

The pair disappeared down the hill, and Aydra took a moment for herself as the navy sky began to lighten. Her heartbeat picking up pace. Her fist clenching and unclenching around her bow. She closed her eyes and felt for the creatures around her. For all the birds she knew had followed her through the woods that morning.

The feeling of a warm body at her side didn't make her jump this time.

"Not bad, Sun Queen," Draven muttered.

Aydra opened her eyes, but she didn't look at him. "Not bad for a Sun Queen or for a woman not versed in battle?"

Draven pulled one of his short swords from its sheath and held it up to the twin crescent moons light, allowing the glow to reflect off the silver. The jagged edge of its blade cut the air, and she noticed the ivory on the handle.

"Both," he replied.

"Are those bones?" she asked about his sword.

He laid the blade in his hands, allowing her to see the handle more clearly. "Portions of phoenix breastbone as the handle."

Her gaze narrowed. "Phoenix?" she repeated. "There hasn't been sighting of a phoenix in decades."

A small smile rose on his lips, and he reached down into the bag on his belt that she'd been curious about earlier. The skeleton head he pulled out made her eyes widen.

A phoenix skull, complete with black horns and spiked bone over the open eyes. It narrowed down to a sharp point at the beak and would have covered his entire face.

"Your true crown," she realized.

His confident smile widened as he held it by its horns and then looked out at the scene before them. "Is your raven already down there?"

"She will tell me when the Honest have taken the boats," she replied. She squinted into the dim light as she started to see sentries dropping like flies down the dunes away from the camp.

"Do you have a before battle ritual you usually do?" she asked him as her nerves began to heighten again.

She heard him scoff under his breath, and she looked sideways just in time to see his hair fall over his shoulder. He fumbled with his hand a moment, and then he turned the ring on his finger three times.

"Ah... Not really," she knew he lied. "What about you? Were you praying to the Sun for help earlier?"

"The only being I ever pray to for salvation is myself."

A low growl that she didn't recognize emitted from his throat, and she saw his fist tighten around the blade in his hand.

"I wish you wouldn't say things like that," he muttered in a raspy voice.

"Why not?" she managed.

He turned to face her fully. Her eyes met his darkened gaze, and she felt her heart arrest at the sight of the smolder resting in his features.

"Because restraint lives poorly in my core," he growled. "And I don't have enough time before this battle to fuck you fitly into oblivion."

If it hadn't been for the sudden screech of her raven overhead, she would have pushed him to the ground right then, had him hold his hand over her throat as he railed her maniacally like the Venari King stories of old— damn whoever was around them.

But she would have to settle for the fantasy of it.

For the raven did screech over their heads. And the battle had begun.

Draven slid the phoenix skull over his face, and Aydra's mouth dried, her thighs squeezing together at the sight of him standing over her, his face hidden behind the great creature's ivory skull, his eyes staring menacingly into her being.

She'd never seen a skull look diabolically sexy until that moment.

And then Draven reached out for her hand. When his lips pressed to her knuckles beneath the skull, her chest caved, her mouth opened, and she inhaled a jagged breath.

The wind picked up around them, her hair billowing from beneath the scarf she'd tied around her head. A low whistle sounded as it pulsed through the forest towards them. But she couldn't look away from him, too entranced by the carnal man standing before her that made her heart constrict with a single look. His wind was pushed down the hill and over the dunes, and she reminded herself to breathe as the raven circled them over once more.

Fucking curses of Duarb.

Focus Aydra.

She forced herself to push her distraction from her mind as her raven cursed at her.

Draven let go of her hand, and together they turned away from each other to face the ocean. Sand was picking up in the wind he'd sent, wrapping itself around the sentries that were left and confusing those coming out from the tents.

Aydra closed her fist at her side, and her eyes rolled back as she felt for the birds in the trees above them.

A ray of sun hit her back.

Every bird in the forest rose from the top of the canopy. Bewildered shouts filled the air. The swarm swallowed the sunlight.

Aydra's eyes opened. The noir of the creatures' cores ate at her insides.

Kill them.

Screams.

The sight of her flock attacking the strangers on the beach filled her vision. Bellows echoed out of the water.

Nadir and his men charged the beach.

The wind pushed hard over the dunes, sweeping men off their feet.

Aydra pulled an arrow from her quiver through her bow. Draven's open hand went up into the air. His wind slowed their side of the dune.

The arrow released from her hand. Draven's fist tightened, and the noise of a hundred more cut the sky. The thud of them hitting their targets reverberated in her ears. Some of his company continued firing as Aydra paused to watch the scene. More and more of the strangers were coming out from their tents. She saw a cluster forming to her right, shrouded around a weapon she knew was a ballista.

"Lex and I will take care of the ballista," Aydra told him as she drew

217

her sword from her belt.

Draven didn't say anything to her. Instead, he thrust his own sword into the air, shouting, "Venari!" to his people. A great bellow echoed back, and Aydra's heart pounded in her ears as she heard him say—

"Show them who you are."

They ran.

Lex already had her sword drawn. Aydra caught up with her at the bottom of the hill. They charged at the front of the throng of Venari soldiers, blood pulsating through their veins.

"We're taking the ballista to the right," Aydra called to her Second, who was smiling maniacally as she ran at her side. "Keep grinning like that and the Venari will think you mad," she mocked.

"No madder than you, my Queen," Lex bantered.

Balandria's company was at the top of the dunes, knelt down and firing arrows down below. At some point, Aydra threw her boots off as her feet were heavy in the sand. Traction caught her steps, and she dove her way down the front of the sandy dune on her back. She met the bottom with a somersault and was immediately in contact with a man running at her.

Loudly.

Her sword struck his kneecaps. She jumped to her feet and thrust her blade into his neck just as another man came running up on her side.

She and Lex made their way to the right, slashing down men coming at them as they pushed through the sand. Blood spattered over its nude innocence, guts spilling onto the ground. She kept one eye on the men charging the ballista at all times. They'd begun to pull the bolt through.

Aydra grasped an arrow from her quiver and sent it flying at one of the men. It struck his neck, and he fell from the weapon. Attentions turned on her. One of them pulled an arrow, aiming in their direction —

Her raven landed on the man's face.

The man screamed and fell backward onto the sand.

"Nice shot," called a familiar voice. Aydra turned, finding Dunthorne watching her, his foot against the chest of a man who was leaned forward towards him, his short swords crossed over the man's neck. The blades sliced his throat, and Dunthorne kicked him to the ground.

"You'll show me that move later," she called to him.

Dunthorne grinned. "With pleasure."

Behind!

Another bird calling to her diverted her attention. She whirled around and struck swords with the man over her head. He shouted as he blocked her advance. And when he pushed her backward, her back caught against someone else's.

"We should start every morning like this," Lex called jovially to her.

Aydra almost laughed, and her sword caught the man's throat then. "Blood. Adrenaline. Beautiful people fighting at our sides." Her gaze caught Lex's, and she grinned. "It's the morning we've always waited for."

Spear!

Aydra yanked herself and Lex to the ground as the thunk of the ballista being fired sounded in her ears. The bolt flew over their heads and went through the man that had been running at them.

The pair stood, watching the men whose faces were pale as they stood frozen on either side of the great crossbow. The women exchanged a short, raised brow glance, and Aydra twirled her sword in her hand.

"I think they want to die," Lex said.

"We should oblige," Aydra agreed.

The men quickly began to load another bolt. Aydra and Lex ran towards them, pushing back any men who got in their way. The men were faster loading it this time. Aydra had to duck once more as the spear came whizzing past her. She didn't look to see where it landed this time.

Would you like me to take them? the raven asked.

This one's mine.

Swords were drawn. The man on the left jumped from the weapon and met her on the beach. Their swords clashed left, grunts sounding as she battled him. She barely saw Lex join her, jumping onto the ballista and striking the lone man left on it.

The tip of Aydra's opponent's blade cut her cheek. Aydra stumbled, her fingers touching the sliced skin, and she felt blood trickle down her flesh. Her angered eyes rolled up to meet the man's.

The man dropped his sword, stepping backward, and he fell to his knees as Aydra took one step towards him. Aydra kicked his sword away. His eyes closed, and he pressed his hands together, muttering words under his breath that she didn't hear. She grasped him by his hair and pulled his head up to look at her.

"Who do you serve?" she demanded.

He opened his eyes, and his brows narrowed. "What—"

"I asked who you serve, stranger," she repeated.

Behind!

Aydra swung her sword backward without looking and felt it hit flesh. The man's head bounced onto the ground and landed at her feet. Aydra was still staring at the man in front of her. His eyes were widened at the sight of his companion's head cut clean on the ground by his knees.

The sight of it must have sent some last minute surge of defiance through his bones, for his eyes rolled up, and he seethed, "Long live King Aeron of Mathis, ruler of Man," before spitting at her.

Her sword cut through his neck, and she let his hair go as the blood rushed out of his body. She looked up to Lex on the ballista.

"Who the fuck is King Aeron?" Lex asked.

Aydra took a short glance around them. "What did he mean by 'Man'?"

The battle continued to rage around them, and Aydra gave Lex a short nod. "Think you can handle that thing?" she asked.

Lex grinned. "Living the dream," she said with a wink.

Aydra smirked at her. "Let's finish this."

Aydra ran from her side then. Her sword met and clashed with man after man as the sun continued to rise. Her birds dove and pecked the eyes of strangers, taking some down whole and eating them alive. She'd just turned her attention to a man coming up on her left when—

"My Queen! Your left!"

The noise of Ash's voice made her cringe. She'd nearly forgotten he was there. She dove under the man's parry, cutting his kneecaps, and then she sliced his head from his body just as Ash paused short beside her.

Aydra nearly sent the crows at him.

"You want to be useful, captain?" Aydra said, her sword pointed at his throat. "Kill the intruders and stop paying attention to what I'm doing."

As to whether he listened to her order or not, she didn't care. She turned on her heel and ran down the beach to the next kill.

Ash intervened a few more times, and each time she tried to run further down the beach away from him.

At one point, she battled a man in the surf, and one of the cannonstinger creatures had wrapped its lightning tentacles around her arm when she fell into the water.

The sand and sting of it made her blood boil.

So she made sure the man died a slow death by raven and crow peck.

Blood sprayed on her face with every kill, and she felt her hair coming undone from beneath the black fabric, the splay of her curls growing with every frustrated breath she took.

"Whoa—"

The noise of Draven's voice didn't startle her. She kicked her opponent to the ground and thrust her blade into his face before turning to Draven behind her. He moved the skull up so she could see his face, and he muttered, "Having some trouble?"

Frustration swelled through her, and she whipped the scarf he'd made her wear off her head. Her curls flayed out and over her shoulders wildly. Another man was coming at them from behind Draven. She pulled an arrow through on her bow, and it zoomed past Draven's shoulder, making him flinch backward as it went whizzing by him.

"Well—" her blade met an oncoming man, and she blocked him above her, then kicked him, "I have sand in my ass—"

Left! the raven called.

She pulled another arrow and smashed it into the stranger's throat to her left, knocking him back.

"—burns on my arm from a *stupid* cannonstinger—"

She grabbed another and hit the man running at them from the water.

"—dealing with Ash trying to save me every few minutes—"

Another arrow flew from her bow.

"—and you're standing there staring at me instead of helping me take the lives of those who want our land—" her blade pushed into the neck of a stranger, and he fell to her feet as she whirled around to Draven again. She blew upwards to puff the hair out of her eyes, and she took a few steps forward to meet his figure. "Are you going to help, or are you going to fuck me here on the beach?"

He seemed to consider it. "Bit of an audience," he decided.

"I doubt it's ever stopped you before."

The raven screeched overhead, and she impetuously pulled an arrow, sending it flying past Draven's ear and into the man running towards them.

Before she could move, Draven pushed her behind and struck

221

swords with the man running towards them. Another met Aydra, and she forgot about the battlefield flirting for a moment as this new opponent dodged her advances. Her short sword cut swiftly across the man's throat, and she kicked him to the ground.

She barely realized Draven had taken her bow from her hands until she felt one of his swords in hers. She whirled around, and he grabbed an arrow and sent it flying into the man running at her back. Another man ran at her, and she bolted down the sand, where she slid and slashed at the man's kneecaps.

Draven was watching her when she stood. She strode a few steps in his direction and tossed his sword back, to which he did the same with her bow.

"Tempting," he growled, eyes blazing through her.

The noise of someone shouting diverted both their attentions. Draven shoved the skull back over his face. They were separated, Draven running in the opposite direction towards where Balandria had been. Aydra's sword clashed with another overhead. She kicked him into the surf and stepped on his hand before he could slash at her. Just as her blade landed in his chest, she caught sight of someone, not of the strangers, falling to his knees.

Her eyes did a double-take up the beach, and her heart sank.

"No!"

The stranger had Dunthorne's curly hair in his hand. Aydra pulled an arrow quickly— but it landed in the man's neck too late.

His sword had already crushed into Dunthorne's side.

Aydra ran and dove to the sand, her knees landing behind him the moment Dunthorne fell sideways. She cradled him desperately in her arms, pleading with him to stay conscious.

"No—No, hang on, Dunthorne—" she begged, grasping his hand. "Stay with me! You'll be okay—HELP!"

But everyone around her was too occupied to aid her. Aydra pulled him further onto her lap, holding his beautiful face in her hand. His eyes were slowly fading before her. A lump rose in her throat as she held him. "Stay with me," she told him. "It's just a scratch. You'll make it—*DRAVEN!*"

Dunthorne's dark golden skin glistened in the sunlight. He squeezed her hand and tried to swallow as the blood began to come up in his throat.

"Tell my king—"

"No, no, you will tell him yourself— *DRAVEN!*"

She didn't know where he was, but she shouted his name anyway, hoping someone would hear her desperate cries.

"Will you sing it?" she heard him whisper.

Her stomach knotted at his request. She drew a raspy breath as she slowly accepted the little time he had left. Her hand wiped the tear off his cheek, and she gave him a small smile. "Yeah... Yeah, I can sing it," she whispered.

"From once a wind... and brisk of leaves—"

The Wyverdraki song flowed from her jagged breaths. Halfway through, she looked up, finding Lex standing a few feet away, seemingly frozen to the spot. Aydra's eyes pleaded at her, hoping she would understand to find Draven.

Lex's feet moved, and Aydra turned back to Dunthorne's fading face. She squeezed his hand again as the last of it came from her breath.

"Set me free," Dunthorne whispered with her.

She stifled the emotion with a clench of her teeth, and Dunthorne reached up to her face, his throat bobbing.

"Save my King," he breathed.

She wasn't sure what he meant, but she didn't have time to question him. She nodded desperately and kissed his palm. "I will," she promised.

With a final breath, Dunthorne's life left his eyes. Aydra's head hung low, and she laid him down onto the sand as swords fell to the ground around her.

And then the scream she'd least wanted to hear filled her ears.

Her heart shattered as the noise of Draven's shout sounded around her as an echo. His knees slid to the ground on the other side of Dunthorne, the skull over his face skidding over the sand as he threw it off him. She barely heard the words he shouted. Draven grasped Dunthorne's vest in his hands, pulling him up off the sand as though it would snap him back to life.

More tears fell down her face as Draven surrendered to the truth of his friend's death, and he buried his head into Dunthorne's chest.

34

The battle barely lasted an hour.

Draven and Balandria had their men pile the bodies of the strangers up on the beach and set them aflame. Aydra, Lex, and Ash helped pile the bodies. Aydra watched Draven as he held his cold, stern face before his own men, giving his kingly commands and instructing his people where they were needed. She recognized his held together facade as one she put on herself.

Their losses were not as significant during this one. Including Dunthorne, the Venari lost three men, and the Honest lost four. After the bodies were piled, they made carts to take the bodies of their loved ones back home.

"Any wounded should stop with me at the Umber," Nadir called to them.

Lex raised an expectant brow in Aydra's direction, and Aydra cursed the canon stinger wound on her arm.

"I'm fine," Aydra assured her in a huff.

"Go with Nadir," Lex insisted. "At any rate, just go so you can meet Lovi."

"What will you do?"

"Find a ledge to throw him off of," Lex said with a nod to Ash.

Aydra raised a brow in agreement. "We miss an opportunity earlier," she muttered.

"True." Lex's hands sat on her hips, and they both watched him try to speak with one of the Honest women. "You should tell him where you're going. He won't listen to me."

"You're right," Aydra grunted. "Hey, Ash—"

The sound of his name coming from her made him alert to her as though he were being called by his master. He excused himself quickly from the woman and came jogging up to her. "Yes, Your Majesty. I am here."

"Thank the Architects," Aydra mumbled under her breath. "You'll go back to the Venari kingdom with Lex. Pack your things. You'll ride out for your Village by nightfall."

"Where will you go?" he asked.

"I am stopping with Nadir by the Umber. Diplomatic mission," she replied.

Ash gave her the first agreeing nod he'd used all day.

Aydra bid Lex goodbye a moment later and then made her way across the sand to where Nadir stood, gathering up their injured people.

"Surviving, Sun Queen?" he mocked upon her approach, a slow smile growing on his face.

As the adrenaline of the morning began to slow, Aydra felt herself start to tire. "I am," she forced herself to say. "Your people fought valiantly," she told him. "The ambush from the reef side was well coordinated. Those men had no idea what to do upon seeing you all rise from the waters."

The smirk on his lips widened. "My people have been guarding this reef for two hundred years—not usually against people, but against creatures and the Infi. We have—"

"You fight creatures?" she balked.

He eyed her. "Don't give me any of that 'creatures are misunderstood' bullshit, Sun Queen. These were vicious animals."

"So is the Ulfram—" a flash of small red caught her eye, and she called out to the cardinal passing her by "—but with the right understanding, they are no more deadly to you than a cardinal," she said as the cardinal landed on her finger.

Nadir's jaw set, and he stared at the small red bird on her finger. "I'm pretty sure that bird helped peck men's eyes out today. So I don't know how innocent I would say it is."

Aydra smirked, and the bird left her. "Tell me, Nadir. Will your giver be at the Umber when we get there?"

"Ah... probably," he finally decided. "No promises. Don't think he will listen to any politics you'd like to talk about."

"No politics." She held up her arm, showing him the canon stinger burn, to which he winced for her.

"Ouch."

"Ouch is correct," she agreed.

He grinned a crooked, mocking grin down at her. "So not all creatures are vicious, huh?"

She nearly rolled her eyes at his happy face, his cerulean gaze dancing at the delight of her pain. "Shut up and take me to your giver."

"Where are your shoes?" he asked.

"Oh." Aydra had forgotten she'd taken them off. "I'm actually not sure."

Nadir laughed at her and then draped his arm around her shoulders. "Good thing the trail is sand. I'm sure one of my sisters will have a pair that will fit."

Draven did not go with them to the Umber. Instead, he helped his people take their dead back to his home. He'd barely looked at her since Dunthorne's death, and she knew he was taking the passing of his friend hard.

She was left to walk the way with Nadir. They spoke of the battle as they walked, of the way the strangers fought. He told her what they'd found on the ships—weapons, even some gold. He had his people sailing them around to the eastern edge of their reef to be raided of goods.

It took an hour to reach his home, and when they finally arrived at the hillside above it, she stopped for a moment to take it in. A smile rose on her face, and she shook her head at the beauty of their peaceful home.

Colorful tents lined the beach, boats pulled up to a line of docks that jetted sporadically into the ocean. The clear water poured softly against the sand on the shore. She could see the reef beneath the water as it spread out further than her eyes could see.

In the distance, she saw carts upon carts, full of goods, fabrics, food, and flowers.

"So you are the traders?" she realized.

Nadir stopped beside her and pointed at a great hill in the distance. "Beyond that hill is our food forest. We can grow a lot of foods here that you're not able to in the northern climates. Most of it trades with the Blackhands and Venari. Your Dreamers only trade for the rarest of goods, as you grow most of your things in the Preymoor," he explained.

She crossed her arms over her chest and raised a brow at him. "Tell me, Nadir… are the rest of your people as beautiful as the home you live in?"

Nadir's face faltered just slightly, and he held his chest. "You don't think I'm pretty?" he asked in a hurt voice.

She rolled her eyes as he fell off balance, faking pain at her words. "Take me to your giver, pretty boy."

The noises of children laughing and playing around the tents danced in her ears. A few came up to her, offering her flowers, and by the time they had reached the big tent, she had near a bouquet of flowers, in the end of her braid that had been woven into, over her shoulder.

Nadir gave her no warning before whipping the curtain door out of his way and barging into the great tent, holding it open only long enough for her to skirt through.

"—*luwee cidefu*—"

"Grand!" Nadir announced with his arms wide, crossing the room to the older gentleman using an elongated staff to cross the tent.

Aydra's ears perked at the language she didn't understand emitting from the old man's lips. But the moment Nadir spoke, the man turned, and a wide smile grew over his face.

"Storn, m'boy!" the man exclaimed, hugging Nadir. He clapped Nadir's shoulders and then pulled back to look at him. "Sun harsh for battle today," the old man said. "Venari must have good intentions."

"Ah... probably not the only reason why the sun was bright for our assault," Nadir said, stepping sideways and revealing Aydra standing at the door.

The old man let go of Nadir, and he took one step towards her. His long white-blonde hair was dreaded down to his waist. The white and blonde beard on his chin thinned as it lengthened to the top of the man's frail chest, and its color stood stark against the darkened olive of his skin. Wrinkles and puffed bags surrounded his eyes. He stared at her with the same cerulean eyes as Nadir. He clutched his hand on the staff, and he slowly crossed the space between them.

Aydra swore she saw water in the footprints he left behind.

"A fire Sun daughter with eyes of the sword," the old man mused as he reached her. He deliberately considered her and reached his hand out to touch hers. Aydra's stomach knotted as his softly wrinkled hands curled around her fingers.

"Your mother prepares for war," he continued.

Aydra frowned, taken aback by the claim and the broken accent in which he spoke. "My mother knows nothing of the war on our shores," she argued.

"So she tell you," the man spoke shortly. A small smile broke onto his face then, and he laughed a high-pitched chortle that made her brows narrow back at Nadir's smirking face. He turned away from her and started moving things on a table nearby.

Nadir leaned in towards her. "Excuse his speech. He's much better versed in the old language," he muttered.

"The old language?" Aydra repeated, "what like, Haerland's original language? Who—"

"My children fond of you," the man cut in then, having apparently not heard Aydra and Nadir talking. "Never they brought a Sun Queen into our home."

Nadir chuckled at the confusion on her features. "Aydra, this is Lovi Piathos," he said simply.

Aydra felt the color drain from her face.

"I'm sorry, what?" she managed, now hugging her arms over her chest.

Nadir laughed again. "Lovi Piathos. Giver of the Honest people. Lesser One and child of the Ghost of the Sea. But here at the Umber, we call him the Grand."

If there had been a chair behind her, she would have sat. But there was no chair, and so she was stuck making herself stay on her feet like a frightened child.

She wasn't sure what she had expected upon meeting him. A warrior, perhaps. A tall, strong man of beauty and grace, whose skin looked of the glittering sea.

The very last thing she had expected was an older man with a tall staff to help him walk.

"Don't let the staff fool you," Nadir said in a hushed voice. "He doesn't really need it. Just thinks it makes him look wiser—*Ow!*"

Lovi had smacked him in the shin with the end of his staff. The high-pitched laugh emitted from Lovi, and he turned with two potions in his hand to mock Nadir.

"Mock and pay," he said with another laugh. He looked to Aydra then and nodded towards a chair on the other side of the tent. "Sit, my dear."

Aydra snapped out of her daze and made her way to the chair. Lovi stood over her, pouring some of the potion onto ribbons. She winced when he pressed it to the wound on her arm.

Lovi started asking Nadir about the battle as he dressed her wound.

He told him about the ships and what they'd found, the weapons they'd used. Lovi asked about the plan they'd used to ambush, and Nadir grinned at Aydra.

"Actually, if it hadn't been for the Sun Queen here, I'm not sure we would have won with the numbers we did," he affirmed.

"I'm sure you would have figured out something," Aydra argued.

"Bickering like the last time," he muttered. "It's nice to have fresh eyes on the field once in a while."

Nadir left them a few moments later, leaving Aydra in the room with only Lovi's company. She shifted nervously as he cleaned the wound on her arm, followed by the cut on her cheek, but his calm energy made her feel more open to speaking truthfully with him than even her own mother.

"Tell me, little Sun. How your mother?" he asked after a few minutes.

"Oh, you know Arbina," she said, shaking her head. "High. Mighty. Manipulative... All the things she says we aren't to trust about every other race in this land."

Lovi chuckled under his breath. "Not have I heard another speak about her like this since Duarb was able to walk the ground." His cerulean eyes met hers, and he paused. "What she says such to make you think this?"

Aydra sighed and ran a hand through her hair. "I'm sorry. I shouldn't speak ill of my giver. It was rude of me."

"Hole open," he bantered. "You spill."

She scoffed as he started blotting her wound again. A long sigh left her lips, and she stared at the ground as she began to admit words to him she'd not shared with another living being.

"Everything I've ever learned about the other races of Haerland has been proven wrong to me in just the last few months," she admitted. "I don't know what to trust. I was injured in the Venari kingdom during the Deads a few months ago. Draven and his people aided me back to health, no questions asked. When I spoke with my mother about it, she told me the reason I'd fallen in the first place was that the Venari had orchestrated it." She paused and met Lovi's narrowed gaze, and she shook her head as the memory of her mother's words radiated through her. "I know she is wrong, but when I accused her of it, I thought she would murder me right then."

Lovi chuckled under his breath. "Your mother always been strong-willed, yet terrified of everything," he said, wrapping the dressing around her forearm. "She always believed everyone after her. She has reasons." He tied the bandage off then and took her hand. "You trust instinct, Sun daughter. And if ever you want full truth of our past, come back to Umber. I take you to the Honest Scrolls."

She stilled as she met his gaze and then gave him a nod. "Thank you."

"Hey, Sun Queen—" Nadir burst through the tent door again, carrying a pair of boots in his hands. "Will these fit?"

Aydra had forgotten about her absent shoes. She took the shoes from his hands and pushed them on her feet. Lovi's chortle echoed in her ears again, and then he reached out for her hands.

"Meet again soon, Sun daughter," he said, kissing her knuckles.

Lovi disappeared through the curtain door a few moments later. Nadir had brought her a simple black cotton dress to change into as well, as her own clothing was covered in blood and sand. He waited for her outside the tent as she changed.

When she emerged, he whistled, obviously not expecting her to pull off the said dress, or perhaps he was attempting to swoon her. "Not bad," he mused with a sly raised brow, to which she resisted the urge to scoff. He grinned at her. "Black is your color, isn't it?" he asked.

"Is there a darker noir I should know about to match my core?" she bantered.

His finger pressed to his lips as though he were thinking. "Not that I'm aware of," he answered.

"Then yes, black is my color," she said proudly.

Nadir huffed, that charming, crooked grin settling on his lips. "I hope they've a crown fit for you back at your home," he said then.

She frowned. "What do you mean?"

"I mean..." He stepped forward, one hand shoving into his pocket. "I've lived through four sets of your elders, of the Promised kings and queens of the past, and you're the first to actually treat our people as... well, people. As allies and not enemies. Equals instead of slaves."

"Four sets?" she balked. "How old are you?"

"Eighty-seven," he replied.

Her face faltered, and she gave his young facade and handsome face a full once over. "Eighty-seven? And you look like this?"

He grinned, white teeth shining at her. "Immortality. Don't you know the stories?"

The noise of children running past them diverted her attention. Aydra's chest swelled at the colorful scene around them. The laughter in the air. The children running in the grass and playing on the beach nearby. The hugs and kisses exchanged as their soldiers came home from the battle.

"It amazes me the freedoms of you and Draven's people," she said as she stood there with him. "The joy they share with one another. I wish to see my people with the same."

"Your people do share this freedom," he argued. "Your Dreamers in the towns and villages across the Preymoor and Hills of Bitratus, they feel such joy. I've been there during festivals, brought supplies in for birth moon celebrations and parties."

Aydra's weight shifted, and she suddenly felt as if she knew nothing of her own people aside from the ones residing at Magnice. "But—"

"The Dreamers residing behind your fortress and those in the outskirts are very different. Why do you think Zoria traveled to the Village of Dreams so often?"

She quieted for a moment and hugged her arms around her chest. Nadir seemed to sense something was wrong, and he stepped forward and draped his arm around her shoulders again.

"Come on. I'll walk you back to the Venari roost. Unless you'd like to stay here," he added with a quirk of his brow.

She rolled her eyes at his attempt at swooning her. "I'd appreciate the escort back."

He grinned widely. "Good. You can tell me about your sister along the way. Whether she's as maniacal and beautiful as you are."

Aydra almost laughed. "More beautiful, and you're not to touch her."

He clutched his chest in his hand. "Come now, Sun Queen. That hurts. You don't trust me?"

"When it comes to my sister? No, not in the least," she said.

35

A few of Nadir's people walked with them back to the Venari kingdom, carrying on about the fight that day, speaking valiantly about their brethren that had been lost to the battle. Nadir told her about their own funeral ritual that she would not see the following day. They would place the bodies of their people on separate rafts with their favored flower and send them up the Impius River aflame. He told her that she would see the rafts if she traveled far enough inside the Forest the next day. Aydra made a mental note to try to time it right so that she would see it.

It was nearly dark by the time they arrived back to the Venari home. A somber energy radiated over the whole of the kingdom, but Nadir and his people quickly changed that with their joyous laughter and fill of stories.

Aydra left Nadir's side and went to Lex, who had settled herself at the bottom of the steps to Draven's home. Her gaze flickered up to the balcony as she stood by Lex's side. Draven was leaned over the banister, his eyes staring absently into the fire, not a single muscle moving on his body.

"Has he been like this since getting back?" Aydra asked as she took a seat next to Lex.

"I've only heard him whisper a few words to Balandria. Nothing more," Lex answered. "I didn't realize he and Dunthorne were so close."

"He was his Third. The strongest of the pure Venari born," Aydra knew. "Also one of his greatest friends." She looked up and watched him a moment, watched the flames flicker in the shadows of his face. "I cannot imagine his pain. It would be as if I lost you," she continued, meeting Lex's gaze.

Lex reached over and squeezed Aydra's thigh. "Never," she promised.

Aydra gave her a small smile, and she laid her head on Lex's shoulder with an audible sigh. Her eyes were beginning to droop, the length of the day finally catching up with her aching body.

"Nadir told of their funeral rituals," she said, sniffling a yawn. "We should rise with the sun to find the river, watch as their boats float upriver."

"Do you know how to get there?" Lex asked.

Aydra yawned audibly. "I don't. Hoping you could use your instincts to take us there," she said as she smiled sleepily at her Second.

An amused huff left Lex's lips. "You should get some sleep if we'll be rising so early," she told her.

"Not yet," Aydra groaned. "Have to send off the Dreamer captain first. Where is he?"

Lex gave an upwards nod towards the other side of the fire. "His bags are packed. He was just waiting on you to come back."

"I suppose I should get rid of him then."

"Have fun," Lex teased.

Aydra made her way across the field to where Ash was standing. He greeted her with a full hug. It was apparent that he'd been drinking with some of the Venari, who she was sure were simply making fun of him.

He wrapped his arm around her shoulders, the slur of his eyes gazing down at her. "You're as beautiful in this forest as you are in your own kingdom, Your Majesty," he cooed in her ear.

Aydra's eyes nearly rolled out of her head. "Come, Ash. I'll escort you out."

She tugged on his hand and led him away from the clearing. In silence, they walked through the darkened trees, all the way to where his horse had been taken and left. The cold of the forest circled them, and she eyed the Venari who were above them in silence in the trees.

"You fought well today," Ash told her as they reached his horse.

Aydra ignored him. "You'll go to the Village and then I will meet you back in Magnice in seven days. We must report to my brother what went on here."

Ash frowned, his balance only wavering a second as he stared at her. "You're staying here another day?"

"I have some things to take care of with the Venari and Honest commanders. Myself and my Second will leave in two sunrises and go straight back to the castle. I expect you there when I arrive."

"Wait—" he grabbed her arm as she started to turn, and he pulled her closer. "Is that how you would leave me? After going into battle today, slaughtering men at my side... and you would let me leave with as cold of an attitude as the winter frost?"

The prickled glare on her face didn't fade. "What would you like, Ash? A private fuck here on the forest floor?"

He leaned forward, whispering, "I'll save it for when we're back in your bed," in her ear.

The kiss he pressed to her lips then, she didn't savor. She pushed just slightly on his chest as he started to deepen their embrace. His eyes narrowed down at her, and she pulled her facade to the surface.

"Don't get too hasty, Captain..." Her hand grazed the front of his pants, and she felt him quiver in her arms. "You'll never make it to your Village in such a state."

He smiled and took a wobbled step back, kissing her hands before letting her go. "I'll see you in a week, my Lady."

Once Ash's shadow disappeared into the forest, Aydra pulled her cloak tighter around her shoulders. She closed her eyes and allowed the noises of the forest to fill her.

Crickets. Birds. Wind rustling the leaves on the ground. There was a peace to it that her being craved. Different from the peace of the kingdom that she so despised. This was an urgent peace, one that both calmed her and filled her with adrenaline.

Ash being in the forest that day and on the battlefield had made her uncomfortable. It was as though she were on the field with someone scrutinizing her every move, trying to shield her from the dangers that she knew how to handle. The last thing she ever wanted was for someone to think she needed help as he'd treated her that day.

She honestly wished she'd accidentally sliced his throat.

Maybe then the mess of it would be over.

The Venari and Honest would never have said anything different, and none would have been the wiser. Her brother would have perhaps listened to her then, but then again... he also may have thought the Venari to have done it on purpose and sent an army to the south.

She groaned inwardly at the thought of having to go back to him.

—"He treats you as a possession."

Aydra's eyes opened, and she turned just slightly as Draven came walking up around her side, stepping over the fallen trees and limbs on the forest floor, hands shoved in his pockets.

"Excuse me?" she asked.

"The Dreamer," he explained. "He treats you as though he is your savior. You know he even tried to step in and save you once today," Draven added with a shake of his head. "And then you chopped the man's head off."

Her lips pursed at the memory. "I'm aware. But I don't need saving."

"I know you don't," he replied. "But he acts as though his being allowed conquest in your bed makes him some higher authority than his lonely rank as captain."

"I have never been anyone's conquest," she growled. "The only reason any person finds themselves in my bed is because I allow them there."

"Nevertheless," he said as he stepped over the last fallen tree towards her, "He thinks he owns you." Draven paused in front of her. "You deserve better."

"How would you know what I deserve?" she breathed haughtily.

"Because you're the fucking *Queen*," he said as though it were obvious. "And I don't just mean the title of it or your birthright. That display today, you leading the attack on those men... you're more of a Queen than your brother will ever be a King. As much as I would have loved to watch you cower before the men running at you in an attempt to kill you, the fact remains that you battled them with more ferocity than even my own Second. You deserve someone who matches that, someone who will treat you with such an equality and recognize your true core."

His eyes darkened as his weight shifted in front of her.

"You deserve nothing less than someone who would burn this entire kingdom to the ground for your salvation."

His voice vibrated her insides. His stare didn't leave hers, and for a few moments, she found herself unable to blink. She crossed her arms over her chest and raised her chin up to meet his.

"Sounds like a fantasy," she finally managed. "Where would I find such a person?"

"Perhaps the Berdijay is looking for a mate."

She couldn't help the smile that rose on her face. "You're utterly ridiculous," she told him. "What are you doing out here anyway?"

"Had to take a piss."

"Ah. Right." She shook her head as a small chuckle left her. "Where at so I don't step in it?"

He huffed under his breath, and when he looked down, his hair fell over the left side of his face. She watched his hand reach out, and he touched one of the flowers that was still in her braided hair.

"Honest kids had a bit of fun with you?" he asked.

"Something like that," she replied, feeling her heart begin to warm at the dilation in his eyes.

"What's this?" he asked as the back of his finger grazed her cheek.

Her breaths danced at the touch of his skin against hers, the way he was staring at her. "One got lucky. I took his head as well."

Draven scoffed. He took a blue flower out of her hair then, and he pushed it behind her ear, the graze of his skin on hers making her nearly forget about the events of the day. His eyes darted over her face, and she thought for a moment he would say something more about the flowers, but instead, he simply turned and held out his arm for her.

"Come," he beckoned. "Nadir is keen on swapping war stories with my men. You'll enjoy his tales of bloodshed."

Her heart fluttered at the quirk of the first smile she'd seen on him since the battle. The touch of his skin against hers when she took his arm. And when she took the deepest inhale of the day as they walked back, she felt the familiar butterflies fill her stomach.

The memory of how he'd looked at her earlier on the field made her thighs squeeze. And when she remembered the look of him in the phoenix skull, she felt goosebumps rise on her flesh. She could have given in to him right there, pulled him to the forest floor, and fucked him in the dark.

But she didn't.

36

Draven's quiet figure only woke her the next morning when he was getting out of the tub. He didn't say anything when she sat up in the bed or when she wrapped her robe around her and made out for the balcony.

She knew it was funeral day, and he would be laying one of his closest friends to rest. She didn't want to crowd him or start any argument. So she stayed quiet and waited for him to take the steps down before she called for her raven to find Lex.

The Venari funeral included walking the hour to Duarb's roots. Aydra and Lex followed at the back of the crowd as they walked through the forest to their giver's tree.

The noise of water rushing perked Aydra's ears as they neared their destination. A few of the Venari parted off to the east, including Draven and Balandria. Aydra tugged Lex's arm to follow, wanting to see the Honest boats Nadir had told her about the day before.

The smell of fire caught her nostrils, smoke wafting through the forest. She'd never seen the Impius River before. It was broad, cutting through the darkened forest like a blade slicing through flesh, splitting it in half. Rocks lined the banks of it.

As they approached the large river, the sight of four boats coming down through the middle of it caught her gaze. Longboats ablaze with soft orange and yellow flames. She could still see some of the flowers they'd laid around the bodies in the boats.

The Venari who had decided to adorn the edge of the river in salute to their Honest brothers all laid their fists across their chests to the left, where the mark of the Honest would have been were they of their kind. Aydra and Lex did the same.

Once the boats were out of sight, Draven and Balandria turned and led them back into the forest towards their giver's tree. The forest swallowed them once more. Aydra's raven fluttered from tree to tree above them as they walked. Within minutes, she could see the Forest begin to open up again, and the sight of the largest tree she'd ever laid eyes upon sat in the middle of the only open clearing in the forest.

Lex grabbed Aydra's arm as they approached, and both of them stopped to stare at the beast of a tree before them.

It was practically a monster. The trunk of it was more significant than any tree in the forest, thirty feet in diameter and black as the dead of night. The sunlight that had just graced the canopy seemed to hide upon their reaching it despite there being an enormous gap between this tree's canopy and the trees around it-- as though the other trees were terrified of their branches curling with this one's.

The limbs were thin and twisting upwards, ivory instead of brown. The trunk, as black as it was, she knew was not made of wood, and neither were the limbs hovering over them.

Because the trunk was made from the tongues of his dead children, overlapping one another and wriggling in the still air like snake tongues.

And the limbs were a twisted mix of vines and curled bones of all the beings Duarb had ever taken back into his roots.

This was the curse Duarb had been forced into a hundred years earlier.

She wondered if his tree had been as beautiful as her own giver's tree before he was cursed.

Draven waved a torch over some of the curling roots jutted out from the earth. The roots seized and shriveled upwards as though in fear of the fire over them. His men brought forward the ones they'd lost, and each was placed beneath Duarb's roots.

The fire touched the cloth the men were wrapped in, and the flames engulfed the air. The ground rumbled. Lex grabbed Aydra's arm.

"You don't think…"

Aydra watched the roots wrap around the bodies then, and the ground quaked again. "I do," Aydra whispered.

Duarb took their bones back from where they were born, and the fire engulfed their flesh.

Draven shifted and lifted his arms up in front of himself, his forearms touching, fists in front of his face. They watched every other Hunter do the same and saw the phoenix markings converge together to make up the whole bird on the backs of their arms.

The Venari people did not stay the entire time to watch their friends burn. But each one went up to Draven and placed their hand on his shoulder or hugged Balandria before making their way back home.

Aydra stayed until it was just she, Balandria, and Draven left in the clearing. Lex left her and walked back with a few of the friends she'd made. Aydra wasn't sure what to say. The flames were dying when she finally mustered the audacity to step closer to them.

Balandria saw her out of the corner of her eye, and she gave Aydra a nod. Balandria squeezed Draven's arm and then kissed his cheek before turning and disappearing into the darkened forest.

Aydra pressed a hesitant hand to Draven's shoulder and came around his side a few moments later. He had to look twice, obviously not expecting her to be at his side. Her heart ached for the pain he was going through, how it stretched over his features, and she reached up to his reddened cheek, feeling her own tears rising at the sight of the strongest man she knew breaking in front of her.

But it was when he dropped the torch and sank his arms around her that her heart shattered for him. He buried his head in the crook of her neck, and she felt the wet of his tears on her skin as she held him there until the flames completely died. She settled into the comforting vulnerability of his warm body, feeling her own relax against him, her hands stroking the back of his neck.

They didn't speak, even after they parted and she pressed her lips to his forehead, they said no words to each other. She held his hand as they walked the hour back through the forest together. Every few moments, she would look back at him, watching his darkened expression as he strode with one hand in his pocket. She would squeeze his fingers and rub the outside of his hand gently when she saw him in a daze, and he would look up at her with a solemness in his features that she wasn't sure how to take. But it was when she heard laughter and the sound of drums ringing in her ears from his forest kingdom, the noise of it echoing off the trunks of the trees, did she turn to him with a confused frown.

He huffed amusedly under his breath, the smallest of smiles rising at the corner of his lips upon hearing the noises of his brethren. "Celebration of their lives," he told her. "We eat their favorite foods, dance their favorite dances, tell our favorite stories of them..." His throat bobbed deliberately as he looked through the trees towards his home. "It's our way of showing appreciation for the life they were given."

"I like that," Aydra said, returning his smile.

She started to walk again, but he tugged gently on her hand, her heart startling at the squeeze of his fingers, and she stepped back towards him with a slight frown. "What?"

His hand ran through his hair, and he pushed it over to the left side. "Thank you," he said simply.

"For what?"

He fumbled with her hand a moment, thumb caressing the top of her knuckles. The sincerity of his hand toying with hers made her breath shorten. As to how he brought her to surrender by such a delicate touch, she didn't understand.

"Holding him while he died," he started. "Fighting with my people when you didn't have to. Not saying any teasing comments while the tears ran down my face—"

"Draven, you're the strongest person I know," she interjected. "If you need to weep, by all means, weep. You don't have to be strong all the time. Especially in front of me."

He chuckled softly, eyes darting to the ground and then back to her. He was silent for a brief moment as his hand squeezed hers again, and the intensity of it pulsated up the back of her arm. She could see his mind working behind his darkened sage eyes, and her heart began to beat loudly in her ears at the gaze he stared at her with.

"Aydra, I—"

"My King!"

His daze broke at the sound of one of his men shouting his name, and he looked past her into the forest. Aydra turned to find two of his men hanging on each other, drinks in their hands, and it was obvious the party was well underway.

Aydra bit her lips together to keep the laughter at bay as she crossed her arms over her chest upon their approach.

"My King!" one of them repeated, nearly tripping on a root. "You're to come with us. Bael has proposed a drinking challenge as Dunthorne liked to do. You must be the one to judge it."

The other shoved a drink into Draven's hand and clapped his shoulder. "You know, he cheats—" the man finally noticed Aydra standing there, and he held his arms open, to which Aydra's eyes widened.

"Sun Queen!" the man exclaimed. "I forgot you were here! Come—" he wrapped his arm around Aydra's shoulders "—you can judge as

given."

"I like that," Aydra said, returning his smile.

well."

Aydra's eyes met Draven's as the Hunter started to lead her back towards their home, and Draven openly laughed at her.

The knot in her stomach didn't waver as she followed him back to camp.

37

Her eyes danced with his above the firelight the rest of the afternoon and into the night. Each time she would look up from her laughter with the Venari people, she would meet the fire in his eyes as he spoke with people across the clearing, hands stuffed in his pockets, shoulders always rounded in her direction. Her cheeks hurt from laughing with the Venari race since darkness had approached, hearing stories of their own inner squabbles, of their dealings with the traders, the weekly food fights they liked to get in.

She watched Draven retire himself after a while, going so high up to the roof above his home that she could not see him. It wasn't too long after that she found her nerve, and she rose from the ground, hugging the blanket around her shoulders as she walked past Lex's figure snuggled up with a few Venari and Honest women. Lex raised her cup to Aydra and gave her a wink upon her passing. Aydra resisted the urge to kick Lex as she stepped over her to the stairs of Draven's home.

Draven was leaning against the banister when she finally made it up the grand winding staircase to the roof. His figure was illuminated in the moons' light, hands pressed into the railing overlooking the whole of the forest below him. She paused at the top to take in the scene.

Moons light danced off the darkening leaves of the trees. There were only two more Dead Moons cycles left in the year, and she knew after the last that the leaves would be gone, and a frost would take the bare forest over, if only for a short period of time.

The only tree taller than the one they stood in was Duarb's great tree to the south.

She hugged her arms around her body at the slight wind breezing through the treetops.

"Did you get lost?" she heard him ask without turning around.

She crossed the space between them and stood at his side, gazing down at the scene below them as he was. "It's beautiful up here," she said, admiring the stars above her.

He didn't say anything, and she felt her brows narrow at his silent figure.

"Something wrong?" she asked.

"Why did you come here?" he asked, turning to face her. "I mean... why come help me after blatantly ignoring me the last time I went to Magnice?"

"What do you mean?"

"You acted as though I didn't exist, as though—"

"I was being followed," she interjected. "Belwarks watching my every move. The last thing I wanted was for them to go back and tell my brother anything that would have inevitably brought harm to you. I needed to make sure to give the illusion of our usual aversion towards one another. Anything different would have been flagged."

"Our usual aversion towards one another usually includes at least the common decency of acknowledgment," he argued.

"What do you want me to say?"

"I want you to tell me why you came here. The truth," he demanded.

"I told you I would come when there was another ship. I told you I would be here. I don't give my word lightly," she answered haughtily. "Is that not enough?"

Something flickered in his eyes that she didn't recognize.

"Is that truly is the only reason you are here?"

Her heart began to throb in her chest. "What do you want me to say, Draven?" she managed breathlessly. "Do you want me to say I am here because I cannot stop thinking about you?—"

His eyes snapped to hers. She should have stopped talking, but the words came vomiting from her mouth quicker than she could stop them.

"—That I am here because having to ignore you in the hallways and act as though you are still my enemy King was tearing a hole through my being? That as fearful as I was about there being another boat on our shores, the thought of getting to see you again in a realm where I could freely be myself filled me with a joy that I hardly understand?"

That stupid left brow elevated on his face, and she hated herself for admitting everything she'd just said.

243

"Because I won't," she added quickly. Her chest was heaving at this point, and she shook her head. "I won't say it. I will not allow you to look upon me with that *stupid* glint of satisfaction that—"

The rising smirk on his face made her fists curl, her teeth set. She wanted to slap the look off his face as much as she wanted him to fuck her into oblivion.

She pointed her finger at him and stepped back. "—*that!* That look there."

He bit his lips together, amusement dancing in his eyes. "I don't know what you mean," he said in a sultry growl that made her knees limp.

Her finger pointed in his direction again. "No. Draven. I came here to help you with the ships. Nothing more."

He paused before her, and his eyes squinted down at her. "So leave," he shrugged. "Leave if that's all you came here for. Your horse is ready. Your bags are packed. Go back to Magnice."

A huff left her.

"Maybe I will," she managed.

He stared at her a moment, and she stood her ground, fighting the pull towards him that her body begged for.

"So go," he said with a nod towards the stairs.

"I will," she managed.

His arms crossed over his chest. "You're still here."

"Oh, *I'm* going," she warned.

"Okay," he said nonchalantly with another shrug.

She pushed past him then, knocking into his shoulder. "Goodbye, Draven."

"Have a safe trip back," he called after her.

She paused at the steps and looked back at him. He wasn't watching her any longer. Instead, he'd turned to face the moons. She stared at him, expecting him to turn and tell her not to leave.

But he never did.

"That's it?" she called out.

He turned and leaned his hips against the banister, arms crossing over his chest, but he didn't speak.

She balked at his quiet figure. "Have a safe trip back?" she repeated. "That's all you have to say to me?"

He shrugged again. "You said you didn't come here for anything else except the ships. I shouldn't like to make assumptions about the Sun Queen's intentions for traveling."

"Assumptions..." she almost laughed at the word. "This is a game to you, isn't it?"

"No games," he replied.

She felt herself stepping towards him, annoyed to her bones with his frustrating antics. "You think you're so irresistible. So powerful. You, with your perfect hair, your strong arms, your *stupidly* handsome face —"

"Handsome?" he repeated, hands shoved in his pockets as he slowly, yet deliberately, began crossing the space between them.

"Oh, shut up," she said with a roll of her eyes.

A faint smile rose on his lips at her frustrated figure, long hair falling over his eyes. He paused in front of her and pushed his hair over to one side before looking her over once more.

"I thought you were leaving," he said softly.

Her heart throbbed in her ears at the feeling of his warm body so close to hers. "Why don't you shut up and kiss me instead."

She could feel her breaths shortening as he paused, apparent that he was working out whether she was serious or not. But a moment later, when his hands gently wrapped behind her throat, thumb stroking her jawline, her knees liquified. The tickle of his fingertips made her eyes flutter. The heat of his skin against her own caused a deliberate tingle from his touch down her neck and over her shoulders. She could feel the sweet of his breath on her open mouth as he leaned down. And then, he pressed his lips to hers.

Curses of Duarb, she'd missed him.

Every pore of her being surrendered to his embrace. She grasped his shirt in her hands to steady her balance, relishing the warming feeling of his lips on hers. Nothing compared to the fluttering of her heart in her chest, the heat radiating from her chest to her stomach, and between her legs just from his kiss.

He pulled back a few seconds later, and she felt herself waiver on the spot in his absence. His calloused fingertips tickled the back of her neck, and she looked up to meet his gaze.

"Like that?" he whispered.

The amused glint had left his eyes, leaving behind a dark smoldering gaze that made the hair on her arms raise.

"Like that," she breathed. "But everywhere."

She grabbed the collar of his shirt and pulled him down to her, her lips capturing his so quickly that he grabbed her waist to stay balanced. Kissing him made her mind blank of everything. As though she were in a hidden shadow dimension. As if the realm around them didn't exist. She groaned into his mouth as she felt his hands grasp her hips, his already hardening length pressing into her lower abdomen. His mouth moved to her throat, and she heard herself curse at the nip of his teeth, the ferocity in which he clinched her waist and backside in his fingers.

She tugged at the bottom of his shirt, and he allowed her to lift it over his head. It fell to the ground, and he paused a moment, entwining her fingers with his as gloves that fit he and only he at their sides as the swell of a genuine smile rose on his lips. Not snarky. Not arrogant. Not mocking.

But a real smile that made her heart flutter.

She felt her own smile rise on her mouth, and with it, she pressed her lips against his, softly this time, savoring his strength around her, memorizing the rough edges of his fingers as they trailed her sides. He fumbled with the strings on the back of her dress, and then she pushed her arms out of it, allowing it to fall to the ground at her feet.

He paused to stare at her, the wandering of his darkened gaze making heat radiate on every muscle. She could practically feel her nipples peaking, her wetness soaking through the light fabric of her undergarments, with just his look upon her.

"What?" she asked.

He stepped forward and cupped her neck gently in his hand again. "I didn't get to see you last time," he whispered. "Even your face… the darkness of the Berdijay…" His voice trailed, and she realized the Berdijay's fog had not lifted completely in the forest.

He'd been as blind as her.

The tips of his fingers trickled down her throat, over her shoulders, and against her sides. Causing a shiver to rise on her skin when his thumb flicked her nipple and then caressed her ribs. Moving to her broad hips, where he slipped his fingers beneath the seam of her garments, tracing the hem around her backside. And when he spread those digits wide across her ass, he gripped that fabric before she could protest, and he ripped it off of her.

Aydra's heart caved at his smirking down at her, chin raised, left brow elevated a fraction, and holding her now shredded underwear in his palm.

"Venari, those were my only ones," she uttered, her own hands fingering the hair on his pectorals and down his taut abdomen to the V at his hips.

He tossed the fabric over his shoulder, and his hands squeezed her ass so firmly this time, she nearly came off the ground. "Honestly surprised you were wearing them," he teased. "You never wear them."

Her mouth nearly dropped. "And exactly how many years have you been staring at my ass to know that?" she bantered.

A crooked smirk plastered to his lips, and he smacked her backside hard in response. His head bent low into the crook of her neck, lips pressing over and over to her throat, his beard tickling her skin, as he continued to squeeze her flesh. Grasping her hard enough, she wavered off-balance until finally, he pulled her up off the ground.

Her legs instinctively wrapped around his waist. She felt herself laugh, and she kissed him again, feeling his smiling lips against hers. Her bare body pressed into his. She could feel him already hardening through the fabric as she moved her hips against him. She could have simply stayed there in his arms, pressed against him, kissing him the rest of the night, and been happy with it.

He laid her on the bed, his mouth tugging and kissing her throat, and she felt her eyes roll into the back of her head. Her thighs bucked at the feeling of his fingers raking the inside of her leg, and when his finger traced her folds, her breath hitched. His mouth was on her breast, and she threaded her hand behind his neck, the other gripping the bedsheets as he barely tickled her clit. Her entire body shuddered into the mattress upon his fingertip pushing inside her, and she couldn't help the moans escaping her throat.

His mouth removed from her flesh, and her eyes opened to see him standing over her at the end of the bed, his finger still slowly moving in and out of her, and his other hand stroking his own elongated length. She sat up and pulled his hand off his cock, only to replace it with her lips.

A great exhale and, "Fuck, Aydra," left his throat. She pulled back just enough to look up at him as her tongue swirled his tip. Just as her fingertips touched him, and she raked his length with her tongue, he grasped hold of her hands. She continued to keep his gaze locked with hers as she sucked on his tip. Watching his chest still and then cave with a deliberate exhale made her suck him deeper into her throat. He let go of her hand, his fingers reaching for her chin, and he pulled her off of him with a weighted swallow.

His thumb brushed her bottom lip, and she wrapped her mouth around it. His eyes fluttered. A low groan escaped him, and he grasped her arms in his hands, tugging her up onto her knees so that she was level with him. He was still holding onto her wrists when she leaned closer to him, her nose brushing his. She started to reach for him again, but his hands tightened around her.

"I want to touch you," she whispered against his lips.

He groaned low, leaning forward to bite her lip, and then he placed her arms around the back of his neck. "You'll have me undone before I can see you," he breathed in her ear.

"Would that be so bad?" she managed in a pleading tone.

His fingertips began to trickle down her arms slowly, to her underarms, to her ribs, down her sides. And then, he grasped her hips with such ferocity that she gasped.

"Later."

His breath licked at her flesh, and the chill that ran down her spine made her muscles weak.

"Tease," she muttered against his lips.

His sly smile made her mouth dry. She couldn't hold herself from kissing him any longer, and her lips slammed into his, passion spreading. His fingers grasping at her hips and butt made her moan into his mouth. She loved how he grabbed her flesh as though it were saving him from falling off the edge of a cliff. His arms wrapped around her body, torsos flush together as they made out, making up for the time they'd missed these last months trying to deny the fire between them.

His length was so close to her wetness that she only had to open her legs to feel it brush against her. He groaned into her mouth as she moved her hips back and forth atop him, feeling herself shake at the thought of it inside her. She pulled back just enough to whisper, "I want you inside me," against his lips, to which he nudged her nose with his in response.

"Say it again."

Her hips bucked against his length, and she started to move her hand between them, but he grabbed her wrist and placed her hand around his neck again.

"Draven…" she felt herself bite her lip as he hooked his arm around her waist, grasping her butt cheek in his fingers, his other hand curling beneath her bent knee and pulling it up off the bed around his waist. "I want to feel you inside me," she managed again.

"Soon."

She wanted to hit him.

But the moment the words left his lips, he pushed her backward onto the bed. Her hair fell over her face. For a brief second, she couldn't see him.

And then she gasped at the sudden feeling of his tongue against her clit.

"Fuck, *Draven*—" Her entire body melted into the mattress, mouth agape with ecstasy as she surrendered to the suck of his mouth, the flitter of his tongue, the burst of his beard against her wetness. Her back arched into the air. Her legs were over his shoulders, his hands once more grasping at her hips. She managed to look down, and her eyes met his. The intensity of his gaze nearly sent her over the edge. His tongue flicked her clit quickly, followed by a deliberate tease, alternating between the two and sucking at her wetness as her head hit the mattress again. Her lip was almost bleeding at the strength in which she bit at it, and as she felt her body reaching and reaching, her hands gripped at the sheets. She tried denying her release, enjoying him between her legs far too much to let herself go.

But her high-pitched moans and strain of her muscles were no match for his tease. And she came apart on his lips with a whole shudder of her body and cry of pleasure that she was sure woke every person in the forest.

He didn't stop. Her legs were shaking, thighs squeezing, the sensitivity of herself radiating through her as he continued to suck on her clit. She made herself sit up, and she ignored his warning not to touch his hair. She grabbed him, only to reveal the ravenous Venari grin that made her heart skip. He rose from his knees, and she pulled his face to hers, kissing him hard and tasting herself on his lips. His arm around her waist tightened, and she managed to take his length in her hand this time before he could push her away.

"Inside me," she growled against his lips. "Now."

His hands grasped her hips, and he pulled her off the bed onto his waist. "Yes, my Queen."

Just as swiftly as he pulled her onto his waist, her back hit the mattress, and his thick length filled her. An audible gasp left her lips, and her thighs squeezed around his waist. They both paused a moment, allowing the familiar moment to wash between them just as it had the first time—the warm chill, the raising hair, the arrested breath in their throats. His groan filled her ears, and she felt goosebumps rise beneath her fingers on his arms. Her legs clenched around him, and then he began to thrust in and out of her, his breath tickling her neck. Her fingers curled in his hair, and with every move, she felt herself once more coming to her end. Her vision blanked, eyes rolling into the back of her head, and her entire body tensed. Air couldn't penetrate her lungs. And then—

Their cries filled the still forest air.

The explosion of it made her shake. Her breath barely returned as he stilled atop her and then collapsed onto the bed at her side. The stars above them danced in her spotty vision. She couldn't move, body exhausted from the pleasure of simply him. She closed her eyes for a moment to let it wash through her, calm her heartbeat.

After a few minutes, she felt the bed move, and she opened her eyes. Draven was stood from her side, and she watched him go to the table on which his pipe was sat. She turned over on her side, head resting in her hand as she watched him pack it with the Blackened herb of his own garden. Her heart swelled as she stared at him, rippled back and taut bare cheeks illuminated in the moons light above them.

This man.

This beautiful man.

With all his flaws, his darkness, his sarcasm, and his passions… he made her feel more alive than she'd ever pushed herself to feel. This man, who had driven her to her angered limits more times than she could count, who she had treated as her enemy for over two decades, was now the only man she ever wanted in her bed again. She wasn't familiar with the full feeling in her chest upon watching him turn around and lean against the tabletop, lighting the pipe with the lit match in his hands. The fire illuminated his features once more, and she felt her mouth go dry again as his head tilted back slightly, and the smoke left his lips. His gaze traveled deliberately back over to her and then over her body, making her thighs squeeze together at the sight of his darkened predatory eyes.

"Are you aware of how much sexier the moons light and that pipe make you?" she asked, "or are you somehow completely oblivious?"

A small huff left his lips, and he slowly crossed over to the bed once more. His hand ran through his thick long hair and pushed it over to the side as he extended the pipe to her, and then he sat on the bed himself. She took it from his hands and took a long draw of it, allowing the herb to swim through her veins as she laid her back on the bed, legs bent sideways toward him. A low sigh of satisfaction left her throat.

Draven pulled one knee into his chest. He reached out, and his fingers traced a scar on her thigh behind her knee, eyes traveling over her body as he'd done earlier in the night.

"What?" she asked as she handed the pipe back to him and sat up on her elbow once more.

"Yesterday, when I saw that Dreamer idiot kissing you..." he started slowly, taking in a draw of the herb, "I had to remind myself not to slice his throat."

She almost smiled. "Jealous, Venari?" she teased.

His eyes danced, and he exhaled the herb again. "He treats you as though you are fragile. As though your crown will break if he taps it too hard."

"And how should someone treat me?"

He paused a moment, apparently considering her words, and he reached out to softly touch her calf. "With respect for the woman you are, not as someone they want you to be. With equality, not as though you should be shielded behind a wall. And as nothing less than the most fearsome woman in all the land."

She tucked her hair behind her ear, heart swelling at the words he'd used. "You know, I would have blamed it on the boats if you had sliced his throat," she told him. "No one would have known it was you."

His smile met hers as he held out the herb for her to smoke once more. "Relentless," he drawled, a teasing gruffness to the tone.

"Mmm..." She fell back on the bed and sighed as she stared at the stars above them. "I grow tired of the fake smiles and false niceties of my brother and all his minions," she admitted. "Every laugh at meetings, every time they shake one another's hands... Every time someone tells me I look lovely, I want to ram a knife across their wrists, watch them bleed out on the floor..."

"Graphic," he said with an inhale of the herb. "If you need help, I'd be happy to oblige."

She almost laughed. "I have a running game with Lex. Sometimes after really terrible meetings, we talk about who would scream the loudest if we started a massacre."

"Ash," Draven affirmed as she exhaled the smoke into the air. "Definitely Ash."

"I'm more inclined to think old man Sauder from Scindo would be the loudest."

"Who does Lex think?" he asked.

She took a long inhale of the herb and grinned. "You."

This obviously took him off-guard.

"Me? Really?"

She turned over sideways, almost onto her stomach. "She thinks you would scream loudly and very high-pitched."

He laughed. "What do you think?"

"I think I would have saved you for last," she said smoothly, "kicked your ass as I did when we were children."

He almost choked on the inhale he'd just taken, and his hair fell over his eyes. "You got lucky that day."

"You think so?" she mocked.

He handed her the pipe once more, and she inhaled it deeply, her muscles falling further into the depth of its haze. Talk of fighting made her head spin, and she remembered the words the man had said to her on the beach.

"The man on the beach that I cornered... he said something weird," she said then.

"I didn't know you cornered one."

"I did. Asked him who they served."

"And?"

"He said... 'Long live King Aeron of Mathis, ruler of Man.'"

Draven took another long draw from the pipe. "Interesting."

"Any ideas?" she asked.

"None," he said with a shake of his head. His eyes flickered over her again, and a small smile quirked at the corner of his lips.

"What?" she asked, seeing the amusement in his gaze.

"You... You're the only person I know capable of making talk of war seducing."

She smirked. "Tricks, Venari," she winked.

A long sigh left him as he watched her once more, the darkened haze of the herb lifting into his eyes and replacing the amused glint. She felt the herb swimming through her the same way, and her eyelids became heavy. She sighed back into the bed on her stomach and sat her head on her hands, staring out at the canopy around them. Draven's head hit the poster of the bed, eyes closing as a long breath emitted from his lungs.

Content.

Perfectly. Content.

The silence between them was a blanket she hugged herself into. She couldn't stop watching him, fascinated by the creature before her that made her feel things she'd dared not think truly existed. Challenged. Fulfilled. Matched.

Equal.

She sat up then and pushed herself beside him, curling her legs behind her. His eyes followed her movements as he took a long inhale of the herb. She leaned in and pressed her lips to his as he began to exhale, and she swallowed the sweet smoke emitting from his lungs. The warm trickle of a honey chill ran down her spine, and she felt his fingers gently touch her knee. Her tongue raked the length of his, savoring the taste of the herb on his breath, of the Venari man sitting before her— a taste of forest and darkness and unchecked desire smothered into this perfect shadow she wanted to envelop her very being. And when she pulled back to look at him, her thighs shifted, and she felt herself growing wetter again at the amorous look on his face.

The tip of his finger reached between her thighs, and he grazed her folds so delicately that she had to take in a sharp breath of air.

"Careful, Venari," she heard herself whisper as his finger brushed against her. "You'll have me undone before I can touch you," she repeated of his own words.

"Thrice."

She balked and pulled back slightly to see the determination in his eyes. "Thrice?" she repeated incredulously.

"Before you can touch me," he confirmed.

She felt her lips gape open slightly at his torture. "This really…" She almost whimpered as his lips brushed the skin of her throat, and his middle finger dipped between her folds, grazing her clit. "This really isn't fair," she finally managed.

He smiled slyly over her. "You are truly used to getting your way, aren't you?" he teased.

"I *am* the Queen."

The low chuckle that emitted from his lips made her thighs squeeze again, and he bent down, his teeth tugging at her earlobe. "My forest. My rules. *My Queen.*"

The growl of his words against her skin made her eyes roll into the back of her head, and she surrendered to him a few times more.

38

The morning came too soon.

They stayed up for hours, enjoying the embrace of one another's company, holding onto it as though it would disappear if they moved apart. They smoked, stared at the sky together, speaking the stories of Haerland's past and the differences between the Chronicles and Honest Scrolls. And when she fell asleep in his arms, her mind rested and was swallowed by a warm, fluttering feeling she was unfamiliar with.

"I wondered where you'd end up last night," Lex teased.

"I don't know what you mean," Aydra lied.

Lex chuckled under her breath. "He's good for you, I think. The only man I've ever met that can actually handle you."

"Do you truly think that, or are you just too scared to tell me otherwise?"

"Well, you'll notice I said man, not person," Lex quipped with a wink.

The pair laughed as Aydra started packing her bag. Words Draven had said two nights before continued to echo in her head.

"What's wrong?" Lex asked, apparently feeling the tension in Aydra's form.

"He said something the other night that I can't stop thinking about…"

"What?"

"He said I deserved someone who would burn down this entire kingdom to save me if I ever needed it," she repeated.

Lex considered the words. "He's not wrong," she agreed. "You think he meant himself?"

"Maybe," she wondered aloud. "Perhaps. I'm not sure. I—"

Lex's hand on her arm made her words cease. "In all seriousness, my Queen," Lex started, "I like him. He's smart, sarcastic, equally as angry and passionate about his people, a fearsome being to behold, and… I've seen the way he makes you laugh. If anyone deserves to see your happiness, it is one who can accomplish such a feat. And if he would burn this kingdom for you… You'd not find many others who would."

"You would," Aydra affirmed.

Lex gave her a crooked smile. "It would be my honor, of course, but you should know my duty as your Second would be to not disobey your orders which I'm sure would be to save your sister first. But as your greatest friend… I'm more inclined to think I'd be standing by your side with the torch as we burnt it to the ground ourselves."

Aydra almost laughed. "Yes, that does sound like us."

Lex gave her a wink and started out of the room. "I'll meet you out front when you're ready."

"Thank you, Lex," Aydra called as Lex left the room.

"Whoa—"

Draven nearly barged into Lex as she turned the corner of the door, and she paused haughtily on the other side of him.

"Sorry. Didn't realize you were up here," continued Draven.

"Queen needed a bit of relief after you failed to satisfy her last night," Lex told him swiftly. "I'm sure you can understand. There are some things a woman just knows how to do better."

Aydra clapped her hand over her mouth to keep herself from bursting with laughter.

A sly smile rose on Draven's face. "You'll have to teach me then."

"Secrets, Venari King. I'm not sure you've earned them." Lex gave him a full once over and stroked her chin with her finger. "Perhaps you will have by your next trip to Magnice. We'll talk."

Draven grinned. "I look forward to it."

Lex gave him a wink and then continued down the stairs, barking orders out to people in her way as she descended. Draven whirled around and met Aydra's amused eyes with his own surprised gaze.

"I really like her," he said happily.

Aydra chuckled under her breath. "She's certainly been my amusement for some years now."

"And you two…" his voice trailed as he shoved his hands in his pockets and raised a brow.

Aydra smirked. "What happened to it not being your business who shares in my pleasures?" she asked.

"Well, that answers that," he said with the suggestive smirk that made her heart flutter.

She smacked his chest. "You're ridiculous."

He took her waist in his hands then and pulled her against him, smiling as he leaned down a breath from her face.

"I have to finish packing," she told him.

"I know." He nudged her nose with his. "But I actually needed to make sure Lex was lying, and you were satisfied without her assistance this morning."

She pulled back and bit down the laughter bubbling to the surface. "What do you think?"

"I think I need another round to be sure."

Laughter emitted from her throat as he began kissing her throat. "Draven... Draven, they are waiting for me—" she had to make herself say the words from her lips as he gripped her backside in his hand. "I can't..." Her willpower was quickly fading, and her eyes rolled into the back of her head as his hand dove between her legs, gently caressing her over the fabric of her pants.

The glimpse of the bag on the bed brought her back to reality. She gripped his shirt in her hands and gave him a gentle nudge. "Draven, wait—"

He pulled back softly and gazed at her face.

"I'm sorry. I have to pack," she told him.

He smirked knowingly and took a step back, still holding onto her fingertips. "What can I do?" he asked.

"Nothing, I... Actually, can you get my things from the tub?" she asked of him.

He nodded and disappeared across the room. Her mind wandered in silence as she continued throwing things into the bag, giving no care to anything being folded or taken care of. All she could think about was what her brother would say upon her return, the kind of trouble he would say she was in... she knew it would be a battle between them when she told him she'd actually seen the ships.

"Don't go back," Draven said as she buckled one bag closed.

She didn't look up at him as she turned and grabbed the last of her things from the top of the dresser. "I have to. I am Queen. I have to go back to tell my brother of the ships. There is so much to do. The Nitesh is coming. More ships—"

"Slow down, Drae," he insisted upon taking her arm.

She sighed and finally paused to face him. "I'm sorry. I just... with everything that's happened..." Her voice trailed, and she looked down at her packed bag on the bed, the thoughts of what awaited her at Magnice trickling through her subconscious once more.

"You could stay," he repeated as his fingers touched hers.

She felt her gaze squint. "You've said that twice now. You know I can't," she told him. "Why don't you want me to leave?"

"Ah..." he muttered nervously, avoiding her gaze. She watched him swallow hard, and then he took her hand in his. "Because I am in love with you," he said simply.

Aydra's heart stopped at the words.

She stared, wide-eyed, and took a step back from his figure as he gazed at her with the most sincere look she'd ever seen on anyone.

"You what?" she managed.

He rubbed the back of his neck nervously, and she watched as an embarrassed smile rose on his lips. "I know. It's... it came as quite a shock to me as well," he said, avoiding her gaze. "But... I've no other explanation for the feelings I've come to have for you. Aydra, I... I can't get you out of my head."

His hand left his neck and slapped his thigh defeatedly as though he were giving up something of great importance. "I can't stop hearing your voice," he continued to admit. "Your laugh... I hear it as the lullaby I fall asleep to every night. I dream of seeing your smile, of holding you in my arms. I dream of feeling complete again, as I did when you were with me before... And then these last few days... despite everything that's happened... I've never felt as alive as I do when I am with you. Last night... last night, I felt like I was home. As though our worlds were at peace somehow, you shrouded in darkness with me. You are the most stubborn, most infuriating, and yet the smartest, bravest, wildest woman I've ever known. You don't know fear, and you love your people and this land with a passion I'm not sure you're even aware of." His chest visibly fell, gaze resting over her once more. "I am unequivocally fallen at your strength and ferocity."

He reached out for her hands again and took her shocked fingers in his. "I know it's a lot. And I realize how crazy it sounds— that I could be in love with someone whom I've been taught my entire life to see as inferior, as my enemy... Aydra, *I know*." His hands squeezed hers, and his weight shifted. "I don't expect you to feel the same, but I think you've felt something, and I wanted— I *needed*— you to know."

She didn't know what to say.

She didn't know what her face was doing.

She didn't know how he could utter the words he'd just said to her. How could he love her?

Years of bickering and loathing each other. And after two weeks of being with her, a few restless nights, and one battle plan later... *he loved her?*

"You can't be serious," she forced out. "You don't *love* me, Draven. You love the small fraction of myself that you've gotten to know here in the Forest. You love the brief carefree moments we shared where I was able to actually be happy—"

"You told me yesterday that you could not stop thinking about me," he interjected, "that you came here because you wanted to be with me —"

"I'd been drinking," she managed.

He gave her a sideways stare, and that stupid, disbelieving brow raised.

"Draven... You can't... you can't love me," she stammered. "Our races are enemies—"

"Is that the only excuse you'll give me for not being allowed to love you?"

Her thoughts flickered to the words of her mother and her brother, the words she'd been fed her entire life. Not to trust him. That he was manipulative.

But in her time in the Forest with him and his people had proved differently...

Everything she'd been told was a lie.

However, that didn't excuse the ludicrousness of him telling her he was in love with her.

"You don't know the rest of it, Draven, of what I am," she continued. "You don't know my past or my darkness."

"Then share it," he said as he stepped forward again, taking her cheek in his hand. "Share your past and your darkness. I want to hear it. Let me in."

The anvil sitting on her chest grew stiffer, and she struggled to take a breath upon speaking. "I can't," she breathed.

Hurt spread through every pore on his face. He avoided her gaze a moment and caressed her knuckles. "Whatever you think you can't tell me, you're wrong." He brought her knuckles to his lips, and he lingeringly kissed them.

He stayed and helped her pack her bags, all the while making his usual sarcastic remarks and jokes that made her stomach flutter and her cheeks hurt with a smile. And once she was all packed, he had one of his men carry it down for her.

Leaving this time was not like the last.

His arms hugged around her as they stood on the porch, and for a few moments, she savored his strength around her. Eyes closing, forehead lying against his.

She wouldn't see him again until the next banquet.

And then he began to hum the Wyverdraki song.

His body started to move side to side, dancing with her, and she almost laughed.

Her voice joined his hum, and she whispered the words softly as he entwined his fingers with hers. He spun her out a time or two, swaying with her when he would bring her back in. And when she finished up the last of it, he wrapped her into him again.

"Who knew the Venari King was such a romantic?" she mused.

He smiled down at her, and his nose nudged hers. "Don't tell anyone. You'll ruin me," he growled.

She reached up to his face, fingers threading into his beard a second before she dared to move further. Her stomach knotted as she felt the softness of his hair against her fingertips, and his eyes closed. A visible chill brushed over his skin, an audible breath leaving him.

"Is this okay?" she asked softly.

"Only you," he whispered, and the way he said it made her heart flee.

She allowed her eyes to memorize his features, this small moment engrained in her consciousness to last her for the next few weeks that she would have to go back to her regular duties. The press of his hand on the small of her back. The fit of his fingers with hers, entwining together and not against. The slight smile on his lips that rose to his dilated eyes.

"I don't even know what to say to you," she whispered.

He pushed her hair off her face and pressed his forehead to hers. "Just don't ignore me when I come to Magnice in a few weeks, and we'll call it even."

39

"I still do not know for sure that is what we saw," Ash said five days later as he stood beside Aydra in the Chamber. Rhaif stared between the pair.

Aydra rounded on Ash. "Are you… you're fucking joking, right?"

Ash did not look away from Rhaif's figure in the chair. "I do not know the tricks of the Venari and Honest. Until we see men on our own shores, I see no reason why we should concern ourselves with the southern seas. The men we fought were half-witted sportsmen at best, not any true army."

A swarm of birds threatened to come inside. Two crows squawked and landed on the windowsill, two more fluttering to the high ceiling. The raven landed on her shoulder just as she felt her mind start to blank.

"Drae—"

Dorian's voice did not heed her. She turned fully to face Ash.

"You… you fought alongside me. Alongside Draven. Nadir. Lex. All of their men. You watched as they and their companies laid their lives on the line. Watched as they died in front of you. We held *funerals* for them the next day. And you think it was all a sham by the Venari?" she nearly screamed. "How, Ash? How can you think such?"

"I never said it was a sham," Ash argued. "I said the men were not a threat. You are blinded by your favoritism for their races," he continued. "These men that died were simply not good fighters. They'd no business on the field to begin with."

"I held Dunthorne's hand as his life passed into the next," she spat shakily. "I shot the arrow that killed the one that killed him. How dare you—"

"Calm yourself, my sister," Rhaif called from his chair.

Aydra realized the crows were circling outside. She took a step back.

"That is all, Ash," Rhaif said then.

"I cornered one of them," Aydra said quickly.

Everyone in the room paused, silence stilling in the room. Aydra's weight shifted as she stared at their confused faces.

"I cornered one of them on the beach. Asked him who they served," she further explained.

Rhaif's brow raised. "And?"

"He spoke only a few words before I sliced his throat," she uttered, eyes darting between their scrutinizing faces. "He said 'Long live King Aeron of Mathis, ruler of Man.'"

Rhaif's hands clenched over the edge of the chair. He looked to Ash, to whom he gave a short nod. Ash bowed low at the King and turned on his heel without looking at Aydra's fuming face, his cloak billowing behind him as he left the room.

Aydra turned to Rhaif. "You cannot possibly believe him over me, believe that these people were nothing," she argued. "I told you what he said. I watched our people die—"

"Those were not our people, my sister," Rhaif interjected.

"You wait until Draven gets here for the next meeting. You will hear him tell it again, of how you ignored his pleas to send aid, of how—"

Rhaif's laugh vibrated the room. And he wasn't the only one that showed amusement. The Belwarks at the back of the room and at his side chuckled under their breath. The noise of it made her insides still.

"If you think the Venari will convince me otherwise, you're wrong, and you know this," Rhaif snapped. "What makes you think I would listen to him any more than I listen to you or the Village captain?"

"Because he has no reason to lie to you," she said breathlessly. "This stupid feud has gone on long enough. Strange ships are knocking at our doors. We must put this behind us and unite against them."

Rhaif stood from his chair and crossed the room towards her, his hands outstretched. "My sister... You've had a long journey back to us. Perhaps you should rest tonight." He leaned in closer as though he were hugging her. "You're embarrassing yourself," he whispered in her ear. "Leave before I'm forced to do something I don't want to."

"Like what, brother?" she hissed. "Burn me? Go ahead. I'd like to see what the others have to say when you do it in front of them."

"If you think they'd be on your side... you're wrong."

His words cut deep, and she was reminded of the portrait paintings of past Kings and Queens on the walls.

An accessory to the true crown.

Intended to be nothing more than a pretty face.

Aydra glared at her brother as he stepped back and grinned at the others in the room. Anger rose inside her, and her raven flapped its wings on her shoulder.

"Drae."

Lex's voice broke her out of her daze. She felt her Second's hand press to her arm.

"Come. We will take our leave," Lex told her with a glare at Rhaif.

Aydra locked the door to her room and put a chair under the handle that night. Her raven was in the room with her. Lex had offered to stay, but she told her not to, knowing she would be in danger if she did. Aydra wasn't stupid. After riding out without telling him along with arguing about the boats that day, she knew that he would want to punish her.

But this time was different.

She didn't feel scared. There was a strength inside her that hadn't been there before. A will to live beyond the scare of his fire and bruises.

Sleep did not find her that night. She sat up in bed, in Draven's shirt, covers pulled up over her, and she tried to read the translated Scrolls book Draven had given her. She'd packed the pipe he'd given her to calm her nerves.

Draven would have murdered every being in the castle if he knew.

It was the only secret she knew she could never tell him.

The handle jiggled twice during the night, both times making her heart skip, her body jolt upright. She knew he was trying to get to her or scare her. Her raven sat at the end of the bed, awake the entire time. She knew she couldn't stay locked in there every night, that she would have to face him in the darkness at some point. But she wanted at least one night to process everything before that happened.

She'd tried to set herself apart over the years, make sure her fate was different from the queens of her past. The accessories. The trophies.

Just a pretty face.

She wanted to be part of it. The dirty. The gruesome. No, there wasn't much crime to deal with there, but she made sure she was trained so that if there ever was, she would be ready. It was why she did not rely on the animals as so many Promised daughters had before her. Why she learned as much as she could about archery and combat, the darkness of any creatures she might face in the Forest... It was why she pushed Nyssa to do the same.

She knew she would have to be the best of them all.

40

She was standing at the edge of her mother's pool on the beach.

Arbina was doting on her, running her hands through Aydra's hair as Aydra pulled an arrow back on her bow.

"Higher," Arbina had instructed Aydra's thirteen-year-old self.

Aydra's weight shifted. She eyed her target at the edge of the fall. Arbina's touch on her arm made her breath catch. Her mother lifted her back elbow just slightly as the noise of splashing water sounded in her ears.

Arbina paused and rolled her eyes at Rhaif practicing his advances in the water. "Dear boy, stop. Your sister is working. Quiet."

Rhaif stopped and straightened but didn't speak. Aydra squinted at her target, and she released her arrow. It struck the fruit they'd placed beside the waterfall on the ground. Arbina squeezed her shoulders, and she turned her head slightly at Rhaif.

"If only you could land such an arrow," Arbina scolded him.

Aydra's arms lowered, and she turned just in time to watch Rhaif scratch the back of his neck, eyes staring at the ground. "I can," he argued.

"Really?" Arbina challenged him. Her arms wrapped over her chest. "Prove it. Prove you're ready for your marking."

Rhaif crossed the space between them, and Aydra handed him her bow.

"Show her, brother," Aydra whispered.

Rhaif gave her a tight-lipped smile, and Aydra squeezed his hands as she placed an arrow in his palm.

Aydra stood off to the side and crossed her fingers, hoping Rhaif's aim would be true this time. Hoping he would finally prove to their mother that he was good enough to be given his mark and fire.

He pulled the arrow back, and Arbina did not help or instruct him. She simply watched him struggle with the arrow, scrutinizing his form without words.

Aydra saw the shake in her brother's hands. She looked between her mother and Rhaif, watching her mother's lips purse at Rhaif trying his hardest before her. Aydra slipped sideways to him and touched his arm.

"Breathe," she said in his ear. "Both eyes open. You can—"

"Don't help him."

Their mother's voice cut the air. She watched Rhaif, arms crossed over her chest as she stared down her nose at him. Aydra took a step back, her face reddening quickly. Rhaif's eye caught hers, and she gave him an encouraging nod.

The arrow tore through the air.

It landed with a thud just above Aydra's own, and Aydra's heart skipped in her chest. She felt her eyes widen with glee, and she bounded to her brother, wrapping her arms around him. He grinned and hugged her, the first time that he'd actually been able to do anything properly in front of their imposing mother.

"I told you!" Aydra exclaimed as she hugged him.

But the happiness of their moment was short-lived. For when they pulled back to look at Arbina, Aydra had hoped to see some sort of pride on her features, anything other than the scold that seemed to rest on it. However, she did not get that reprieve.

Arbina gave Rhaif a full once over, chin lifting in his direction.

"Weak," she accused. "Again."

—"Drae?"

The noise of Dorian's voice pulled Aydra out of the daydream she'd been entranced in. A full breath entered her lungs, and she looked back from the edge of the cliff she stood on to find him coming up behind her, sword drawn and sitting lazily over his shoulder.

"Dorian," Aydra breathed, giving him a small smile.

Dorian's eyes narrowed, but he didn't press her. "Lex told me you wished to see me. Something about... learning to fight like the strangers?"

Aydra forced another breath into her lungs, and she nodded. "Come on. We'll go to the stadium."

Rhaif didn't touch her in the days between her arrival back at Magnice and the next Council meeting.

Aydra tried to surround herself with her family, teaching Nyssa more on her bow, battling Dorian with the sword. After fighting the men on the ships, she knew they would need to be even stronger than they'd been brought up to be.

"They're fast," Aydra said, her sword clanking with Dorian's. "Fumbling, but fast."

Dorian blocked her overhead parry. "What do you mean fumbling?"

"I mean—" she jabbed right, and he swerved. The somersault he did beneath her next slash made her pause. "Where did you learn that?"

"Sometimes I practice with Lex," he grinned.

"That sounds about right." Their swords clashed back and forth, her pushing him back and back. "The men were also vocal," she told him. "Could hear them coming up on you without turning."

Dorian blocked her again and slashed right. "I know the Hunters are, but what of the strangers?"

"You'll never have to fight the Hunters," she told him. "Especially you. Sir best friend with the Venari King," she teased.

"You know, I heard a rumor," he said, dodging her advance. "I heard you were fucking him."

The question caught Aydra so off-guard that Dorian knocked her sword out of her hand. He was grinning at her when she straightened from picking her sword up from the ground.

"All right, little brother. I see you." She twirled her sword in her hand, ready for him to advance, but he simply stood there.

"That was a blatant dodge of my statement," he declared.

"What was?"

Dorian's eyes widened as though he'd just discovered her deepest and darkest secret, and he was determined to use it against her somehow. "You *like* him."

"Okay, that's enough parrying today." She rolled her eyes and put her sword away. "Let's go find your sister."

"No—" Dorian pushed her off as she went to drape her arm around his shoulders. "Don't dodge me. Answer my question."

"I'm not answering anything," she countered, arms hugging over her chest. "Who I keep in my bed is not your concern. I dare not ask who you keep in yours."

The confident smirk he gave her then would have rivaled Draven's. Aydra scoffed and shook her head.

"Come on. We'll—"

"Ash's sister," he said then, twirling his sword as he stepped towards her. "Councilman Burdo's wife. Councilman Engle's son. Councilwoman Ebonrath. The Scindo twins. Ambassador Tarwin's son. And Lex... but only for *training*, as she puts it."

Aydra's mouth nearly dropped. Dorian chuckled lightly and then placed his hand on her shoulder.

"Now that you know my list... I believe my question is a fair one."

Aydra crossed her arms over her chest as she dared the smile she knew wanted to place itself on her lips to rise. "Fuck off, Dorian," she bantered.

Dorian grinned. "So you *really* like him."

His arm hugged around her when she didn't argue this time, and he sighed arrogantly. "Who knew my beautiful, rebellious elder would be the one to bring peace between our fighting races."

From that day on, Dorian made fun of her every chance he got. She knew it could have been his hanging around her so much that deterred Rhaif from harming her, and whether Dorian truly knew that was happening, she wasn't sure.

But Dorian clung to her, asked her to read from the Scrolls book Draven had sent, shared the herb he'd grown from his own garden, and begged her to tell him about the creatures in the forest. Some days they would go to the cliffs, and on those days, they took Nyssa with them. Aydra would set up makeshift targets for her sister to practice with, helping her with her stance and confidence.

It made her miss the days she and Rhaif had shared together like that.

41

On the night before the next Council meeting, Aydra couldn't sleep.

Her stomach was in knots. She'd not had a moment to see Draven before that hour, having been so consumed with duties and pre-meetings with the Nobles about the securities of their towns.

The dress she'd chosen for that meeting was solid black, long fitted sleeves that went down over her hands, capped shoulders, and a plunging V that didn't stop until it pointed beneath her breasts at her waist. The bottom was full and flared over her hips, a high slit on the right leg that went all the way up to her mid-thigh. The dress trailed behind her when she walked.

"Fallen at your feet, my Queen," Lex said as Aydra emerged from her room.

"Maye truly knows me, I think," Aydra said, speaking of the seamstress she favored.

Lex fell in step with her as they walked. Aydra couldn't stop fumbling with the ring on her finger.

"Your fidgeting is making *me* nervous," Lex said.

"I haven't seen him in over a month," Aydra managed.

Lex chuckled under her breath. "Funny. He said the same."

Aydra stopped and stared at her. "You saw him?"

"Passed him on the way up to your room," Lex answered. "He is also looking rather delicious today. This will be fun."

Upon their reaching the doors of the Chamber, she paused and turned the ring on her finger over three times as she'd started doing. She nodded at the Belwarks, and the doors opened.

Gold reflection bounced off her crown from the windows' lights as she walked inside. Heads turned, and they bowed upon her passing.

Her eyes found her sister on the other side of the room, and she and Lex made their way over.

Aydra grabbed a wine on the way over, downing it before even reaching her sister.

"Drae!" Nyssa exclaimed, crossing the space between them. "You're early for once."

Aydra laughed. "Ready to get this meeting over with, more like," she answered.

Nyssa began talking to her about something, but Aydra's attention faltered completely. Her heart skipped upon seeing his relaxed figure across the room.

Draven was standing by the window, gold goblet in his hand. His teeth tugged on his bottom lip as he took the drink away from his lips. One of the Nobles was standing in front of him trying to talk to him about something, but she knew he hadn't heard any more of the man's conversation than she was hearing of her own sister's.

His gaze found hers, and he stilled. He looked over her, and she watched as his tongue darted over his lips—

"—hear me? Drae?" Nyssa's voice entered her ears.

Aydra snapped herself out of her daze and pushed Nyssa's hair back, giving her a small smile. "I'm sorry, Nys. I just need to speak with the Venari before the meeting. About the Infi," she lied.

Lex almost choked on her drink, and Aydra glared at her.

Draven was already moving across the room to her. She met him halfway, and the noise of her heart thudding in her chest nearly made her ears bleed.

She didn't know what to say.

His eyes traveling up and down her figure didn't help matters.

Another jagged breath filled her lungs, and she felt her mouth open just slightly to let out the air she could barely breathe in the first place. She wanted to reach out and touch him, feel the burn of his skin against hers. A small smile rose on her lips as his eyes finally locked with hers.

"You know this would look a lot less suspicious if the two of you would say something instead of simply eye-fucking each other," came Lex's nudging voice behind Aydra. Aydra nearly jumped, and Lex gave her a smile upon pressing a drink into her hands. Lex left them just as quickly as she'd appeared, and Draven smirked as she sauntered away.

"She's right," he said.

Aydra gulped the red wine in her cup. "She usually is," she muttered.

He took two steps forward, his shoulder meeting hers as though he were going to walk past her. Her breath caught in her throat, and she felt her hair fall over her face as he leaned down.

"You're mesmerizing, Aydra," he whispered. "I'm not sure how you expect me to hear anything these people have to say with you sitting across from me like this today or any day hereafter."

The growl of his words sent a shiver down her spine. She tucked her hair behind her ear and looked up at him.

"The same, but about you," she managed breathlessly.

Draven stared at her a moment, words sitting on his tongue, and then he shifted. "Aydra—"

"Is there something happening here that I should know about?"

The sound of her brother's voice made Aydra jump. She felt heat rise on her chest as Draven turned fully towards him, his body tensing at Aydra's side.

"Not at all, brother," Aydra said with a tilt of her head. "Draven was just telling me of the Wyverdraki mating ritual," she lied, regaining the confidence in her voice. She took a good step back and wrapped her hand around her brother's arm. She felt her shy facade fade and the wall she so desperately clung to with the crown on her head veil over her face.

"Sounds barbaric," Rhaif said with a glare at Draven.

"It's actually quite beautiful," she mused, smiling genuinely at Draven's softened features. "Should you like to hear it?"

Rhaif's gaze danced over Draven's figure just noticeably before turning his attention to Aydra. "Take your seat, sister. We need to end this meeting on time for once."

Her brother took her arm and began leading her towards the table, but not before she gave Draven a smile over her shoulder. Her heart fluttered in her chest upon seeing the crooked smirk he returned.

Aydra hardly heard what the meeting was about.

Every time Draven's eyes met hers, she had to shift in her seat. The stare he gave her across the table had her dripping with the fantasies of what he would do to her later. She could see the vein straining on his neck, the short breaths he would take when he shifted in his own seat.

The only thing she remembered was when her brother began to adjourn the meeting without bringing up the safety of their kingdom.

"Wait—" Aydra called as her brother tried to stop the meeting. "We have to talk about the ships."

Draven sat up in his chair as the rest of the room began to murmur together.

"Ships? What ships?" Councilwoman Reid asked.

"Are there ships on the shores of Magnice?" another member asked.

Aydra's eyes darted between Ash and Draven, then landed back on Rhaif's flared irises. "Well, no, but—"

"Ships arrived on the shores of the Honest Sea a few weeks ago," Ash cut in then. "The Venari King and his Honest friends handled the incursion. I was there with the Queen myself and witnessed the strangers be taken down."

"There is no need to concern yourselves, Council, Nobles," Rhaif cut in. "The Queen has a slight obsession with these ships," Rhaif said with a laugh. "You'll excuse her paranoia. The Venari and his men have the situation under control, do you not?" he asked Draven pointedly.

Draven's lips pressed together thinly as he looked around the men and women at the table. He finally took a deep inhale and met Aydra's gaze. "The ships have arrived twice on our shores. My men and the Honest have battled them both times. I will not pretend to know when or if they will be back."

"Who are they? What do they want?" one of the Ambassadors asked.

Aydra chanced a glance at Draven. "We're not sure."

Murmurs broke out around the table.

"You're not sure what they want? You've simply met them on the beach and killed them instead of asking what they wanted?"

"The man said, 'Long live King Aeron of Mathis, ruler of Man'," Aydra said.

Voices paused around the room, and they all stared at her.

"What does that even mean? Who is King Aeron?" asked one of the councilmen.

"I don't know," Aydra said. "That's the point. These people are not to be trusted. They obviously want our lands."

"The Venari should bring some of them in for torture and questioning if there is a next time. Find out information rather than simply killing them as you've done so recklessly these last times. Perhaps these men could be useful," said Reid.

"Of what use could people not of our own be? They are clearly not Haerlandian and come from somewhere far across the seas. We don't know from where they were born, what they did to their land there, or why they would be traveling so far away from their homes," argued Aydra. "You cannot take this lightly. We must—"

"I'm not sure I understand why we are having this discussion," Ash interjected. "The strangers are not on the shores of Magnice."

"The Captain is right," said one of the Nobles before he turned to face Draven. "Do you have this situation handled, or are you and your men as worthless as the Chronicles say you are?"

Draven's fist curled in on itself. He glared at the standing people around him.

"We have it handled," he growled. "For now."

Rhaif clapped his hands over the table and said something, but Aydra didn't hear it. The people all stood and began chatting with each other absentmindedly. An audible restriction of frustration sounded in the back of her throat. That these were the ignorant leaders supposedly in charge of their people. Dismissing the very thought of war and strangers taking their shores as though they were safe.

Aydra fought the urge to slam her fist on the table or throw the glass at the wall.

A glass of wine was sat in front of her then, and she turned just in time to see Dorian sit in the chair at her side.

"They'll figure it out when they've got an army taking over their towns," he said to her.

Aydra lifted the cup to her lips and drank it in one swift gulp. "Idiots," she mumbled. "You would think an invasion would alarm them."

"They don't care unless it's on their land," Dorian insisted. "Also, Reid is right. We really should find out what they want."

Aydra sighed. "Yeah. Yeah, fine."

"I know, sister. It's one less instantaneous spill of blood your sword will meet," he mocked, "but you might find diplomacy can be an option."

"Killjoy," she bantered.

Dorian almost laughed at her. "Perhaps you should take Nyssa with you next time they come," he added.

A frown slipped onto her face. "Why?"

"Because she might be a twat half the time, but her negotiating skills have come to rival Rhaif's," he answered. "And she could use some time away from this place. See the land. Meet the people. Just remember to bring a bottle of nyghtfire."

"Why's that?"

"She gets a bit shy in front of crowds."

Aydra almost laughed, but the serious face Dorian had strewn across his own made her pause. "Oh, you're not joking."

"I'm not." He traded out his full cup for her empty one then and stood, holding out his arm. "Come on. Don't give them the satisfaction of your being bothered by their idiocy."

Aydra made her rounds with full glasses of wine, putting on the facade her crown so demanded she wear in front of the Council she knew would take it from her if given the chance.

No one spoke of the ships. No one spoke of politics. The only thing they seemed to want to talk to her about was she and Rhaif's birthing moons coming up in the next month, wanting to know if they'd decided on a party theme or decor. She had to lie and tell them all she was looking forward to it, that they'd planned a grand celebration for it.

Her reprieve came in the smell of herb once she escaped their clenches.

"There you are," she said in relief when she found him by the open window of the hall.

Lust rose in his eyes as he puffed on the pipe and looked at her deliberately. She felt her shoulders relax upon reaching him, and he held out the pipe to her.

"Careful, Venari," she uttered as she took the pipe from his hands. "Your gaze deceives you."

"Funny," he mused, turning back to the window. "I'm sure I saw you climax at least twice simply sitting at that table."

"Mm… Only the once actually," she said, feeling the swim of the herb and wine through her veins. "You're losing your touch."

"I doubt you'll be saying the same later."

The jagged breath left her lips, and she had to stifle a moan at the look he was giving her. Her arms hugged her chest. "Promise?" she managed in a quiet voice.

He scoffed quietly before he took another inhale, and he shifted his weight against the window. "Seems your brother is still in denial about the ships."

"It would seem he believes us to have killed ghosts of our own men."

"Pretty sure Belwarks' heads would just turn to ashes upon their beheading. Duarb would have claimed the bones of any of my men.

Their ears would have been pointed had they been Dreamers. And the Honest… well their necks would have had gills."

"Don't you think I've said all of these things to him?"

"Have you?"

She gave him a sideways glare and wrapped her arm over her chest, swirling the wine in her cup. "You're just trying to get a rise out of me," she muttered.

"I'm not," he replied simply. "Simply wondering what you've been doing here for a month when your brother acts as though—"

"You know he will not listen to me."

"Then make him."

"How exactly do you propose I do that? Ash told him the strangers were barely swordsmen. I showed Rhaif my own battle scars. Had Lex recount and affirm my story—"

"You could summon Nadir," he interjected.

She balked at him. "Summon Nadir? As if he would ever step into this kingdom without the use of force."

"He might. Offer him something he can't refuse."

"Like what? His life?"

He chucked under his breath. "I said summon. Not threaten."

"He's your friend. You summon him."

"I cannot summon anyone to a kingdom that isn't mine."

She paused and stared at him a moment, a plan formulating in her head. "Could you bring him to the meeting with the Nitesh if I asked it of him?"

"You mean escort the favored son of Lovi Piathos and commander of the Honest Army across the Preymoor and Bitratus Hills all the way to Magnice to ambush a meeting with the most powerful woman in all of the land?"

She raised an expectant brow at him and tilted her head.

He contemplated it a moment.

"Yeah, all right," he gave in with a shrug.

She almost laughed at his nonchalance.

His weight shifted, and he straightened to stand over her.

"You wanted danger in your life, my Queen… allow me to oblige."

"Knew there was another reason I kept you around," she grinned.

A huff of amusement left him, and he took one step closer to her, allowing his hair to fall over his face when he paused at her side. "Do you know what I'm going to do to you later?"

The chill ran down her spine with his breath tickling her ear. She turned around as he leaned his shoulder against the wall on the other side of her, and she took the pipe from his hand again.

The shyness she'd felt upon first seeing him had long faded with the swim of the herb and wine pulsing through her body, and she felt back to her regular self at his banter.

"Do tell, Hunter," she said wickedly.

His gaze deliberately danced over her as she exhaled the smoke from her lips. "Your Second will have to carry you to breakfast once I'm done."

"I'd rather have breakfast in bed."

Draven allowed a smirk to rise on his lips. "Have you ever begged, my Queen?"

"Never."

The corner of his lips rose higher. "Not even for your end?"

"The last time I needed such words, I threatened to hang the woman from her thumbs in the tower, and then I finished myself."

"You'll be too tied up to finish yourself tonight."

She liked where this was going.

"Tied up?" She nodded towards the buffet table. "I suggest you gain your strength, Hunter. You'll need to eat before such a night."

"No need. I've my feast right here in front of me," he purred as he leaned down to her ear. "I can smell your wetness, my Queen," he whispered. "You're lucky there are other people in this room."

Her thighs squeezed together as her fingers gripped the stone, eyes fluttering involuntarily at the vibration of his voice. Her hair raised on her arms and on the back of her neck, and she looked up at him through her curls. The servant's door in the shadows caught her eye.

"What people?" she uttered.

On her heel, she turned, leaving him standing there to stare after her as she disappeared through the back doorway.

Her back planted against the stone wall, and she waited for him to join her, feeling her thighs already squeezing together as the fantasy of him ripping her to shreds in the servants' hall flooded her mind.

So when the door opened and shut quietly ten minutes later, her breath quickened, and he wasted no time in pressing his lips to hers. The desperation of his kiss poured into her, and she couldn't stop herself from devouring him as she'd fantasized about doing for weeks.

She could already feel him firm against her abdomen. His hand quickly moved the slit in her dress to the side. He pulled back just briefly, the darkened smirk on his features making her wetter than she already was.

"Dirty girl," he uttered upon finding she'd worn no undergarments.

"Stop flirting and fuck me," she demanded.

He tugged the roots of her hair in response, causing her chin to lift towards him. His finger slipped torturously inside her. She leaned forward to kiss him, but he pulled back, keeping his face an inch away from hers as his thumb caressed her clit, two fingers plunging slowly in and out of her. She hardly realized her leg pulling up around his hip, granting him further access.

She tried concentrating on the moons light outside the window to keep herself from emitting the moans threatening her throat.

His hand moved from her hair and clapped over her lips. "Quiet, my Queen," he growled into her neck.

The warmth of his growl sent a shiver over her flesh. Her hands found their way to his neck, and he pressed himself flush against her, still torturing her with his hands. Her muscles tensed, and she gripped his hair in her fingers as she felt her undoing come so close.

But then he stepped back and let her go, leaving her standing breathlessly against the wall, unfinished. She had to grip the stone with her fingers to keep from stumbling forward.

His brows heightened in a dominating manner as he stared at her from across the walkway.

"If you think I'm going to beg…"

"I think that's exactly what you'll do."

She gave him a full once over and then brought her finger to her lips, sucking on her middle finger. "I told you, Venari—" she reached between her own legs and felt her hardened clit, continuing to stare at him as she threatened to finish herself. "—I am perfectly capable of finishing myself."

His face faltered only noticeably to her as she was staring at him so intently. She allowed her finger to slowly rub herself side-to-side, watching as his mouth slack, his eyes darken… Her eyes rolled in the back of her head as she bucked her hips against her own fingers, and she reminded herself to keep quiet.

She could have ended herself so quickly, but she was enjoying watching him stare at her. And when she opened her eyes, she hated him all over again. He'd taken his great length from his pants and was stroking it in his hand as he watched her. Her chest heaved, feeling heat rise on her throat. She rubbed herself harder, allowing her mouth to open slightly, a low moan emitting from her throat. And then, she willed herself to cross the space between them.

His eyes danced over her face from beneath his hooded brows. She reached out to touch her hand against his on his cock. His eyes fluttered as she moved his hand and teased the tip of him, already feeling the stick of his own on his head. He leaned down to kiss her, but she pressed a finger to his lips.

"Let's see how quiet our Venari King can be."

Her knees hit the cold stone, and she took him into her mouth before he could utter a response. She heard an audible breath leave him, along with a slew of curse words. Her tongue played with his tip, finger barely touching him as she enjoyed the noise of his quickened breaths in her ears. She felt his hand in her hair, and she tilted her head back to gaze up and him. He'd clapped his own hand over his mouth and closed his eyes. She paused and reached up for his other hand, making him look down at her as she sucked on one of his fingers.

"My castle. My rules. I want you to watch as I bring you to your end. *My King.*"

A deep growl emitted from his throat, and she moved his hands to her head as she took his length deep down her throat, mouth almost struggling around his girth. His weight shifted, and she heard him mutter a low, "Fuck, Aydra," under his breath. She moved his length moved in and out of her mouth, allowing her tongue to continue to rake the underside of him and tease the tip of him between strokes.

She grasped his backside with one of her hands, the other wrapping itself around his length as she tongued the tip. His grunts filled her ears, and she knew he was getting close. The curl and dig of his fingertips in her hair made her own moan emit from her throat, sucking him harder.

And when he finally came apart in her throat, she didn't stop. Continuing to savor and swallow and choke on the juices flowing from his insides. An audible moan emitted from him, and he grasped at her hair in an attempt to pull her away. She allowed her tongue to rake him again as she licked the last bit of him off, sucking on his length until he began to flinch in her mouth. He yanked her hair back, and she was forced up onto her feet, a chill of goosebumps running over her skin at the tug he had on the roots of her hair.

"So not very quiet," she said, pleased that she had caused him to lose himself.

The bliss of his undoing continued to radiate over his features. He merely stared at her a moment, his fingertips grazing her throat as his breaths evened.

"What?" she asked.

"Fucking... *You*..." He was staring at her as though she was something new, as though it was the first time he'd looked upon her face, and he was trying to figure out her darkest secrets.

"Draven?" she said, feeling her weight shift.

His thumb grazed the corner of her lip, and his eyes danced over her a moment more before he once again kissed her. Desperately, this time. He grasped her hips hard in his hands and hoisted her up onto his waist, fingertips digging into her flesh as he turned them so that her back crashed into the glass of the window with an audible echo in the quiet hall. His mouth was on her throat, fingers between her legs, and she felt him growing once more against her.

She grabbed hold of the rough window siding, the rock scratching her palms. Her eyes closed as his finger delved between her thighs, and then she felt him tug on himself. He pulled back to meet her eyes, the look in his gaze something maniacal she'd not seen before. She gasped as she felt him fill her, and her body limped on the spot, mouth agape just as his was.

His teeth tugged at the skin of her collarbone, pushing her flush against him as he began to thrust inside her. The stone ravaged her bared butt. A moan threatened her lips, and he shoved his hand over her mouth. Her fingers gripped so tightly to the rock she felt it break beneath her nail beds. The back of her head hit the glass, and she arched herself against his torso, feeling her end coming close. And then he kissed her fiercely as he fell apart with her, both their moans stifled by the mouth of the other.

Her legs wobbled when her feet hit the ground. She blinked as she brought herself back to reality, forcing her breaths to even.

"Perhaps you should come to my room later instead of yours," he said as he buttoned his pants.

She pushed her hand through her hair to try and tame it, staring at the window to see her reflection. "Why's that?" she breathed.

He stepped forward and pulled her hoisted dress down around her hips to hide the scuffle, then straightened over her, his torso flush against her back, fingers wrapping softly around her waist.

"Because I want to hear your screams when I taste you."

His breath on her neck made a chill rise on her skin, and the words made her heart flutter. She gulped as she turned, and then she reached up to straighten his ivory bone crown.

"Careful, Venari," she muttered. "We'll never make it to dinner."

His arms settled on either side of her, palms pressing into the stone as he leaned over her figure. "Would that be so bad?" he said against her cheek.

Her lips twisted upwards just slightly, and her chin tilted up, nose nudging his. "It wouldn't."

He kissed her again, and her heart faltered in her chest. It was hard to pull away from him, hard to distract herself from the magnetism of his kiss, his touch. It was nothing like any other relationship she'd ever bothered herself with before. He did something to her that she couldn't explain, as though his touch made her body weaken and strengthen all at once, as though his simply being near her made her feel more alive than ever.

She forced herself to pull away from him a few moments later, and he grabbed her backside in his hands, roughly and forcefully enough that she felt her mouth sag, the corners of her lips quirk upwards in a playful manner. He leaned forward and bit her bottom lip just as he smacked her bottom, and she fought the urge to shove him back against the wall again.

"I'll find you later," she whispered as she let him go.

Her breath left her as she stepped away, and he held onto her hand for as long as he could, fingertips burning with his skin against hers. She caught a final glimpse of him in the light of the moons, and the domineering smirk on his face as he gave her a slow once over, caused heat to rise on her cheeks.

She could have stayed in his arms the rest of the night as she'd done in the forest. She could have surrendered herself to his embrace for the rest of her life. But teasing him was fun as well. And she liked the game they were playing.

"I see you had a pre-dinner snack," came a voice the moment she stepped out into the light of the room again.

Her heart skipped, but then she realized who it was. She paused her step and straightened her sleeve. "Lex."

"My Queen." Lex stepped in front of her and reached up to Aydra's crown to straighten it. "The next time you decide to have a romp in the servants' tunnel, you'll tell me. You don't know how many I had to stop from going through the doorway. And be a bit swifter next time. People were beginning to wonder where you'd run off to." She pushed her fingers through Aydra's hair and then stepped back, but Aydra didn't miss the curl of her nostrils.

"What?" Aydra asked.

"You smell like sex," Lex muttered. "Let's talk a walk outside before Ash comes pouncing."

"Let's hope he knows better than to think I would allow him anywhere near my bed after his display after the battle," Aydra said.

Lex almost laughed. "Men are stupid. He probably has no idea."

42

"Is that what you do?" Draven asked the next morning.

They were on the beach, tucked away around the bend where she usually liked to take her swim. Aydra stripped to her underwear and the lace fabric triangles over her breasts that corseted down around her waist. The surf came up and tickled her as she grinned at Draven over her shoulder.

"Take your clothes off," she told him.

"Shouldn't you be doing Queen things?" he asked. "Like taking care of your people? Seeing the Ambassadors and the Council off?"

"I have never been the one to send them off. Rhaif usually deals with that. I am the security commander. I deal with criminals, which, let's be honest, there aren't many of those here. So, therefore, I am allowed a few hours a day of peace should I choose to take it," she said as she pulled her thick hair up into a messy bun with a strip of fabric.

His arms crossed over his chest. "Is that actually true?" he asked.

"Not at all." She sighed upon looking back at him, seeing him watching her apprehensively. "Come on, Draven. Get out of your head. Have a bit of fun. You're allowed to indulge yourself once in a while."

His feet hit the edge of the water, and she noticed his hesitation.

"You've never been in this ocean, have you?" she asked.

"These are the bleeding waters of my giver's enemy," he replied with a nod towards the waterfall coming down beneath Arbina's roots high on the cliffside. "So no, I've not been in this one. Only Lovi's waters."

"Is there a difference?"

"Lovi's water doesn't try to kill me."

She grinned and walked out of the water towards him. Her lips pressed to his, kissing him deeply and chilling as his fingertips tickled her bare skin. She pulled back after a few moments, biting her lip as their eyes locked. "You're with me," she promised. "The creatures like me. Nothing will hurt you."

"Except you?" he asked, eyeing the blade on the garter attached around her thigh.

She almost laughed. "Only me."

The water lapped at their chests moments later as she wrapped her legs around him, unable to keep herself from kissing his lips as the sun cascaded onto their bodies. Him. In her home. In her waters. The sun glistening and reflecting back to her in the pale of his sage eyes. Her heart filled when she would pull back to stare at him. The look he would give her, the one that he'd had on his face the day before. As though he were confused about her presence, unbelieving of her in front of him made her entire body warm and not from the sunlight.

"Why do you look at me like that?" she whispered.

His hand pressed to her cheek. "I didn't expect you," he admitted. "You. This person. This… amazing, fearless, stunning, compassionate woman… Each time I look upon your face, it is as though it is my first time seeing it. These years before, when we hated each other, I feel as though I hated a different person."

Her hands wrapped behind his neck, and her nose nudged his. "As do I."

"Do you know what I used to do when I came out here?" she asked later once they'd settled onto the sand.

"Talk to the fish?"

She huffed amusedly under her breath. "No. The fish don't really talk back. They just stare at me like I'm crazy."

"Maybe they have a point."

She nudged him in the side and then stared back at the ocean, allowing a long sigh to leave her lips before she spoke again.

"I used to hold myself beneath the water," she admitted. "Stay there until I began to panic. To feel my own lungs struggle against the current over my head, wondering if I'd be enough to bring myself above the water again." She looked down at her hands, nervousness spreading. "I know it sounds stupid. Childish—"

"It's not stupid," he interjected.

She glanced sideways to see the sincere expression on his face. "After so many years here of just... *nothing*. Being told by my olders and the Council to sit beside my brother and keep quiet. To listen behind closed doors as men discussed things they thought me not capable of comprehending. To have to be numb to feelings I should have allowed myself to sink beneath. That no matter how special our mother may have treated me, that I was still nothing more than a simple princess. I have craved so much more for so long. To feel something. Anything." The squeeze of his hand around hers made her heart constrict. "Don't coddle me, Draven," she begged in a soft voice. "Don't agree with me for the sake of agreement."

"You should know well enough that coddling is not exactly my strong suit."

"I mean... what I tell you. Don't pity me. I have lived a great life here. My core simply craves more. To feel my heart beat at a faster pace than this resting rate. To feel adrenaline in my bones. A restlessness in my muscles. Being out there on the field with you, with those soldiers... I've never felt such life as I did in those few days. To live life rustling through the trees, combating each other with swords and laughter. To be adventurous. It's what I was meant to do. Not sit here on a throne in pretty dresses."

Draven didn't speak. He didn't turn towards her, instead simply staring out at the ocean. She noticed a daze wash over his features as though he were thinking of something far away. His fist clenched and unclenched at his side, and she saw the vein in his neck straining just noticeably to the surface. The sight of it made her wary, and she started to reach for him.

"Draven?"

"I wish I knew the peace you speak of," he said in a quiet voice, his hand moving away from hers. "You've no idea how lucky you have it here. To not have to worry about crime in your streets, the largest threat being when the sheepherders do not have enough of the luxury milks your Dreamers crave. You've no idea this adrenaline you crave, this so-called adventure you say you want. I live in that every day. If you wanted true darkness, all you had to do was stay in the forest a little longer. I can show you darkness."

Her heart emptied as she thought about the things he did not know. Blue flames flashed before her eyes, and a ringing began in her ears.

"What— with the creatures that crowd your forest?" she managed. "The shadows?"

"No," he said firmly. "Not the creatures."

"Then what?" she argued, feeling the frustration rise as he seemed to mock her. "The ships? Having to defend the realm against strangers? Your Infi broth—"

A knife found the skin of her throat. Her heart dropped, and he pulled her head back by her hair, exposing her throat.

"You want to know darkness, my Queen?" he growled over her. "Tell me how many infants you've stuck your own blade through," he dared in a quiet voice. "Tell me how many wailing children's bones you've watched be ripped from their insides and pulled into the dirt beneath your giver's roots. Tell me how you would look upon the face of a child you've watched grow for ten years, only to have him marked with the cursed fate instead of the Venari, to be forced with the choice of killing it or allowing it live and its life threaten this entire land."

He released her with such force that she fell into the sand. The knife landed in the ground at her feet, and her body chilled at the glare he stared at her with as he stood.

"Do not wish for a darkness you know nothing of," he breathed.

"Perhaps you should point this darkness towards your own giver instead of taking it out on—"

"Why would I point this on my giver?" Draven spat. "My giver has been the scapegoat of every race on this land. He has been accused of things over the last Age he never did."

"Like what? Like seducing my own mother into slavery? Betraying her for his creatures?"

"Lies of your Chronicles," he hissed.

"Then tell me the truth of it. Tell me what your Honest Scrolls say of it."

Draven sighed heavily, and she could see the vein in his neck pulsating. "I should have known this would never work," he uttered under his breath.

Aydra's stomach dropped. "Excuse me?" she managed.

His hands were on his hips, and he turned back towards her, gaze darting over her heaving figure. "I have to go," he breathed.

Her heart throbbed in her ears as she stared after his retreating figure.

"I told you you wouldn't love me after," she called.

He paused in his step, seemingly frozen to the ground on which he stood. His fist tightened and released at his side once more. His head turned just slightly, and she met his eyes over his shoulder.

"You're wrong."

43

Aydra tried not to let her broken heart show in her features in the weeks between the meetings.

She poured herself into helping Lex prepare for the Belwark trials happening in the coming days, trying to keep her mind off her own stupidity of allowing Draven to leave her kingdom in anger. But at night, she found herself hardly able to sleep, curled up in his shirt and toying with the pipe he'd given her as she stared at the ceiling or the moons outside.

During the Dead Moons cycle, she crawled outside onto the roof of one of the towers each night, and she sat in silence, wishing she could hear the Noctuan cries and songs from the Forest in her ears. On one of these nights, Nyssa followed her and sat with her, her head lying on her sister's shoulder as they stared at the bright stars above them.

"You didn't want to go to the forest for this turn?" Nyssa asked her.

The thought made Aydra's stomach knot. "Not this time."

Nyssa rolled over to her stomach then and began to play with Aydra's hair. "You seem… not yourself these last couple of weeks," she said, avoiding Aydra's gaze.

Aydra's heart skipped. "What do you mean?"

"I mean… You were you, and then there were a few weeks when you were a lot happier, and now these last couple of weeks… I'm—I'm not sure. You seem sort of… sad."

Aydra had thought she did well at hiding the things her core dared not show even herself. "Blame it on the pressures of the kingdom," she sighed, giving her sister a forced smile.

A small smirk rose on Nyssa's lips at her sister's lie. "You know, Dorian told me a secret. He said you met someone."

"Dorian exaggerates," Aydra mumbled. "Besides, it doesn't matter. He and I had a fight. It's over. I don't know that he'll ever want to speak with me again."

"I doubt that's true," Nyssa argued. "It's you."

Aydra sighed and settled back onto the blanket they'd brought with them. Nyssa sank back down beside her, and Aydra wrapped an arm around her shoulders.

They fell asleep talking about the stars that night.

The week before the great meeting came the Belwark Trial day.

Lex had been excited about it for weeks, training with Dorian and Aydra on their downtime to keep her skills sharp. She wasn't expected to participate, but she'd volunteered to be one of the opponents Belwarks would fight to climb in their ranks. She and Rhaif's Second, Bard, were, after all, the fiercest fighters in the kingdom. If any lower-ranked Belwark could take either, they would be put forth as contenders for the prince or princess to choose as their Seconds.

There were ten fighting for the role of Dorian's Second that day.

Lex was already standing outside Aydra's door when she was ready. Aydra's hair was braided back on one side, the gold of her crown sitting in the thickness of her curls. She'd picked an outfit the day before that she felt represented her own Second well— thigh-high lace-up black boots, a fitted sheath dress that hugged her curves and landed just above the boots on her thighs, leather braces and small belts wrapped around her waist, and a garter to hold up the thick cotton stockings above her boots. Her black leather belt hung low on her hips— her sword dangling against her exposed thigh. The matching cotton arm sleeves pulled from her hands up to the inside of her biceps. She'd found a single shoulder pad adorned with spikes. The long black cape billowed behind her when she walked.

"Well, well," Lex said, brows elevated as she pushed off the wall, "Didn't realize you were competing as well," she added with a wink.

Aydra forced a smirk to the surface despite her depleting heart. "Thought I would show my support for my favorite person, let the greenhorns know who they're truly challenging today." She reached out, stroking her finger on the pointed winged shoulder pads Lex adorned on her shoulders. "I do love these."

Lex smiled at her. "As do I."

Nyssa met them in the next hall. Lex and Aydra both stopped in their tracks upon seeing her. She was wearing knee-high boots with buckles, slim navy pants, a brown corset wrapped tight around her petite waist above her hips, creating a silhouette Aydra had rarely seen on her sister. The navy shirt she wore sat off her shoulders, dark brown fur along the trim, long snug sleeves wrapped with small brown belts around her arms. Her sword dangled on her hip as Aydra's did. Her hair was pulled halfway up, tiny braids on either side of her head. Her thick sideways bangs swept over her left eye, and she was adjusting the buckle on her arm when she saw them.

Nyssa's cheeks reddened upon catching their eyes, and she shifted the weight on her feet. "It's too much, isn't it?" she asked shakily.

Aydra's eyes traveled over her sister's attire, feeling a smile rise on her face. "Did you pick this out or Dorian?" she asked.

Nyssa fumbled with her sleeve, avoiding Aydra's gaze. "I did."

Aydra stepped forward. "I love it."

Nyssa's honey orbs lit up, and her chest swelled with a great inhale. Aydra ran her hand through Nyssa's hair, giving it a fluff over her shoulders and taming the strays that had fallen out of her braids. She reached for Nyssa's black and gold tiara, straightening it in her thick cinnamon hair.

"Chin up, shoulders back," Aydra told her. "Don't let them see you fumble or blush. Everything you do is on purpose. If you trip, you meant to. If you stumble on words, you meant to. You are their next Queen. Make them remember it."

Nyssa gave her a deliberate nod. "Right," she managed.

"Just channel your inner Aydra," Lex said with a wink as she came to stand beside them.

Aydra's expression furrowed back at her. "What does that mean?"

Lex smirked down at Nyssa, and Nyssa grinned a grin Aydra hardly recognized.

Aydra looked between them. "I leave you two alone for ten days, and now you've inside jokes," she mocked.

Lex chuckled under her breath. "Come on. You'll both make me late for my fight."

The stadium was high on the cliff east of their castle. The road around the castle walls was steep. Dreamers and Belwarks both made the trek up the path and filled the great seats. Aydra and Nyssa entered the stadium to their platform. The crowd gave a great cheer upon their entering. A few of the Village Nobles had made the journey, each giving bows and widened eyes upon seeing the pair reach where they would stand. Shortly behind them approached Rhaif and Dorian. A wide smile was spread on Dorian's face as he waved at the jeering people, as the day was for him, after all.

Aydra swore he was getting taller by the day.

She turned her attention to Lex standing at her side, watching her Second as she examined her sword in the bright glint of sunlight coming down on them.

"Are you sure about this?" Aydra asked her.

Lex whirled her sword in her hand, staring out at the coliseum. "Looks like a good day to slit kneecaps, don't you think?" she answered with a coy brow.

A deep breath entered Aydra's lungs, and she nodded. "Yes, it does." She gave her Second a deliberate once over, allowing a smile to rise on her lips. "Show them the ferocity they'll need to be worthy of the Second Sun position."

Lex winked at Aydra one last time before turning on her heel and going back down the steps towards the tunnel entrance.

The words Rhaif spoke as he announced the trials, Aydra barely heard. Her raven landed on her shoulder, Nyssa's eagle on the banister. The crowd cheered upon his announcing Lex as the champion volunteer. Her reputation preceded her, and Aydra's chest swelled with pride.

Dorian's figure came to stand beside her and Nyssa, and Dorian pressed a goblet of wine into her hands. Aydra glanced sideways at him. She noticed how calm he seemed, the cool of his white blue gaze staring at the rumble of people around them, smile spread over his growing features.

"For someone whose Second is being chosen, you certainly are calm," Aydra muttered to Dorian.

"It's Corbin," Dorian muttered as he pressed the goblet to his lips.

"Come again?" Aydra said, brows creasing.

"Discussed it with Lex yesterday," he answered. "I want Corbin. He's of your company and not Rhaif's. He's trained beneath Lex on more than one occasion. He's bold, brave, loyal..." He paused a moment, the pair watching the Belwarks warm up and stretch around Lex below them. "These trials are simply a formality on this round. Something to keep the people entertained."

Aydra stared at her younger brother. "Why are you growing up so quickly?" she mused.

Dorian smiled a crooked smirk at her, but did not respond directly to her question. "Tell me, sister... why did your lover run off so hastily last he was here?" he chose to ask. "Did you scare him?"

Aydra froze at the mention of it, but she tried to brush it off. "You know me. Scaring is what I do best," she managed.

The horns blew, and Aydra looked back to the stadium. Lex crouched in the middle of the Belwark circle, eyes darting around her as she dared each of them to storm at her.

"Are you nervous?" Nyssa asked her.

"About Lex fighting? No," Aydra said fast.

"You're a terrible liar."

"Shut up," Aydra grumbled. "As are you." She pushed her arms behind her back pointedly and watched Lex as she moved, knees bent, sword drawn. "Pay attention to how Lex remembers where each of them is at all time," she told Nyssa. "She's no powers of an eagle or otherwise to tell her where her enemy is approaching from. She must use her senses. When *you* fight, you'll have your eagle—" Aydra reached a finger up to her raven, giving him a scratch under his neck "—he will watch out for you, let you know from what side your enemy is approaching."

The fight began, and the shouts of the Belwarks echoed in the air.

Swords clashed. Some fought with each other, each of them charging at Lex on their own time. Lex was fast. She dodged and moved from their advances, bouncing around them and running at the ones who annoyed her with sweeping glances.

"Do they ever use bows in Belwark trials?" Nyssa asked.

"I've never seen it," Aydra answered. "How are you doing with your training?" she asked, having been absent from her sessions since before the last meeting due to helping Lex prepare for the trials.

"Fantastic," Dorian said from the other side of her. He beamed around Aydra at his sister, and Nyssa rolled her eyes at his proud face. Aydra smiled at the tug Nyssa had on her lips, biting back the grin that so obviously threatened her.

"He's exaggerating as usual," Nyssa argued.

"She's being modest," Dorian muttered. "Should have seen her yesterday on the cliffs. Firing arrows three at a time now."

Aydra's smile widened. "Perhaps I'll join you tomorrow. See how much your brother is truly exaggerating."

"No—"

"You don't want me to come?" Aydra asked, confused by Nyssa's quick reply.

"It's not that. It's just..." Nyssa tucked her hair behind her ear, and Aydra could see her chest beginning to heave. "I mean—"

"She thinks you're intimidating," Dorian butted in.

Aydra frowned between them. "What? Intimidating?"

"Shut up, Dorian," Nyssa hissed through clenched teeth.

"Wants to be the best she can be before she shows you anything," Dorian continued.

"I swear, Dorian, if you don't shut your trap—"

"I'm quite sure she thinks you'll disown her if she's a disappointment."

The eagle screeched and fluttered his great wings in Dorian's direction.

Dorian balked at the beast. "Down, bird," he muttered, shaking his hands at him.

Aydra took a long swig of her wine, using it to cover the laughter threatening her lips.

Dorian leaned closer to Aydra, whispering in her ear. "She also has a plan and wants to go back to the Forest so she can show up—"

Nyssa grabbed something on her side. The glint of iron in the sunlight made Aydra snap into motion, but she wasn't fast enough. A tiny sliver of silver rushed in front of her face—

Dorian caught it between his flamed fingers.

"There's my sister," he grinned.

"What the Infi is going on down there?" they heard Rhaif hiss. "Behave yourselves!"

Aydra pressed her amused lips together and looked between her youngers. She took the weapon out of Dorian's hand, noticing the proud smile spread across his features as he smirked at Nyssa. The weapon was not larger than her pinky. A small blade shaped like a feather, razor-sharp at the tip and on the sides. Aydra handed it back to her sister.

"Careful. We'll make mother mad," Aydra muttered, glaring at Rhaif over her shoulder.

Their attentions turned back to the fight below then, and they saw only five left to battle Lex. Lex knocked through the remaining ones, forcing two to yield. Aydra moved closer to the banister, out of line with her brother and sister, and she began to pace slowly despite herself at the sight of Lex beginning to tire. The last three in the stadium were nearly as fast as her.

"I thought you told me not to pace," Nyssa muttered behind her.

Aydra took her finger out of her mouth and bit the inside of her cheek instead. "I lied." She paused and wrapped her hands around her chest, forcing herself to stand stationary as she watched the scene.

Lex was heaving, the scratch on her face showing the reddened ash insides of a Belwark. The three left to yield were dancing around her. The final two would battle one another instead of her. She only had the one left to put on the ground.

Aydra knew she was favoring Corbin, trying to strike down the other two from Bard's company.

Give her a reminder, Aydra told her raven.

Her raven flew off the railing. He circled over the stadium and gave a chortle she knew Lex would hear. Lex straightened and cracked her neck, sword whirling in her hand again.

Bard's Belwarks charged at her. She blocked their advances and shoved them. They gathered themselves up off the ground and rushed at her again and again. Corbin jumped in, taking care of one for her as Lex struck with the other. And when it was finally only she, Corbin, and the last, Bard bellowed a horn to cease the battle.

"Our final challengers for the title of Second Sun to the Prince," Rhaif announced. "Belwark Corbin, and Belwark Jhost. A round of pride for our Queen's Second, Hilexi."

The crowd cheered loudly. Lex was doubled-over at the knees, but she jolted her sword high into the air upon hearing her name. As she walked off towards the tunnel entrance, Aydra gave her siblings a squeeze.

"Can you two not fight long enough for Corbin to be given the title?" she asked them.

"Where are you going?" Nyssa asked.

"Find Lex. Make sure she's okay."

Aydra gave Dorian one more ruffle of his hair and kissed Nyssa's temple hard before turning and practically running out of the box. She skipped down the steps towards the tunnel, hoping to catch her Second before she went too far.

Lex was leaning against the wall, clutching at her chest as she tried to regain her breath. She did a double-take upon seeing Aydra approach, and a smile spread over her face. "You were worried," she mocked.

"I wasn't," Aydra argued.

"Sending your raven to screech over my head says otherwise," Lex grinned.

Aydra nearly laughed as she reached her. The scratch on Lex's face was gaped open, but blood did not trickle from her insides. A look of fire poured from inside the wound, black ash around it like molten rock. Aydra reached out and took the great sword from Lex's hands, pushing it into her belt. She helped take her shoulder pads off and then draped them across her forearm.

As Lex straightened and finally regained her breath, Aydra wrapped an arm around her. "Come along, my Sun. I'll make you food myself."

"Should we wait on Corbin?" Lex asked.

Aydra glanced at the deteriorating battle going on still in the stadium. "Dorian can make his own Second victory food. I'm making my best friend a meal."

"So raw carrots in bone broth?"

"No," Aydra glared. "Thought I would try a Venari recipe. One of Balandria's. Maybe I won't burn them."

Lex snorted.

"Shut up."

44

It was the next Council meeting before she heard from Draven again.

The big Council meeting.

Every race from Haerland convened in one castle.

The meeting that would go down in the Honest Scrolls and the Chronicles as The Gathering.

They'd even asked that the High Elders from the Blackhand mountains join them, as well as sent invitations to the Honest people instead of her simply hoping Draven would bring him.

Her nerves were already getting the better of her. After not hearing from Draven, she was more than concerned about his simply not wanting to be with her. She worried about the peace they'd come to share, whether he would treat her as his equal as he'd done before or if a feud would start over dinner.

Aydra wondered if perhaps he'd decided to let her go.

Her stomach was in knots as the day of his arrival came. She hugged her arms around her chest and stared out of the window on that morn, desperate to see him come in on horseback.

"You're being ludicrous," Lex said, lying on Aydra's bed and popping grapes into her mouth. "Draven isn't stupid."

"What do you mean?"

"I mean, no man ever gets to know you, enjoys your company, and then runs away from you," Lex replied.

"They do if they're scared," Aydra argued.

Lex huffed amusedly. "This is the Venari King... Your match. Your equal. Your death of moons in the Noctuans' eyes," she said dramatically with a roll of her eyes. "I highly doubt you could scare him."

Aydra's brows elevated at her over her shoulder, and Lex chuckled.

"Right, okay, maybe you could scare him a bit, but—"

The door opened, and in walked Bard, his hands pushed behind his back. Lex sat up, and Aydra frowned from the window.

"Good morning, Bard," Aydra said, crossing her arms over her chest. "To what—"

"The king wishes to see you in his study," Bard said simply.

Aydra exchanged a look with Lex, and Lex stood from the bed.

"I'll escort her—"

"I'm fine," Aydra insisted, pressing her hand to Lex's chest.

"I am coming with you," Lex argued.

"No," Aydra affirmed. "You will find my youngers and make sure they are ready for the meeting."

"My Queen—"

"Now, Hilexi," Aydra demanded.

Lex's eyes softened, but she gave Aydra a bow nonetheless. "Yes, ma'am."

Lex left out the door, and Aydra turned to Bard with a forced smile. "Very well, Bard. Take me to him."

Rhaif was pacing in front of his great fireplace when she was announced. She stepped inside his study without a word and stationed herself a few steps from the door as they shut behind her. Only when he paused and came around the front of his desk did she say anything.

"You needed something?" she asked.

Rhaif fumbled with the ring on his finger and stared downwards in silence for a few moments. She didn't know whether to be wary of his silence or if, perhaps, he was figuring out the words to speak.

"This week..." he finally began. "This week, you are not to bring up the ships. You are not to bring up becoming allies. You are not to bring up your silly notion of this... this *Echelon* you've so spewed about."

The darkened tone in which he spoke made her ears ring. "You expect me to sit back and speak nothing while you and the Council talk about trading routes and qualities of goods in front of the rest of the races of our land instead of discussing an enemy coming on our shores? Instead of discussing the unity across all our races that we will need to possess to truly strike these people down?"

His eyes traveled over her, and he pushed his shoulders back. "Yes."

"You can't be serious."

"I am," he affirmed.

"And if I refuse?"

His eyes flashed fire, and she watched his fingertips blacken.

But his threat would not back her down this time.

"If you think you can subdue me in front of people I have gone into battle with, you're wrong. These people are my friends—"

Rhaif's low laughter filled her ears. "Friends..." he mocked, shaking his head. "You're the Sun Queen. You have no friends."

"Your inability to make people love you is not my problem."

He grasped her arms in his hands and shoved her against the mantle, her head banging backward into the bookcase.

"Do not make me subdue you," he warned.

"You cannot silence me."

Aydra's forehead met his nose, and Rhaif dropped her, doubling over and holding his bleeding nose in his hands. Aydra ran for the door.

The floor turned to fire beneath her.

It paralyzed her feet, and she fell to her knees as the pain seized her entire body. Breath stopped in her throat. She pulled in every direction for the crows, the ravens, anything to help her.

A swarm of crows poured in through the window, and she heard him cry out as they attacked.

But fire engulfed the room. Cores voided and broke around her. Her heart stung, and she opened her eyes.

Black feathers filled the air like snow.

"NO!"

He grasped her neck in his hands and lifted her to her feet. His lip was broken. Scratches covered his forehead and cheeks. His nose continued to bleed.

But the rage in his eyes did not fade.

"Perhaps this will remind you of your place," he hissed.

"—Put her down."

Rhaif looked twice towards the door. Aydra seized the lapse in his grip and kicked. Her foot struck his side, and he doubled-over, clenching his rib. Her burned knees hit the floor again. She winced in the agony of her painful flesh, barely able to keep her eyes open as Dorian emerged from the shadows of the now open door.

"Stay out of this," Rhaif warned.

Dorian's irises turned black, his own lightning form streaking around his eyes, and Aydra could just see the tips of his fingers turning charcoal. He stood his ground over her.

"Get out," Dorian said as navy fire flared on his fingertips.

A warning.

Rhaif straightened, eyes blazing at Dorian's defiant figure. "This doesn't concern you."

"I said get out," Dorian repeated. "Or should you like me to tell the kingdom how you truly earned the high crown at eighteen?"

Rhaif stared at the Prince, but he didn't argue. He grabbed a handkerchief from atop his desk and held it to his bleeding nose. "Council meeting in an hour," he uttered. "I expect you to be there, Prince."

The servants' entry door closed behind him at the back of the room. Aydra pushed herself up to her elbows just as Dorian knelt beside her.

She swatted his hand away when he went to grab her. "Don't you *ever* interfere again," she hissed at him.

Dorian's entire body caved at her words. "What?" he asked, voice barely above a whisper.

"I said—" She forced herself up to a seated position as she grasped onto the chaise to try and pull herself to her feet. "—Do not *ever* interfere with our fighting again. It is not your place—"

"He was hurting you," Dorian argued.

"And if you ever see it again, you are to walk the other way. Let him finish, and then you can come in after he is gone with our mother's waters for healing. You are *never* to walk in on it, *never* to put yourself in his line of fire."

"You are my sister—"

Her knees gave out from under her as she pleaded, "I cannot lose you, Dorian!" in such a broken shout that a lump rose in her throat.

Dorian put his hands under her arms, and he helped her into the chair. She sucked in the tears threatening her as he sat at her side, and then she reached out to cup his cheek in her hand.

"I cannot lose you too."

Draven was late arriving in Magnice.

He and Balandria had slept in longer than they should have on the journey up, so he'd barely any time to do more than change his clothes upon their arrival. He was nervous. He'd not spoken with Aydra since the last he'd been at Magnice, and he had meant to get there early enough to talk with her before showing up at the meeting.

But he didn't have time.

Dorian met him just outside the Chamber doors as he, too, rounded the corner in haste.

"Prince," Draven called to him.

"Forest King," Dorian acknowledged, taking Draven's hand and then hugging him.

Dorian's face was pale. Draven squinted at the Prince upon parting from him.

"What's wrong?" Draven asked.

Dorian started to speak, but his mouth shut just as he saw someone over Draven's shoulder. Draven turned to find Rhaif coming towards them, his purple cloak billowing out behind him.

"Tell you later," Dorian mumbled as he pushed open the door.

Draven fell in behind him and took his seat at the quiet table. Dorian joined Nyssa at the back of the room, where he said something to her, and her eyes widened.

The air was thick with an energy that made him wary. The Council spoke in hushed tones around him. The doors opened once more. Rhaif came striding in, the rest of the table standing for him, and Draven felt his eyes narrow as he saw Rhaif's face more clearly.

His nose seemed slightly off-center, but there was no bruise. His bottom lip was red as though it had recently been healed of a deep scratch. There were red markings on his cheeks and forehead.

Rhaif snapped his finger and pointed at the chair Aydra usually sat in, and a Belwark came forward to remove it.

"Will the Queen not be joining us?" Ash asked.

"Ah—" Rhaif took his seat and clasped his hands together atop the table. "My sister is feeling a bit under the weather today. She sends her regards. Not to worry, though. She'll be at the meeting with the Nitesh at the end of the week."

Draven's eyes flickered to Dorian's at the back of the room, and

Jack Whitney

Dorian's head moved just noticeably.

"I do thank you all for coming earlier. We have much to discuss before she arrives. I'd like to make sure we are all on the same page." Rhaif leaned forward and clasped his hands above the table.

"We have also requested for the Elders of the Blackhand Mountains to join us, and I have received word that the leaders of the Honest army, as well as Lovi Piathos, will also be arriving." His gaze moved to Draven, and Draven watched his jaw flinch, obviously hiding something, as he shifted in his seat. "This meeting... It will be a celebration of our uniting lands. Every race of Haerland in one room. This is what we have planned for."

Draven sat in a haze for much of the meeting, his mind unable to concentrate on anything. He tapped his middle finger on the table the entire time, itching to get away from the fake laughs emitting from Rhaif's lips.

When Rhaif finally stood from his seat and announced they would retire for dinner, Draven started to leave the room without glancing back at the staring Council.

An arm grabbed him as he reached the door, and he nearly ran into it at the strength in which the person held him back.

Lex's green eyes tore through him.

He paused and straightened in front of her. "Where is she?"

"She's okay," Lex promised. "Do not go bursting in as though you are there to save her."

Draven ran his hand through his hair, and he took the crown off his head. "Right," he finally breathed. "Why was she not here?" he asked.

Lex's eyes darted to Rhaif, and her weight shifted as she turned back to him. "That is not my place to say."

"Hilexi..."

"Using my full name will get you no further to the truth," she assured him. "Evacuate the urgency from your core. She needs her equal. Not her savior."

45

Aydra watched the sun go down from beneath the poisoned waters of the tub. For a long while, she wondered what lie Rhaif had made up about her not being there. She wondered what Lex had told Draven and whether he'd cared that she wasn't there.

Dorian helped her raven bring the water up to her tub after the fight that morning. The look on his face made Aydra's heart weep every time she met his eyes.

"You shouldn't see me like this," she told him. "I am fine. Go to the meeting."

"You shouldn't *be* like this," he argued. "I don't understand—"

"No, you don't," Aydra insisted. She met his stark blue eyes, and she reached out for his hand. "Promise me you'll always support your sister. No matter if she ever does anything stupid or anything the Council may deem 'out of turn'. Promise me you'll always stand at her side."

He wrapped his hand around hers and reached out to wipe the burn on her cheek with his thumb. "I promise."

She made Dorian leave her soon after, and she surrendered her body to the pin-needle healing of her mother's waters.

Hours after, she found herself staring out of the window at the shining moons, her black silk robe wrapped around her healing body. She felt emptier than she had in a long time.

The door opened and closed just as she wiped the tears from her face. Aydra barely turned from the window, expecting it to be Lex coming back with news from the meeting.

"I didn't think you'd be here so soon," she said as she stared out at the ocean. "What happened? Did my brother not go on and on about the sheep this time?"

"Oh, he did," said the voice not of Lex's. "Wouldn't shut up about the quality of the wool not being great enough for the coming winter."

Her heart skipped at the sound of his voice. She turned, finding Draven holding one of the trinkets on the table by the door, turning it over in his hand with squinted eyes. Her chest began to heave, and she felt an ache for him that made a smile rise on her lips.

"It's not like you people really need heavy wool around here," he continued absentmindedly. "Your winters are no more horrid than—" he paused as they locked eyes, and she realized she was smiling.

"What?" he asked.

"Nothing, it's just..." she felt her breath skip, her eyes glisten. "You're standing there talking about wool as though... " she bit her lips together, and his expression softened. "As though the last we saw each other, I wasn't... we weren't..."

"Fighting?" he finished for her. He sat the trinket back down. "Aydra, if you think you can scare me away by sharing with me the darkest parts of yourself, then you're going to have to do a lot better than being fearful of a boring life."

"Like what?"

He shoved his hands in his pockets and gave her a full once over. "Like telling me you feel nothing between us... or perhaps that you rape children for fun in the streets, that might do it."

She allowed a ludicrous smile to rise on her lips. "You're ridiculous."

The grin that made her knees weak spread over his features, and he started to step towards her. "So you do feel something."

A warmth filled her at the sight of his beautiful face, and she reminded herself to hold it together as he reached her. His hand pushed a hair back behind her ear, and she felt his smile against her lips before he kissed her. The shiver ran down her spine with the heat of his embrace. She gripped his shirt in her hands to steady herself.

He pulled back after a moment, biting his lip as he stared down at her. "I'm sorry about the last time I was here," he whispered. "I had no right to get angry with you."

"You did," she assured him. "I didn't realize the true pain of the Infi. And I'm sorry I said those things about your giver."

A darkened shadow flickered in his features. "Aydra, I love you. And I want you to share with me those parts of yourself you think I cannot handle. I—"

She hugged her arms around him to cease his rambling, burying her face in his chest just below his neck, and surrendered to his embrace. For the first time in weeks, her body relaxed, and peace filled her insides.

"I was worried about you," he whispered. "When I didn't see you at the meeting... I thought... No one would tell me what had happened... What did happen?"

"I haven't felt well for a few days," she lied. "Didn't much feel like putting on the facade today."

He eyed her a moment, gaze narrowing. "Liar," he accused.

"It's nothing," she sighed. "Just a fight with my brother."

"Should I be concerned about these fights? I heard what you said to him the last time he was in my realm... Aydra, if he's—"

"It's fine," she affirmed, squeezing his hands. "He just... he's changed so much over the last few years. Becoming someone I hardly recognize. Angry. Scared. Thinking someone will betray him at any moment. Becoming more like the kings of our past..." She stopped herself and drew a deep breath before she revealed too much. "I love my brother. But it hurts so much to see him morphing into someone he swore not to be."

He paused to consider her a moment, but he didn't push it. "He doesn't deserve your grief."

"I know," she whispered.

He pressed his lips to her palm and held her hand against his cheek. "And so the dying moons said to the sun..."

"Set me free," she finished. She leaned her forehead against his and sighed again. "I have to tell you something."

"Do you think you can hold that thought for an hour or so?" he asked.

"I can, but why?"

"Because Balandria came with me, and I need to go check to make sure she hasn't murdered any Dreamers."

It was not the response she expected, and it amused her nonetheless. "Yeah, you'd better check on that." Her fingers curled in the soft hair on his jaw. A quiet moment between them, rare and unfleeting, a moment she allowed her eyes to memorize every pore on his face, the scar above his cheek, the hazel flecks in his sage eyes... He leaned his forehead against hers. His soft walnut and caramel locks felt like water on her skin as they fell on her shoulder. She inhaled the scent of the forest, and she closed her eyes.

"I thought you were leaving," she muttered as they stood there.

"You distracted me," he murmured against her lips.

Her knees weakened as he pressed his lips to hers, and air returned to her lungs. His hands fell below her hips, and he squeezed her backside, pushing himself into her, and she couldn't help the groan that emitted from her throat. Her heart fluttered in her chest, ears warming with the rise in her blood pressure. She pulled him closer to deepen the embrace, desperate to forget about the world.

"My sister— *Oh.*"

The plate in Nyssa's hands dropped to the floor in the doorway.

Aydra was barely startled, too entranced by his figure in front of her to care about her sister bursting into the room. She pulled back just as the noise of the rolling bowl echoed on the floor.

"Oh… Oh—what? Wait. *Him?!*" Nyssa asked, still standing in the door.

Aydra didn't look away from the smoldering gaze on Draven's face. "Close your mouth, sister," she said. "You'll catch flies."

Nyssa blinked as though trying to wake herself up. "*Him?!* This is the secret man Dorian told me about?!"

Aydra turned around towards her sister, and she almost laughed at the bewilderment written in Nyssa's features.

Draven's breath tickled her ear when he leaned down and muttered, "I'll let you two talk," in her ear.

"Yeah, you should check on Balandria," she agreed.

He huffed amusedly under his breath and squeezed her backside in his hand, making her jump in surprise. "I'll come back later," he said before leaving her side.

He gave Nyssa a quick wink upon passing her.

"Venari," she uttered in a paralyzed voice.

"Princess," he returned. He opened the door but paused just before exiting. "Oh, you'll forgive your sister for any screams you may hear later. Don't worry. She's in good hands."

Nyssa's eyes widened, a startled yip leaving her lips, and she clasped her hand over her mouth. As the click of the door sounded behind him, Nyssa stared at Aydra in disbelief.

"What— What was— *Him?!* He is the one you told me about?"

Aydra almost laughed. She slumped back onto the bed and patted the seat beside her.

"Come sit," she asked of her.

Nyssa's brows raised. "Sit?" she balked. "You want me to just sit after... after... *Him?!*"

"Would you think me crazy if I said I loved him?" Aydra admitted.

The word slipped from her lips so easily before she had a chance to stop it. The warmth of her heart spread through to her extremities as a restless ache, and she knew it was true.

"Yes," Nyssa replied quickly, wavering on the spot. "Yes, I would. I would ask what bewitchment he has placed on you to make you think such."

Aydra smiled, feeling a blush rise on her cheeks that she was unfamiliar with.

"Wait... You're serious," Nyssa realized.

Aydra bit back the emotion threatening to surface as she felt her sister sit down beside her. Nyssa reached out and grasped her hands.

"Drae?"

"I don't expect you to understand it," Aydra managed. "I know... after all these years of hate being poured into us, the lies of the Chronicles and the feuds like wildfire spreading between our races... I know it is crazy, but..." Her voice trailed, and she met her sister's eyes. "He makes me feel more like myself than I knew I was. I can be free with him, tell him the things on my mind that I haven't been able to tell anyone—"

"You could have told me," Nyssa begged.

Aydra squeezed her hands. "No. No, I couldn't. Nyssa, the things I've been made to go through for this kingdom... I dare not see you go through the same. A new war will be upon us by the time you are crowned. I need you to be the fearless woman you will be in facing the new enemy on our shores."

Aydra watched her expression soften, and then Nyssa gave her a small smile.

"What?" Aydra asked upon seeing her eyes light up.

"He's the reason you were so happy those few weeks," Nyssa noted. "I mean, you've always been you, but... this was different. You were glowing. And I've never seen you blush in my life. I didn't know your cheeks knew to redden."

Aydra chuckled under her breath, and she sighed heavily, staring at their entwined hands. "It's certainly a new sensation," she admitted.

"Why didn't you tell me it was him?" Nyssa asked.

Aydra's head tilted with the smile she gave her sister. "I didn't think you would understand. And because I wasn't sure there was anything to tell. We'd just fought. He'd left in anger..."

"What about the stories? What the Chronicles say about his kind?" Nyssa asked.

"Lies," Aydra affirmed. "Draven is different. He is not like the kings of his past."

The smile on Nyssa's face grew, and Aydra watched as amusement rose in her eyes. "And the other stories? Are those as much lies as these?" she asked with a sly brow.

Aydra's eyes widened. "Nyssari Eaglefyre!" She laughed and wrapped her arm around Nyssa's shoulders. "I'm not sure what you've done with my little sister, but I like the direction this is going." She kissed her cheek hard. "What do you say we raid the kitchens, and I'll tell you the truth of those stories?"

Nyssa grinned. "I'd like that."

"I take it you made up with her," Balandria said when Draven joined her on the balcony outside the room he always stayed in.

Draven sighed as he allowed his forearms to rest against the stone banister. "I did."

Balandria's eyes danced over his figure. "You truly love her, don't you?"

Draven couldn't help the minor quirk of a smile his lips twisted into at the question. "I do," he said, meeting her eyes. "I know. It's... odd."

"That's one word to describe it," she muttered. "What about the plan?"

Draven paused and looked out at the ocean waves. "Parkyr's plans didn't include my falling in love with the Queen," he admitted.

"You would abandon his plans for love?"

He sighed and gave her a once over. "Rhaif will still get what's coming to him, but it won't be by Parkyr's plan to take over his kingdom any longer. Things have changed. What matters now is keeping those ships at bay."

"Those ships have not condemned our people for over a century."

"And what do I keep saying about our reigns?" he snapped.

For a moment, she looked as though she would argue, but then her fists relaxed, and she exhaled a long breath. "That we are to be better."

"We don't have to be our predecessors, Bal. We don't have to continue this cycle of manipulation and revenge on those who have staked us for being who we are. We can choose to be more than what his followers wanted—"

"None of these people see us for the people you want us to be," Balandria argued.

"Is battle what you want?" he asked her. "To start a war with these people while strangers come on our shores?" He stalled again, pushing his hair off his face. "Do you remember what I told you about there not being any more Infinari children?"

"About Duarb knowing something is coming?"

He nodded. "Arbina has missed her own traditional cycle," he informed her. "Something is coming. Something big."

"What are you saying?" Balandria asked.

He took something out from beneath his gambeson. The emerald and black streaked rock of the Venari King, enveloped in thin golden wire, hung on a leather chain. "I have a feeling my time on this land is coming to a close."

"Why would you say that?" she asked.

"Because as soon as Rhaif finds out about Aydra and I, he'll think her seduced by me, that this has all been part of my plan to take his crown. Unless she somehow convinces him differently, he's likely to come up with some bogus charge against me. I am certain I'll find myself in chains before this year is out."

Balandria's hand tightened around her sword. "I'd like to see him try—"

"No," Draven cut in. "You are much too valuable to this Age to risk your life."

"If you expect me to sit back and watch my King rot in some cell above this ridiculous castle, you're—"

"Oh, you won't have to," he interjected. "I'm sure my death will be a swift one."

Balandria glared at him. "Now is not the time to joke, Draven."

"No jokes," he told her. "If that day does come, you are not to do anything to prevent it. You will take my place as Alpha, become the Venari King you have long known yourself to be." He reached for her shoulder. "Your word, Balandria. Swear on our giver you will do nothing to save me when that day comes."

"You are my King," she managed. "You cannot expect me to do nothing and allow him to kill you for something as ludicrous as simply falling in love with his sister. He doesn't deserve your life."

"No, he doesn't," he agreed. "But I am not the one destined to lead our people to a greater war than even our ancestors could fathom. You are. And as such, I need your word. Swear to me, Balandria."

Her stern gaze weakened, and he could see the clench in her jaw. "I swear," she finally said.

He pulled the necklace off his head and started to place it over her neck, but she pushed his hands back.

"You are not dead yet," she told him. "You are still my King. Until this life rips you from me, you will keep the honor of this stone."

She closed his hand around the stone, and then he pulled her into his chest, hugging her close.

"I couldn't have asked for better than you," he whispered in her hair. He pulled back and cupped her face in his hand. "I have no doubts that you'll be the greatest of us."

He could see the apprehension in her dark eyes. She opened her mouth to speak, but he held up a hand.

"Get some rest," he told her. "We have a long week ahead of us. You'll need to learn the in's and out's of the meetings, the castle, handling the guards. But, your first job, tomorrow, will be to get to know the Prince and Princess. I have a feeling you'll need them as allies soon."

"What will you do?" she asked.

Draven began walking backward. "Enjoy my time with her while we have it."

He'd nearly reached the door when he heard Balandria call out for him again. He paused at the threshold and looked back at her over his shoulder. Her arms were wrapped around her chest, a cautious look in her gaze.

"Is she worth it?" she asked.

Aydra's face filled his mind. The warmth, security, and love he felt when he was with her radiated through him.

"Only her."

46

Each time she woke in his arms, she settled into it instead of rising. And each time her morning started with his hardened length pressing against her backside, she surrendered to the ravenous moments, relishing the way he held her firmly against him. He would be gone in a few days, and she wanted to savor him.

Draven left Aydra's bed before the sun rose to go to Balandria. He had plans for her, wanting to show her around, let her get to know the rest of the Council. Aydra offered Lex to him to help her get adjusted to things. She wasn't sure why Draven had decided to now bring Balandria into the mix of things, but she wasn't about to argue or push him for reasons.

She trusted him.

Whatever he was thinking, she knew it was for the better of their kingdoms, for both their people.

Rain pelted the windowsill when Aydra finally rose. She smiled at the sight of it and pulled on her riding clothes, along with her cloak.

"Ah, should have known," Lex mused as she stepped inside Aydra's bedroom. "Shall I tell your lover where you're off to?"

Aydra smiled as she opened the grand window in her room and stepped onto the windowsill. "Please do."

Her eyes closed, and she pulled for the core of the Aenean Orel. And then she fell into the air out of her window.

Great golden feathers flashed in her sightline as the air consumed her. But the Orel was faster, and the immense four-legged golden eagle swooped beneath her falling body mere feet from the ground and rocketed them into the air.

Her falling figure out of her window made Draven's heart stop.

But he watched as the Orel's great eagle body swept beneath her and launched back up into the clouds, and then his breath returned.

Dorian clapped his hand on Draven's shoulder. "Yeah, she does that."

"Where do they go?"

"Ah... Cliffs usually. Not sure exactly where, though. Lex knows. You'll have to ask her," Dorian replied.

"Get out of here," Nyssa interjected then. She was smiling at him when Draven met her gaze, and she nodded her head towards the door. "Balandria is in better hands learning from us than she is hearing it from you. We will take care of her." Nyssa wrapped an arm into Balandria's, and she nodded towards the door again. "Go. Be with her."

"I didn't think you approved," he said, eyeing her.

Nyssa tucked her hair behind her ear, and her smile widened. "I didn't. But... I've never seen my sister with such happiness. True happiness. She loves you. I cannot stand in the way of that."

Draven's heart skipped at the word, unsure of if he'd heard her correctly. "She what?" he managed in a crack of a voice.

Nyssa's face paled. "Oh shit," she managed. "Oh, fucking curses. She hasn't told you."

His heart was in his throat, and he felt his breath shortening. "She hasn't, no."

Dorian's chuckle filled his ears, and he clapped Draven on his shoulder again. "Go get her."

Draven left them soon after and made his way through the castle looking for Lex. He found her leaving Aydra's room, her head shaking as she closed the door.

She grinned upon seeing him. "Forest King," she drawled, her arms crossing over her chest. "She's not here."

"No, I saw her jump from a window," he said with raised brows.

Lex laughed fondly. "My Queen has many activities that allow her heart to pump at a greater pace than it ever should. Tempting death by hoping the Orel will catch her is one of them."

"Where did she go?"

"Follow the shore south for an hour on horse. You'll find a great hill and trail leading to the top there, and that is where you will find her. At the top. Probably naked. Basking in the pelting rain."

"Tell me something, Hilexi…"

"Ooo…" she cooed playfully. "Must be serious. Using my full name," she bantered. "What bothers you, Hunter?"

"Am I completely mental for loving her?"

Lex chuckled under her breath, blonde hair falling over her eyes. "She's a free spirit who craves danger and blood. Passionate about her people. Fanatical about the relationships she keeps. Itching to feel freedom and poison all at once beneath her skin." She paused a moment and then grasped the top of his shoulder in her hand. "It'd be hard not to fall for her."

Thunder clapped loudly overhead.

Aydra closed her eyes and inhaled the cold scent of the rain around her soaking body. The water dripping on her face reminded her that she was capable of feeling more than just the numbness she'd held to for so long, of serenity and peace clouding out the thoughts that threatened her mind. Her toes gripped to the edge of the rocky cliffside beneath her feet. One wrong move, one little slip, and the five hundred-foot drop would take her life hostage into the depths of the ocean.

You've company, her raven told her.

She could hear the horse galloping against the wet grass, puddles splashing beneath its great hooves. She didn't bother opening her eyes. The only person crazy enough to follow her an hour from Magnice in the middle of a rainstorm was the Hunter.

Lightning cracked into the ocean.

The hooves slowed, and she turned just in time to see Draven dismount his horse. His white shirt was soaked to his firm body, and he strode towards her.

Thunder roared into the air.

"You're crazy," he shouted.

She almost laughed. "Would you love me if I wasn't?" she called back.

The curl of a smile rose on his lips as he stared down his nose at her, head tilted up just slightly. His eyes flickered up and down her figure, and then he crossed the space between them. His arms pulled her into his wet chest. Her eyes fluttered at the press of his solid chest to hers, the grasp of his fingers digging into her hips. He leaned down, water dripping down his nose as she reached up to his lips—

The screech of a bird sounded overhead.

Aydra grabbed his shirt.

"Hold tight," she uttered.

"What?"

—She dove them both off the side of the cliff.

Draven's arms latched frantically around her waist as the noise of his cursing shouts sounded into the wind circling their falling bodies. Aydra closed her eyes, a grin on her face, and she felt for the Orel, willing it to catch them.

The Aenean Orel swooped beneath them, and she grasped to its feathers. They were whisked upwards into the air. Draven clasped his arms around her waist, and she looked back over her shoulder at him. His eyes were closed tight, head buried in the crook of her neck. She laughed and squeezed her hands around his, and she felt him breathe a great exhale into her neck. She watched as he opened his eyes a few moments later, and when his gaze met hers, she smiled and kissed him.

No words needed to be spoken as the great eagle soared through the air. Aydra leaned her back into him, and he pressed his lips to her throat, hugging his arms tighter around her. Her body filled with the warming ache she'd felt the Rhamocour look at him with. A love that she sank into as though she were sinking into the water's abyss. She'd never felt her heart so full, heat streaking up her arms and settling around her neck and cheeks.

This was the crave she'd been searching for her entire life.

For how long they soared, she wasn't sure. It was only when the rain started to let up, and the sun began to peek through the clouds that the Orel landed on the cliffside, and the pair dismounted the great beast.

Aydra gave it a scratch on the side of its head as her feet hit the ground. The eagle leaned its head into her hand, and then she pressed her forehead against its head and closed her eyes.

I must go, the Orel told her.

Thank you, she told it.

The Orel didn't say anything, but she felt the sun shining from within it. It shook off the water from its feathers and took flight after. Aydra felt Draven come to stand at her side as they watched it fly off over the ocean, and then it disappeared into the rays of sunlight peeking out.

No matter how many times she'd seen the rays cut through the air and ripple onto the surface of the water, no matter how many times she'd seen the dark grey and blue clouds stand stark against the cerulean of the ocean, the golden light of the sun… her breath still skipped when she viewed it from the high of the cliffs. The water was slowly drying on her skin. Petrichor entered her nostrils, and she closed her eyes for a brief moment.

"It's beautiful," Draven said at her side.

Her eyes opened, and she looked at him. His long hair was matted soaking wet to his head, droplets of water resting on his chestnut beard. His white tunic was pressed wetly against his skin. Peace rested in his strong features. It was a different peace than she'd seen on him in the forest. This was the mesmerizing facade she craved, as though he'd lost his kingly identity on the way to the cliffs to meet her. This was Draven as he was. Raw. Unfiltered. Beautiful.

She reached out for his hand, and he met her gaze, a small smile rising on his lips.

"Perfect," she agreed without looking away from him.

47

It was late when they finally made their way back to the castle. Still soaking wet from the rain, Draven lit a fire and laid a blanket out for them in front of it in her room. She packed the pipe as she watched him ignite the hearth, and then he sat beside her with a sigh.

"What did the Berdijay show you when you spoke to it?" he asked as he wrapped his arms in hers.

"Serious question, my King," she said, lifting her head off his shoulder. "Why do you ask?"

He leaned back against the bottom of the chaise and moved one of his arms behind her shoulders. "Because you jumped off that cliff with me in your arms today as though you were ready to die."

"Sounds like you were scared."

"Terrified," he admitted.

She exhaled the smoke from the pipe and laid her head on his shoulder again. "Do you fear death?" she asked.

"That depends," he told her.

"How does fearing death depend on something?"

"It depends on if it is by my choosing," he explained. "I have always sworn my death would be of my own design, not at the request or notion of any other. But... if I died tomorrow, by my choosing or by another's, I would die happily knowing I spent my last days with you."

Her head lifted, and she shook it amusedly at him. "Such a *romantic*, Venari," she mocked him.

He chuckled under his breath and his nose nudged hers. "Breathe a word of it and I'll have you in ropes," he warned.

"Promises, promises," she cooed.

313

"You still didn't answer my question," he said.

She sighed heavily as he passed her the pipe again. The flames danced in her eyes as the memory of the Berdijay filled her mind, and she exhaled the smoke into the air.

"Nothing," she said simply. "I saw… me. Doing nothing. Forced into silence, into submission. Unable to speak. Forced into marriage to quiet my words. Told to take my place as the crown's accessory… A sedentary life in invisible chains."

She felt Draven huff behind her, and she frowned as she turned to see his face.

"Do my fears amuse you?" she asked.

"No. It's just… most people when they meet the Berdijay, they're shown death, darkened creatures, abuses… but you. You fear none of those things."

"Death is but another chapter in this abyss of life, and the darkened creatures these people fear are usually misunderstood, not dangerous."

He toyed with her fingers in his hands. "Is there any creature you will not stand up for?"

Her chin laid on his chest, and she gave him a small smile. "Shadow thieves," she bantered.

The amusement radiated over his features as he exhaled the herb and raised that sly brow down at her. She relaxed and laid her ear against his chest, feeling his heart beat against her cheek. Staring at their entwined fingers again, she caressed the inside of his palm and then said, "So… about these ropes…"

Draven's chest moved, and she knew he was chuckling under his breath. She looked up just in time to see him exhale again, and she watched as his gaze turned from playful to sultry, pupils dilating despite the fire raging before them. His tongue darted out over his lips as his head leaned down, and she thought he would kiss her, but he paused, open-mouthed an inch from her lips.

"What about belts?" he uttered.

Her chest caved in on itself at the growl of his words, and she felt the drip of her own wetness between her legs. His touch was delicate on her exposed thigh, and the tickle of his fingertips running up her leg made her breath arrest. She moved her own hand to the front of his pants, and she could already feel his thick length awakening through the fabric. He groaned as she began to stroke him.

"I like leather," she managed.

His other hand threaded itself around her throat, thumb delicately stroking her skin beneath her jaw, and she felt her eyes flutter as she inhaled the sweet smell of the smoke around them.

He was shadow and angst.

Carnal and capricious.

Her own brand of poison.

And she wanted to unleash him upon her flesh.

Their eyes met, and at the same time, they released each other to stand. Her heart pounded in her chest upon moving to her dresser. She fumbled with the drawer to find her leathers at the anticipation of his promises. She'd barely gotten it open when she felt him press against her back, hands latching around her waist and gripping at her hips. She paused, letting out a deep breath, and his mouth bit onto her earlobe. Her body sighed back into his, and she forgot her reason for being at the dresser. She pushed back against him, teasing his slowly hardening cock with her bottom. His fingers moved over the fabric of her dress, grasping the flesh of her hips between them. She reached back to thread her hand in his hair, making him groan against her skin, and she surrendered to the tease of his fingers on her breast. His mouth sucking at her jaw.

"Belts, my Queen," he whispered in her ear.

"Stop distracting me," she breathed.

She could feel the smile on his lips against her jaw. But he stepped back, and wind swept over her neck as he removed his shirt behind her. Her heart began to thud again. She forced herself to search for the belts and not peek over her shoulder, knowing as soon as she did that she might come apart at the sight of the ravenous Venari King she knew would be staring at her.

The subtle noise of iron clanking caught her ears. She paused, remembering where she'd left the braces upon taking them off after the Belwark trials.

Over the accordion screen by her tub.

She willed her breaths to even as she turned, and her chest caved upon seeing him. The firelight reflected off the ripples of his chest, shadows settling in the crevices and scars across his torso and arms. He toyed with the small belts in his large hands, hair falling over his left shoulder and shrouding the left of him in darkness, only allowing the light to find the right side of his face.

The buckles were undone, and he lifted his darkened eyes to meet hers.

Leather snapped when he pulled them taut between his hands. The noise of it made her jump and caused the beat of her heart to flee.

"Come here."

Fucking Infi.

She forced a deep breath to enter her lungs, and her feet led her the rest of the way to him, pausing and lifting her chin to meet his downward gaze. His head tilted, eyes traveling over her, suggestive brow elevated. Then his lips pressed hard to hers.

She almost stumbled, but his arms caught her. He pulled her flush against him. She felt the cold of the buckles in his hands through the dress. But he tossed them sideways, and his hands dug into her back, the fabric of her dress stretching beneath the weight of his grip. As his mouth moved to her throat, she heard the cotton begin to rip. His teeth bit at her skin, making her knees weaken, and cold air rushed around her as one of her favorite day dresses was ripped in half and tossed beneath her feet.

She opened her mouth to say something, but her arms were seized in his hands. She was lifted stiff off the ground and then shoved onto the edge of the bed. He towered over her, hand on her cheek. Her face sank into his palm as her mouth opened at the sight of his dominating figure over her. The temptation to touch his elongating length made her muscles whimper. She reached out, wanting to feel him in her hands, but he grabbed her wrists just as her fingertips grazed him.

He bent low, hands pressing into the bed on either side of her, and she almost fell into the mattress. His breath rasped against her skin. She thought he might kiss her, but instead, he grabbed the leather belts from beside her that she'd not even seen. The leather breezed over her thighs when he straightened, and he pulled her hands in front of her.

"What are your plans for tomorrow?" he asked as he deliberately began wrapping the thin belts around her wrists.

A short breath entered her lungs, her thighs squeezing at his touch. "Does that matter?" she breathed.

Her wrists were forced together hard, and that brow elevated as he tightened and fastened the belts.

"It matters in that I should know how much you'll need to use your legs."

A small smile crept up onto her lips, and she bit her bottom lip upon meeting his eyes. "You once promised to fuck me fitly into oblivion," she dared. "So I expect to be railed valiantly over the Edge."

A soft smirk pressed onto his lips, rising to his eyes, and the smolder that settled in his features made her breath arrest.

—He shoved her backward into the bed.

She hardly had a moment to register it. His lips were on hers, and her bound hands were thrown over her head onto the pillows. He seized her wrists in his hand, and for a moment, she forgot she was bound. The desperation in his kiss made her head spin, her legs bend around him. His free hand wrapped around the back of her thigh around his waist. She groaned upon feeling his length against her thigh.

But then he stood on his knees over her and pulled her up hard by her hands, forcing her arms over his head. Her legs latched around his waist. Open hands gripped at her bottom, fingers splaying over her flesh. It was the hard smack of his hand against her skin that made her moan into his mouth.

He moved, and her back hit the mattress again, higher on it this time. He removed himself from beneath her arms and reached over to the table. She watched as he whirled his knife between his fingers over her, eyes lit with delight.

The blade was jammed between the buckles of the belts and into her headboard, locking her arms in place over her head.

The smirk on his lips made her entire body whimper.

He bent low, and she craned her neck up, wanting to feel his kiss on her lips. But the tickle of his fingertips ran up and down her sides. Until one hand was around her throat, and he smiled against her mouth as one of his thumbs stroked her trachea and the other grazing her clit.

She felt her legs open wider, her hips move up against his touch as he teased her, staring over her and watching her as he tortured her. Ragged breaths drew through her lungs. She wanted to feel him between her legs, feel his length inside her and buried in her body.

But his hand pressed into her throat, and two fingers thrust hard inside her, and she fought for breath and composure. Her legs squirmed, hips shaking. The desperation of her insides made her feel ready to combust. He didn't let up. Fingers thrusting faster and faster in and out of her, the weight of his other hand burying her neck into the mattress. Her vision began to black, and she wasn't sure what she would fall victim to first: her orgasm or a blackout.

—He released her throat. Desperate breath entered her lungs, but she couldn't keep herself from succumbing to the ecstasy of his hand still inside her. He moved. Her arms strained against the belts over her head, and then she felt his mouth on her clit. The entirety of her body shuddered, and she melted as she came apart against his lips.

The brace of her hands above her made her body shake, as she was in dire need of gripping onto something and having to settle for the dig of her own nails into her palms. She was still regaining her breath when she felt him grab her ankles in his hands, and she opened her eyes to him on his knees below her, pants shredded off his body and his length taut. His darkened gaze danced over her still shaking body, and he lifted her legs off the bed in his hands, bringing her hips with it.

The torture of him filling her sensitive sex made her groan in a higher pitch than she was used to hearing of herself. He gripped her ankles tight in his hand, her hip in the other as he bent forward, forcing her legs straight and flush against his torso. Her body shook. His length hit something inside her with every slow stroke that made her whimper. And when he began to pick up pace, she forgot how to stay quiet. His hips hit her backside hard, over and over, the fill of him moving inside her making her chest constrict. She felt her arms and legs turning to liquid at the strength of her trying to deny herself release. Toes pointed. Nails drawing blood on her palms.

She heard him groan, and the next thing she knew, the knife was removed from the headboard. She sprang into action, thrusting her arms around his neck, sitting up, and kissing him hard. He slipped from inside her, and his arms wrapped perilously around her body. But she was only allowed the reprieve of his kiss a moment, for she was whirled in one movement onto her stomach.

Her arms were thrust above her head again, and the knife was once more lodged into the headboard. She could feel the heat of his body over hers as she lay there. The touch of his light fingers on her thigh forced her body to flinch with a moan. His fingers traveled deliberately up the back of her leg and then between her cheeks, dipping into her dripping sex. Her heart throbbed unevenly in her chest as the restlessness of her muscles squirmed beneath his tease.

"Bend, my Queen."

The growl of his voice in her ear made her body cave. She forced her knees beneath her just as his hand slapped her backside hard. The bed moved again, and she felt the softness of his lips on her flesh where he'd just spanked her. The air brushed her wet skin, her thighs squeezing as he kissed lower and lower until his tongue licked at her clit again, and she heard an involuntary high-pitched noise come from her throat.

"Tell me what you want, Aydra," he breathed against her throbbing sex.

She could hardly contain herself long enough to answer, shaking at the tip of his tongue darting over her flesh as he kissed her thighs, his hands splayed over her backside.

"Oblivion," she managed.

He smiled against her leg, and she felt the bed move, his body coming flush against hers as he bent at her side.

"There's my Queen," he purred in her ear.

Then, he moved her hips in his hands as he straightened between her spread legs, his tip tickling her sex again. His fingertips dug into the bend at her hips, and then his length filled her.

A slew of curses left her lips, and she tugged on the brace of her hands, greedily wanting to take back some control. She moved her own body up and down his length, relishing the noise of his groans and firm of his fingers as she toyed with him, circling herself on his tip and then slamming her cheeks against his hips.

He allowed her the control of it for only a few moments before he smacked her backside with his open hand. Her movement paused, and he took advantage of her lapse and began to move quickly in and out of her, the slaps of their bodies echoing over the cackle of the fireplace.

Her arms were liquid above her. She felt herself reaching and reaching again as she tightened around him. But he abruptly leaned over her and removed the knife from the headboard. He tugged her up, and she practically fell back against him as he pushed her bound hands behind his head. She felt the bed move again and knew he was standing behind her instead of kneeling. His length filled her slowly, and she closed her eyes. His hand wrapped delicately around her throat, the other dipping low between her legs. His teeth pressed to her neck, length moving in and out of her with deliberate tension. But it was when his hand tightened around her throat, and his finger stroked her clit that her insides began to truly shatter. Her body reached and reached, and she felt every muscle seize.

"Come with me."

The vibration of his words sent her over the edge. A noise she'd never heard herself make emitted from her lips, and her entire body shook as she came apart just before he did. His hand tightened around her throat, and she felt him shudder inside her with a loud groan.

For a moment, they stilled, allowing their bodies to fall down from the high together. His hand relaxed, and his forehead fell against her neck. She could feel the sweat on his brow, the unevenness of his breaths on her skin. She sank exhaustedly back against him, unable to move her strained muscles as they continued to tremble. His lips pressed softly to the top of her spine, and he reached for her hands around his neck.

He held onto her, helping her steady as she sank sideways onto the mattress, rolling down onto her side with her knees bent. Draven crawled beside her, and she watched as he undid the belts around her wrists. Even when he'd released her of them, she still couldn't move. His fingers massaged her skin, and he kissed her knuckles. He reached out and moved her matted hair off her face. She met his dilated gaze as he gave her a small smile.

"That was for nearly killing me today," he told her.

She wanted to laugh, but all she could manage was a huff and a smile. "I should try to kill you more often," she bantered.

He leaned down and kissed her, tucking her hair back as he did. The only movement she could manage was scooting closer to him when he laid down, and she laid herself into his arms.

She fell asleep snuggled against his chest as he delicately stroked her bare back, the sound of him humming the Wyverdraki song in her ears a lullaby she allowed herself to drown in.

48

Her legs ached from the night before, and she wanted to lay in the shadows of his tightened embrace for the entire day. But she rose upon seeing the light come in her room, and as she tried to stretch her arms, she sank into the angst of it with a pleased groan.

His touch was delicate on her spine, and she turned to look at him, allowing her hair to sleepily fall over her shoulder. He was watching her with a slight smile on his lips, the edge of his knuckle grazing her skin at the small of her back.

"Hi," she whispered.

"Hi," he managed back.

She closed her eyes, cracking her neck and stretching her back with an arch. Draven moved sideways, his lips pressing briefly to her shoulder before he rose from the bed. His naked body was cascaded in sunlight upon his rising, and she sighed as she stared at the beautiful sight of him.

"What will you do today?" she asked him.

He pushed his arms through a shirt and pulled pants on without answering her. She watched as he picked up the shreds of her dress on the floor, and then he smirked at her.

"Where are your day dresses?"

Her head tilted in confusion at his question, but she pointed to the wardrobe in the corner nonetheless. He stretched over to it and pulled one of the black cotton ones from the front. It was tossed at her, and he gave her an upwards nod.

"What do you say to breakfast?" he asked. "You completely famished me last night."

Her chest swelled at the pure grin on his face. She shoved the dress over her head and took his outstretched hands. He pulled her off the bed and flush against him, her hands threading into his at their sides. She couldn't fight her smile against his lips as he bent his head low to hers, hair tickling her shoulders, as he pressed his mouth lightly against her own.

It was brief, and her heart fluttered at the taste of him, muscles sinking into the warmth of his embrace. When they parted, she took a step back and tugged on his hands, still smiling as her chest bled of the love filling her.

"Come on," she urged him. She grabbed a scarf from the chair it was thrown on, and then she led him out of her room towards the kitchens.

It was the noise of laughter that made Aydra and Draven pause at the door. Aydra recognized her own brother and sister, but the sight of the smile that lit up Draven's eyes upon hearing the third voice made Aydra want to hug him.

"Is that who I think it is?" she asked him.

He chuckled under his breath, hair falling over his eyes as he glanced at the floor and then back to her. "Leave her alone for a day with those two, and they're suddenly inseparable."

"Isn't that what you wanted?" she asked.

He smiled at the door, inhaling a deep breath, and then pulled her against him snugly to kiss her temple. "Yeah, it is," he breathed.

The smell of the breakfast pastries hit them as they opened up the door. Dorian, Nyssa, and Balandria were already seated at the small table they liked to share, a splay of breakfast treats, meats, and cheeses out on the top.

Nyssa was throwing part of her bread at Dorian's face when they entered.

"—shut up," Nyssa was laughing. "I did not say that."

"You definitely did," Balandria mocked from the other side of the table.

Nyssa's mouth dropped, and Balandria dodged the food that was thrown towards her. Balandria was mid-laughter when her eyes landed on the door, and the sight of her king coming into the room must have startled her, for she immediately jumped to her feet.

"My King," Balandria breathed.

"Sister!" Dorian announced loudly, his hands in the air.

"Drae! Sit here," Nyssa moved over, patting the seat beside her.

Draven went over to Balandria. What he said, Aydra didn't hear.

Aydra shook her head at her brother and then pressed her hands into Nyssa's shoulders.

"Did you leave us any food?" she asked them.

"Barely," Nyssa replied. "Dorian thinks he's a starving Ulfram."

Dorian grinned widely at the pair, twirling the fork in his hand. "Growing men need sustenance," he said with a wink.

"Grown men also need sustenance," Draven said, sitting down at the end of the bench Nyssa sat on. Balandria sat back down beside Dorian, and Aydra sat between Nyssa and Draven across from Balandria. Dorian shoved a plate of food toward the end of the table at them.

"Try those," he said, pointing to the wide pocket pastries. "One of my own recipes."

"You wish it was your recipe," Nyssa mocked. "You've never cooked a thing in your life."

Her youngers continued to banter together as Aydra and Draven filled their plates. Aydra couldn't stop stealing glances from him, feeling like a giggling teenager when she would meet his smiling yet domineering gaze.

"So, tell us, Balandria," Aydra finally began once she'd forced her eyes from his, "what kind of trouble did my youngers get you into yesterday?"

"Ah," Balandria picked at the food in front of her, smiling at her plate, "define trouble," she replied.

"Did they actually show you some of the castle and their duties, or did they skip those off for obstacle practice?" Aydra asked.

"Definitely obstacle practice," Balandria replied.

"Sounds like skipping duties runs in the family," Draven muttered from behind his tea.

"It was a perfect day for it," Dorian affirmed. "Rain. Lightning. Nyssa cheated."

"I did not cheat," Nyssa argued.

"Wait—" Aydra's narrowed gaze turned towards her sister. "You let Balandria see you practice, and you won't allow me to go with you?"

Nyssa's cheeks reddened just slightly. "I'm not ready," she insisted, reaching for the fruit.

"She's ready," Balandria and Dorian said at the same time.

Aydra stared between the pair, seeing the raised brows and affirming stares on their faces. "Okay, the Venari Second says you're ready. That isn't nothing."

"Bala spent too much time with Dorian yesterday," Nyssa bantered. "She's picked up his exaggerations already."

Draven snorted.

Balandria's bottom lip dropped, and she tapped her cup on the table as she turned her head slightly in her king's direction. "Something you'd like to add, my King?" she asked him.

Draven lifted his cup to his lips, hiding his smirk behind it. Incomprehensible words muttered from his mouth, but they could understand none.

Aydra reached over and tipped the cup towards his face.

Draven jumped, startled at the liquid on his skin and falling down the front of his shirt. Stifled laughter filled her ears as she watched him fumble, grabbing at the table and hitting the cup on the wood with a thud. Balandria's eyes were wide, her hand slapped over her mouth to conceal the laughter on her features.

Aydra and Draven's eyes locked. She grabbed a napkin off the table and began mockingly wiping his face of the tea. "You have something on your face," she bantered.

The dare in his gaze made her chest tighten.

He grabbed at her legs under the table and pinched her thighs. A yip emitted from her lips, followed by laughter she didn't know she was capable of, and his fingers tickled at her flesh. She laughed, burying her head against his chest, the feeling of his tickling fingers grabbing at her and making her cheeks redden, her chest swell, and her muscles jump. She grabbed his hands and pushed them away as she felt his smile against her cheek. And after a moment, she willed her heart to stop skipping, and she straightened up beside him as he reached for a pastry on the tray.

Dorian and Nyssa were staring at her when she moved her hair out of her face. She sighed a strangled breath and took a long swig of her tea, eyes darting between her youngers' mesmerized facades as she poorly attempted to rid herself of the scarlet on her cheeks.

"I didn't know you could laugh like that," Dorian mused.

"Neither did I," Nyssa agreed.

She felt Draven's light touch on the small of her back, the feeling of it making her eyes flutter with her fast-beating heart, the rise of the hair on her flesh and up her spine, and she couldn't help the unfamiliar heat pulsing up her neck to her cheeks. He was chewing on the pastry in his hand when she turned to look at him again, his right elbow propped up on the table, hair swept over the right side of him.

Her lungs swelled, aching with the amorous restlessness of his gaze in her bones, and as she smiled sideways at him, he gave her a quick wink.

She turned back to her siblings, and she bit her lips at the cheeky grins on their faces. She threw a piece of fruit at Dorian's face and muttered, "Shut up and eat your food," to the pair.

Aydra and Draven listened quietly to the three speak animatedly of their wins and Nyssa's supposed cheating from the day before. After a while, Aydra found herself in quiet conversation with Draven, picking at her food almost more than eating it as she couldn't stop chuckling under her breath. She'd asked about the Blackhands, who were due to arrive the next morning, and what she should expect from them, as well as when Nadir would be coming.

"Who is Nadir?" Nyssa asked, having heard their conversation.

"Someone you're not to concern yourself with," Aydra answered quickly.

"Good luck with that," Balandria muttered under her breath.

Aydra met the Venari Second's eyes, and Balandria looked as though she might smile or mock Aydra. Draven cleared his throat and shifted on the bench.

"What? She's his type, isn't she?" Balandria argued to Draven. Draven rubbed his neck and avoided glancing at Aydra. "That she is," he mumbled.

"What does that mean?" Aydra asked.

"Fiery. Petite. Beautiful. Determined." Balandria paused and looked at Aydra. "Nadir is a great man. What is your concern?"

"I think that is her concern," Draven said.

"I am nineteen," Nyssa chimed in. "I think I can choose the right sort of man for myself, thank you all."

Balandria paused, and then she took a long drink of her tea as she met Aydra's 'I told you so' gaze.

"Right. You should hide her," Balandria finally agreed.

Aydra nodded knowingly at Balandria, a single brow lifted, and she picked up another piece of fruit to eat.

The food quickly vanished before them as they continued to speak of the Honest, of the Blackhand friends of Draven and Balandria's that would be arriving the following morning. The pair had stories to tell of their own trips to the mountains, of meeting the Blackhands on their yearly graduation journeys into the Forest of Darkness to bring back a Noctuan. Draven had tried to cease the tradition years earlier but had almost started a war between the races in trying. Draven had been forced to table the discussion for fear of losing his own realm.

When the food was gone, Aydra sighed into Draven's chest, wanting to stay in their bubble of peace and freedom a bit longer rather than start the day she wasn't looking forward to. His lips pressed to her temple, and she hugged his arms as they wrapped around her. He spoke in whispers in her ear so only she could hear, his hand squeezing her waist, the other grazing her lower abdomen. He told her how he would splay her on the table they sat at before starting the day, of how his tongue would have her moaning so loudly the servants would think her being attacked, and he promised them a show. Her eyes fluttered at his words, and she could feel him firming behind her.

"Do you think you two could not fuck at the table while we're present?" Dorian asked them after a few moments.

The pair snapped out of their bubble, both chuckling under their breath as they came back into reality.

"What are your plans for today?" Aydra chose to ask the others.

"Choosing foods for banquet tomorrow," Dorian answered. He paused and stared at the empty plates on the table. "I should have probably stopped eating earlier."

"That would have been the smart thing," Nyssa mocked.

"We need to go find you a dress for banquet tomorrow," Draven told Balandria.

"You're not putting Balandria in a dress," Aydra argued. "She'll cut your throat."

Balandria raised her glass to Aydra. "I knew I liked her," she said to Draven.

"What do you suggest instead?" Draven asked.

"I have something that would suit her better," she replied. "You'll just need to take it to my seamstress, Maye, to have it taken in, make it her own." Her eyes flickered to Nyssa. "Can you take them? Make sure Maye doesn't have any attitude for helping Venari?"

Nyssa nodded. "I can do that."

"What will you do today?" Dorian asked Aydra as he started to stand.

Aydra paused a moment, eyes lingering on her plate. "Ah... I have been summoned to help Rhaif with choosing decorations for the celebration."

Dorian stared at her from across the table, apparent worry

stretching over his features. "Is Lex going with you?" he asked.

"She is," Aydra affirmed. "Speaking of which, I should really find her."

49

"I think you're being ridiculous," Aydra argued with Rhaif hours later as they walked through the flower shops. "It's a celebration. Not a wedding."

"A wedding would stress me less," Rhaif mumbled as he picked up another flower. "What about these?" he asked, holding up a long stem with a small black flower on the end.

She stared at the flower he was twirling in his hand. "Where has that been all my life?" she muttered as she took it from his fingers.

"Figures," he said under his breath.

She pressed the black flower to her nose and inhaled the scent of it, allowing it to fill her insides. "Figures what?" she dared ask, eyes flickering to Lex who was standing near.

"That you would be attracted to a noir flower."

"Matches my core," she muttered. She paused a moment and looked him over as he picked another flower from the next cart. "I honestly don't think these people will care whether the decorations in the Great Hall are blue, black, or pink. The only thing the Blackhands will care for is the food."

"Which is why I've Dorian handling that," Rhaif replied.

Aydra felt a smile rise on her lips, and she almost laughed. "Yes, he is the expert."

The first smile she'd seen on Rhaif's face in months met her own, and for a moment, she was reminded of the brother she'd once known.

The flash of a memory of them walking down that same street at the age of seventeen filled her mind. She could hear his laugh, feel his arm wrapped into hers. He'd bought her flowers and placed them in her hair that day.

But the memory of how that afternoon had ended made her heart constrict.

"I promise, it's the last time," he had sworn.

"You said that last month," she had whispered.

"Drae, please." His hand wrapped around her cheek, thumb stroking her lips. "You know I love you." His lips kissed her hands, and her heart fell for the promise he whispered.

Aydra nearly vomited in the street as the angst of the memory making her stomach knot. The flash of his ashen face from two days before entered her mind, and she forced herself to straighten.

Rhaif turned away from her then and pushed his hands behind his back, and Aydra was glad she had not allowed such a memory to rest in her features.

"What about these?" he asked with an upwards nod towards a bouquet of burgundy flowers.

Aydra sighed as she paid for the stem in her hand, and then she turned to see the flowers he was looking at. "Whatever you want, Rhaif," she said, feeling sadness fill her core. "I'm sure it will be beautiful whatever you choose."

The ache stayed in her stomach throughout the day. Each time he would try and get her to speak with him normally, she found herself unable, and when night came, she did not join him and her siblings at supper.

She bid Lex goodnight, urging her to look after Nyssa the rest of the night instead of herself, and she then retired to the silence of her bedroom. She had not seen Draven or Balandria since the morning, not even a glimpse of them in the hall.

Being around Rhaif for so long that day and having to act as though they were as they'd always been in front of people had been overwhelming. She'd kept her facade, pushed her pain to the back of her mind, and forced herself to smile in front of him and their people.

So when the water of her bath wrapped around her that night, her heart broke, and she wept into the warmth of it.

Her core emptied to a numbing she'd never wanted to feel again, and soon she fell asleep in the water.

The dreams that filled her were of her own past.

The first being the day after Dorian and Nyssa were marked— together— two months before Rhaif had been given his own marking and fire.

"She doesn't mean it," Aydra managed as they stood atop the cliff they liked to go to.

"Doesn't she?" he argued, and she could hear the pain in his voice.

The bow sagged in her extended arms, and she stared sideways at him. "Rhaif—"

"Drae, she marked our youngers before me," he cut her off. "Both of them. *Together*."

She could see the frustration in his face, his tense arms as he tugged at his hair, pacing back and forth at the edge of the cliff. She began to reach for him, but he jerked away from her, his hands in the air.

"You don't understand," he argued. "You've been her favorite since we were children. You've not had to work as hard as I, just to in turn be completely ignored. You don't know what it is like to be humiliated in front of your own kingdom. To watch as your eight-year-old brother and sister are given a surname and powers before you are. Do you know what Vasilis said to me this morning?"

"I was there," she said in a whisper, remembering the way their older had spoken to him that morning. Calling him cowardly and unworthy. Shouting at him and saying what a failure he'd become.

Rhaif's hands ran through his hair, and he stopped abruptly, pausing at the edge of the cliff. Aydra sat the bow on the ground. She stepped up behind him and placed a soft hand on his shoulder. "Rhaif —"

—He seized her neck in his hand.

She struggled, slapping his taut arm beneath her hands, bewildered by the sudden turn in his attitude. "Rhaif, I can't breathe—"

The darkness in his wide eyes poured through her.

"What is it you have that I do not?" he said in a lower voice than she'd ever heard from him, his head tilting just sideways. "You're not special. Simply because you beat the Venari child in combat, you're somehow more worthy of her love than I?"

Her breath wouldn't catch. She dug her fingers into his arm. "Rhaif, please—"

But her feet were lifted off the ground.

"Look at you—"

Her eyes began to droop.

"—No more indestructible than any other—"

She struggled for breath, her feet kicking into the open air.

"—a whore and a pet—"

Her raven screeched over her head.

"—I could snap your neck with one swift move—"

Help, she called out.

"—But I wonder how she would weep if you were dropped off this cliff—"

The raven dove at his face.

Rhaif cried out, and his hand slipped from around her throat.

Her ankles hit the grass hard, and she looked up just in time to see blood trickling down her brother's face. He shoved her raven off him finally as Aydra stood from the ground. Bewildered eyes met hers as though he were waking from the trance he'd been under only a moment before.

For a few seconds, neither moved. Aydra rubbed her throat, feeling her muscles shaking as she wrapped her head around the reality of what had just happened. The gaze in his eyes softened, and she watched as his chest began to heave, and then he reached out for her.

"Drae—"

She flinched away from him and started walking backward down the trail. "Don't touch me," she whispered.

He'd apologized and wept in her arms that night, swearing to her he would never do it again. Swearing he'd just been frustrated at their youngers' markings the day before.

Lies.

Her dream morphed, and she was on the Throne Room floor, Rhaif standing above her triumphantly.

It was the day Rhaif had finally been marked of his sign and given his abilities— ten years after Aydra's own marking, and a full Dead Moons cycle after their youngers had been given their markings.

Summer had been in full bloom. Aydra could still smell the flowers on the vines that had entangled themselves around the stone of the Throne Room.

Arbina walked along the edge of her pool, her feet hardly making ripples in the surface as she watched Aydra and Rhaif parry. They'd had a good morning, went swimming down around the bend, chased each other over the sand when Aydra had told the seagulls to annoy him more than usual.

Rhaif grinned and extended a hand to Aydra's fallen figure. Aydra paused, her confused gaze washing over the pride in her brother's features. Her chest swelled at his smile, and she took his hand.

"You've been practicing without me," she noted.

Rhaif chuckled under his breath and pulled her up off the floor. "I don't always need your help, favored daughter," he said with a wink.

Aydra rolled her eyes but did not deter the smirk from her lips. She whirled her sword in her hand and grinned at her brother's smug facade.

"We'll see how long that lasts."

He lunged forward, striking swords with her again and again, this time more fiercely than the times before. Aydra was pushed backward. Her brows narrowed at this newfound strength, but she continued to fight him anyway. He was fast, much faster than she was accustomed to him being.

"Rhaif—"

A wildness filled his dilated pupils. She tried to push forward, to strike him above her.

But the edge of the Throne Room met her feet.

Aydra yelped as her heels hit nothing but air, and the wooden sword in her hand fell into the waterfall.

"Rhaif!"

Her scream echoed off the stone. Her raven screeched.

Aydra's hands caught herself on the stone edge. Her feet dangled. She stretched for anything to help her push herself up.

But Rhaif was standing at the edge of the room over her, and Aydra froze at the sight of his eighteen-year-old self staring at her with such malice in his gaze.

"Very good, my son."

The coo of her mother's voice sent a chill down Aydra's spine.

She'd never heard her call him 'my son' before.

Aydra watched Arbina stretch the space between them and wrap an arm around Rhaif's shoulders, ignoring Aydra's struggling figure hanging from the edge. Aydra grappled with her slipping grip.

Arbina led Rhaif over to the edge of her pool.

"You are ready," Arbina told him, a smile on her face.

Rhaif's chest swelled, and Arbina led him deeper into the water.

Aydra's feet finally found a rock to sink in to. She hoisted herself up, pulling her body up and over the white stone. She rolled onto the floor just as she saw her brother's head dive beneath the liquid. Bubbles erupted onto the surface. She could hear his screams, see the blood from the waters cutting through his skin as he was marked.

Blue flames engulfed the surface.

Aydra's eyes widened. Her raven landed beside her, and it gave her finger a comforting nip.

It was the sight of her brother walking out of the pool that made her heart stop.

His clothes had been ripped off him. He was soaking wet, his navy black hair matted down over his daring eyes. Streaks of black ran up his torso like veins beneath his skin. His hands and wrists were blackened with the ash of the Promised King.

His chest heaved up and down with deliberate labored breaths.

But in his hand was something she didn't expect—the gleam of a bright silver sword danced in the sunlight, and his fist curled around the handle.

Arbina stepped up to him, her arms crossed over her chest, chin raised in the air. She reached out and stroked his cheek.

"Show your form, Rhafian Sunfire."

Rhaif's shout bellowed through the air. Blue flames erupted onto his skin.

Aydra's insides drained as she watched her brother take his true form.

Their elder, Vasilis, had died that night.

The moons were shining brightly through her window when Aydra's eyes fluttered open. She thought she'd heard something. A shadow passed between herself and the window, and she jumped so fiercely, water splashed onto the floor.

Draven was staring down at her.

"*Sweet Arbina*, Draven," she breathed, willing her heart to beat at a normal pace.

"Why are you asleep in the tub?" he asked.

She sighed heavily and rubbed her face, the memory of why she was there and the dreams she'd just had filling her mind. Her hands grasped to the sides of the tub, and she shook her head.

"It's nothing," she managed. "Just a bit overwhelmed."

He reached for her robe and held it for her as she stood. The look on his face made her heart tighten.

"Don't look at me like that, Draven," she said, slipping her arms into the warmth of the thicker robe. "I simply had a long day."

"I saw you in the streets with him," he said as she stepped from the bath.

She pulled the robe tighter around herself and avoided his eyes. "Choosing decorations for the celebration tomorrow," she explained. "It's apparently going to be an extravagant affair." She noted the look on his face as he stood in the light of the window. She knew he could tell there was something more wrong, but she wasn't ready to tell him everything.

"Don't," she warned.

"I didn't—"

"I mean, do not look at me as though I am some broken filly," she managed, feeling her chest begin to heave.

"Why would you think I would look at you as such?" he asked softly.

"Because—because you saw me having to act with him today, and you have to know how much that hurt," she admitted, feeling a lump rise in her throat. "To have to walk beside someone who would condemn me tomorrow if given the chance. Act as though he has not turned into the monster kings of our past... as though nothing has changed and he has not become someone he promised not to be—"

"You cannot save him," Draven whispered.

Her heart shattered into bits as she met his eyes. "But why can't I?" she managed. "He is my brother. We grew up playing, laughing... We loved each other. We promised to be *so much* better. What happened? Why can't I save him from the madness of our predecessors?"

Draven stepped closer and held her hands in his. "Fear is our greatest enemy. It causes you to do things you never thought yourself capable of. Your brother is lost to the gravity of it. Everything you are, he fears. You are smart, strong, confident, intrepid... you could be the greatest leader this Echelon has ever known. And tomorrow, when our friends from the east and south get here, his jealousy of you will only get worse."

He paused and pressed his lips to her knuckles. "I've no doubt every race will be calling you their Queen before the week is over."

"I would never ask them to," she whispered.

"And that is why they will."

She fell into his arms, and he hugged her against his chest. "And what about when this week is over? When our guests have left, and you have returned to the Forest?" she said.

"Then you kill him," he said with a shrug.

"I am not killing my brother."

Draven sighed heavily, a low growl emitting from his throat. "It would save us a lot of grief."

"And it would also start a war we do not need."

"Killjoy."

She started to smile, but the door opened then, and Lex burst into the room.

"My Queen— Venari King, you both need to hear this—"

Aydra froze at the sight of her Second's widened eyes and bewildered gaze. She wasn't sure she'd ever seen such fear on her features before.

Her arms fell from Draven. "Lex, what's wrong?"

Lex stopped at the edge of the bed, swallowing hard as she stared between them. Draven's weight shifted towards her.

"Spit it out, Second Sun," he demanded.

"Infi," Lex said with a heave of her chest. "Infi reported in the smithing streets."

50

"What—*again?!*"

Aydra grabbed a dress from the closet and shoved it over her head. Draven tossed her her boots.

"How many?" he asked.

"Three."

A low grunt of frustration left his throat, and he pushed his hands through his hair. Aydra watched him a moment, and for the briefest of seconds, the memory of past Venari betrayals entered her mind.

She pushed past him and followed Lex from the room.

Their quick footsteps echoed in the silent hall. Aydra couldn't stop turning her ring over and over on her finger, a knot forming in her stomach as the thoughts of betrayal invaded her mind.

Her raven screeched over her head.

She was wrong... right?

"Is there something you should be telling me?" Aydra asked as they reached the next hall.

"Like what?" he asked.

"I think you know."

"Like telling you as in you think I've unleashed these creatures on your kingdom?" Draven knew.

"Have you?" she dared to ask.

"There was once such a plan, yes—"

Aydra stalled in her steps and rounded on him. "Excuse me?"

His eyes flickered to the ground. And when he didn't speak, her heart began to throb in her ears.

"You speak about such a plan so causally," she hissed. "Has this all been a rouse? Our entire relationship? A trick to take over the

336

Promised crown?"

His gaze met hers, and the sadness resting in his pupils made her chest constrict. "Is that what you think of me?" he said in a voice barely audible.

"It's not what I *want* to think—"

"Then why would you say it?"

"For the same reason you once asked me if I'd called my brother to invade your realm," she spat. Her gaze washed over his figure, and she pressed her hands to her hips. "Given our own history and the history of our races, I have to ask."

He straightened, and a blank expression filled his shadowed features. "So ask it."

Her arms crossed over her chest, and the words she was forced to speak broke her heart. "Have you allowed Infi to live and brought them here? To invade our towns and my kingdom in an attempt to take over this realm as kings of your past have done?"

"Not during my reign," he answered.

"But there was a plan?"

"We don't have time for this," Lex interjected.

"A plan I abandoned," Draven continued. "I have not let any Infi live during my time as King. You saw me the morning after during the Deads."

"And are there any of his old supporters in your ranks? Anyone who would—"

"The people now in my kingdom would not go against my leadership," he insisted. "You know them. You have spent time with them."

She wanted to believe him. She wanted to take his words as truth.

"Drae!"

Dorian was running at them down the hall. She reached out as he caught up, and he nearly bounded into her. "What's happened? Where are they?"

"A few of the smiths cornered them, locked them up," said Lex.

"How did they know they were Infi?" Dorian asked.

"I wasn't told much," Lex admitted. "Just that they'd been found and the men were calling up for support."

"We need to hurry before word spreads," Aydra said. "Guests will be here in the morning. We don't need them knowing about this, nor do we need Rhaif finding out. Come—" the sudden look Aydra saw on Draven's face made her words cease.

His hands were on his hips, and he was staring at the ground with widened eyes as though something had just occurred to him that he'd not thought of before.

Frozen.

Paralyzed.

"Draven?" Dorian sounded.

Draven's widened eyes rose to meet Aydra's, and she saw the color had drained from his face. He didn't speak but instead rubbed his face in his hands, starting to pace on the carpet as he tugged at the roots of his hair. "I'm so stupid—"

The wind began to pick up around them, and one of the windows burst open, hitting the walls hard. Dorian and Lex jumped, ducking slightly at the sound of it. Aydra's chest constricted, and she watched with a tightened jaw as Draven's frustration nearly caused the rug beneath their feet to billow off the stone.

"We need to go," Aydra insisted.

The four of them ran through the castle in silence with their cloaks high over their heads as they headed into the darkened streets. Most Dreamers had gone to sleep, but the fires were still lit outside one of the shops on the smithing street. As they neared, she could hear a rumble of people speaking inside.

Lex opened the door and went inside first. Aydra allowed Dorian to walk in before her, followed by herself and lastly Draven. Twenty Dreamers were gathered around the fire-lit room. They spoke animatedly in hushed, harsh, voices. They barely seemed to notice the four coming inside. She recognized the one she knew as Grey towards the back of the room, arms folded over his chest.

Three men were tied up and subdued in the middle of the circle. Aydra froze at the sight of their reddened faces, the streaks of blackened blood where it looked like men had beaten and struck them with irons to keep them from running.

One man spotted them at the door, and he said, "Who let you in, Belwark?"

A brow raised on Aydra's face, and she whipped her hood off her head. "I believe it is my kingdom. My Second can go wherever she pleases."

"Your Majesty's—"

Dreamers dropped to one knee around them. Dorian removed his hood then, and he slowly started walking around the three Infi in the middle of the room. He paused in front of one, pressing a finger to its face and pushing its head sideways, looking over the beaten streaks on its face.

"Where did you find them?" Dorian asked aloud.

"It was just past sunset," answered Grey from his knees. "They were sneaking around the back of my shop."

"Stand," Aydra told the Dreamers.

"How did you know what they were?" Dorian continued, pausing over the next one. He grabbed its hair and lifted the Infi's head, revealing the slow blink of the yellow eyes Aydra sometimes saw in her nightmares.

"You see those eyes once..." Grey said as he stood from his knee, "you can't really get them out of your head."

"I thought we were rid of this filth," said one of the women.

"The Infi are possibly growing bolder and coming down from the mountain towns," Draven said then, slowly removing his hood. "They —"

"What's he doing here?" said someone.

"Venari King— He has unleashed these beasts into our streets!"

"You are not welcome here, traitor!"

"Get out—"

The noises of their protests filled Aydra's ears to the point that her heart shattered in her chest. She looked at Draven, seeing the crestfallen expression in his features, his fists tightening at his sides.

He had not asked for this.

"Cease!" Aydra shouted.

Their voices silenced, and she pressed her hand to Draven's arm.

Dorian's cloak whipped around him as he stared at the faces in the room. Aydra could see the fire rising in his gaze, the tips of his fingers darkening as he turned in a circle and dared any of the Dreamers in the room to speak.

"The Venari King is the only person with the knowledge of how to rid our streets of these creatures," Dorian affirmed. "He has not unleashed anything on our kingdom. You'll do well to remember it next time you see him."

"Wait outside," Aydra whispered to Draven with a slight squeeze of his bicep.

Draven didn't look at her when he exited the shop.

Her eyes met her brother's as she hugged the cloak around her chest, and then she looked around at the people staring at her. "Elders of the Blackhand mountains are to arrive tomorrow. We will have a long discussion with them about the way they allow these creatures to stay alive."

"How do you know that is where they come from?" asked one of the women. "How do you know it is not a trick of the Venari—"

"The Venari do not allow the Infi to walk among them," Aydra snapped, eyes glaring through the woman that had brought up the notion. The woman sank back into the shadows, and Aydra stepped forward to stand beside her brother.

"Does anyone else have any opinions they would like to get out?" she dared to ask.

The room stilled, Dreamers glancing between one another but saying nothing in response.

"You can get rid of them?" asked Grey.

The three Infi men began to groan groggily. One of them shook its head as though it were waking up from a blackout. Dorian grabbed slowly for the knife on his belt.

"Get these people out," he muttered to Aydra and Lex. "I do not wish for them to witness beating hearts being pulled from these lifeless bodies."

Aydra nodded before looking around the room. "Go home. All of you. You've seen enough for tonight."

The people filed out quietly until only Grey was left in the room with them. He refused to leave, and so Aydra had warned him of what was to come. She had Lex signal Draven that he could go inside once the others had gone.

Grey tensed the moment Draven stepped in. "Why is he here? Has he come to claim his brothers?"

"He is with me, Grey," Aydra said pointedly. "And these creatures are not his brothers."

Draven didn't say anything in response to Grey's query, almost as though he hadn't heard him. He simply stepped forward to Dorian's side. The force at which he pulled each of the Infi's heads up to look at them was abrupt. Aydra couldn't stop staring at the shamed shadows resting in his features.

He sighed heavily and looked to Dorian.

"You know what to do," he said in a low tone.

Dorian twirled the knife in his fingers as he stared at the creatures. "Hey, Grey—"

"Yes, Your Majesty," Grey replied.

"You may want to cover your ears."

The noise of the first one's piercing scream reverberated through the small shop, and a chill ran down Aydra's spine. Dorian had pushed his knife into the man's throat. Dark, nearly black blood spurted from the vein he had cut, and it poured out onto the side of his body, trailing over Dorian's hands and onto his feet.

Which was when the other two woke up.

They shifted features. True forms coming to the surface. Disfigured and molten-skinned, red burns plaguing their faces. Their wails echoed off the walls, making Aydra wince at the ear-piercing sound of it.

"You're going to wake up the whole village, brother," Aydra muttered as she hugged her arms around her chest.

Dorian's knife met the necks of the other two, and their wailing ceased—but they knew it was only brief if he did not work fast.

"Quickly," Draven said over his shoulder.

"You could help," Dorian argued as he cut the chest of the first.

"What do you need?" Grey asked.

"Three bags," Dorian managed, pulling the first's heart from his chest. He tossed the still beating muscle into Grey's hands, and Grey nearly dropped it as he realized what it was doing.

"What—"

"Bags, Grey," Aydra reminded him.

She watched her brother work, the determined expression on his face that she knew he'd earned while on his time with Draven vanquishing those in the village towns. Draven was pushing him to do this on his own, as she was sure he'd done while he and Dorian had been on the road together. Grey brought forward two more bags for them, and Dorian took them from his hands.

The blood spattered on his young features, sitting stark against his alabaster skin and large white blue eyes. His thick black hair was quickly matted, the tips of his bangs falling into his right eye. He had a firm clench of his wide mouth, teeth showing as he worked determinedly to get the heart out of the second Infi.

The ribcage broke, and Dorian pulled the heart out, pushing open the bag on the floor with his elbow. The beating heart dropped inside it, and he moved on his knees to the third.

—The Infi surged back to life.

Its shriek made Aydra jump.

The creature grasped onto Dorian's cloak and yanked him forward. It snarled in Dorian's face, saliva dripping from its pointed teeth.

"Dorian…" Aydra said slowly, not wanting to interfere if he didn't need it.

"I've got it."

Dorian resisted the pull of the creature and—

His knife plunged into its neck once again.

She watched him take the last heart as the bodies lay limp on the ground, the rope around them unfurled. Dorian sighed and sank back on his knees, apparently willing his breaths to catch after having to wrestle with them.

"Look at that." Draven gave Dorian a firm clap on his shoulder. "A King worthy of the crown not yet on his head."

51

The ordeal of the Infi was exhausting.

It was well past midnight by the time they wrapped the bodies up and stowed them away in the stables so they could take them to the Hills of Bitratus after the meeting. Aydra walked with her arm around Dorian, back up the streets, and sent him to bed, insisting he remember to wash himself up.

Draven didn't speak as they walked back into the castle. Once Lex left their side, Draven turned as well, and Aydra stared at the back of his head as he descended down the hall.

"Where are you going?" she called.

"My room," he said simply. "I shouldn't like to think the Queen wants to consort with the enemy king now that she thinks I've unleashed terror in her streets."

Her stomach knotted, and a sourness poured into her core. "How exactly did you expect me to react?" she said in a voice higher pitched than she meant to.

Draven stilled, and when he turned to look at her over his shoulder, she saw a fear and surrender in his eyes that made her weight shift.

"You once asked me a similar question," she said slowly. "Did you not think such a thought would cross my mind?"

"I asked you that well before—"

"It shouldn't matter when it was," she cut in. She paused a moment, her body feeling numb of the positivity and equableness she usually felt around him. Her heart now stretching in all different directions at once.

"I worried about this," she managed under her breath.

"What?" he asked, turning fully to face her.

343

"That we would be forced to one day choose between each other and our people. That the mistakes of our past kings would come between us—"

"Aydra, do you trust me?"

The sternness of his brows made her shift. She avoided his gaze as she pondered the question. He'd risked the love of his people to help her more than once. He'd not done anything to make her think he wanted her kingdom. The way he'd stared at the Infi creatures with sadness and fear in his eyes, with the betrayals of his predecessors on his mind, filled her thoughts. And then she remembered how he would look upon her face, smiling that smile that made her heart melt and her mind cease of worry. The way he would look at her… it was something she knew could not be faked.

"I do," she said upon meeting his sage orbs.

A great sigh left him as she closed the space between them, and he closed his eyes upon laying his forehead against hers. She pressed her hands to his cheeks and kissed his forehead before taking his hands in hers once more, and then she led him to her room.

There was no late night of lust, no smoldering jokes or teasing arguments. Draven stripped himself of the bloodied clothes, and he got into bed without saying a word. At first, she wasn't sure what to do, how to act. But she sat up in the bed against the headboard, and he laid down atop the sheet with his back to her.

She watched his body rise and fall, obvious he was still awake as he lay there in silence. And when he finally readjusted himself, turning over to face her, she reached for his hand and gave it a squeeze. His eyes avoided hers, but he moved, and her entire body shattered when he wrapped his arms around her and laid his head against her stomach. She could feel the rapid beat of his heart, the tenseness in his body.

She wept for him.

So she hummed the Wyverdraki song, absentmindedly allowing her fingers to graze over his back, tracing the jagged extensions of his phoenix marking on his shoulder blade and bicep, her other hand laying over his forearm.

"Will you run?" he whispered after a while.

"I won't," she promised.

He exhaled heavily, and for a moment, she thought he might not speak. But he sat up in front of her, and her heart shattered at the sight of his struggling figure sitting before her.

"Do you know how it feels to have people look at you as the Dreamers did tonight?" he asked in a rasp, meeting her eyes. "To be condemned for the mistakes of your giver, of previous kings who spread nothing more than ill-witted violence and terror into other parts of our world? To know no matter how much of a different life I may want for my people, that they will never be looked upon by others as anything more than traitors and thieves?"

He paused, and she nearly broke at the look in his eyes. His jaw was taut, frustration spread over his features. She could see the battle beneath the facade he so desperately clung to, the fight of whether he should go with previous kings or start a new journey for his people.

"I don't," she whispered.

He fumbled with his hands a moment, muscles straining to keep his emotions at bay, and she felt the wind encircle the room.

"When Parkyr died... I wasn't crowned immediately. There was pressure from the older generation to change tradition and choose a new king, one of Venari instead of Infinari. They thought me unworthy of the phoenix crown because I was young. They cut my hair. I was challenged for my leadership. I was forced to execute one of my own in combat beneath our giver's tree. Even after I'd won the title, they didn't respect me, but those of my own age defended me. During the first Dead Moons of my reign, I took Dunthorne and Bael out with me to Duarb. Parkyr had only ever allowed me to go with him to the birthings once. Said he would take me when I turned eighteen. But he died when I was sixteen, and I didn't know what I was going to find. What we saw... those blistered red-skinned creatures that barely resembled infants. Yellow eyes and wailing screams. I decided right then, I would allow none to live, that if an Infinari child was born and then marked of the Infi fate instead of Venari, that I would take its life, no matter how hard it might be. A few years later, we received news of the Promised crown being passed to the next. That you were crowned." He paused and met her gaze a moment, and she could see him bite back words. "There was immediate pressure from the olders. They wanted to continue with Parkyr's plan. They wanted... they wanted me to seduce you, to find the Infi hideout in the mountains and ask them to invade your walls when your guard was down."

Her insides began to freeze again.

"Aydra, I swear—"

"Was it orchestrated?" she asked softly. "My falling in your forest?"

"No," he said as his eyes met hers.

"Draven—"

"I swear on my life," he affirmed.

The wind whipped around the room with his stare, and then he sighed heavily, shaking his head. "I always told myself I could be better than the greed of my predecessors, that I could lead our family into prosperity and belonging without the need of war and invasion. That we could reverse the curses of our past, no longer be the people the Chronicles said we were."

"How did you convince the olders to not invade with the Infi?"

"I didn't," he admitted. His hand ran through his hair, and he sighed again. "Parkyr's followers left us the night you fell in my forest."

The room stilled.

She blinked, unsure of what he'd just said.

"What?"

His fingers tugged at the roots of his hair. "There is a faction of Venari, the older generation and followers of the old ways... They didn't like my unwillingness to go along with the plans to seduce you and unleash the Infi. When you fell... they urged me to go through with it or kill you. When I refused, they left. I'm not sure where they've been."

The news made Aydra's heart pause. She stared at the blanket, the moons light reflecting into her room and casting shadows on his grieving face. She hurt. She was unsure what to feel, what to believe.

"Aydra, you have to understand..." he started again, "the pressures of what my people wanted, of the ridicule and slander bestowed upon us simply because of what we are... It's hard not to go through with such a plan when you have been condemned for it before it even happens."

"So why haven't you?"

He sighed and looked at the bed again. "You," he admitted, his eyes rising to hers.

She stilled, her heart skipping in her chest. "Draven... tell me this wasn't a dream," she managed. "Tell me this was real. That you actually love me and it wasn't just for some plan to take over the crown."

He stared at her, eyes narrowing, and he sighed as the wind died down around them. "If this is a dream, I never want to wake from it," he whispered.

"That's not an answer," she breathed.

"How do you suppose I prove to you my love is not orchestrated?" he asked.

She fumbled with her hands in her lap a moment, contemplating the knot her heart had woven itself into. The feeling of his skin against hers caused her breath to arrest, and she watched as he brought her knuckles to his lips, his hands caressing her own.

"I once told you you deserved nothing less than someone who would burn this entire kingdom to the ground for your salvation," he repeated. "Aydra, I know better than to think you'll ever need saving or that you would ever allow me to try to even if you did. But... I cannot promise to never bring harm to your kingdom."

She felt the frown slip onto her face. He squeezed her hands, and she swallowed hard.

"Why's that?" she managed.

"Because if it ever means vengeance for you, I will do it," he swore. "I will burn this kingdom to nothing more than rubble against the cliffside. It will turn to ash and smoke beneath the weight of purple and orange flames. And not for want of your brother's crown or redemption for my giver. Those things I care nothing of. But you... I would light a match beneath your giver's roots and bring this all down if it meant avenging you. If that isn't proof enough of my love for you being real, then I am at a loss."

She stared at their entwined hands a moment before meeting his gaze again. The sincerity and ferocity in his eyes made her chest swell with something she wasn't sure how to put into words. The knot in her stomach. The heat on her cheeks. The fluttering in her chest and equal passion in his words.

She believed him.

She watched as he squeezed her hands once more, eyes avoiding hers. "If you want me to leave—"

"You asked if I trusted you," she interjected. "I said I do."

"And do you still?"

A lump rose in her throat, and she allowed the jagged breath to enter her lungs.

"I do," she whispered.

She leaned forward, pressing her lips softly to his in response. He hugged himself into her arms upon pulling back, and for the rest of the night, they held each other, allowing their breath to sync and be at peace.

Her King.

52

Aydra and Draven were awoken the following morning by Willow bursting into the room after knocking more than once. She was spewing incoherent babble that Aydra wanted to slap out of her mouth when she rounded the bed.

Which was when she saw Draven in the bed by Aydra's side and began to scream.

"—guard! Intru—"

"Shut up, Willow," Aydra groaned loudly at her.

Willow's startled eyes and paled face did not waver. She shifted on her feet, nearly falling over the rug as Aydra rose from the bed.

"But—but, Your Majesty—why—"

"Who lays in my bed is not your concern," Aydra spat. "You'll keep your mouth quiet about it and anything else you see unless you'd like to find yourself falling out the window to the Edge."

Willow's mouth snapped closed, but her eyes kept darting to Draven's groaning figure now sitting up in the bed.

"It is barely dawn, lady," Draven grumbled in his raspy morning voice, rubbing his face in his hands. "Why have you come barging in? Don't you know how to knock?"

Willow's arms crossed over her chest. "I did. Multiple times."

"And?" Aydra asked expectantly as she pulled her robe around her body.

"The Blackhands are coming up through the streets as we speak," Willow said. "They will be on our doorstep within the hour."

Aydra's stomach knotted. "Fucking curses of Durab," she muttered.

Draven fell backward into the bed. "Should have known they'd be early."

"Thank you, Willow," Aydra told her. "If you'll go and wake Lex, I would appreciate it."

Willow nodded but didn't respond. She gave Aydra a low bow and then turned out of the room, closing the door behind her.

Aydra quickly grabbed a day dress from her closet and changed, throwing her hair up and allowing a few stray curls to fall from her thick updo over her face and ears. She shoved her day crown on her head just as Lex burst into the room.

"My Queen—"

"I'm ready." Aydra started out the door but paused to watch Draven leisurely pack his morning pipe by the window. "Are you not coming?"

"Not my kingdom," he shrugged. "If they want to see me, they can wait on me to get through my morning routine."

The memory of the night before invaded her mind at the sight of the shadows beneath his eyes. He must have seen the look on her face, for she heard him sigh heavily and mutter, "I'm fine, Aydra."

"Liar," she accused.

A small smile slipped onto his lips as he struck the match against the wall. "Get out of here, my Queen," he said in a rasp. "I'll meet you in the Great Hall soon."

Rhaif was pacing in front of the great doors when she arrived, and a sleepy Dorian was coming down the adjacent hall when she turned. She paused in front of Dorian to straighten his crown and the shirt he'd obviously grabbed off the floor to put on.

She was wiping a stain off his jaw and cursing at him for not bathing properly after the night they'd had when she suddenly felt Rhaif standing over her shoulder. Aydra tensed at his annoyed energy.

"Something you'd like to say, brother dear?" she miffed.

Rhaif's huff hit her neck, but he didn't have time to utter a word as Nyssa came running up behind them then.

"I'm sorry!" she exclaimed, holding her crown on her head. "I'm sorry. Willow, she—"

Aydra brushed Dorian's shoulders and then turned to Nyssa to finish fixing her. "How long before they're here?" she asked Rhaif.

"Minutes," he replied.

"And have you heard how many they are bringing with them?" she asked.

"Thirty total." He stared at her as she finally turned and joined him at the top of the steps by his side. "Perhaps if you'd come to my study last night once I'd received word—"

"What, so you could burn me again?" she spat.

"—and not gone off galavanting with the Venari King, you would know more about the nature and number of our guests."

Her eyes met his, and for a moment, she felt the agony of his words fill her. But she pushed it to the back of her mind before it tore through the surface, and she turned and held her chin high in the air.

"I don't know what you mean," she affirmed.

He leaned closer, breath on her shoulder as he hissed in her ear. "You think I haven't noticed the pair of you? Heard the pair of you? Moans and screams echoing in our halls as though you are *animals*?"

"Sounds like you're jealous."

"I am not—"

She watched as his hand clenched and unclenched just above her arm, and she could feel the heat from his body against hers. He straightened himself up.

"You will end it," he hissed quietly.

She almost laughed. "I will not."

"He is using you," Rhaif accused. "Do you not remember all the times past Venari Kings have tried to take over our kingdom? How Duarb tried to seduce our mother? The time when their Infi brothers walked our streets without restraint, raping and pillaging our kingdom, and how long it took our ancestors to rid us of their filth?"

"Exaggerations of the Chronicles," Aydra spat, the story of the night before filling her thoughts.

"You invite that kind of madness back into our walls by consorting with him. You are weak, my sister. He has manipulated and seduced you—"

"Do you two think you could put aside your bickering long enough for us to meet our guests?" Dorian interjected as he leaned around Rhaif.

The great gate opened then, and Aydra clasped her hands in front of her and straightened her dress.

Rhaif glared sideways at her. "We'll talk about this when they've left."

"There is nothing to discuss," she argued under her breath as the carriages came closer.

"There is," he hissed. "There is the fact that you have betrayed your kingdom for the taste of a foreign fuck."

"I am not discussing this with you here," she whispered, meeting his gaze. "We have guests."

"Guests whom you'll surely drop the Venari for tonight and wrap your legs around their heads instead. You are playing with the safety of our kingdom by letting him into your bed. What do you think will happen when you inevitably leave him for your next conquest? Do you think he will stand by and allow our kingdom to go on without punishing it?"

"I love him."

The words seethed from her clenched mouth in such a dark voice that she felt the birds stop chirping overhead.

Color evacuated from Rhaif's face. Her gaze blazed through his empty eyes, daring him to question it. His stare fluttered back into reality, and then he turned straight ahead, the veins in his neck bursting to the surface. He straightened his cloak and fumbled once with the sleeves of his shirt.

"We will talk about this in two days."

Dorian's widened blue eyes met Aydra's, and she felt Nyssa's hand wrap around her own.

The noise of the horse hooves on the stone as the carriages pulled up diverted all their attention, but Aydra couldn't help the nagging in the back of her mind at the look on her brother's face when she'd said it.

It sat there the entire time she introduced herself to the Blackhand Elders and their guests.

There were seven Blackhand Elders between the four Blackhand towns. The Elders were much like their Bedrani Council, only they did not have a King and Queen in charge, only a High Elder who had the last vote on matters. The largest of their towns was Dahrkenhill, where four of the Elders, including the High Elder, resided, followed by Monsburne, Greathill, and the Bryn.

Aydra had only met Blackhand people once in her life, and that was the last time their Elders had traveled to their kingdom when she was ten years old. There were a few characteristics about them that she remembered. She remembered their beards, their all rugged mountain appearances, and lastly, their charm.

She remembered Zoria had taken two to bed with her the night they came, and Vasilis had been so furious that the burns he'd punished her with the next morning had made Zoria bedridden for a week.

So when she found herself grinning at the men and women who exited the carriages and felt her brows heighten at the mere charismatic smiles on their faces, she understood why her late mentor had risked such.

She leaned closer to her sister at one point, who was already blushing, and whispered, "Choose *one*."

Nyssa smiled up at her, and Aydra watched a look grow in her eyes that she recognized all too well.

"What happened to a queen taking multiple pleasures in her bed whenever she likes?" Nyssa asked with a raised brow.

Aydra stared at her, pride swelling in her chest. *"Nyssari Eaglefyre,"* she mused mockingly, wrapping her arm around her shoulders. "What have you done with my little sister?"

Nyssa chuckled under her breath as one of the men approached. He bowed to both of them, the braids in his long tawny hair falling over his shoulders when he did. He introduced himself as the Elder from the town of Monsburne, a small farming town that was closest to Magnice at the edge of the Blackhand Mountains.

Aydra couldn't help the laughter growing inside her as the man spoke with her sister. She bit her lip as she looked around, the Elders and their company chatting with her siblings and their own Belwark guard.

"We've a great breakfast prepared in our dining hall," Rhaif told them after a few minutes. "Please, if you'll join us. I'm sure you're tired after your long journey."

One of the gruff men Aydra had heard bellow a loud laugh earlier pushed past Rhaif up the stairs. "Which way?" he asked.

Aydra bit her lips together, denying the laughter that threatened to emit from her.

"You'll excuse Dag," came the voice of the High Elder behind her at the bottom of the steps. "He's new to the Elder guard. Never been one to turn down food."

Aydra turned full towards the man as he stepped up to her, and she took in his figure deliberately. The sides of his head were shaved, leaving only his straight darkened mahogany hair in the middle to be braided down the center of his head. He was only a couple of inches taller than her, with strong shoulders that struggled against the black v-neck tunic he wore.

"I make no judgments," she assured him. "At least his appetite is healthy."

The handsome Elder chuckled, one stray short hair falling out of the braid and over his eye. "That it is." He took her hand then and kissed the top of it. "Hagen Vairgrey, High Elder of the Blackhands, at your service."

Aydra eyed the Blackhand's light brown eyes as his long red beard brushed her hand. "I'll have none of that, Elder. The days you are here are not about services. They are about celebrating the Echelon coming together for the first time in this Age. Repairing relationships we've long squandered."

His full lips twisted into a smirk, thick brows raising. "Tell me, Sun Queen, how is it we will be celebrating such a relationship?" he asked in a gruff voice.

She felt her lips press together at the sultry gaze he stared at her with. "Dancing," she replied simply. "I've been told your brethren are quite fond of it."

The Blackhand flashed her a wide grin. "You should visit Dahrkenhill for such a celebration," he mused, holding out an arm for her to take. "Dancing. Ale. Herb. None of these fancy dresses and uptight decorations. Simply a gathering of our family. Celebrating life, love, and freedom as we should."

Aydra tucked her arm into his. "Sounds like my kind of party."

The noise of Lex clearing her throat behind her diverted Aydra's attention from the Blackhand on her arm. Aydra's head tilted at her friend, who nodded silently towards the corner. Aydra excused herself from Hagen and darted to the corner with her Second.

"What is it? What's wrong?" Aydra asked in a hushed voice.

Lex's gaze darted around the thinning throng of foreigners near them and then back to Aydra. "The Chronicles are *lies*."

Aydra frowned. "Excuse me?"

"The Chronicles failed to mention that I would be questioning my entire sexual history upon meeting these Blackhand men."

Aydra clapped her hand over her mouth, unable to hold back her laughter. "*Hilexi Ashbourne!*"

"And you... will you be having a guest join you and the Venari tonight? Because he is—"

"No, no," Aydra interrupted. "I need you to handle that for me and give me details."

Lex straightened up and ran her hand through her short blonde hair, her eyes darting back to Hagen standing waiting on them. Aydra grabbed Lex's arm as Hagen turned and smiled at them.

"*Details*," Aydra said in an exaggerated tone. "Details, Lex. I need them."

"Perhaps we should all have a go together."

Aydra gave it deliberate thought, the notion already making her stomach flutter and thighs squeeze. "That's… that's certainly not a bad idea."

Lex looked back to their guest. "Escort him to breakfast. Let's see how he and your Venari get on before we suggest such a thing," she said with a wink.

Aydra joined Hagen a few moments later. They were the last ones to leave the comfort of the outdoor theater. She allowed him to escort her all the way to the dining hall, telling her about the celebrations they had in his town the entire way. And when they finally entered the dining hall, she was immediately met with the loud laughter of the one she'd left in her own bed that morning.

It was a look of joy on Draven's face that she'd never seen within these kingdom walls, a freedom that reminded her of the poor relationship her own people shared with the rest of the beings of Haerland. She envied the camaraderie these races seemed to share despite the distances between them.

Her chest swelled when Draven looked in her direction, and his tongue darted out over his lips as his eyes danced between her and Hagen on her arm.

"Who let this guy in your walls?" Hagen said loudly as they approached. "It was my impression the Promised and Venari didn't exactly get along."

Draven turned towards Hagen, chin rising as he set his cup down. "Funny. I was under the impression trash was immediately dumped from their window to the Edge."

Aydra wasn't sure what was happening until—

Grins broke on both their faces, and Hagen dropped her arm.

Great bellows of what she assumed were their hello's echoed in the hall as they embraced one another, their hands clapping each other on their backs.

"It's great to see you, mate!" Hagen exclaimed.

Draven laughed as he pulled back and grasped Hagen's face. "I didn't know you could get uglier," he bantered.

Hagen let a great chortle out that nearly shook the room. "Mate, you're greying. What've these people got you into that you're already begun growing salt in your beard?"

"You've no idea," Draven muttered.

Hagen laughed as he hugged Draven once more. "Ah, it is great to see a familiar face," he declared. "I was terrified of having to walk these halls with only the Queen here as my escort."

Draven smirked and gave her a full once over again, his hands shoving in his pockets. "And what an escort that would have been," he said, winking at her.

Her chest swelled to its capacity at the familiar bantering Draven standing before her, and she played along.

"Treading on fire, my King," she warned playfully.

"Hold on. Wait, wait—" Hagen's eyes darted between them, holding his hands up. "You two..." he considered them both, a slow smile lifting on his lips, and then he hit Draven's stomach. "You animal!" he exclaimed. Hagen draped his arm around Draven's shoulders and met Aydra's eyes. "Venari King in bed with his Promised enemy Queen. This is something the Chronicles won't tell us about," he bantered.

"You've a problem with who I keep in my bed, Elder?" Aydra asked.

Hagen chuckled under his breath. "The fact he is the one in your bed says a lot more about your ability to love those not of your own kingdom than anything else you could have dared tell me these next few days."

He removed his arm from Draven and held out a hand to her once more, which she hesitantly took.

"You have my attention, Sun Queen."

Aydra smirked at Draven over Hagen's shoulder. "Who knew fucking the Venari King would have such diplomatic perks," she bantered.

The laughter from the Blackhands echoed in the room, and Draven grinned, shaking his head slightly at her.

"Ropes, my Queen," he growled.

"Looking forward to it," she winked.

Hagen wiped his face of the tears, and he draped his arm around Aydra's shoulders once more. "Oh, this is brilliant," he said, turning her towards the middle of the room. "You know, it's actually better that you're taken. Now you can show me who I should and shouldn't flirt with for fear of death."

Aydra pulled his arm off her shoulders so that she could tuck her own arm into his. "No one warned me how much of a handful you all were."

Hagen grinned at her. "Oh, my lovely Sun Queen... You've only just met us. This is only the beginning. We've many more adventures to come."

53

The Blackhands were settled into their rooms an hour after breakfast. Aydra hadn't laughed so much since her days in the Forest with Draven's kind. Dorian and Lex had joined them as they ate food, not in the dining hall, but on one of the balconies adjacent to it, the Blackhands sitting on the ledges, legs swinging off as though they did not fear the fall from the wall.

The Nitesh and Honest were due to arrive at lunch. Aydra soon excused herself so she could clean herself up and change dresses before their arrival.

Her heart was whole upon leaving them.

Aydra waited nervously with her family in the Throne Room for the Nitesh to arrive a few hours later. Her brother's foot wouldn't stop tapping on the floor, making it echo around the still room.

"Glad to know someone can still strike fear into your poisonous veins," she mumbled just loud enough he could hear it.

"You will behave in front of them," he muttered back.

She almost laughed. "You'll need to do a better job at defining 'behave'."

"I mean, you will not embarrass our race in front of the Nitesh," he said as he leaned closer to her. "We need her to see us as her leaders, nothing less."

"Her leaders?" she balked. "You expect the Nitesh to bow before our crown? Haerland's chosen daughter, the most powerful woman in this land, and the only person who could, in fact, curse you... *You want her to bow?*"

He settled back in his chair and exhaled deeply, staring out at Arbina's tree. "If she knows what is best for her people."

357

This time, Aydra laughed audibly and shook her head. "What's best... I hope she turns you into a frog," she said with a roll of her eyes.

The doors opened then, and a line of Belwarks filed inside. They came to stand in lines on either side of the door as a pathway to the thrones. Aydra stood, followed by her youngers, and then finally by Rhaif.

The Belwark Corbin came forward, helmet in his hand at his hip. "Your guests have arrived, Your Majestys," he told them.

The first one to burst in through the doors made Aydra fight a smile.

"The Hones—"

Nadir pushed the Belwark out of the way. "Yeah, yeah," he cut Corbin off. "Put a sock in it, will you? I can announce my own people."

Aydra straightened her dress and clasped her hands in front of her as she fought the grin threatening her lips. Nadir's strides caught the room, and he hopped right up the steps to them. He paused for a moment in front of Aydra.

And then he gently tapped the crown on her head.

"Look at that," he mused, a grin spreading over his features. "You do actually own the crown you deserve."

A swell of gratitude filled her, and she stifled her laughter. "Hello, Nadir."

His face furrowed. "Just a hello? That's all I get? Here I thought we were better battle friends than that," he said with a wink. His gaze looked past Aydra, and he found Lex standing behind her. "Second Sun—" he gave her a deliberate once over "—I like this armor on you."

"I'm sure you do," Aydra heard Lex respond.

Nadir grinned, but then it slowly fell from his face upon a double-take to his left, and Aydra knew he'd seen Nyssa standing beside her. His narrowing eyes flickered back to Aydra for a split.

"Such lies from you, Sun Queen..." he began, attempting to hide the obvious smolder on his features as he turned back to Nyssa and gave her a full once over, and Aydra watched him shift on his feet.

"You said your sister was beautiful, but you failed to mention how she would bewitch me upon finally meeting her," he purred. His hand started to reach for Nyssa's as he said, "Hello, Princess," in a breath-like rasp that Aydra wanted to knock out of him.

Aydra grabbed his arm and twisted it back towards her before he could touch Nyssa, snatching him off-balance.

"No," she warned him.

The smirk slipped onto his lips, and he smiled at the ground briefly before meeting her gaze again. "You still don't trust me?" he asked, playfulness in his tone.

Aydra chanced a glance back at her sister, who was biting her lip in an attempt not to grin at the handsome man before her. But Nadir didn't press. He winked at Nyssa before turning back to Aydra, towering in front of her as he gave her a nod.

"All right, Sun Queen."

The deliberate clearing of someone's throat to Aydra's left made her eyes roll. She met Nadir's eyes and gave him a fake smile that he caught. "Nadir—" Aydra stepped back and turned slightly toward her brother. "—this is my brother. King Rhaifian Sunfire."

Nadir took a deliberate step towards him, his figure standing inches over Rhaif's, and he stared down his nose at him. "King?" he sneered, the word like poison on his tongue. He glanced briefly back at Aydra and then to Rhaif again. His weight shifted, and he practically glared at Rhaif's figure. "The same king that refused to send aid and allowed my men to walk into battle against strangers we knew nothing of with only the people of the Venari at our side and thus caused a loss of life that could have been prevented had he merely sent a patrol of Belwarks to protect our shores— that King?"

Aydra had never been more satisfied in her life.

Nadir gave Rhaif a long once over, and then he backed down the steps one at a time, never losing gaze with him.

A group of Honest filed into the room behind him, some of whom Aydra recognized from the Forest. Nadir paused on the bottom step, and he crossed his arm over his chest, resting his fist at his left breast. "Nadir Storn, Commander of the Honest Army. The Grand will be along with the Nitesh."

"Grand?" Dorian repeated.

Nadir's gaze cut to Dorian. "Lovi Piathos," he answered. "And you must be the little prince that the Venari King has declared to be worthy of the high crown."

Aydra snorted, and she heard the same come from Lex behind her.

A flash of blue flame caught Aydra's eye beside her, and her laughter ceased. She leaned closer to her brother, turning her head so that only he could hear. "You dare threaten our guests?" Aydra whispered.

"*I should have all of you burned for mockery,*" he hissed back.

"It is not a problem of ours if you've made yourself a laughing stock outside these walls," she argued.

He opened his mouth to say more, but the doors opening again made both their voices cease. Intense silence filled the room, and thunder clapped outside.

A woman of dark ebony skin pulled a navy hood off her head. Draven was standing beside her, and he untied the cloak around her neck and threw it into one of the Belwark's hands.

The woman was small, more petite than Nyssa. She barely reached Draven's pectoral muscles. Golden flecks danced in her tightly wound textured black curls. Aydra could see the streaks of gold embedded in her burnet skin like sparkling tattoos on dark flesh. She wore a black dress that Aydra strained to see, as though smoke shrouded around her skin, and it curled as she walked.

The Honest parted ways and took a step back as Draven escorted her forward.

This was the Nitesh. Haerland's favored Martyr daughter of this Age. She was the only being with direct contact with their motherland, and as such, was the most powerful sorceress in all of Haerland.

Aydra's stomach knotted as the woman's golden eyes met hers, and a nervousness radiated through her.

Draven released the Nitesh's arm at the bottom of the steps, and as the woman strode up to them, Aydra quickly bowed her head. She saw Nyssa and Dorian do the same from the corners of her eyes, but Rhaif did not.

She wanted to punch him.

Cold hands on her own diverted her attention. "Rise, Sun child," came the thick foreign accent she hadn't expected.

Her head rose, and she met the stark gaze of the Nitesh before her, causing her words to catch in her throat. A faint smile grew in the Nitesh's eyes, and Aydra watched the woman's full lips twist upwards.

"A number of great friends you have in the south," the Nitesh continued. "Respect of one named such a Queen."

Aydra's chest swelled, and she looked past the Nitesh toward Draven, who was standing with his hands behind his back, and he gave her a quiet wink. Nadir stood at Draven's side with a wide grin spread over his face.

"Nitesh, I wish to thank you for—"

Rhaif's voice was cut short as the Nitesh turned so quickly that

Aydra didn't see her move. "Speak not unless you are spoken to, Fire child," she hissed.

For a swift moment, Aydra thought the flames might rise on his chest. But they didn't, and instead, he did something she did not believe he would ever do.

He bowed.

The doors once more opened, and behind them were Balandria and an older man Aydra recognized immediately.

Lovi Piathos.

His staff pressed into the stone as he walked, and the noise of it echoed in the still room. Balandria paused beside Draven and allowed Lovi to continue, where he met the Nitesh at the bottom of the steps.

"Beautiful as ever, my love," Lovi said in his shaking voice. His eyes darted up towards Aydra then, and he grinned in her direction.

"I think that's enough pompous grander for today," Aydra said as she started to make her way down the steps. "Don't you think, Grand?"

Lovi laughed his high-pitched chortle as she swept her arms around his frail body and hugged him. "Yes, quite enough," he told her. "We be frozen statues if lasted much longer."

Aydra pulled back and held his hands a moment. "Belwarks," she began, looking around the room. "You'll show our guests to their chambers so they can take rest before the celebration tonight."

"Have the Blackhands arrived?" Nadir asked.

Aydra nodded. "This morning."

A smile broke out on Nadir's handsome face, and he clapped Draven on his shoulder. "You know where I'll be," he said with a wink. Aydra watched Nadir's gaze sweep up to the thrones, where she knew he was glancing at Nyssa once more as he stepped backward, biting his bottom lip as he deliberately looked her over, and then he turned on his heel.

"Hey— you, Belwark—"

Aydra nearly rolled her eyes as Nadir wrapped his arm around Corbin and tried to convince him to take him to the Blackhands' rooms. Draven's gaze met hers, and she wrapped her arms over her chest.

"Remind me why I invited him," she said.

Draven chuckled under his breath, his hands pushing into his pockets as he stepped closer to her. His eyes flickered up towards the throne chairs once more where her siblings stood, and he leaned closer to her ear. "How long do you think before your brother has a meltdown?"

"He's already had one this morning," she told him. She sighed audibly and then turned to her youngers, motioning them to come join her with a nod of her head.

Introductions of her youngers to the friends she'd made in the south made Aydra's chest swell with pride for her them. They well respected the power of the Nitesh and the Honest, giving them bows, and responding with polite smiles. After a few moments, Aydra found herself simply staring at the pair talking to the other races from the side of the crowd, Dorian with one hand behind his back as he laughed at whatever joke it was Lovi had just told, Nyssa entranced as the Nitesh spoke with her and held her hands. Draven joined her at her side eventually, obviously watching Balandria do the same.

It was with the realization of her youngers knowing and exceeding her expectations that she made a decision she knew might cost her her life. She wrapped an arm into Draven's, and his hand fell over hers with a squeeze.

"The best of us," he said quietly.

She looked up and met his gaze, her chin resting against his shoulder. "Shall we go for a swim before the celebration?"

He gave her a small smile as his hair fell over his shoulder. "As appealing as that sounds, I need to do a few things before. I'll come to your room to get ready."

She nodded and turned back towards the others. Nyssa's gaze caught her's, and Nyssa smiled as she pushed through the crowd towards them.

"That was terrifying," she informed them. "I can't believe you introduced and then left me."

Aydra scoffed. "You're doing great," she told her with a laugh.

"Just stay away from Nadir," Draven told her. "And Hagen. And Dag. Damien. Hagen's Second. And possibly my Second as well."

Aydra met Draven's gaze then, and she frowned. "It's certainly too late for that. Besides, I think Balandria would be a great match," she argued. "Fearless. Beautiful. Certainly had my attention when first I met her."

"Should I have her meet you for a swim instead?" he suggested.

"Mmm… perhaps we ask her to join us later. Compare my Second to yours," she proposed.

He chuckled under his breath and squeezed her hand. "Tempting," he growled.

54

Aydra bumped into a couple of the Blackhands in the halls on her way back to her room, both of whom stopped and asked her to promise them a dance, to which she certainly obliged at their enthusiasm.

Willow had drawn her another warm lavender bath when she arrived, and she was laying out the dress Aydra had had specifically made on her bed.

"What do you think, Willow?" Aydra asked her. "Will it be enough?"

Willow's eyes danced over the black and gold dress, allowing her fingers to brush over the golden lines like lightning that would adorn Aydra's chest. "I think Maye has outdone herself this time," she replied.

Aydra relished the long bath she took, staring out the window as it began to rain halfway through it. She closed her eyes and sank back into the tub, allowing the noise of it to fill her ears. Thunder clapped in the distance often. She savored the comfortableness of it for as long as the water remained tolerable.

The dress hugged her body as she slipped into it and pulled the long black sleeves up on her arms. A chill from the coldness of the room swept over her bare back. She carefully unpinned her hair from the updo she'd put it in to bathe. Just as the last of her ringlets cascaded down, she heard the creak of the door open.

"Enthralling."

Aydra looked to the door, catching Draven's shadow as he leaned against the back of the door, hands in the pockets of the black pants he wore. She smiled and turned back to the mirror, continuing to try and fix her hair.

"You're not dressed," she stated.

"I thought I would get here early enough for a snack before banquet," he said, slowly crossing the room. "But it appears someone is actually on time for once."

She stopped and eyed him in the mirror, feeling a warmth begin to radiate between her thighs as his eyes watched her deliberately, pupils dilated. And when he adjusted the front of his pants, she bit her lip.

"It comes off, you know."

He tossed the clothes he carried in his hand across the bench beside her. She watched as he acted as though he hadn't heard her. He pushed his feet out of his boots and removed his shirt, then picked up the black shirt he'd bought in town for the banquet.

She straightened, confused by his movements. "I thought we were having a snack?"

He paused, eyes lingering on her hips. "I highly suggest you be the one to take off that dress if that's what's happening."

"Why's that?"

"Because it's taking everything in me not to rip it off you."

She smirked at the daring lust in his eyes, the animal in him tugging visibly at the surface as he held the Venari King at bay.

"And here I thought you liked this dress," she said in a low voice.

"I love this dress," he insisted. "But if you think that would keep me from tearing it to shreds to get to you, you're wrong."

Her mouth dried, and she licked her lips. "Tempting," she mused as she started slowly taking her arms out of the sleeves.

Draven stepped forward just as her dress fell to the ground at her feet. His lust poured through to the surface, and when he wrapped his hands around her neck, she pulled his body flush against hers and kissed him hard.

It didn't take long for him to grasp her ass in one hand and pull her up off the ground, thumb pressing into her throat as he begged her legs to wrap around him. Her back slammed hard into the poster at the corner of the bed, and she felt him grow beneath her. She groaned into his mouth, and his teeth tugged on her bottom lip as he pushed against her.

Aydra barely noticed when the door opened.

"Oh—*Oh*, will you two get on with it," Lex said tiredly from the door. "How are your mouths not completely chapped and your legs not wobbling weakly after this week? Every time I come in, you're in compromising positions."

Draven groaned and turned slightly towards Lex. "So stop barging in," he suggested.

Lex smirked and leaned against the doorframe, her long bangs falling over her eyes. "Where's the fun in that?" Lex purred.

"Then, by all means, join in."

"Oh, you wouldn't want that, Forest King," Lex teased. "You'd lose your Queen."

The dance in Draven's smiling eyes made Aydra's heart quicken, her chest fill. She bit her lip as she watched the crooked smile grow on his confident face. He turned his head from her throat, gaze darting over Lex's figure.

"Try me."

Lex's brow raised, and her eyes darted between Draven and Aydra for a moment. "You're serious."

Aydra felt a wide grin spread on her face at Lex's surprise. Draven turned back to her, and he nudged her nose with his. "Would you mind added company?" he asked.

Aydra rubbed her hands up his chest, fingering the hair on it as her eyes danced with his, and then she turned her head to meet Lex's amused eyes. "I never mind the company of my Second's pleasures."

Aydra released herself from Draven's hips, and he gave her ass a smack. Her fingers lingered on Draven's own as she crossed the space to Lex. And when she pressed her lips to hers, Lex immediately surrendered. Lex grabbed around Aydra's naked waist as Aydra began stripping her and walking her backward toward the bed. As her knees hit the mattress, Lex's mouth moved to her throat, and she felt her finger slip between her legs. Aydra's mouth opened, and she met Draven's gaze over Lex's shoulder.

She grabbed him and pulled him to her mouth, kissing him as her hand grasped his length. She heard Lex moan against her neck, and she knew Draven had pressed his hand between her thighs. Aydra's legs opened widely as she backed herself onto the bed, and then Draven released her to whirl Lex into him. He bit at her throat, and Aydra watched his hand flatten against her clit, a finger slipping deep inside her. Aydra backed up onto the bed and teased herself as she watched them.

After a moment, Draven pushed Lex back onto the bed, his dominating gaze towering over her. Lex pressed herself up to her elbows, and Aydra met Draven's smirk.

"Guests first," he growled.

Aydra wrapped her arms beneath Lex and urged her up onto the bed, Lex's back lying on Aydra's chest. She held her there, reaching around to tease a nipple as Draven crawled over them. He slipped his finger inside Lex again and gave Aydra a fierce kiss, reminding her that he was hers, and then he moved to work his way down Lex's body with deliberate kisses. And when his mouth met Lex's sex, her head threw back onto Aydra's shoulder, and she cried out in pleasure.

Aydra's eyes met Draven's, and she knew the thing that he was doing with his tongue well by now, remembering the first time she'd felt it and what Lex had to be feeling then. Lex grasped onto Aydra's thighs tightly, and Aydra continued to play with one of her breasts.

"Oh, fuck—*there*—" Lex's body limped into Aydra's grasp, and Aydra knew she was quickly reaching her end, much quicker than she was sure Lex was accustomed to. Lex was biting her bottom lip, watching Draven with moans emitting from her insides that Aydra had never heard before. Aydra kissed Lex's cheek and then turned her jaw so that she could kiss her full-on, feeling the vibrations of Lex's moans.

"Come for us, Lex," Aydra whispered against her lips.

Draven's eyes met hers, and she watched him suck her clit as he'd done on her, and she knew what came next.

Lex's head threw back onto her shoulder, and the whimpered cry of ecstasy from the Venari's pleasures radiated through her to a shudder.

Draven sat up, licking his lips as he stared over them. Lex fell sideways back onto the bed, and Aydra almost laughed as she watched her attempt to regain herself. Draven crawled up beside her and pressed his smiling lips to hers, grasping her face in his hands. Lex moved, and Aydra shoved Draven back onto the bed where she herself had just been sitting. She reached down and teased his tip with her fingers, causing a low growl to emit from his throat. Which was when she felt Lex's tongue by her fingers on Draven's length.

Draven's arm wrapped around Aydra, and he kissed her harder as Lex's mouth devoured him. Aydra pulled back, smiling at him, and then leaned down where she ran her tongue down the length of his cock, opposite from Lex. Draven groaned into the bed as Lex grasped Aydra and pulled her mouth to hers, sitting up on either side of Draven's legs.

Aydra felt Draven's hands grasp her hips, and she allowed him to move her until she could feel his length teasing between her cheeks. She inhaled sharply, and he sat up behind her, his fingers teasing her wetness. "Relax," he whispered in her ear.

The deliberate chill ran down her spine, and she nearly melted into him as he slipped a finger into her ass. It was a different sensation that made a restlessness fill her body, and for a moment, she forgot about Lex being in the room.

But his hands grasped her hips again, and he slowly lowered her cheeks down onto his length. An audible gasp left her. Lex didn't seem to notice. She kissed Aydra's throat and made her way down her front. Aydra's heart fluttered in her chest at the feelings happening to her, her breaths shortening. Draven grasped her hands in his and held her up as he gently moved his hips up and then torturously down inside her.

It was when Lex's mouth pressed to her clit that she saw stars. The flickering of her tongue made her whimper as Draven continued his own. She heard him groaning familiarly behind her, and his hands tightened around hers. Aydra looked down and watched Lex play with Draven's sack as she continued to tongue her.

"Fucking—" Draven's words didn't finish. Lex pressed a finger inside Aydra, and Aydra's breath altogether ceased.

They fell apart together with screams that would have awoken Arbina herself.

Aydra practically fell onto the bed at Draven's side and stayed there a moment, unable to gather herself together as her heart started to beat again. Lex sat back and leaned against the poster of the bed opposite her, a wide smile spread over her lips.

After a few moments, she felt Draven move, and he clasped her butt cheek in one of his hands upon sitting up. She watched him take Lex's hand and kiss her knuckles.

"Fair enough, Venari," Lex managed, flipping her hair out of her face.

"Satisfied with my performance enough I can keep my Queen?" Draven asked Lex.

Lex chuckled under her breath. "Exceeding expectations," she said with a wink. She stood from the bed then and started to pick her clothes up off the floor. "If you'll excuse me, I need to refresh myself before the banquet." She shoved her pants on and grinned at them. "I'll be back soon. Try not to squander that time doing more of this while I'm gone."

Aydra met Draven's eyes, and he laid down on his stomach beside her, the grin he had been wearing now softened. He reached out, his fingertips delicately tracing her hip. Her eyes fluttered. She didn't know how he made her want him more by just the touch of his thumb, the wanton of his gaze.

"Did I hurt you?" he asked.

Her eyes flickered over him, and a small smirk rose in her features. " Leather two nights ago, and you're worried about hurting me with a bit of ass play, Venari?" she mocked.

A huff of amusement left his lips, and his fingers tightened around her flesh, and then he smacked her backside. He pushed himself up onto his hands, hovering over her body. A serious gaze quickly replaced the playful one, and the air intensified around them as she raked her hands up his chest, threading her fingers into the hair on it. She wanted to take him again, to feel the pleasure of his filling her once more, but she wasn't sure they had time.

"Stare at me much longer and we'll never make it tonight," she informed him.

He leaned down, his lips pressing softly to her throat. "I thought you wanted ropes," he muttered against her skin.

Her fingers entwined in his hair as she inhaled the forest scent of him, her legs instinctively bending up on either side of his waist. The feeling of his rippled back muscles beneath her fingers made her eyes close, her hips arch upwards against his.

She reached for his length and gave it a tug, stroking it back to life. "Quickly, my King," she whispered in his ear.

He groaned into her neck, and she felt him stiffen in her grasp. He nipped down her collarbone and sucked on her breast, teeth tugging on her hardened nipple. But she pushed on his chest, legs gripping around him, and she turned him on his back. Her hands grappled to the poster behind his head, and she sank herself onto his hardened cock with a rock of her hips. He cursed under his breath, eyes tightening, and she surrendered as his hands splayed over her hips, fingertips digging into the thick flesh of her backside.

It was a half-hour more before they were both dressed in their banquet garb again. He mocked her the entire time they were dressing, telling her of the dances he was sure the Blackhands would try to teach them. She'd just finished twisting her hair when she heard the words he was speaking trail, and she glanced back at his face as he stared at her. The smile on his face faltered, replaced by the dilated pupils and look of inherent surprise that she'd only seen on him a few times.

"What?" she asked.

369

"You've no idea how powerfully striking yet diabolically terrifying you are, do you?" he said to her.

The words caught her off guard, but the smile rose on her lips nonetheless, and she sighed into the swelling in her chest. "Do you not realize you're the same?" she asked him, almost chuckling under her breath. "Beautiful, dominating, and amorous all at once. Wrapped in shadows of inherent angst and carnal desire, poised to strike at any moment."

A smile tugged at the corner of his lips, hair falling over his face as though he wasn't used to anyone saying such things about him.

"Now who's being ridiculous?" he bantered in such a low quiver that a chill pulsed down her spine.

Her smile widened as he stepped forward and wrapped his arms around her waist, and she almost closed her eyes at the sweep of his hands digging into her hips. He didn't say anymore as the thunder clapped outside, and she began to run her hands up and down his arms, surrendered into the quiet of their shared ardor, the content of their equality.

"Are you ready for this?" she whispered.

Draven's weight shifted in front of her, and he looked past her out the window. "Thunder. Clouds. Lightning. Rain… Looks like as good of a day as any to die."

She shoved his arm. "Be serious. For once, Venari."

His hair fell over his face, tickling her shoulders, as he pressed his forehead against hers. "I am serious. *My Queen.*"

The door opened then, but it didn't startle them.

"Well. You two are certainly looking to make an entrance," Lex said as she crossed the room. "Is there some sort of joint venture that I should be warned about?"

"The fewer people who know, the better," Draven said as Aydra took a step back to look at herself in the full-length mirror again.

"If it makes you feel any better, I don't even know," Aydra said with a raised brow.

"All right. Keep your secrets," Lex said. "But hurry it up. We're late."

Aydra's stomach knotted as she stared at herself in the mirror, blocking out Draven and Lex's bantering beside her. She looked down at the form-fitted black and gold gown, the twisted dark golden vine pattern wrapped within the stark black velvet material glistened of the waning sun outside. It fit around her curves and flared out below the knee as her favorites usually did. The sleeves hugged her arms, and the golden pattern leapt off the black fabric around her shoulders, wrapping up over her collarbone and neck like tree limbs.

Her hand reached for her hair. The fire had returned in her eyes in the last few days that she'd felt more alive than she'd ever felt here in this castle. Draven appeared behind her then, the black high collared gambeson he had bought fitting snugly around his form. The collar cut low on his chest, revealing the bottom edge of the taut muscles of his pecks, the dark hair creeping up on his skin. The leather of his skinny pants glimmered in the sunlight coming through the window. The great sword on his belt hit his leg when he moved. His black and ivory-boned crown already sat embedded in his dark sun-streaked hair, as though it had been made to fit on his head and his head alone.

He reached for the thick golden twigged crown in her hands, and she turned towards him. It was placed on her hair, and she rubbed her hands against his chest and up to his face as his arms slid around her waist.

"I love you," she whispered.

A look of startled surprise pressed into every pore of his features. "What?"

She bit back the smile threatening her lips. "I'm sorry, I forgot I hadn't told you."

His weight shifted, still blinking as though he couldn't believe what she had said. A short inhale caught in his throat, and his head tilted just noticeably. "That's not..." She heard a deep growl-like exhale leave him, and he pressed his forehead against hers, eyes closing. "I am going to pretend you didn't say that... And we can circle back later," he suggested.

She almost laughed at his nervousness, but she reached a hand up to his cheek instead, pausing a moment to savor the look in his eyes, the look of overwhelming disbelief that she'd said what she said written in them. A twinge of pink rose on her cheeks, and unfamiliar amorous words filled her. She couldn't help but sigh into the feeling, allowing them to release from her lips.

"Draven, I... I feel as a Noctuan in your arms," she whispered, meeting his gaze, "and you... you're the rise of the dying moons. Breaking the curses this land has shrouded us in. My freedom and my salvation. The King I never have to fear inequality of. *My* King."

She watched as his chest rose, and he shifted again, a swell of something in his eyes when he opened them that she hadn't expected.

Another great exhale left his body, and he cupped her neck in his hands again. The kiss he pressed to her lips was gentle, and she felt the tremble of his mouth against her skin.

"You shouldn't have said that," he managed upon pulling back.

Her smile faltered just slightly.

"Why?"

"Because now I'm really going to burn this kingdom to the ground."

55

Draven could not escort her to the great hall. He was intended to meet Balandria and Nadir before walking in, and so once they left Aydra's room, he paused in the hall before her, to which Lex laughed and leaned on the wall to wait.

Draven kissed Aydra's cheek. "Don't let the Blackhands charm you before I've arrived," he told her.

She smiled and gave him a full once over, feeling herself bite her lip. "Find me for a dance later."

"A dance?" he repeated, obviously taking him off guard. "I hope the scribes have their quills ready," he continued, glancing fleetingly back at Lex. "We're re-writing history tonight."

"No," Aydra said with a shake of her head. "We're breaking the Chronicles at the spine."

Draven's head tilted at her, and before she could blink, his lips pressed hard against hers. She wavered on the spot at the ferocity exuding from him into her, and when he pulled back, his hand pressed into her cheek.

"I fucking love you," he growled.

She didn't have a chance to respond. He kissed her again, and once more with such an intensity that she had to grab his waist to stay steady. After a moment, he let her go, and he backed away, continuing to shake his head and look the whole of her body over. Words refused to escape her lips as she watched him, and then when he finally turned on his heel and walked down the hall, the breath she'd held inside finally exhaled from her body.

Her balance staggered, and she felt Lex's hands on her arms to keep her on her feet. A mocking grin had spread on Lex's face when she came to stand before Aydra, hands still holding onto her.

"Have we recovered?" Lex bantered.

Aydra was still staring at the door Draven had left through. "I may have to go back in my room and take care of something before banquet," she breathed, eyes widened up at Lex.

Lex snorted and wrapped an arm around Aydra's shoulders, staring at the door as Aydra was. "Same, my Queen. Same," she agreed with a grin. "But we are late. So I think the both of us will have to go with mental release until tonight."

Aydra nodded and squeezed Lex's hand. "Right. To our inevitable deaths, then?"

"After you, Your Majesty," Lex mocked.

"Dance with you?" Nyssa repeated, brows furrowed. "What—"

Aydra grabbed her hand and pulled her to the middle of the floor. "Don't worry, I'll lead," she told her with a smile.

A short squeak emitted from Nyssa's lips when Aydra twirled her and then pulled her back in. The wild look on Nyssa's face made Aydra laugh.

"What's wrong, sister?" Aydra mocked. "Should two women not be allowed to dance together for fear of mockery or scorn?"

"It is quite unorthodox," Nyssa said.

Aydra chuckled under her breath. "Since when has anything I have done been by the rules?"

Nyssa seemed to relax, and she squeezed Aydra's hand as she smiled at her. "Never."

A full grin spread on Aydra's face, and she pushed Nyssa out to twirl her once more. "Besides—" Aydra wrapped Nyssa into her and then twirled her back out, "—this dress favors much better with the wind in it."

The laughter that emitted from Nyssa's lips made Aydra's chest tighten, and when Aydra pulled her back in and held her hands, she felt her head shake at her younger sister.

"You should get to know more of these people, especially Balandria and Nadir," Aydra told her.

Nyssa's gaze narrowed before moving past Aydra to where she knew Nadir was standing on the other side of the room. "I thought I was to stay away from Nadir."

Aydra paused, her gaze squinting at her sister. "You think he's cute, don't you?"

"Yes," Nyssa answered quickly. Aydra's brows raised, and Nyssa's cheeks flushed. "I mean… I do— Have you seen him? He's—"

Aydra cut her off with a laugh, and she shook her head. "No," she told her.

"But he's gorgeous," Nyssa argued, eyes flickering towards him in the corner.

"*Nyssari!*" Aydra laughed.

The twisted disappointed smirk Nyssa gave her then reminded Aydra of the time she'd taken away Nyssa's first sword at the age of nine. Aydra shook her head and hugged Nyssa tightly, inhaling the scent of her sister's cinnamon hair. When she pulled back, she pressed her hands to Nyssa's cheeks and scrunched up her face amusedly at her.

"No," she laughed. "He's the worst sort of man."

"What do you mean?"

"Well… He's handsome. Smart. Confident. Leading commander of an army." Aydra chanced a glance across the room towards where Nadir was leaning against a column. "And he's quite funny," she finished. "You'll be in love with him before you realize what's happening."

A lone laugh left Nyssa's lips, and she sighed as she smiled fondly at Aydra. "I'm glad to see you so happy again," she noted.

Aydra paused, allowing the grief of her actions the last month to wash through her. "I know I've been intense lately with the training and pushing you… Believe me, I do. But, preparing you and your brother for the possibility of what's coming on our shores has overwhelmed my mind. I cannot stop thinking about the weapons on their ships. What the man said to me. How armed they were just to be sailing over an ocean. Dorian thinks I should bring you the next they come. To chat with them instead of beheading them on the beach."

"Dorian said that?" Nyssa asked.

"He believes in you," Aydra affirmed. She reached over and pushed Nyssa's hair back off her face. "You're going to be such a Queen, my sister. Beauty. Grace. Honor. Compassion. You and Dorian will rule in the fairness and equality this crown has been absent of for years now."

Nyssa's head tilted, and she eyed Aydra. "Why are you telling me this?"

A long sigh emitted from Aydra, and she took a turn looking around the room at all the faces watching them, finally landing on Rhaif's shadowed figure as he flirted with one of the Blackhand women. His eyes met hers, and she squeezed Nyssa's hands once more.

"It's nothing," she managed, meeting her sister's gaze once more. "Now, tell me, what is it you and Dorian want to do for your birth moons coming up?"

Nyssa told her excitedly about the plans she'd been trying to put forth in the next week for their birth moons. Aydra memorized the happiness on her sister's face. She wanted to remember this day for as long as she could, just as it was.

After another dance, one of the Blackhands came between her and Nyssa to ask her sister for a dance. Aydra gave her sister a wink and let her go. Her eyes wandered a bit around the room, finding Dorian dancing with one of the Scindo twins, Lex chatting with Balandria by the buffet…

But it was the sight of the three most handsome men she was sure Haerland had to offer standing in the corner together, laughter on their faces, that a smile rose on her lips, and she shook her head at them.

Draven's gaze met hers as Hagen clapped his shoulder, doubling over at whatever joke it was Nadir had just said. She felt as though he were fucking her in the back of his mind, taking her somewhere she hadn't been before. His hand tightened around his drink, and his other shoved into his pocket. When he winked at her, she forced a jagged inhale to her lungs, gaze darting over him deliberately as her thighs squeezed, and then she finished crossing the space between them.

"Why do I get the feeling you three together is more trouble than any town knows how to deal with?" she asked upon reaching them.

Draven's chin rose, and he looked down at her with a sly smirk that made her heart flutter. Nadir and Hagen were still laughing, but they straightened upon her words, the pair of them shaking their heads.

"Mm… wouldn't you like to know, Sun Queen?" Hagen bantered, swirling his drink in his hand.

"I would, actually," she admitted.

She noticed the smile on Nadir's face then. He was looking past her shoulder. There was a softening in his eyes, his lips twisted upwards just at the corner, revealing the small dimple on his cheek...

She punched him in the stomach.

"Hey!" Nadir balked, throwing his hands in the air.

"Stop staring at her," Aydra warned.

"What—*she's staring at me!*" he argued.

"He's not wrong," interjected Hagen.

Aydra opened her mouth to speak, but Hagen had already taken her hand. "What—"

"Leave him alone, Sun Queen," Hagen said as he tugged her around. "Let's have some fun."

Her eyes widened to Draven, and he laughed softly at her as she was dragged by the Blackhand onto the dance floor. Hagen whirled her out and back into him, causing laughter to emit from her lips despite herself. She was shaking her head at him when he pulled at her hands.

"Shouldn't you be dancing with one of the women I pointed out to you earlier?" she asked.

He met her smile. "I will. But first—" he twirled her in a circle before taking her hand again "—I needed to clear a bet with my mates."

She fought the knowing grin threatening her lips. "What kind of bet?" she dared to ask.

"How long it would take before the Venari King came and interrupted us."

Aydra shook her head. "I'm afraid to say you'll be owing your men money tonight, Elder," she said.

"Yeah? Why's that?"

"Because the Venari King cares little of who I dance with. Jealousy does not live on his public features. He knows he will be the one in my bed later. Who should try and swoon or tempt me otherwise simply does so in foolishness."

Hagen grinned. "And that's exactly why I'll be winning the bet and not the others."

Hagen told her more of the Blackhand celebrations as they danced, comparing the dance they were having then to their own, promising her they were less formal and more of a grand family gathering.

"Perhaps you and your youngers could travel to our town for one," he told her. "We'll put you up in the Temple. Finest rooms at the tallest point in Dahrkenhill. It is most beautiful during the Deads. The stars go on for ages."

"And when will the next celebration be?" she asked.

"Come in the spring. The fields of flowers are bountiful. The snows will be gone. It's the perfect time and place."

Aydra's chest swelled at the thought of seeing it. "I'd like that."

"Don't worry, you can bring your forest lover as well," Hagen said with a wink.

Aydra laughed. "Thank you."

Dorian came and took her from Hagen's arms after another dance, insisting he go and ask Lex for a dance. Aydra tried and failed to keep her composure as Dorian spun her around repeatedly, attempting to dizzy her to the point that she could not see.

"You are glowing today, my sister," Dorian said finally as he held her so she did not fall. "Tell me your secrets."

Aydra's chest filled as she steadied herself. "One day, I hope you and your sister find the truth that was once written in these walls… how the first of our race was happy, fearless, and gracious to all the people of Haerland. Not what I was told was our truth, not what my Olders had been told was our truth… I have tried to protect you both for as long as I can remember. You deserve so much more than the past atrocities of this kingdom."

His eyes softened just so as he twirled her around again and then back into him. "You deserve everything, Drae. Love. Freedom. Happiness…"

A smile rose on her face as she saw Draven's figure heading towards them, and Aydra forgot about the rest of the room. "Someone to walk this life equally with," she added.

Dorian's eyes squinted, and he turned her so that he could see exactly who it was she was staring at. She heard him laugh under his breath, and he shook his head knowingly. "Exactly."

The smile on Draven's face made her heart quiver. It was as though she were seeing him for the first time—the swelling in her chest, jagged breath leaving her lungs…

Tunnel-vision surrounded her.

It was only them.

Draven clapped Dorian on his shoulder. "Do you mind if I steal her?" he asked her younger.

Dorian let go of her waist and held out her hand to Draven. "By all means," Dorian said, giving him a short bow.

Aydra hardly noticed her brother leaving as Draven pulled her hand to his lips, and he kissed her knuckles. The cold air brushed over her wet skin, causing her muscles to ache.

"My Queen," he muttered against her flesh.

A deliberate warmth spread from his kiss up her arm and then down her spine, and she felt her thighs squeeze as he stared through her with dilated pupils.

"You really shouldn't call me that when there are other people in the room," she managed.

A quirk of a smile rose on his lips, and he slipped a hand around her waist, grasping her flesh just noticeably and sending heat directly to her stomach. "Why's that?"

"Because I find myself dripping whenever you say it," she breathed in his ear.

She felt the goosebumps rise on his arm, and he stared at her with a dark smolder that made her hair raise. "If I can't call you my queen in public—" he twirled her once and then pulled her back into him "—then you certainly can't say things like that."

She almost laughed. "We'll call it even."

She could feel the eyes of those around them staring, heads turning as they danced in circles, him occasionally spinning her out and then into him just as the men had done that danced with her previously in the night.

But her chest swelled every time he would smile at her, pull her flush against his torso. And more times than once, she felt her heartbeat quicken when he would touch the bare flesh on her back.

"I need to tell you something," he said in a breath.

Her eyes narrowed just slightly. "Don't tell me you've fallen for one of the Blackhand women already," she said in a playful tone.

He chuckled under his breath. "As appealing as they've made themselves, no. Nothing like that." He pulled her close and held her hand against his chest. She could see a seriousness rise in his gaze, and he sighed audibly.

"It's actually more of a question," he clarified.

"Okay…"

"Will you help Nadir with one of the water serpents?"

Her face faltered, and she wanted to slap the rising smirk off his lips. "Seriously," she muttered, unable to keep herself from smiling. "You are such an *ass*, Draven." She pushed his chest slightly as he continued to chuckle at her. "I thought it was something serious!"

"I am serious," he argued. "He wanted me to ask. Apparently, it's terrorizing the children because of the ships."

She shook her head and felt her lips twist up at his grinning face. "Maybe it is he who is terrorizing it," she uttered. "I can't believe you just tricked me like that. I thought something was wrong. Like you were suddenly going to tell me you didn't love me or that—"

"If I ever tell you that, something is very, *very* wrong. Someone is trying to kill me or worse," he interjected, squeezing her hand. A different seriousness rose in his gaze.

"Aydra, you... You are my equal core. My partner. My comforted darkness in a world of deafening light." He paused as they swayed, and she watched him exhale deeply and give her a slight shake of his head. "Shrouded with you in the shadows of our Sun is the only place I ever want to be."

A rasp of a breath left her as her heart caved in her chest. "How am I not supposed to tell you I love you when you say things like that?" she whispered.

He cupped her cheek in his hand, jaw tightening distractedly as his throat bobbed. The glistening in his eyes made her own tear up, and he looked as though he would shake his head again, but instead, he sighed audibly.

"Restraint," he uttered.

She barely heard the quiet laugh that escaped her, feeling her eyes dance as she gazed up at him. "You're ridiculous."

He smiled and laid his forehead against hers. "Say it again," she heard him whisper.

Her hands wrapped around his neck beneath his hair, and she pulled back just slightly so she could see his eyes.

And then she pressed her lips to his.

Ancient enemy races, the Queen of Promise and Venari King of the South, kissing before every race in Haerland.

She felt him smile against her lips, and he grasped her tightly in his arms before picking her up off the ground.

Aydra didn't care that everyone in the room was staring at them. She didn't care that the music had stopped playing, that a bewildering intensity had filled the air. All, except for the Blackhands, whose noises of cat-calls and whistles were echoing around the room, were silent.

Kissing him in front of every being in Haerland was the best way she knew how to express how much she loved him.

Her feet hit the ground, and he wrapped a hand on her cheek as he pulled back, a grin spread over his features. "So much for restraint," he mumbled.

She huffed amusedly under her breath. "You should know by now, restraint has little place in my core."

He pulled her flush against him again, and his nose nudged hers. "My Queen."

The words once more sent chills down her spine as she inhaled the forest scent of him. "My King."

"*Ahem.*"

The deliberate clearing of someone's throat brought her back to the reality of the room. Every couple around them was staring. Aydra caught Nadir's gaze, knowing he was the one that had cleared his throat, and he gave her an amused wink from where he stood. Calls from the Blackhands of 'Get a room!' and whistling continued. But it was the silence of her own people that made Aydra's stomach knot.

Aydra caught Lex's eyes towards the door, and she gave her a large grin. Aydra fought the returning smile and stepped back from Draven to look around at her own people, who looked as though they were frozen to the spot on which they stood.

"Why have we stopped dancing? Has the band died, or is that what they are asking for with this silence?" Her eyes cut to the corner where the band was sitting, and they started back up.

A few of the Blackhands started trying to dance again, but the Dreamers they stood with were rooted to the floor. They continued to stare at the pair.

Aydra's eyes wandered around them, meeting every Dreamer's gaze. "If you value breath, you'll dance," she warned.

Slowly, the people took each other's hands, and once more, the room filled with moving bodies all around them.

Draven's brows were elevated when she turned back to him. She heard a growl emit from his throat as he wrapped his arms fully around her waist and bent his head. "I love when you talk like that," he muttered into her hair.

She smiled and nudged his nose. "Wait until tonight," she whispered.

And so they danced. They danced until it was only they and the Blackhands left in the room.

And when they retired for the evening, her body surrendered to a restless ache that she swore made her heart pump faster, her body more sensitive to his touch. A night different from other nights, one where they allowed their love to live in their bodies together, not simply a lust-filled passion, but more.

Because she couldn't stop kissing him. She couldn't stop touching him. Her sitting on his lap on the lounger as he caressed her body, moving to the bed and to every surface. As long as she was touching him, she was free. His skin felt of a radiant heat on hers she couldn't explain. It was an overwhelming feeling she never wanted to be rid of, a race of her heart that made her feel alive. An out of body alive that she had to remind herself was real more than once.

This was the home she'd been missing her entire life.

Wherever he was.

And she swore it was the happiest day she would ever know.

56

Aydra and Draven met with the staff early before the sun so that they could instruct them on how to set up the room for the meeting that afternoon.

It was the largest gathering of minds Magnice had ever seen.

The four royals of Magnice. The Venari King and his Second. The Nitesh and her army commander. Nadir and Lovi Piathos. The seven Blackhand Elders. The Bedrani Council. And finally, every Dreamer Noble and company commander of the Dreamer army.

A table set for thirty-four was not an easy feat.

Aydra and Draven were the only ones who knew where to sit everyone so that a war did not break out over the last roasted turkey leg.

They helped the servants create a great rectangle with the tables. Ten persons each on the longest sides, seven on the other two. She made a point to have the Blackhand Elders on one side, opposite the Nitesh and Honest.

But when she sat her own chair beside Draven's facing opposite where Rhaif was to be seated, Draven raised his brows.

"I thought we were keen on not starting a war," he said.

Her lips pressed together, and she fought a smile. "I like to look my enemies in the eye when bringing them to their knees."

A low growl emitted from his throat. "It is entirely too early in the day for you to be speaking like that."

She almost laughed, and she continued instructing the servants where to put chairs. "My sister will be beside me, Dorian beside Rhaif on the opposite side with the Council surrounding on both sides. We'll have the Nobles on either side of my sister and Balandria."

"You're giving Balandria a spot at the table?" he asked.

"She's your next King," Aydra confirmed. "She deserves it."

A sleepy Dorian strode into the room then, apparently unaware that they were prepping the room for the meeting. He stopped mid-yawn and frowned around him.

"What's happening…" he managed.

"Good morning, brother," Aydra said, giving his hair a fluff. One sniff of him and her nose curled. "Disgusting, Dorian. You smell of sex. Who did you get into trouble with last night?"

He smiled sleepily at her, eyelids halfway over his prominent blue eyes. "My secrets," he told her. He wrapped his robe tighter around him and looked around the room again. "What are you two doing?"

"Making sure no wars are started tonight," Draven replied as he continued to set plates on the tables.

"Why not?" Dorian asked with a yawn. "I thought a great war was what we were preparing for," he replied.

"That's a different war," Aydra argued. "One that we need to have everyone on the same page for."

Draven's gaze narrowed. "You're going to bring up the ships, aren't you?" he asked.

She stopped moving for only a brief second and then quickly started folding the napkins in her hands. "Maybe."

"Aydra—"

She turned away from him, creasing the cloth violently in her hands as she waited for the words she knew he would utter. "You cannot stop me."

"Aydra, you can't—"

She started across the room, and he grasped her arm, whirling her back around to face him.

"You don't know the Blackhands," he argued. "If you start off talking about war, they will think they have been ambushed into this meeting to bow at your feet. You will start something you cannot control. Do you not remember the last time you brought them up?"

"Then what is the point of all this?" she almost shouted, wrenching her arm away from him. "What is the point of bringing every leading member of the Echelon together in this room if not to talk about the strangers on our shores? What else is there to discuss?"

"Trading routes, goods, the slaves of the northern Blackhand town, Infi persons in the streets, peacekeeping initiatives—"

She almost laughed, her head shaking at his last words.

"Peacekeeping initiatives…" Her head shook, and she sat her hands on her hips. "The only peace these people will ever see is if we get rid of the strangers on our shores. We have to talk about it."

"And we will—" he stepped forward and took her hand in his. "But we have to play their games first. You cannot run out of the gate talking about war and invasion. Let them talk their politics, and when your brother tries to end the meeting, bring it up as a last note. You have my full support. You have the word of Nadir and his men, along with Lovi. But you have to be smart about it. We have to present this as something we merely need aid to prevent. Not as the start of a great war between the entirety of this land and some strangers. The only thing we know about them is that they refer to themselves as Man—"

"It will become a great war if we do not handle it."

"I know," he affirmed, squeezing her hands. "I know. And I agree. But we have to play the politics."

A great exhale left her in a huff, and she muttered, "Fine."

Dorian was still standing beside them, and his gaze darted between the pair. A servant walked by with food on a tray, and he grabbed it out of her hands, popping a grape back in his mouth.

"So what food have you two ordered for this meeting? Anything good?"

Aydra's tense body relaxed, and a great sigh left her as she felt Draven wrap his arms sideways around her. She tossed one of the grapes from the tray playfully at Dorian's face.

"You're the worst," she muttered at him.

The creak of the servants' door at the back of the room opened, and in walked a petite hooded figure that Aydra frowned at the sight of. None of the servants walking around seemed to be bothered by the person coming in.

"Nyssa?" she called out.

Nyssa jumped, and scarlet hair fell from beneath the hood. She grabbed onto her chest and turned to face them, obvious she had just been startled. "Drae," she managed, widened eyes looking around them. "I didn't expect—" she paused and looked around them then, apparently just noticing the grand table being set up. "What's going on here?"

"No, no," Aydra argued, brows furrowed as she slowly stepped towards her sister. "Why are you sneaking around through the servants' tunnels with your hood up?"

Nyssa's mouth opened and closed, weight shifting under Aydra's gaze. "I—I was just going to the kitchens for food," she stammered, fumbling with her fingers. "Bit famished and light-headed after banquet last night. I can still feel the wine going through me—"

Nyssa's eyes darted anxiously from her hands, to the floor, and to Aydra's own. Her cheeks were as flushed as her hair, and Aydra slowed her stride as she stepped up to face her. Aydra's arms hugged around her chest, and she gave her sister a full once over.

"Mmhmm…" Aydra muttered through her closed mouth, eyeing Nyssa's avoided gaze.

Dorian snorted behind them, and Nyssa cut her eyes at him over Aydra's shoulder.

It was then Aydra noticed why Nyssa had her hood up.

Aydra reached forward and pushed Nyssa's hood back, followed by her hair. She felt her lips twisting, and she raised a brow at the raised blood marks on her sister's throat.

"You're a terrible liar," Aydra mocked.

Dorian burst into laughter that echoed around the room.

"Shut up, Dorian!" Nyssa nearly shouted.

At first, Aydra smirked at her blushing sister, obviously flushed that she'd been caught out of sorts and bringing food back to whatever person it was that had adorned her bed the night before. But the way her sister avoided her gaze made Aydra pause.

And then, the realization of who it was that she was sure had joined Nyssa in her bed hit her like an anvil.

Aydra audibly gasped, eyes widened. "*No!*—what— *Nyssa!*"

"And we're leaving," Draven's hands grasped Aydra's shoulders, and he tried to pull her away.

Aydra pulled her arms away from him, mouth still agape. "The one person—"

"Drae—"

"—I told you to be careful of—"

"Sister, please—"

"—you took him back to bed?!—"

"*Will you—*"

"—What happened? Did he lure you with his stupid jokes?"

"Oh, what did you think was going to happen?" Nyssa spat.

Aydra's words ceased at her sister's scolding rolled eyes.

"You tell me I can't have something, I'm obviously going to go after it!" Nyssa continued.

The defiance written in Nyssa's features made Aydra's chest swell.

Aydra shook her head, feeling her lips slowly twist upwards as the words her sister had just said repeated in her head.

"Something tells me she didn't have to do much 'going after'," came Dorian's amused mutter.

"Shut up, Dorian," they said at the same time.

A laugh sounded under Aydra's breath when she turned back around, and she met Nyssa's gaze. "That's the first time you've truly stood up to me," she mused.

Nyssa inhaled deeply, and Aydra watched as a small yet nervous smile lit up her sister's face. "I'm learning," she managed in a breath.

Aydra grinned. "Yeah? How did it feel?" she asked.

Nyssa's chest began to heave, gaze darting between Aydra and Draven standing behind her. "Terrifying," she admitted, "but a good terrifying?" Her voice was high-pitched, as though she were fighting anxiety. She shook out her hands, nerves possessing her. "If that makes sense. I—"

Aydra laughed as her sister steadied herself. "It does make sense," she told her. She wrapped her arms around her sister and hugged her tight a few moments before parting. And then she held Nyssa's face in her hands.

"I'm going to kill him," Aydra said with a full grin on her face.

"You're not," Draven said, sinking his arm around Aydra's shoulders as she dropped her hands from Nyssa. "If I remember correctly, your sister can decide the right sort of man for herself," he added with a wink at Nyssa. "Besides, Nadir would somehow charm his way back into your good graces before you got the drop on him."

An audible sigh left Aydra's lips, and she reluctantly resigned the notion. "Fine."

Dorian came up beside them then. The grin on his face was spread into his features. He started to reach for Nyssa's chin so he could see the marks on her throat, but Nyssa slapped his hands.

"Ass," Nyssa muttered.

Dorian chuckled under his breath and held out his arm for her to take. "Come on, let's go get you that food for you to take back to bed."

The pair started off down the hall, Nyssa shoving his arm off her after a few moments and Dorian laughing at her as they playfully argued down the tunnel.

Aydra was still in shock. Draven laughed and pressed his lips to her temple. "Leave it," he urged her. "She can take care of herself."

Aydra hugged her arms over her chest. "That's what I'm worried about," she admitted. "They're growing up too fast."

"Nineteen. A great war on our horizon. I'd be worried if they weren't," Draven told her.

She hated that he was right. "True." She sighed and took his hand then, taking another look around the room as the servants went back to putting things out for the meeting. "Let's go get some food. I think they have things handled—Hey, Willow—" she called to her lady "—if you need us, we'll be in the kitchen. Please do not deviate from where I've placed everyone. My axe was sharpened yesterday, and I've been itching to strike it through something." She paused and looked around the room at the Dreamers who stared at her. "You've been warned."

57

Aydra chose the pantsuit outfit to wear to the meeting.

The black pants hugged her curves, and the thick peplum caped shirt clung to her torso until it flared out and away from her hips. Draven placed the crown on her head as she was dressed, and she nervously turned her ring three times around her finger before they set out of her room.

"Stop fidgeting," Draven said under his breath as they walked.

"I'm not," she argued as she stretched her fingers at her sides.

"Liar."

"Shut up."

The Council was already seated around the table with the Dreamer captains. The Blackhands and Honest were mingled in the corner, the Nitesh standing off to the side speaking with Nyssa. Aydra and Draven greeted them with hugs and smiles. Aydra's nerves stayed bottled up, only waning just slightly when she spotted Dorian talking to Nadir.

She slipped out of the Blackhands' conversation to go and hug her brother. Dorian kissed her cheek and then gave her a tight-lipped smile.

"Why did you sit me next to him?" he said without moving his mouth.

"Because you can handle it," she argued, keeping the smile on her own face. She gave him a wink and pressed her palm to his cheek. "Just keep him from engulfing all of us in flames."

Nadir came up then, smiling widely as he gripped onto Dorian's shoulders and shook them jovially. "Sun Queen," he uttered. "What is on our agenda for this meeting? Trading routes and food, or are we speaking of our beloved ships?"

Aydra's arms crossed over her chest, and she stared at his smiling figure. "Nadir, tell me something," she said, stepping closer to him.

Dorian slipped out of Nadir's grasp just as Aydra reached him.

"What's the last thing I said to you yesterday when you arrived?" she asked, voice edging.

Nadir sat his chin in his hand, and he looked up at the ceiling as though he were recounting their words. "You introduced me to your brother."

Aydra grabbed the napkin off the table. "I told you—" she smacked his arm three times "—don't—go near—my—sister!"

Nadir winced and blocked her blows. "What—*she came on to me!*" he whispered fast. "I was weak!"

Aydra glared at him. "Sure you were," she mumbled. "And my sister is terrified of everything. There's no way she would have come on to you."

Nadir's brows narrowed slightly. "Maybe you should get to know your sister a little better then—" she smacked him again "—*hey!* Enough with the hitting!"

"You're lucky my King asked me not to castrate you," Aydra warned.

The deliberate clearing of Draven's throat at her side made her pause. Aydra took a deep breath, feeling herself calm as Draven's hand landed on the small of her back. "I'm fine," Aydra made herself say.

Draven stared at his best friend, and Nadir lowered his arms. "What the Infi, Naddi?" he whispered.

"What? You're mad at me too?" Nadir argued. "It's not my fault. I was avoiding her, doing as I'd been told. She— She— *I was weak*—We spent most of the night talking anyway—"

Aydra balked, and Nadir backed away before she could hit him.

"Not that that's any better!" he said fast. He pushed his hair back off his face and sighed heavily. "I'm not apologizing," he finally said. "I know what you said… but… it was nice. Talking to her."

Aydra hugged her arms over her chest and gave him a pursed lips once over. "Break her heart, and I'll break your neck," she finally told him.

The door opened then, and the Belwarks announced Rhaif's entrance.

The three looked between each other, and Nadir clapped her shoulder as he moved past her towards his own seat. Draven squeezed

Aydra's hands.

"Ready?" he asked one final time.

Aydra exhaled a breath through her mouth, and Draven reached up to her cup her cheek in his hand. "Ready," she said, sinking her face into his palm.

The rest of the group took their seats around the table, the last of which being Draven and then finally Aydra.

Rhaif stared at her across the table.

And Aydra couldn't stop smirking at him.

Rhaif's hands steepled together atop the table, and he leaned forward to look at the scribe in the corner of the room. "Scribe, please record the date and time of this historic meeting, along with the names of all those in attendance," he said mechanically. "As a first order, I would like to thank all of you for coming. It has been too long since our races were united as one."

A Belwark came forward then and placed a piece of parchment down in front of the High Councilwoman, Reid. She nodded and thanked the Belwark before clearing her throat.

"A first matter— trading routes," she began.

Aydra tapped her fingers absently on the table as they spoke of goods, of trading with new places, of the new stock the Blackhands could offer if Magnice would allow them to trade in their streets as well as the Honest.

Once the trading routes were mulled over and a declaration had been put forth for the new goods, things turned towards the discussion of the Infi. The Council wanted an update on any Infi in their streets, as well as an update on Draven's end—whether they'd found more in his Forest.

"We took care of it," Aydra argued at the Council. Her eyes flickered to the Elder from the Bryn. "But I'm told your town has more Infi in it than you dare to admit."

Draven squeezed her thigh under the table.

The Bryn Elder stared at her, and the woman sat up at the table. "We have a few, yes. Can't seem to get rid of the filth. They hide on the higher peaks, only coming into our town at night or in the winter."

"I can help with disposal," Draven interjected. "It will be a long journey for you to be rid of them, though. I can explain what you'll need to do before you leave."

The Bryn Elder gave him a nod. "That would be much appreciated."

"There is an easier way," came the Nitesh's voice.

Frowns slipped onto Aydra and Draven's faces as they leaned forward to see her.

"What do you mean?" Draven asked.

Lovi's laughter echoed around the room, and they all turned to see him shaking his head. "Secrets, Nari," he mused. "You've too many."

"Can one of you please tell us what we're missing?" Hagen piped in.

"Disposal of Infi," the Nitesh began. "Duarb's roots connected to the Knotted Caves. Mons welcomes his presence."

"So… they just have to take the bodies to the caves?" Draven asked. "Not the Hills?"

The Nitesh nodded.

Draven sighed back in his chair and nodded to the Bryn Elder. "That makes things simpler. I'll tell you how it's done when we're finished."

"Or I could go," Dorian chimed in.

Chairs moved as people tilted their heads at him. Aydra bit her lips to keep from smiling. He met her gaze, and she gave him a nod.

"I can travel to the Bryn in a week. Help you dispose of the bodies. I accompanied the Venari King when he disposed of those in our streets," Dorian said.

"I will go with him," chimed in the Belwark Corbin.

Rhaif's hands were tightened together atop the table. "Then it's settled," he said. "The Prince will ride with his guard to the Bryn next week. We can be rid of this filth before it takes a whole town."

"Are there any other matters to speak of?" Rhaif asked, his gaze darting around the room.

Draven grasped Aydra's hand above the table and leaned back in his chair, gazing down his nose at the Promised King before him.

"I think you know," Draven said in a low voice.

Aydra leaned forward. "Let's not dance around it."

Rhaif's eyes cut at her. "There is nothing to dance around," he hissed.

"Were you trying to keep it quiet?" came Nadir's voice. "Did you think we wouldn't bring it up?"

"Bring what up?" asked Hagen. "What's going on?"

"It's no longer a concern," Rhaif said quickly.

"No longer a concern…" Nadir repeated the words and sank back into his chair. "So sixteen of my men dying. Eight of the Venari… their lives being lost to strangers invading our shores, that is not a concern to you?"

"Invasion?" the Nitesh repeated.

"It was my understanding," Councilwoman Reid interjected loudly, "that this situation was taken care of."

"The situation was taken care of," Draven said. "Only because your own Queen rode out to help defend those not of her own and came up with a battle plan that saved our asses."

"There will be more," Nadir chimed in.

"When did they come?" Hagen asked. "Where?"

"They've landed west of our reef twice now," Nadir said. "More and more ships are coming. It is only a matter of time before they start coming in from the west as well to Magnice."

"Is that a threat?" asked one of the Bedrani.

Nadir stared at him. "How can it be a threat from my people? We are the ones fighting them."

"These strangers were no more versed in combat than our queen in battle plans," announced Ash.

Chairs slid and swords drew.

Ash suddenly found himself staring down the length of Draven's blade with Lex's knife at his throat. Balandria and Nadir's hands clenched around their own as they also stood.

"So, what you're saying is… these men were well skilled with their blades," came Nyssa's voice.

A flicker of a smile met Nyssa from Nadir, and he winked just noticeably at her. Aydra didn't lose her stare with Rhaif's annoyed face.

"Enough," Aydra finally announced, her hand on Draven's side.

Draven slowly placed his sword back in its hold, and Lex took a step back. When Draven sat again, he grasped Aydra's hand above the table.

"Has anyone spoken with these strangers?" asked Hagen. "Found out what they want?"

"Since when should we speak with people coming in not of our own and setting up their own camps without asking?" asked Nadir.

"Since maybe they were run away from their own homes and are simply looking for refuge," argued Hagan. "And you people have been slaughtering them when perhaps they need help."

Draven's hand tightened around Aydra's. "Then perhaps they shouldn't travel wearing armor and sporting crossbows on their ships," he practically growled.

"I spoke briefly with one," Aydra affirmed.

"And he said?" asked Hagen, arms crossing over his chest.

"He said, 'Long live King Aeron of Mathis, ruler of Man'," Aydra repeated.

Hagen stared at her expectantly. "What else?"

"There was nothing else," she replied. "He spat at me, and I cut his throat."

Hagen scoffed and settled back into his chair. "All right. So you learned nothing—"

"A great deal more from this encounter did she learn than she realizes," cued in the Nitesh.

Silence enveloped the room, and they all stared at the golden-gazed woman sitting at the end of the table.

"You know them?" Aydra asked.

The Nitesh sat up in her chair, and her eyes darted around them. "Man is a race born across our seas, not made of the land as we but rather of shared blood of each other, a long way from here. If they have discovered our lands, they will not stop."

Aydra met Draven's bewildered gaze, and she squeezed his hand as the wash of worry ran through her.

"What do you propose we do about this?" Hagen asked then. "Why should our people be concerned if they are simply on the shores?"

Aydra's gaze flickered around the table, meeting the eyes of Nadir and Dorian before turning back to Hagen. "We do not ask you to bring your soldiers down here until we know more. We will find out more the next time they arrive… what they want, how many they are, why they have come to our land. You have my word. But we thought you should know the situation. If they come onto our shores here at Magnice, and their intention is revealed, that they intend to take our land, we only have our Belwarks and a few Dreamer companies to defend our kingdom. If they break past us, they are likely to be in your realms within just a few months," she continued with an eye on Hagen.

"We can only do so much from our side," Draven added. "All we ask right now is that you think about sending aid should we need it. Supplies. Weapons. Possibly Belwark patrols since you are the closest," he said with a look towards Rhaif.

Mutters between races filled the air. Aydra glanced at Draven, and he squeezed her hand again.

A few moments passed, and she watched Hagen sit back in his chair, arms crossed over his chest. "All right, Sun Queen. You've got your supplies should you need them."

"We will see what we can spare for the Venari," announced Councilwoman Reid. "Perhaps a Dreamer company or two."

Aydra's heart swelled, and she leaned forward at the table as Nyssa grabbed her arm. Eyes flickered to the Nitesh at the end of the table, and she straightened up from speaking with her guard.

"This not the fight of our Martyrs. Not yet," she told them plainly. Her hands stretched together above the table, and she sighed. "However... should you need supplies... we will send with Honest traders."

Breath returned to Aydra's lungs. She met Dorian's proud gaze, and he smiled at her across the table.

"All this talk of war has me starving," announced Hagen as he stood. "Where is this grand food the king promised us?"

As the rest of the people stood around them, Aydra's chest continued to flutter. She turned slowly to Draven, unable to keep the smile from her face. His jaw twitched as he fought a grin, and his hair fell over his face as he winked at her.

She wanted him to fuck her on the table right then as the exhilaration of moment swam through her, but she settled for the grand kiss he gave her upon standing.

58

The night of the meeting consisted of joyous laughter and promises from the Blackhands, excited about the possibility of spilling the blood of strangers. She and Draven laughed with them, retiring only when everyone else had broken off to their bedding partners.

Aydra didn't want to rise the next morning, too comfortable in Draven's arms to move upon the rising sun. But she knew she had to. She would need to get Lex out of bed, find out where her siblings were, gather everyone before their guests left for the day.

"Stay," he muttered as she moved.

"We can't," she argued. "We have to get up. You need to find Balandria."

Draven groaned as he sat up and rubbed his face in his hands. "For someone who skives off Queen duties on the regular, you certainly do make yourself responsible for people waking."

"I do not know where my youngers ended up last night. I have to find them. And Lex will have who knows in her bed."

"Probably my Second," Draven mumbled. "Perhaps your younger brother."

Aydra gave her hair another fluff and then headed out of the bedroom, walking barefoot over the black rug floor down the hall and up the staircases to the rooms of the personal Belwark guards. She didn't pause before bursting in, not caring who it was that had accompanied her Second the night before.

"Lex, are you awake yet? My brother— *Oh.*"

Her brain stopped computing upon seeing the people in Lex's bed.

Balandria. One of the Council's Dreamer daughters. And Hagen.

"*Oh,*" was all Aydra could manage.

Hagen moved slightly, his arms rising over his head as he laid between Balandria and the Dreamer daughter.

"Morning, Sun Queen," he mused with a smile.

Aydra fought the grin threatening her lips. "Morning, High Elder. I'm glad to know you've not really a type."

Hagen huffed under his breath. "My type is strong women." He slapped Balandria's butt as he rose from the bed, stark naked, and Aydra couldn't stop her eyes from wandering as he crossed the space towards her.

"If the Venari hadn't already had you in his bed, you'd have been here with us."

She smirked at him. "Believe me when I tell you, Blackhand. It would not have been your idea to grace my bed. It would have been mine."

He reached for her hand and kissed her knuckles. "Come to Dahrkenhill. Bring the Venari and your Second. We could have fun."

She allowed her eyes to dance with his a moment. "Get your clothes and find your way to your own room. I've been told you all are leaving in an hour." Her eyes flickered back to the Dreamer daughter stirring in the bed, and she said, "That goes for you as well, Skye," to the girl. "Your father will be wondering where you are."

The Dreamer, Skye, jolted up and grabbed her dress off the ground, eyes wild at seeing Aydra standing in the room with her. "My Queen —" she looked in the mirror and fluffed her long blonde hair, "—my Queen, I'm so sorry. Please—"

Aydra chuckled under her breath and held up a hand. "I did not see you," she told her.

Skye grasped her arm. "Thank you," she whispered before running out of the door.

Aydra woke the Seconds then and hurried them both to get ready. Hagen quickly excused himself upon their rising and darted from the room.

Lex exchanged a knowing smile with Aydra as the door closed.

"Tell me he's as good with that tongue everywhere else as he is in his charms," Aydra demanded.

Balandria and Lex looked at each other and then grinned at her. "Exceeding expectations," Lex mused.

"Rivaling my own King," Balandria added, winking at Aydra.

Aydra's brows heightened. "Really?"

"Really," Lex agreed.

Balandria stood from the bed and came around to face Aydra. "Do you know the twist Draven does—"

"Hey Lex, have you seen—" Draven burst into the room without knocking, and Balandria stopped speaking. Draven frowned as he looked between them.

"No one told me about this morning party," he said in a low tone, eyes darting between the three.

Aydra grabbed Lex's shirt off the floor. "Get your clothes on, Seconds. We're seeing the rest of these people off in an hour."

Seeing off their guests that morning was different than the times before. The courtyard seemed to be divided, only Dorian and Nyssa being the two that darted between the separated guests. Aydra did not speak any more to the Council or the Dreamer captains than usual, but she mingled with her friends, hugging and telling them goodbye individually.

Hagen had her promise to visit their town soon. Nadir told her he would expect her there to see him during the next Deads so she could talk to the water serpent she'd promised to help with. Aydra eyed him as he told Nyssa goodbye, watching as a blush rose on Nyssa's cheeks as she laughed under her breath at whatever joke Nadir had said. Nadir had kissed her hand, and he gave her a wink before turning away from her finally.

Lovi hugged Aydra tightly, telling her he would take her to see the Scrolls when she came to help with the serpent. And when the Nitesh finally reached her, Aydra didn't know what to say.

The Nitesh reached up to Aydra's face and pushed her hair off her cheek. "Informed of any lies from your mother, tell me. You have my support for whatever path you should choose to take next, my Queen."

Aydra heart jumped in her throat, for Hagen had called her the same only moments before.

Draven draped his arm around her as the last of the carriages left, and she hugged him from the side. "Looks like we have plans," she said with a sigh.

"I told you they would call you their Queen," he said as they locked eyes.

A small smile spread over her lips, and he bent his head down to kiss her. She sighed into his embrace, cherishing the small moment of freedom and warmth in front of the rest of the kingdom.

"All right, enough with the public displays," came Dorian's voice as he pushed past them.

Aydra laughed and pulled away from Draven, sinking her arm into her brother's bent elbow. "I'm so proud of you," she told him as she reached up to fluff his hair.

He grinned and started to walk with her into the castle doors. "What do you say to a pastry breakfast?" he asked her. "In the kitchens at our table."

"Am I allowed a guest?" she asked, eyes flickering to Draven behind them.

Dorian paused, squinted eyes darting over Draven's silent figure. "I guess he can come."

"Nice to know one member of the family likes me," Draven mused under his breath.

"My sister—"

The sound of Rhaif's voice made Aydra stop in her tracks. She stopped, and Dorian's arm tensed around her. She squeezed his arm back and gave him a nod as she turned and stepped away towards her brother.

"Rhaif," she said, stepping up to him on the other side of the door.

Rhaif pushed his hands behind his back. "You'll meet me in the Chamber in an hour," he demanded.

"Why would I do that?" she asked.

"Because we've much to discuss after the meeting yesterday," he replied.

She bit the inside of her cheeks at his gaze, and she finally gave him a nod. "Very well."

Aydra couldn't stop pacing, a nervous energy pouring through her.

Draven and Lex were with her in her room. He was leaned against the poster of her bed, Lex sitting down at the end of the mattress.

"I don't like it," Draven argued. "What does he want?"

"One or both of two things," Aydra said. "He either truly wants to discuss the meeting, or he means to punish me."

"Punish you?" Draven repeated with a balk of his head.

"If he touches you—"

Aydra held a hand up to Lex. "No. You'll do nothing. Your orders are to protect my sister. No matter what happens, you protect her."

"Wait," Draven interjected. "What—"

"I will not—"

"Swear it," Aydra demanded, stopping in front of Lex and ignoring Draven. "If you love me, you will swear it. Nyssa and Dorian must stay safe. And you cannot kill him if something happens."

Lex stared at her. "If he kills you—"

"Why the fuck is this even a conversation?" Draven interjected, stepping forward. "Kills her—"

"—I am to simply sit back and do nothing?" Lex continued. "How —"

"The same goes for you," Aydra told Draven.

Draven stilled as though he were paralyzed against the post, arms crossed over his chest. "What have you not told me?" he asked deliberately.

"If he hurts me, you are to do nothing," she said.

The glare in which he stared at her with then made her bones tingle, the hair on her arms stand on end. "I will rip him to shreds with my bare hands," he uttered.

"You won't get the chance with his fire," she argued.

Wind knocked the grand window open so violently that one of them shattered against the stone.

"Why do you think Duarb gave the Venari King wind?" he said in a low growl.

"If you kill him, you will start a war," Aydra said. "The Belwarks and Dreamers will not listen to Dorian even if he tells them not to go to war with you. They will want vengeance for him."

"And they won't if you die?"

"The Bedrani Council has wanted me subdued for some time. His killing me would be a welcome reprieve, especially after this week." She looked between the pair and crossed her arms over her chest. "Swear to me. Both of you."

Lex exchanged a glance with Draven, and at the same time, they both said, "No."

"Please—"

"We shouldn't even be having this conversation," Draven interjected.

A knock on the door signified that it was time.

"I have to go."

She disappeared from the room without looking at them.

59

The raven flew in one of the open windows and perched on her shoulder as she walked down to the Council Chambers.

Plan? he asked her.

Buy time. I do not wish to make a saint out of him.

Rhaif was sitting at the long table when she arrived. A Belwark led her inside, and she took Draven's seat across from him. His chin sat against his hand, and he was leaning back lazily in his seat.

"Close the windows," Rhaif instructed the Belwarks from his chair. "Then leave us."

Aydra's entire body stilled, heart skipping.

He did mean to hurt her.

"Think they don't know how to break glass?" she asked, knowing why he was closing the panes.

Rhaif's eyes locked on her, but he did not utter another word. Each grand window closed, and throughout it, she nor he moved or blinked.

But once the doors shut, she felt her breath stop.

Rhaif sighed, and he allowed his hand to hit the end of the chair arm. "What is your plan, sister?" he asked across the table.

Her brows narrowed. "Excuse me?"

"Your plan," he repeated. "I know better than to think you actually love the Venari brute, not to mention the display the past two days, your fraternizing with our eastern enemies... flirting and speaking to them as though you truly mean to be their allies. I do not dare to think you mean to truly bring the old Echelon together. And besides... You wouldn't know what love was if it was thrown at your feet."

"How would you know what love is? The only thing you've ever loved is yourself."

"Wrong," he argued upon his standing. "The only things I have ever loved are our giver mother and you. Everything I have ever done has been for you. Your safety."

Aydra's hands curled in on themselves. "Burning me is not love. Manipulating me is not love. You do not trust me. You sent an army after me because I went to help our allies to the south—"

"You betrayed me and all of your people to travel south for an orgy all because you thought I was being mean to you," he mocked. A sarcastic smile rose on his face, and he started crossing the space between them. "Ash told me about the two of you as soon as he and his company returned here. They told me of you with the Hunter, with the Honest commander... how you stuck so close to them throughout the battle, revealed your secrets, demanded the Dreamer company lay down their lives for a cause they'd been ordered to not have any part in." He paused and towered over her. "So tell me, my *dear* sister. What is your plan?"

She stared at him, feeling the raven watching her from the top of one of the chairs, waiting on its orders to attack. But she didn't give it.

She stood from the chair and walked deliberately around him, and she answered in the only way she knew might save her from war.

Lies.

"Patience, brother," she replied slowly. "Allow them to think they have a place at our table. Bide our time. And then eventually... once we have them where we want them, we strike. Hard. Take the southern realm as ours." She started to pace around him. "Can you see it?" she whispered. "Hunters on their knees at our feet. A summer castle on Lovi's shores. After we have the south, we can set our eyes on the eastern mountains. The Blackhands will never know our strength. They will not stand a chance. And when they are ours, we will only have one piece to conquer. Haerland's own Martyrs would rather kill themselves than start a war. You will be King of all Haerland." She rounded in front of him again and pressed her hands to his cheeks. "Arbina's roots will freeze. The Nitesh will grant you immortality for your sparing her people. You, my brother, can be the King who never dies."

"Immortality, you say?" he repeated, his gaze hazing over as he looked out the window.

"A gift for your generosity," she whispered. "For the greatest and last King Haerland will ever know. Rhaifian Sunfire. Ruler of the

Seven Realms. Conqueror of Ghosts. Defender of the Lost." She pulled back and stared determinedly into his eyes.

"High King of Haerland."

Her brother grasped her cheeks softly in his hands, smiling proudly, his pupils dilated with darkened glee. He leaned closer, his lips tickling hers, and she waited for the moment in which he would kiss her crudely as he'd done before.

And then he laughed under his breath.

"Lies."

He yanked the roots of her hair and threw her back into the table. Her hip hit the edge of it, and she winced, her hair falling over her face.

"Why—*why* would you lie to me?! What are you up to that you would need to create such an elaborate false scheme?" he growled.

"Because I knew it was what you wanted to hear! I wasn't stupid enough to think that you would actually believe me when I say I love him," she blurted.

"You—" a chair flew away from his hand and crashed into the floor, "you actually... *love* him?" he dared ask as he continued stepping towards her.

Aydra straightened herself up, her chest heaving. "I do."

Blue fire pushed up from beneath his gambeson and onto his neck as his breaths became shorter and shorter. Black engulfed his fingertips and began splintering up his arms. Aydra felt her eyes fluttering back, and she heard the crows echoing in her ears.

"Stand down," she warned him. "Don't make me do this—"

"No, my sister," he said as the black reached his eyes. "Don't make me."

And then he screamed.

Windows shattered. She flung herself to the floor into a ball and shielded her head in her hands. She heard the rapture of her crows dive into the room. She expected the flames to engulf her, to take her into their grasp and burn her alive.

But she never even felt the heat.

—The screech of her raven echoed in the room.

Her eyes opened just in time to see the blue flames consume its black body.

"NO!"

Black feathers fell in the air in front of her in slow motion. The flames recessed back into Rhaif's body, but she barely heard him stepping backward.

Her raven was gone.

"No…"

Her heart shattered.

"No—*no!*"

Her raven's ashes were in a pile at her folded knees.

She screamed as a feather fell in her trembling hand.

"*NO!*"

Her raven. Her namesake. The first creature to ever speak with her. The one that had been with her since she was a mere three years old.

Dead.

His ashes stained her shaking fingers.

She barely heard the clip-clapping of her brother's shoes on the stone as he left her screaming on the floor.

"*NO!*"

Reduced to ashes.

By her own brother.

She couldn't stop the agonizing screams emitting from her throat. Her shaking hands curled around the black feathers before her, and tears poured down her face.

Strong arms grasped her from behind. She continued to scream, not even aware of the audible sobs and horrifying noises emitting from her insides.

An emptiness filled her.

She surrendered to the arms around her and buried herself in what she realized was Draven's chest, clutching his shirt in her hands.

Every emotion she'd ever suppressed boiled to the surface.

"You were right," she whispered into Draven's chest.

"About what?" he asked.

"Your being here when my wall came shattering down."

His arms hugged tighter around her, and he kissed her forehead. "I didn't mean like this."

She didn't know how long they sat there. But Draven didn't move. He didn't speak. He just held her there, occasionally rubbing her back or kissing her forehead.

Aydra sat up finally, avoiding Draven's gaze. Her eyes found the ashes of the raven again, and she bit back another bout of tears.

"He was the first creature I ever heard," she managed as she reached out to the ashes again. "I was three. He was only still a baby himself." A small smile rose on her lips at the memory. "I found him in the hanging tower. He'd tried to fly out of the nest, but he was too small to keep up with his siblings. His mother left his there. You should have seen Zoria's face when I brought him back," she remembered fondly.

"I'll take him back to the Forest," he promised.

She met his eyes. "Why the Forest?" she asked.

"Ravens are all born in darkness. The only reason they are not part of the Noctuans is because they do not share the bloodthirst." He reached down and took one of its feathers between his fingers. "The Sun commissioned them long ago to be the bridge between the light and the dark."

Aydra frowned. "How do you know this?"

"The Honest Scrolls," he answered.

She realized they were not the only ones in the room. The crows she'd heard earlier were all perched around the Chamber. A hundred of them at least, all sitting quietly as though in mourning of the one slain.

"Take me with you," she breathed.

Draven sat up slowly, his eyes narrowing at her. "Is that what you want?"

"I cannot stay here. Not after this... He'll make up something and have me in chains by the end of the month," she said. "And Nyssa should come as well," she begged.

"I doubt your sister would agree to that."

Aydra looked at the ground again and nodded. "Then I must go to her and explain."

"And Dorian?"

"He will understand."

60

"You're leaving, aren't you?" Lex asked in her doorway.

Aydra stopped moving, inhaling the tears that had just fallen down her cheek. "I am," she whispered.

"Will you allow me to come with you?"

"I need to know you're here protecting my sister. You know what he is capable of. I need someone I trust to look after her."

Lex nodded as she crossed the space between them. Her hands reached out and squeezed Aydra's hands in hers. "I swear it."

Aydra hugged Lex then, wrapping her arms around her tightly, realizing it would be the first time she would be away from her for longer than two weeks. She wasn't sure what to say to her.

"I know it will not be the last I will see of you, and as such, I will not tell you goodbye," Lex said into her hair.

"I would let you do no such thing," Aydra said as she pulled back. "Thank you. For everything."

Lex leaned in and kissed her then, cupping her cheeks in her hands as a tear stretched down her cheek. "My Queen," she whispered.

Draven appeared in the door soon after, with Nyssa and Dorian at his side. Nyssa crossed the room and wrapped her arms around Aydra with force.

"Dorian told me everything," Nyssa whispered in her hair. "I'm so sorry I didn't know."

Aydra pulled back and wiped the tear from Nyssa's face, giving her sister a small smile. "It wasn't your place to know, to try and protect me. But I cannot stay here. You understand why?"

Nyssa nodded. "I do," she whispered.

Nyssa hugged her again, and then Dorian's hand came to a rest on

Aydra's shoulder. She couldn't hold back the emotion as she wrapped her arms around him.

"You remember what I told you?" she said into his hair. "Keep her safe. Keep yourself safe. Lex will be here with you." She pulled back and wrapped a hand around his cheek. "Take care of your sister. Let me know of anything that happens. I will be back for the next meeting."

Dorian visibly bit back the emotion burning his cheeks and nodded. "Okay."

She hugged him tightly again, fighting the tears that threatened her insides.

Lex took Nyssa and Dorian away from her not long after. Draven stayed, helping her finish packing her bags. And when she was done, he took her hand and kissed her palm.

"Are you ready?" he asked, hoisting her bag onto his shoulder.

She took one more look around her room, making sure she did not miss anything and also taking in the home she'd always known.

"I am."

He held her hand as they walked from her room and down staircases and halls through the castle, not saying anything more as she memorized every stone around her. Her home. Her kingdom.

And she was forced to run from it.

"Fleeing off to the Forest, are you?"

The noise of Rhaif's voice made her fists curl as they reached the last hallway. Draven snapped around at her side—

The bag on his shoulder fell to the ground. Draven's fist collided with Rhaif's face, and the noise of Rhaif's breaking nose vibrated in Aydra's ears.

"Ah!" Rhaif grunted and stumbled, hands clenching at his nose. Flames pulsed to life, but Draven didn't care. He shoved Rhaif backward, and Rhaif fell onto the floor on his back.

"Little shit of a King—" His fist railed into Rhaif's face again— "Is this how you rule? Cowering behind your fire like a—"

"Draven!"

Draven grabbed Rhaif up by his shirt and slammed his back into the ground, the wind billowing around them and pushing Rhaif's flames low. His arm drew back again, but Aydra grabbed Draven's arm before he could strike into her brother a third time. The noise of armor sounded in her ears, and she pulled Draven to his feet, pushing herself between the pair.

"Not now."

"You would rather I do nothing after what—"

"*I don't want to see you in chains,*" she said through gritted teeth, just as she noticed two Belwarks come around the corner. "Wait for me at the gates," she pleaded with him.

The veins in his neck pulsed as he stared at Rhaif over her shoulder.

"Draven, please—"

Breath left him, and he stepped forward again, towering over her. She thought for a moment he would push past her, dive into Rhaif's face again, but then he took a step back and met her gaze.

"If you're not with me in five minutes, I'm coming back to slit his throat," he promised.

Draven turned on his heel.

—Every great double window in the hall burst as the wind broke through their glass, and Draven slammed the door behind him.

The two Belwarks at the other end of the hall stopped in their strides, hands on their swords. Aydra held up a hand to them.

"Go back to where you came," she demanded. "There is nothing to see here."

The pair gave her a short bow and turned on their heels.

Aydra watched Rhaif pick himself up off the floor. He held to his bleeding nose, flames and ashen skin receding back.

"He will pay—"

"Come after he or I, and you'll never see daylight again," she promised.

Rhaif stared at her and wiped his face with his sleeve, gaze fuming through her. "Go ahead, sister. Have your fun in the forest. But when he hurts you, don't come running back here looking for your crown."

"My crown comes with me," she argued. "I go to the southern realm not only to get away from you but also to help them protect our borders, to fulfill my duty."

"If you leave this kingdom, you forfeit your place as Queen."

Aydra stared at him. "That crown is my birthright."

"For the Queen of our realm, yes. But if you leave, you'll no longer serve this realm."

"That is not up to you to decide," she shouted. "You cannot demote me simply because I choose to leave the abuses of this realm to protect our people."

His eyes cut at her. "Is that what you think this kingdom has done to you?"

She clenched her jaw, not wanting to start with hearing the manipulation she knew was coming. "What I think…" She paused and shook her head, allowing the emptiness she'd felt these last years to wash through her.

"You've been raping me since we turned fourteen. Threatening to end my life simply because our mother spent more time with me. Because you were jealous. I am *sorry* she treated you as such. I am sorry she turned you into this person and made you feel inferior. But… I cannot blame myself for it any longer. We promised to love each other, to be better. We promised we would not be the kings of our past. And now look at you—"

"How would you know what love is?"

She paused, biting back the lump in her throat. "I know it is not anything I have ever felt whilst living here in these walls," she managed. "You have become your own poison, Rhaif. I cannot stand to be swallowed whole by your fury."

"Then I am sure your sister will—"

Her blade pulled from her waist, and she shoved it beneath his jaw before he could blink. "You dare touch our sister… I will kill you."

"Do it," he dared. "Strike me down as you know you want to. Secure your place as High Queen. Take what you have long waited for."

"I have never wanted the High crown. I have never thirsted for the power as you do."

"Then what do you want, sister?"

She released him like hot iron burning her skin, and his feet clapped on the floor upon his landing. She took a step back, blinking back the bewildered feeling in her bones.

"Freedom," she breathed.

Her crown thudded on the stone floor at his feet.

61

Her palms wiped her face harshly as she emerged from the doors, her head feeling empty, heart void of the queenly title she'd grown to know. Draven stared questioningly as she descended the steps to his side.

"Where is your—" Draven paused from placing the bags on the saddle and stared at her as his face began to pale. "Your crown. Where is it?"

"Forgotten," she said sternly. "I can protect my people just as well without a crown as I can with one," she said as she took up tacking on the bag to the saddle.

"Wait—*what?*" Draven reached for her arm and whirled her back around. She swallowed the tears threatening her eyes.

"I am no longer Aydra Ravenspeak, Promised Queen," she managed. "I am simply a daughter of Arbina, a survivor of Magnice."

"He took your crown?"

Aydra didn't respond.

"That crown is your birth—"

"It doesn't matter," she interjected softly. "What's done is done."

Their eyes locked, and Draven sighed.

"Then I feel no hesitation in offering you refuge within my realm, my Queen," he said as he took her hand in his and kissed her palm.

"I am no longer a Queen," she whispered.

"You're the only one of your past siblings to have ever earned the title," he breathed back.

"You're just saying that—"

"You should know well by now I do not say any words simply because of what I feel for you," he interjected. "I would have said it a

411

year ago."

She bit back her tears and looked past his shoulder to the gates, heart numbing in her chest.

"Let's go," she managed.

Aydra tried not to look around her as they made their way through the shop streets; the sight of their Queen without her crown accompanied by the two Venari leaders she knew was bewildering to every Dreamer walking their streets.

She wondered what lie Rhaif would come up with when people began to ask where she'd gone.

As the fortress gate closed behind them, Aydra paused and turned her horse around. She gazed up at the kingdom she left behind. The white stone castle. The halls she'd grown up playing in. The merchants she'd grown to love and cherish. The Dreamers she'd sworn to protect.

She reminded herself she could still protect these people from the southern shores. That this was not the last time she would look upon the brilliance of the kingdom she loved so much.

Magnice had been her home, her entire world. Her giver was there. Her kingdom. She'd sunbathed on the shores and grown up speaking with the seagulls and crabs that would dust the beaches.

Her home that she could call home no longer.

Red hair caught her gaze at the highest tower.

She held up a hand and brought her fingers into a tight fist. She saw Dorian join Nyssa in the doorway, and she hoped he would heed her warning.

"Drae?" she heard Draven said from behind her.

Her heart finished breaking, and she tore her gaze around to him. "Yeah," she managed. "I'm ready."

Aydra didn't speak much as they rode across the Hills of Bitratus. Draven didn't ask anything of her. He and Balandria spoke their usual banter, speaking of their plans once they returned and what needed to be done around their kingdom. She was grateful he did not push her, try to make her talk to him about what had happened.

As they talked and ate, she simply sat by his side. Occasionally he would reach over and squeeze her thigh or graze her hand. But he never crowded her. He packed the pipe every night, but despite smoking the herb she craved so much for escape, all she wanted to do at night was try to sleep.

For four days, they traveled, and on the night they finally reached the edge of the Forest, he begged her to eat something more than a few bites of bread. But she couldn't.

Her heart ached for the comfort of her raven. To hear his voice, his screech over her head as he watched over her.

"Can I do anything?" Draven finally asked once they'd settled in for their final night on the road.

She looked up at him, and he simply kissed her forehead, not needing to hear anything from her lips. She sighed into his arms and laid her head on his chest, unable to even breathe words on her tongue.

As she laid there against his chest, she heard him humming the Wyverdraki song. Her eyes closed, and she nuzzled her head into his chest.

"What will your men say when I return with you?" she whispered.

"Doesn't matter," he replied softly.

"It does." She sat up and looked at him. "To me. It does."

He sighed heavily, his thumb brushing her hands. "After you helped us with the ships, I think my men have earned a new respect for you," he replied. "Once they learn of what you sacrificed to be there, you will find no more loyal a group of people."

She reached up and kissed him then, the first time she'd kissed him since their leaving her castle, and she threaded her fingers in his beard, savoring the taste of his lips.

"Thank you," she whispered upon pulling back.

He squeezed her waist. "Only for you," he breathed.

She laid back against his chest once more, and he hummed the Wyverdraki song again. Laying in his arms, the safety of the Hills around them, surrounded by darkness and firelight...

She wanted to tell him.

She wanted to tell him everything.

Her heart began to thump loudly in her ears. She almost vomited at the thought, but something inside her had the urge to get it out. The humiliation of her truth tugged at her heart. But this was Draven.

And she needed to say it.

"Draven…" she managed, squeezing his hand. "I need to tell you something… something I should have told you a long time ago."

He brought her hands to his lips and kissed her knuckles gently, brows furrowing. "What?"

She sat up then, allowing her hair to fall over her face, avoiding his eyes as the shame she felt cracked and splintered her numb body. "Do you remember the darkness you said I knew nothing of?" she asked in a shakier voice than she knew herself capable of.

"I didn't mean—"

"Draven, please…" she begged.

He stopped talking and simply held her hands in his, and she found herself trembling at the thought of telling him. Her heart raced, the noise of it throbbing in her ears. The first time Vasilis touched her flashed in her memory, and the flames turned blue in front of her as she stared at them.

"Aydra?"

The sound of Draven's soft voice slashed the flames back to orange. An icy breath cut through her lungs, and she wiped a tear forcefully from her face. "What I tell you," she managed, "you have to understand. I've never actually told anyone. Dorian and Lex know, but… it is because they saw it. Not because I told them."

"Whatever it is—"

"Draven, don't coddle me," she whispered. "Don't try to save me. I just… I need you to *hear* me."

Draven stilled a moment, obvious he was thinking of every little thing she might be about to reveal to him and preparing himself as his eyes traveling over her face.

But he gave her a reassuring nod and whispered, "Okay."

The words vomited from her mouth.

Before she knew what was happening, she was telling him everything. Everything. From the first time Vasilis put his hands on her and Zoria told her it was normal, to the last time Rhaif had burned her and forced her to her knees. She told him of how she'd blamed herself for it for years, of how she'd only just allowed herself to escape from the condemnation of it.

The words caught in her throat. The knot folded in her stomach. She thought she would actually vomit a time or two, and Draven would rub her arm and squeeze her hand in response, not saying a word as she worked through it.

And when she was done, she watched as his own tears ran down his silent face. The angst of revealing her true self to him ripped through her insides, and seeing the hurt on his face made her flesh redden. She reached out and wiped his face, to which he took her hand and kissed her palm hard.

"I'm sorry," he choked. "I'm sorry I didn't realize the extent of it… Of what was happening… I thought it was just squabbling between you, normal fights of a brother and sister, I—"

"It's fine," she whispered. She avoided his gaze, terrified if she looked too hard into his eyes that she would see her own shame written back at her in his pupils.

"Aydra, it isn't fine," he argued. The wind picked up, but only for a second. His form squirmed as though he were trying to keep some part of himself shoved inside, trying not to allow his powers to exude at the frustration and anger he felt. "What he did to you… what they have all done to each other… if the people knew how Arbina treated you both —"

"Do you truly think the people would believe me over him or our mother?" she breathed, feeling the heat creep on her cheeks at the thought of what the people would say if she even tried to accuse their wonderful king of such horror. Their perfect king. Honorable and generous. To accuse all the kings before him, those whom her people had practically worshiped in those walls, forcing their queen to stand alone in his shadows without realizing what they were doing to them.

"Do you think they'd believe the word of the promiscuous Queen over their beloved Chronicles and honorable King?" she continued.

Draven's fist tightened at his side, and he stared into the darkness, a firmness rising in his jaw. "He will pay for this," he promised. "I will break every bone in his body before slitting his throat if ever I get him alone."

"No, you won't," she affirmed.

"You expect me to sit back and not rip him to shreds the next I see him?"

She stared pointedly at him, their eyes not moving until finally he sighed heavily and surrendered a, "Yeah, fine," despite his apparent

want to spill her brother's blood through every hall of her castle.

"If you were to kill him, it would take away from what we should be truly focused on," she insisted. "These ships. The strangers. 'Man' if you will. If you kill him, it will start a war between us, between all our friends we just brought together, and we cannot lose any men before the true battle comes. You know this, Draven."

A growl emitted from under his breath. "I never liked being the hero," he told her. "It's much more fun being the villain."

The upwards quirk of her lips was brief, and an exhausted breath left her lungs. He exhaled deliberately as she sank against him, her body washed with the relief of telling him the truth, getting it out so there were no secrets between them. Her skin tingled with the waking of her numb core. As though her flesh was being pricked with needles as it awoke in a new day and life. Just a little freer than it had been before.

62

The murmurs of the forest welcomed her two mornings later.

She could not keep the tiny smile from herself upon smelling the forest air around her. It was just darkening when they'd arrived the night before, and Draven had brought her in under the light of the moons overhead. She hardly remembered it, being so exhausted from the mental anguish of her leaving and then the restless nights she'd received on her journey. She wasn't sure how she made it up the stairs.

But when the rays of sun came through the ragged curtains over the windows, she felt herself stir, and she turned over and opened her eyes, only to find Draven standing in the wide doorway across the room from her, his figure leaning on the doorframe facing out towards the forest.

She watched him a moment, allowing the day to sink in, allowing her mind to grasp on to why she was there and not in her own black sheets beneath the golden canopy of her four-poster bed. The smell of the forest entered her nostrils, but she could not make herself get up.

Her heart ached for the sound of her raven's morning cackle.

A tear fell down her cheek, and she pulled the blanket up around her once more.

A few minutes later, she felt the bed shift, and she knew Draven had sat down beside her. She didn't move, pretending to be asleep, not wanting to see any pity he might have for her on his features.

He didn't shake her. He didn't push her. He simply leaned down and kissed her shoulder, giving her hip a squeeze through the blanket before rising once more.

She stayed in bed the rest of the day, and the next, not even rising when he would bring food up. She felt drained, void of the presence

417

that had so long been with her.

It was weird. She was so accustomed to hearing her raven's voice, feeling his comforting presence at her side at all times of the day and night. A small piece of her had vanished. The comfort blanket she shielded herself with now gone.

She felt terrible for not getting up and at least speaking to Draven, but she didn't know what to do, what to say, even how to act. She was grateful for him, not only because he'd aided her but because he wasn't being pushy about anything. He wasn't crowding her, forcing her to be whatever normal was.

At night, he simply laid beside her and kissed her shoulder, not wrapping her up in his arms until she was the one to snuggle against him. And when she would snuggle into him or take his arm and wrap it around her, he would sigh heavily and kiss her neck, just softly enough that she knew he was there. She appreciated him more than she could put into the words she wanted to tell him. Telling him she loved him did not seem enough to express what she'd come to feel.

He saw her.

The real her.

He *heard* her.

It was on the third morning that she finally rose from the sheets. Her frazzled hair was matted on the right side of her head, the rest of it poking out in a wild mane of curls. She could feel knots in the ends and on the back of her head. The shirt Draven had given her hung loose on her deteriorating body.

But the smell of the forest intoxicated her. It was a cool morning, the kind of cool morning where you want to sit on your balcony snuggled in a blanket, a warm cup of tea in your hands. She rubbed her face in her palms a moment as she sat up, allowing the blood to flow back to her insides.

She allowed her legs to dangle over the side of the bed, waking her toes up one by one. The cool wood touched her feet, and she made herself get up.

Sunlight flooded through the canopy of the trees, the rust of the turning leaves catching in the rays. The light cascaded down and hit the wooden rail of the balcony. Birds' songs flittered in her ears.

This was the new morning she would remember for the remainder of her days. Her first truly quiet morning that she actually accepted without the struggle of the crown on her head or the comfort of her raven at her side.

She hugged her arms to her chest as she felt a tear fall down her cheek. A quiet sigh left her, and she leaned herself on the banister of the railing. Below, she could see men and women enjoying themselves as they ate their breakfasts, the laughter of the men making her smile inwardly. The sun hit her face, and she had to close her eyes as its warmth penetrated her skin. It was as though the Sun herself were speaking to her, telling her it would be okay.

When her eyes opened once more, she found Draven's figure standing in the middle of a conversation with Balandria and Bael on the other side of the clearing between the trees.

It was Balandria who saw her first. Her small eyes smiled at her. She nudged Draven's chest and gave an upwards nod towards the balcony. Aydra's stomach fluttered upon meeting his gaze. The ghost of a smile spread across his lips.

Another Hunter joined them, and Draven's attention was turned as the man shook his shoulders jovially. She felt a laugh rise on her lips as she watched them. A few moments later, she found herself sitting on the balcony floor, leaning against one of the railings with her legs tucked into her chest. A lizard had found her, and she was speaking with it about what it had planned for its day when she heard footsteps on the stairs.

The warmth of Draven's smile met hers as he slowed and took the last few steps up to the platform. Her heart knotted at the look in his eyes. The look she so cherished.

"Making friends?" he asked with a nod to the lizard.

She put the lizard back on the railing. "Always."

He reached out his hands, which she gladly took, and the rush at which he pulled her to her feet made her fall into his arms. She laughed as he hugged her into him, her forearms lying on his chest, the hug of his hand at the small of her back.

"Hi," he whispered.

The curl of his fingers in her matted hair made her knees weaken. "Hi," she managed in a voice she barely heard.

His nose nudged against hers, and she closed her eyes in response to the jagged breaths now threatening her lungs.

"Your heart is beating really fast," he muttered.

"Only for you," she breathed.

She could feel him smiling when he finally kissed her. And for a moment, she forgot they were on the balcony, in full view of his men, the sun beating against their skin as a spotlight on their public display.

It didn't matter how many times he'd kissed her before. Every time, she found herself surprised by the fluttering in her stomach, the honey warmth radiating over her skin, the skipping of her heart…

But the noise of catcalls and howls from the clearing below echoed, and she felt his hand leave her waist. She pulled back to find him flipping off his men, and she laughed at the grinning faces on all the people below.

"Ignore them." His voice tickled her ear. She found Balandria in the crowd, and the woman raised her drink to her and then took a sip.

"I certainly didn't think you'd be getting this response for my being here," she said as he pulled back to see his face.

"I told you they liked you," he insisted. He took a step back and let her go, simply holding onto her hands as he gave her a full once over. "You're a mess," he joked. "What is happening with your hair?"

Her stomach knotted at his banter, heart enlarging in her chest so that she inhaled another jagged breath. "I'm sorry. Does my morning appearance not live up to the Venari standard?"

He laughed, and he pulled her back to him. "Exceeding it," he said against her lips.

For a moment, he simply held her there, his eyes darting over her face as she wrapped a finger against his bearded cheek.

"Will you join us for breakfast?" he asked.

She avoided his gaze as she thought it through. Of whether she was ready to go out and be with people without the reassuring comfort blanket her raven had been her entire life.

She missed him terribly.

Draven squeezed her hands, bringing her back to the present. "No pressure," he insisted. "Only if you're up for it."

Her stomach rumbled, and she squeezed his hands back. "Can I bathe first?" she asked.

He reached up and pulled a leaf from her hair, twirling it between his fingers in front of her. "Probably a good idea."

It was the breakfast she didn't know she needed.

But as she stared around them, enjoying her time with their smiling faces, she was reminded of her youngers, and for a moment, she felt her heart constrict at the thought of them being back at the castle.

After breakfast, a few of Draven's men came up to him with things they needed his help with.

"Yeah, I'm coming. Two minutes," he told them before turning back to her. "I have some things I need to take care of. After, I'm yours."

"Oh—" She had not expected him to think she wanted him to stop his duties for her. "Take your time, please. You're still king. I dare not take away from your duties and your people," she insisted. "I'll see you tonight."

"What will you do?" he asked.

She shrugged and looked around them. "It's a beautiful day. Perhaps I'll take a walk. Get my feet dirty."

His eyes narrowed just slightly, but he didn't protest. "Okay."

"Okay?" she said, fully expecting some sort of argument from him that she shouldn't wander into the forest alone. "That's it? No ordering someone to look after me or—"

"Should I have?" he asked, clearly confused by her question.

"Ah… no, no, it's just…"

He pulled her close and kissed her forehead, making her cease her ramblings. "You're not in Magnice anymore, Drae," he said. "You can go wherever you like. Just be careful of the forest's tricks." He leaned in and kissed her fleetingly before turning on his heel. "Oh—" he paused mid-stride and held up a finger, "—and don't listen to the nymphs."

She frowned. "The nymphs?" she repeated.

"Yeah. Tiny things. I'm sure you'll be fine. Just swat them like flies. And—" he pulled his knife from his belt and tossed it into her hands "—just in case."

She stared at the knife in her hands. "Wait—*what?*" she called as he turned on his heel again and started walking faster.

"You'll be fine. I'll find you later!"

She stared after his retreating figure with a blank stare.

"He's joking," said one of the Hunters behind her. "Nymphs aren't bad. Just like annoying mosquitoes that talk. It's really the Kopies you want to watch out for."

She raised an amused brow at the slender man sitting beneath the tree, whittling away at a large branch in his hands. "Kopies. Right. I'll be sure to keep an eye out."

63

Her bare feet led her southeast into the forest's depths.

She hugged her cloak around her shoulders as she walked, relishing the animals around her as she allowed them to fill her. She had no destination in mind, but when she found herself in the clearing she'd visited with the Venari people for the funerals, she wasn't surprised.

"Hello, Duarb," she said upon seeing the mangled tree.

She should have felt scared. She should have felt the darkness. But all she felt was the sun on her back as she sat down in front of the great tree in the ray of light that had made its way into the forest.

The tongues on its trunk didn't wiggle as ferociously as they had when the Venari had been there. As she stared at it, she started to think her eyes were deceiving her, for it looked as though the tree were breathing. She pulled her knees into her chest and sighed.

"This is weird," she muttered. "I'm used to Arbina simply appearing whether I need her or not. But you... you can't. Trapped inside your own mind except when called upon."

She suddenly felt so sorry for Duarb, being cursed into the tree he had sprung from. She sighed and stared at it another moment before lying down on the ground. Her eyes closed, and she reached out for any creatures in the forest, allowing her core to release from her body.

For how long she laid there, knotting herself with different creatures to escape, she wasn't sure. But halfway through the day, she felt a familiar energy come near, and she nearly screamed out into the sky.

The Aenean Orel landed beside her and bowed its head.

And she fell into its feathers.

The great bird stayed with her until the sun began to set, allowing her to lay against it, its head nuzzling hers as they sat beneath the tree they'd both been instructed was their enemy. When the sun waned, the Orel gave her another bow, and it lifted up off the ground to follow the sunlight. Aydra knew she should have started heading back, but she couldn't move, too at peace with the wrap of darkness and creatures around her that she wanted to settle there for the rest of her days. She allowed the moons light to greet her through the trees, and she sighed into the darkened wood.

"I thought I might find you here," came a voice in the darkness.

She looked up and met Draven's eyes as he emerged into the light. He carried a box with him that she didn't recognize.

"Daughter of his enemy. Of course, I had to come and see him," she said as he crossed the space between them. "What's in the box?"

"Ah—" he sat down beside her and put the box in front of her feet. "It's your raven."

Her heart constricted, and she reached out to trace the lid.

"Thought you might want to give him a proper Noctuan burial."

She turned and met his gaze. "There is a Noctuan burial?"

"Well… normally, it would be during the Deads, but because it was able to live during the moons, I see no reason why this shouldn't work."

A deep inhale left her body as she stared at the box. "Okay."

She allowed him to do the burial in silence. The ashes were spread into Duarb's roots at his base. She felt the tears coming down her face as she watched him work. He ripped a piece of his shirt and gave it to her to wipe them from her cheeks.

Once they were scattered, he lit a match against a rock and tossed it into the roots. Fire blazed in her watery vision.

"Where is the fabric I gave you?" he asked.

She frowned but held out the fabric in her clenched fist nonetheless.

"Draven, what—"

"Trust me," he asked sincerely of her.

He tossed the fabric in the flames, and then he pulled something from the bag he'd had on his shoulder.

The phoenix skull.

He set it down at the edge of the roots and then stepped back to her side. The flames flickered in her eyes, and she buried herself in his chest as the smell of it filled her nostrils. His lips pressed to her forehead, and he hugged her against him.

But then something reached out for her, and she bolted backward, nearly stumbling, her eyes unable to leave the fire.

"What—"

Nausea swept her. A cold chill took over her body. Her knees hit the dirt. A radiating flame started in her toes and vibrated through each muscle, an inch at a time until it rose into her chest.

The greatest gasp she'd ever taken filled her lungs, and she was thrown onto her back.

What threw her the most, though, was the indifferent look Draven had on his face. He crouched beside her and held out a hand. Her gaze narrowed at him, unsure of what was happening.

A screech so high-pitched her ears rang sounded in the air.

The flames at the base of the tree burst upwards. Wind brushed through and extinguished the fire at the roots, but one flame remained in the air, as though a fireball had been launched into the darkness.

Something tugged at her core, filling the emptiness she'd felt since the absence of her raven. It was familiar, yet something completely different from what she'd felt before.

The burst of fire turned black in the silhouette of the moons, and her heart throbbed at the sudden realization of what had soared upwards from the flames.

"A phoenix?" she breathed.

Draven's hands wrapped under her arms, and he pulled her to her feet. She was stiff, frozen as the black flames of it disappeared again into the darkness of the forest. But she could feel its core as it dove down to the earth before her.

The ground shook. It landed in front of her in the moons light, and her stomach knotted as its neck rose high. The whisp of its tail feathers wrapped around her feet. Its great black horns glistened in the moons light.

The amber of its eyes stared at her down its great long beak.

She reached out hesitantly. *What is your name?* she asked it.

It is not the time for you to learn it.

Her brows began to narrow, but when the phoenix's nose nudged her hand, her heart skipped, and then she nearly collapsed at the rate at which her head melted against its head.

She sighed into the comfort of its warm black flames, the wisps of its energy filling her chest. A tear streaked down her face as she settled into it, allowing it to complete her once more, to bond with her as she'd bonded with her raven. After a moment, she took two steps back, and she gave the creature a bow.

Take your flight.

The phoenix burst into shadow and dove into the air.

Aydra watched it soar, collecting its first flight above her head in the silence of the moons. A joy filled her chest that made her emotions edge, and she felt her hands trembling.

The sight of Draven caught the corner of her eye as the phoenix left her sightline. He was standing off to the side of Duarb's tree, his body reflecting back in the light, hands shoved in his pockets as he simply watched the bird soar with a small smile on his face.

"How did you know?" she asked breathlessly.

His gaze flickered to meet hers, and he didn't say anything as he raised an expectant brow.

A wash of understanding came over her. "The Honest Scrolls," she realized.

He nodded slowly and started to walk towards her. "If more people read them, they might uncover the true magic of this land. This world is more than our minuscule squabbles and fights. Living here in the Forest, you learn to appreciate everything Haerland did before vanishing. The phoenix represents not just the Venari. She is the corp —"

Aydra cut him off with a hard press of her lips to his, nearly jumping into his arms as he stepped before her. His startled figure relaxed only after a moment, and then he pulled her flush against him. Her chest swelled with all the things she had no idea how to put into words, and when she finally pulled back, she pressed her hand to his cheek.

"Thank you," she managed.

He took her palm off his cheek and kissed it, closing his eyes just for a moment. His weight shifted, and he held her hand in his. "I know you need time," he started. "I know this is all new, and you're possibly overwhelmed with all that's happened, but—"

"Draven, I love you," she blurted.

His weight shifted again, a great inhale filling his lungs, the same look on his face that he'd had in the castle when she told him spreading across his features. His jaw clenched distractedly, and she watched the glisten take over his eyes.

She squeezed his hands before he could speak. "I love you," she repeated. "I've known it for a while now, and I should have told you so many times before, but... I didn't want it to come across as my saying it out of a darkness I knew I had settled into. I wanted it to be when I knew it would mean more than just the words. I had to be sure you didn't just love me for the reasons I'd said before. After these last few weeks, after… everything… I realize I was wrong. It wasn't just circumstance. It's real. More real than I truly think I understand."

She reached up to his face, and his weight shifted again. "Draven you… you see me. The real me. Crown or no crown. Queen or civilian. You see me for who I am, not who I am supposed to be. You fill me with a strength and trust I'm not used to."

He kissed her hands, allowing his lips to linger against her skin. "So, to be clear, you love me because I'm everything Magnice isn't."

Her heart sank, and she felt the color drain from her face. "What? No—I mean—*what?* Draven, I love you because… because you don't treat me as though I'm some child. You never have—"

"So you've loved me since we were kids?"

She couldn't believe what he was saying.

"I just told you I *love* you, and you're asking for reasons?" she nearly snapped. "Why— I told you. You actually see me—"

"Yes, you're standing right here," he mocked.

"I mean—*you know what I mean!* And when we're together, you… I feel safe with you—"

"So I'm just another safety precaution for you?"

"What—no—*Draven!*" she practically stamped her foot in frustration at the questions he was drilling her with. She did a circle, staring at the moons with words stuck in her throat. "I don't know what you want me to say. I love you. You… you challenge me, you trust me, you don't try and change me, you know when I need time to get myself together, you… you make me laugh, which is actually quite a feat if I am honest, I—" she did a double-take at him standing there with his hand clapped over his mouth "—*is this funny to you?!*"

The amused glint in his eyes made her fume. She smacked his arm hard, causing his hand to fall from his mouth, revealing the broad smile on his face. Laughter spewed from his lips, and she hated him for it.

"I hate you," she muttered as he cackled in front of her.

"Oh—*Oh*, I'm sorry, Aydra," he said through his laughter. "I'm sorry, it was too good of an opportunity to pass up—"

She hit his shoulder again, nearly pushing him backward this time.

"You are such an ass, Draven Greenwood," she muttered as she pushed him back again.

He caught her hands in his and pulled her flush against him, his laughter still radiating through the air as he wrapped his arms around her. Her frustrations waned with the press of his lips to hers, and when he pulled back, she avoided his eyes and bit back the smile threatening her lips. He pushed her hair back, tilting her chin up to meet his eyes. The smile in his gaze made her stomach flutter.

"You'll be the death of me," she muttered.

"We've been planning how to kill each other since we were eight. Of course, I'll be the death of you," he grinned.

She laughed under her breath and then sighed into his embrace. For a few moments, she simply hugged him, closing her eyes and relishing the feeling of his body against hers, the weight on her shoulders now gone.

"What do you say we go back? The boys were working on a feast when I left," he whispered in her hair.

She pulled back and looked up at him. The noise of the phoenix sounded in her ears. It sent a shiver down her spine. "Anywhere with you."

Dinner was potatoes with rosemary and freshly caught rabbit. Aydra wasn't keen on the rabbit. She quite enjoyed the potatoes, but mostly… it was the laughter and stories filling the table that she craved.

Draven pulled her a chair beside him at the table. But by the end of the meal, her head was lying on his shoulder with his arm wrapped around her. The smell of black herb filled the air as they passed pipes between them. They all relaxed as Draven did at banquets: legs thrown over the sides of the armchairs, with their hair down, slumped into the backs of the seats.

Aydra inhaled the herb from Draven's pipe and let her eyes close at the swim of it. His hair fell over her face each time he would look down at her, nudging her cheek with his nose when he would laugh, entwining their hands together as their eyes dazed and the voices around them became distant echoes.

It was some time later that she found herself lying on his chest beneath the stars, the warmth of the fire at their feet, and the cool of the dirt on their backs.

"They dance," she whispered as the herb went to her head.

He chuckled under his breath, his fingers delicately drawing circles on her hip. "Occasionally," he replied.

"How do you think the Architects choose who to place in the stars?" she asked him.

Draven sighed, silence encompassing the moment as he contemplated his answer. "Perhaps Haerland presents them with those she chooses to be worthy."

"No Lesser being has ever been chosen," she noted.

"Name one that's ever earned such," he bantered.

She smiled despite herself. Draven brought her hand up on his chest, and she felt him looking down at her.

"You will be," he told her.

Aydra sat up slightly on her elbow. "Me? The runaway Queen? Traitor to her people, lover of her enemy?"

"The first true Queen of Haerland," he corrected.

Her hand softened against his, and his fingers squeezed her hip just so. "Then you'll be beside me," she whispered. "The true King."

A deep exhale left him, and his eyes darted over her face. "Burning traitorous kingdoms, breaking curses, crushing the Chronicles, and shifting the cosmos… what else can we do together?"

A smile enveloped her face, and her heart swelled with him in her arms. "Everything."

64

A full moon and a crescent met Aydra's eyes as she allowed herself the silence of the balcony. She'd been in the forest two weeks, and it was the most freeing two weeks she'd ever felt.

Not only because she could be with Draven, but because she felt... free. Welcome. Wanted. The Venari people didn't treat her as though she were fragile, as though she would break or snap at them if they said something out of turn. She appreciated the equal respect they treated her with. Even when they would poke fun at her expense once in a while.

She'd filled some of her time reading stories from the Honest Scrolls books and drawings Draven had piled into crooked shelves behind his desk. Other times, walking the forest or chatting with Balandria and the rest of Draven's people. She felt more at home within their darkened kingdom than she'd ever felt in her own.

There had been word of more ships on the horizon. Draven poured over the maps, determining where they might be coming from and where they may decide to dock. They spoke of it together, him trusting her with ideas and plans she had never been trusted with before. He would stress over whether the youngers in the Venari company were ready for such a war. Aydra had seen the younger members of his legion fight, and she assured him they were.

Draven made time to spend with her away from the pressures of his kingdom when he could, even if it was only their sneaking off at night to sit at the river's edge. The phoenix would follow in the shadows, only appearing when she spoke to it. Draven knew everything about his forest. Every tree, every flower, every creature. He would pick some of them, showing her medicinal properties and even telling tall tales of sorcery he swore that some possessed.

It amazed her how much she didn't know about the land.

At night, they would occasionally sleep on the roof, Aydra desperate to see the stars she knew her youngers would also be looking at. She missed them. She wondered how Dorian had done with the Bryn and the Blackhand Elders, whether he'd helped them actually vanquish the Infi in their streets or if he'd made it back to Magnice in one piece.

As happy as she was, she couldn't get the thought of Nyssa being at Magnice alone out of her head, wondering if she and Dorian were okay, wondering if Lex was okay… Aydra had sent the Orel out with a letter to the castle that morning but had heard nothing back yet.

Aydra's hands wrapped around the banister of the roof as she stared at the moons above her on that night, and she felt a tear trickle down her cheek.

"—finishing up dinner if you're hungry—*whoa.*" Draven slowed as he reached the top of the steps, and he crossed to her quickly. "What's wrong? Did Bael say something out of turn?"

"No. Nothing like that," she promised.

"Is everything okay?" he asked.

"Yeah," she whispered, reaching out to place her hand over his on the banister. "Overwhelmingly perfect."

He eyed her. "And that made you cry?"

The comical confusion on his face made her sink into his arms and sigh heavily as she laid her head against his shoulder. "I cannot express how grateful I am for you. For your people… they've treated me as nothing less than their equal. I wish my youngers could feel such equality and love."

His lips pressed to her forehead, and he squeezed her against him. "We can bring them with us after the meeting in a few weeks," he insisted. "Have them stay for a time. They deserve the travel."

She pulled back and looked at him, her chest once more filling with the look he gazed at her with. "Have I told you how fucking much I love you today?" she managed, leaning closer.

His hands curled around her waist, eyes darting from her eyes to her mouth, and she watched as a smoldering smile rose on his lips.

"You haven't," he rasped, nudging her nose with his.

An urgent hunger filled her from her stomach up into her extremities. She curled her hands in his hair, gently tugging on the roots of it. A deep groan vibrated his throat, their lips grazing but not touching. His nose traced her jaw, and she felt his tongue on her skin.

"I have a request," she breathed.

He pulled back slightly, head tilting at her. "Demanding, but go on," he replied.

She grasped his hair between her fingers, standing up taller to move her head beside his ear. "Put on the skull," she requested.

She felt the goosebumps rise on his flesh, the shudder wash over his body. She pulled back just as a low growl emitted from his throat. His fingers dug into her hips as he looked down at her with dilated eyes that made her thighs squeeze.

"You don't know what you ask for with that," he told her.

"I know I want you to fuck me without this restraint you've been putting on the last two weeks."

His brows narrowed just slightly. "I told you restraint lives poorly in my core."

"And you're a liar," she accused.

The smirk that rose in his eyes made her weight shift. They danced with the sadistic delight that she melted for.

"You think I've been treating you as something fragile?" he asked.

"I think you didn't want to scare me."

The smirk met his lips then, and the darkening of his gaze caused a chill to run down her spine. "Careful what you wish for, my Queen," he growled against her cheek.

She leaned in, her lips barely a breath from his. "Put on the skull... *my King.*"

65

"Nadir will be here in an hour," Draven told her the following morning.

Aydra paused while sharpening her sword and frowned up at him. "Why? Is something wrong?"

"He says you agreed to help him with the water serpent," he replied. "And... another ship came in, further west this time, not by the reef. He wants a second opinion on what we should do."

She could see the nervousness in his eyes. She sat her sword on the ground, standing up level with him. Her hand reached up to his cheek, and he covered it with his own, kissing her palm.

"They're ready," she told him.

"We're not fighting this time, remember?" he reminded her.

"Oh, right," she mumbled, almost rolling her eyes. "Diplomacy."

He huffed and wrapped his arm around her. "You'll get your chance to behead them when they inevitably piss you off. I'll have my men sharpen an axe."

"We should bring it with us," she insisted. "You know, just as a precaution."

He grinned, head leaning down towards her. "Wouldn't leave here without it."

A shadow passed over the sun then, quickly diverting her attention.

Aydra pulled back and squinted up, just in time to see the Orel drop something from its talons. A letter.

Aydra unfurled the parchment quickly.

"Magnice?" Draven asked.

"Lex—"

Rupture and rapture
The flames blow
What do we do when the eagle grows cold?

Aydra's stomach dropped.

Eagle.

Eagle.

—*Nyssa.*

Draven's hand tightened around her waist. "Why is she speaking in Berdijay riddles?"

Her breath shortened as she gripped onto his arm. "He's hurt Nyssa."

Aydra crumbled the letter in her hand and bounded up the stairs to Draven's home. She started throwing things onto the bed, pulling her bag from the corner to pack it quickly.

"How do you know that?" Draven said from the door.

"Her core is an eagle," she replied quickly. "Flames are Rhaif. He's hurt her somehow. I have to go back," Aydra argued.

"And if this is a trap?" Draven stated. "What if this is his way of pulling you back in? What if he is using her to get to you?"

"And what if he is?" she wept. "I cannot let her suffer. She is my sister. She doesn't deserve to live beneath him as I did."

"Your sister is strong."

"I know she is. But that doesn't mean she has to suffer in silence."

"What about the ship?"

She paused, her heart tearing in two places as she contemplated her choices. "The ship can wait. This is my sister," she answered. "Besides, I always told her she could come with me for the negotiations when they arrived again. I will get her and bring her back here."

"They will consider that kidnapping and take her crown too," he affirmed.

"What would you have me do, Draven?" she snapped, rounding on him. "Would you have me sit back and do nothing while he hurts her? Ignore her as my olders did me when I voiced my own pains?"

Draven ran his hands through his hair, tugging at the roots. "Aydra, I cannot lose you again."

The reality of why he didn't want her to leave set in, and she crossed the space between them, taking his hands in hers.

"You're not losing me," she promised.

"If you go back there... You know he will try to hurt you. Punish you for leaving or imprison you in your own castle." He paused, his thumbs rubbing her hands. "Are you ready for that?"

433

"My brother has hurt me for the last time," she swore.

The noise of great wings flapped in the air outside the balcony, and the phoenix dove into the room. It stared down its long beak at her, amber eyes staring into her. She felt its ferocity inside her own, and it gave her a slow blink.

She squeezed Draven's hands and looked back at him. "He won't know what's coming."

Draven sighed and rested his forehead against hers. She closed her eyes, inhaling the scent of the forest around them.

"I love you so much," she whispered.

He pulled back slightly and brought her hand to his lips. "I love you," he said before kissing her palm. "And I support you. If this is what you need to do… I will not stand in your way."

66

Aydra took the phoenix back to Magnice.

Anger flowed from her and into the phoenix's. Its black, heating flames tickled her legs and hands. Black flames that wrapped her as a cool breeze, that tickled her flesh as wind would.

They flew in shadow, the whispers of its feathers beneath her hands as they crossed the Preymoor in a matter of hours instead of days.

They flew over the town, all the way up to the castle gates.

She pulled her sword and jumped from the creature's back upon reaching the courtyard.

Belwarks drew their swords as she landed.

Aydra straightened and whirled her blade in her hand. "Do you really want to do this?" she asked the men.

Behind, called the phoenix.

Her sword clashed overhead with the one behind her. He pushed her forward, their swords crashing together. Aydra ducked low and struck his knees, wiping him out to the ground. Her blade landed in his throat. As the crack of his neck filled her ears, she straightened and looked around her again.

The phoenix chirped overhead and circled the courtyard. A chill ran down Aydra's spine at its anger filling her.

"One last warning, Belwarks," Aydra dared the men.

Two of them crouched low, swords at the ready. Aydra held a hand up.

Her fist closed as they launched at her.

Black flames swallowed the courtyard.

Aydra stepped through the cold fire and pushed her way into the castle.

Servants moved out of the way. A few of the Belwarks started to draw their swords, but the sudden sight of the phoenix flying beside her out the windows made them stop in their tracks. She kept her sword in her hand, all the way up to her sister's room. Her foot met the door upon reaching it.

Nyssa yelped upon seeing Aydra, and then her gaze softened. "Aydra—"

She bounded across the room and dove into Aydra's arms, wrapping her arms tightly around her. Aydra hugged her close and then pulled back to see her face.

"Where are you hurt?" Aydra asked quickly. "Where did he—"

"It wasn't like with you," Nyssa cut her off. "It was just my arm."

"It is never *just* your arm," Aydra affirmed. "Don't ever let me hear that it was 'just' anything from you again. Do you understand?"

Nyssa's chest visibly caved, shoulders slouching, but she nodded, and Aydra hugged her again. She held her head to her chest a moment, letting that fear run through her, letting the relief that Nyssa was okay settle in her heart.

"What happened?" Aydra asked upon parting with her.

"I was arguing with him about you," Nyssa answered. "I let it slip that I knew what he'd done to you. The flames grew on him instantly —"

"Where was your eagle?" Aydra cut in.

"He was with me."

"Did he defend you?"

A flicker of a smile found Nyssa's lips. "You haven't seen him yet."

"I came straight to you."

The phoenix landed in Nyssa's great window. Nyssa yelped and threw herself into Aydra's arms.

"What—what is that?!" she shouted.

Aydra smiled at the beast. "She's mine."

"—Nyssa, are you okay—"

Lex froze in the door. "Aydra?" she breathed.

A broad smile rose on Aydra's face, and she bounded into Lex's grasp, hugging her best friend tightly as her chest swelled at the sight of her.

Lex pulled back and grasped Aydra's face in her hands. "You're burning the kingdom without me?"

"Just the courtyard," Aydra smiled.

Lex pushed her hair back and wrapped her arms around her again, lips pressing hard to Aydra's forehead. "Dammit, I missed you," Lex managed.

"I got your letter," Aydra told her. "Knew I couldn't stay there knowing what was happening."

"But I just sent the letter this morning," Lex argued as they parted. "I— *what of Duarb's cursed is that?!*"

The phoenix screeched, and Aydra watched a visible chill run down Nyssa's spine.

"Whoa," Nyssa said, her eyes widened at her sister.

"I know," Aydra agreed with a smile.

"What's the plan?" Lex asked.

"Nope," Aydra argued. "This does not concern either of you. This is my fight. You'll both stay here—no arguments," she added with a glare at Lex.

"I think you'll need this," Nyssa said as she pulled something off her dresser.

Aydra's crown glimmered in the sunlight coming through the window. Her fingertips trickled over the rough-edged limbs, and the weight of it sat heavy in her hands.

"Take back your seat, sister."

Aydra fumbled with it in her hands a moment longer before placing it on her head. The mirror caught her gaze, and she found herself staring at the woman in the mirror. The dark of her hair against the shadows of the creature. The steel of her eyes reflected back in her sword.

Her chin lifted, and she looked up at the phoenix.

Follow me, she told it.

Rhaif was waiting for her in the Council Chambers.

She ignored the outbursts of the Belwarks, her sword already pulled as she threatened them.

"Out of my way," she demanded.

"Aydra, you are not allowed in—"

She thrust the Belwark into the wall and shoved her sword beneath his throat. "Why? Because he told you I am a Queen no longer?" she hissed at him.

The guard visibly gulped. "Y-Yes."

"Allow me to remind you who I am."

Her sword sliced through his throat, and his head rolled onto the ground.

His torso dropped out of her hand, fiery ash staining the white rock floor. She turned slowly towards the other guards.

"On your knees," she growled at them.

The guards didn't dare look between one another. Slowly, they each reached for their helmets and took them off as they knelt before her.

"My name," she asked of them.

"Aydra Ravenspeak—"

"Your Majesty—"

"My Queen—"

Aydra stepped forward in front of the one that had called her by simply her name, and she felt her head tilt down at him. The tip of her sword raked gently against his skin. "What was that, Belwark?"

The guard's eyes rolled up to meet hers.

And then he spat at her.

Her sword met his throat without hesitation, and his head rolled cleanly to the floor.

Fire from his rocky insides caught the rug, and she stamped it out with her boot. She turned on her heel towards the door. A deep breath entered her lungs as blue flames flashed in her memory, but she squashed it with the adrenaline of the phoenix coursing through her bones.

Lies.

The word reverberated through her consciousness.

And she kicked in the door.

Rhaif was standing on the other side of the room, staring out of the window. His arm lazily crossed over his chest, one hand stroking the un-kept stubble on his chin. He barely turned his head in her direction upon hearing her come in.

Rhaif's brow elevated as he looked her over, eyes lingering around her midsection and hips. "Got a bit comfy in the Forest, did we?"

Aydra thrust her sword back into her belt and began to take her riding gloves off one finger at a time. "Spit it out, Rhaif," she dared him. "Say what you really mean."

He looked her over once more, watching her as she stripped herself of the leather braces on her arms, the tight belted corset around her midsection.

"Have you come to kill me?" he asked as he faced her.

She threw the leathers off her body and onto the floor across the room. "Is that what you think?"

"I think you came running in here after you found your sister had been hurt. Not a fault of mine, despite what she may say."

Aydra almost laughed. "Not a fault of yours?" She reached for her sword on her belt and twirled it in her hand a few times. "Is that huge scratch across your face not from her eagle defending her?" she said with a point of her blade.

"Why are you here then if not to avenge your beloved sister?"

"You know, I did initially come for her. I did come to avenge her, to protect her, as I thought she needed. But my sister has proved she can take care of herself." She paused and allowed her eyes to flicker towards the window, seeing the shadow that passed over the sun, and she felt a fire rising inside her that she'd not anticipated.

"I am not here for her any longer. I am here for me," she warned him.

"For you?" His eyes flashed fire as she gripped the hilt of her sword tighter in her fist. "What will you do? Call the crows?"

Her neck cracked as she took a step back. She felt out into the void for the phoenix, feeling her eyes begin to flutter. Its energy ran through her down to her bones.

"What do you say to a fair fight this time?" she mused. "No pushing me off ledges or killing my creatures. Fair. Flame for flame."

Rhaif stepped away from the window, fingertips blackening by the second. He pushed his shirt over his head, and the blue flames began to wrap around his lightning-streaked torso. He pulled his own sword from his belt, and the blade heated beneath his grip.

"By all means," he mocked.

Her sword clashed with his above his head. Rhaif's shouts and grunts echoed off the walls as he pushed her backward. Aydra ducked and pivoted back, her sword barely missing his chest. She lunged forward and swung hard. His sword caught hers before she could slice his waist.

She rammed her head into his.

Rhaif stumbled on his feet, chest heaving. Aydra straightened and dusted off her shirt.

"You're getting slow, sister," he breathed.

Rhaif lunged at her again. Her blade struck his again and again, backing him up and then backing her up, over and over until she felt her arm begin to feel heavy. She felt for the phoenix outside, and its purr reverberated through her insides.

"Enough of this."

Glass shattered in slow motion behind their heads. Rhaif ducked to his knees. The phoenix came swooping inside the room. Its black shadow invaded every corner, and it landed behind Aydra. Aydra's chest heaved. She didn't bother shaking the glass from her hair. She could feel the heat of its feathers behind her, and its tail swept across the floor.

Rhaif's eyes bulged upon his seeing the beast. "What—Where—"

"This is for my sister—" she drove the hilt of her sword into his nose. Rhaif screamed in agony, but Aydra didn't pause.

"—This is for my raven—"

Her knife thrust into his eye.

Rhaif wailed with pain, his screams echoing off the walls. She straightened once more, watching as he grasped his face in his hands, blood pouring through his fingers.

"And this…" The phoenix wrapped her in cold black flames that felt of water and satin, and she allowed her hands to open at her sides. "This is for me."

The black flames wrapped into his blue ones, and she watched as they devoured his fire. His skin singed red. She felt her body shaking at the scene of the blisters rising on his skin, the black flame eating his skin. His screams pulsed around the room. The screech of it shattered her, and nausea swept her at the sight of him cowering on the ground.

The memory of his younger self in that same position beneath their mother's grasp pulsed through her mind, and she couldn't shake it.

Stop, she told the phoenix.

The flames evaporated slowly on his flesh. Rhaif continued to scream and shake in agony. He hugged his legs into his chest, face askew with terror. A glisten rose in her eyes that she wasn't prepared for. Her heart shattered at the sight of him, the brother she'd once loved so much withering in pain.

After a few moments, he laid his arm down, propping himself on his elbow as he found a sliver of strength. His trembling body kicked, and he looked up at her through the tangles of his navy hair.

"Kill me," he begged. "Do it. Strike me down. Send me to the Edge."

Her breath choked on the snotted-nose sob she didn't know she possessed. She didn't realize she was screaming until the noise of it sounded in her ears, bawling tears and cries emitting from her strained throat.

"Do it!" he begged.

The agony of his words tore through her. Her muscles edged, and she bent at the waist as another mortified sob left her lips. The memory of the smile he used to look at her with broke her heart. The promises and the laughter. Her body came crumbling down, and she felt herself sinking into an abyss.

Her brother. Desperate for love. Desperate to prove himself worthy of their mother's love. Desperate not to be who he would inevitably become.

This was not her brother.

This was not the same brother who had once promised her life without fear of fire.

This was not the brother that she had once loved.

This was the King of Promise.

The monster in his true form.

Consumed by fear.

Finally brought to his knees by all the Queens of their past.

She forced herself to straighten with the wrap of the phoenix's cold flames hugging her from behind, and she pushed the screaming sobs away. Her jaw trembled, and she sucked in a jagged breath as he moved to his knees, his fire flickering around his body.

A final tear dropped down her cheek and landed on the stone.

"You don't deserve the freedom of it," she managed.

Her sword clattered to the ground. The noise of it reverberated off the walls as her senses paused at the scene.

Iron chains clanked behind her.

A sharp pain pulsed through her, and she nearly fell to her knees.

The phoenix cried out.

Arms grabbed her from behind.

Leave me! she shouted to the beast.

The phoenix screamed, black fire filling the chamber.

Now!

Her eyes met its amber gaze over her shoulder, and the great bird gave her a slow blink.

I will see you again, she whispered to it.

The phoenix's wings flapped violently as it rose off the ground. Shadow pulsed through the chamber, and the bird disappeared into nothing more than wisps of black fire.

Aydra sank to her knees as a void filled her insides.

And the arms of Belwarks beneath her dragged her from the room.

67

It had been three weeks since Draven had heard from Aydra.

Three weeks since she'd left to take care of her brother.

Draven knew she didn't want him checking in. He would give her the independence she needed to take her throne back, to take back her kingdom. If she had died, he would have heard. He worried for her, but he knew she could take care of herself.

However, it was the letter he'd received from Dorian the day he and Balandria had set out for Magnice that made his stomach turn.

Aydra was sick.

He'd never ridden so quickly across the land to his enemy kingdom before.

At the castle gates, he pulled his sword on the Belwarks that tried to stop him from going in. He barged through the doors and bounded up the stairs and hallways to her room.

"She's not there," came Dorian's voice upon Draven's reaching her floor.

Draven froze and turned to face the young prince but did not get a word out upon first seeing him.

Dorian's round eyes had darkened bags beneath them. His cheeks looked sullen, his usual sun-kissed face now paled. Draven's fist tightened in on itself, and he started to step towards him.

"Little Prince," he acknowledged. "You look terrible," he said as he gave him a hug.

Dorian clapped him on his back and then pulled away, shaking his head. "It's been a long month."

"What happened?"

Dorian rubbed his neck, staring past Draven towards the other end of the hall. "After Aydra attacked Rhaif, the guards took her. She was locked in her room. Only Nyssa and I were able to go in and see her. Lex has not been able to see her until earlier today. Rhaif... he's scared. The castle has been a fortress—"

"She should have killed him," Draven growled.

"If she had, she would already be dead," Dorian interjected. "The Bedrani Council has taken over while he heals. They would not allow me to take my own crown."

Draven couldn't believe what he was hearing. "Not allow you... What is happening here?"

An audible exhale left Dorian, and his eyes darted up and down the hall. "I'm not sure. But I do know you and Balandria need to leave. You should not have come. I have a feeling they'll put you in chains."

"I'm not running. Where is Aydra?"

"She should be back soon. Nyssa took her to our mother's waters to see if it would help heal her."

"I'll go there—"

"No—" Dorian pulled on Draven's arm and tugged him back around. "You'll hide. Here. In her room. Wait for her. Do not go galavanting off into these halls without myself, Nyssa, or Lex. Where is Balandria?"

"With the horses," Draven replied. "You cannot expect me to sit in waiting while my love is hurting—"

"If you want to see her again without bars between you, you will," Dorian demanded.

Draven's hand clenched and unclenched at his side. "What is wrong with her?"

"She's sick," Dorian said.

"What do you mean, sick?" Draven asked.

"I mean, one day she's fine, and the next she is vomiting all over the castle," Dorian said. "Something is wrong."

"What do the surgeons say?" Draven asked, stomach knotting.

"Nothing. They tell her she has eaten something wrong. Idiots. They put her on liquids to try and stop the turning of her stomach."

Draven's heart twisted. Dorian clapped his shoulder again.

"Wait for her here," he repeated. "I'll find your Second."

Arbina's waters, if anything, made the turn of Aydra's stomach worse. She'd scrambled to the edge of the Throne room and vomited off the side of the cliff the second her body had been wrapped in the water.

Nyssa watched her helplessly, holding her hair back and then wrapping her arms around Aydra's shoulders when she finally sat back. Lex was with them, standing guard so that no one else entered or found out they were there.

Aydra didn't understand what was happening to her. She felt dizzy, couldn't keep anything down. Her stomach felt of knives ripping through her flesh. Her phoenix had come to her both times she'd visited the Throne room, and in its few moments of reprieve, she'd found herself relaxed in its cold flames.

Nyssa helped her clothe herself, then she and Lex escorted her back through the halls, Aydra's hood up on her the entire time they walked. Aydra paused in front of her door, tired of the attention for the day.

"I will be fine, Nys," Aydra assured her. "Go. You have to continue on as if nothing is wrong."

Nyssa took a deep breath and nodded. "I'll come back tonight with the liquids." She pressed her forehead to Aydra's just briefly and then turned on her heel down the hall.

"Will you allow me to stay?" Lex begged.

"You're the only one here not pitying me every second," Aydra grunted. "You can stay."

Lex smiled and kissed Aydra's forehead. "I've never been the pitying type."

Aydra opened the door to her room and nearly tripped at the sight of someone standing up from her bed. A knot formed in her chest, and her knees weakened.

"Draven."

He bounded across the room to her, and she nearly jumped into his arms. His grasp tightened around her, and he whirled her off the floor.

"Are you real?" she whispered into his hair.

Her feet hit the ground, and he pulled back, his hands resting on her cheeks. Urgency swam in his gaze as it darted over her face. He opened his mouth to speak, but words didn't emit. He pulled her into his chest again, hugging her flush against himself.

"And I'll come not pity you later," Lex said from the door. She heard the click of it closing, but she didn't turn to see Lex leave.

Aydra pulled back to see Draven's face again. A small smile rose on his lips as he pushed her hair back.

"Hi," he whispered.

Her breath skipped. She melted her head into his palm and inhaled deeply.

But the reality of their situation filled her head, and her heart tightened in her chest. "You shouldn't be here," she told him.

"Why does everyone keep telling me this when no one told me not to come?" Draven argued.

The first true smile she'd felt in a month almost made its way to her lips. "Would that have stopped you?"

"Not at all, but it would have been nice to know what I was walking into."

She leaned up then and felt her body melt into his grasp. "I missed you," she whispered.

His nose nudged hers, and his fingers wrapped into her hair. "I missed you," he managed.

Her heart bled at having him in her arms again. She pressed her smiling lips to his, savoring the taste of him on her skin after so long.

—Her stomach turned. She let him go and ran all the way across her room to the window, where she vomited out into the open air. A cold sweat broke on her forehead as she grabbed the stone.

"So… you *are* sick," Draven said as he crossed the room towards her.

Aydra steadied herself against the wall and looked back over her shoulder to see him slowly walking her way, hands in his pockets.

"Something stupid like that, yes," she muttered, sinking her back against the cold wall. "I have vomited over nearly every inch of these halls. I feel dizzy. Sweating all over. My sister won't stop looking at me like I'm dying." She sighed and looked up at him, her head leaning back. "It's all very annoying."

He looked as though he would laugh. "Only you would define being this sick as an annoyance," he mocked.

She huffed amusedly under her breath, and he kissed her forehead.

"What can I do?" he asked.

She shrugged, hugging her arms over her chest. "The surgeons say it is something I ate. But I've been like this a week. Getting worse every day. I'm not sure there's anything you can do besides wait for it to pass."

"Where is your phoenix?" he asked, looking out the window.

"Ah... not sure. I see her shadow once a day at least. Where she stays the rest of the time, I'm not sure."

"Call her," he said. "I have an idea."

68

Draven sent a letter off with the phoenix without telling her who it was for. She didn't question him. She was happy he was there, happy to have someone around that would not treat her as though she were fragile.

For the remainder of the day, and well into the night, he held her on the floor. Nyssa brought food to her room before night fell, but Aydra could hardly keep it down. The smell of it repulsed her, and Nyssa promised to bring up actual food instead of the medicined mush the surgeons had prescribed in the morning. When she left, Draven packed the pipe, insisting it would help with the nausea, and they sat together on the floor once more.

He told her what was going on in his forest, about their inner gossips, the squabble two men had tried to settle over a woman, who ended up choosing another woman instead of one of them. He told her Nadir was waiting on her before going to the ships again, that they were scouting things out and watching their every move. They would know what they were walking into when they finally did decide to speak with them. Two more ships had arrived west of the reef, but they looked to be supply ships this time, only carrying food and materials, not weapons.

"What about you? You didn't tell me what happened when you got here," he said after a while.

She stared down at their entwined hands. "I fought my brother. Took one of his eyes. Then found myself on lockdown by my own guard."

"But you didn't kill him."

"I didn't, no," she sighed, still looking down. Her head shook as she contemplated her next words. "Killing him would have secured the Bedrani Council taking over, as they already have in his absence. They don't trust Dorian. I fear he will have a harder time getting his crown than I previously thought."

"I don't understand how they can do that. It's his crown."

"But they are the Bedrani Council. They represent the Dreamers of our land. You forget, there are only four Promised children. The only reason we have crowns is because Dreamers gave them to us. They can also take them away."

Draven sank his head against her temple. "You people and your politics," he muttered. "We should kill them all and take over," he added under his breath.

Aydra almost laughed despite the pain that had just sharpened through her abdomen. "Burn the kingdom to the ground," she muttered.

"Purple, orange, and black flames lighting up the sky," he said dreamily.

She hugged his arms tighter around herself and rocked into his chest. His lips pressed to her temple again, the tickle of his beard making her chuckle softly.

Home surrounded her heart, and she sighed into his embrace.

The window burst open.

Both of them shot to their feet. Draven grabbed his sword off the dresser, Aydra taking a candleholder off the desk.

A whirl of wind concentrated in the window, black smoke building from within it. It moved inside the room, and then it dissipated as quickly as it had arrived.

The Nitesh was standing in her room.

The candlestick dropped from Aydra's hands, and her eyes widened at Draven beside her. "You called the Nitesh?" she hissed.

"You're sick. Of course I called the Nitesh," he argued.

"But—"

"Stop your babbling, Aydra Ravenspeak," the Nitesh cut in.

Aydra's insides froze at her hiss. "It's really not that bad. He shouldn't have bothered you."

"Nevertheless, he did," the Nitesh said as she pulled her hood and cloak off and threw it into the chair beside her. "Sit. Now."

Aydra laid down in the bed as another pain shot through her stomach. She pushed it from her mind, not wanting Draven to see the pain in her features. The Nitesh's hands were cold as she pressed her palms to her forehead. A golden glow radiated from her hands and over Aydra's body. Draven stood at the end of the bed, one arm crossed over his chest, chewing on his thumb on the other hand as he watched.

"Don't glare at me like that," Draven muttered to her after a few minutes.

"You called the Nitesh because I have been puking," Aydra grumbled. "I am not dying."

"No," the Nitesh agreed as her hands hovered over Aydra's abdomen. "You are not." The gold lines on her skin flashed as though anger pulsed to the surface, and her eyes grew a wild gold in color.

Aydra's heart skipped at the sudden bewilderment on the Nitesh's face. "Nitesh?"

The Nitesh rose slowly from Aydra's bedside, her widened eyes never leaving Aydra's stomach.

She turned to Draven.

"Take me to Promregis," she hissed. "Now."

69

Draven didn't argue.

It was only a few hours before the sunrise. The only people in the halls were Belwarks and Dreamer servants waking for morning chores. Lex was sitting outside Aydra's door in the hall when Draven emerged.

"Draven—" her words ceased, nearly balking at the sight of the Nitesh behind him. "What—"

"No time. I have to get her to the Throne Room. I could use the escort," he cut in.

Lex nodded. "Done."

Lex led them through the castle, waving off any guards who questioned where she was going. Draven's heart was beating hard in his chest. The look the Nitesh had had on her face when she stood now seared in his mind.

When they reached the Throne Room, the Nitesh did not stop until she was standing at the front of Arbina's pool.

"Back," the Nitesh warned. "Both of you."

They took steps back behind her, and the Nitesh plunged her staff so forcefully into the water that it swelled into a great tidal wave.

The golden streaks on her skin glowed like nerves on the surface. The wave splashed onto the great white tree, and from its depths, a woman formed out of the mist.

His giver's enemy. The reason his own maker was cursed.

Arbina Promregis Amaris.

He'd never seen her in her corporeal form. Long white-blonde wavy hair billowed in the wind that encircled the room. Her icy eyes stared at the Nitesh, and a slow smile spread over her beautiful face.

451

"Nari," Arbina called the Nitesh by her true name. "I did not realize you were the new pet."

"What. Have. You. *Done?*" the Nitesh asked wildly.

Arbina picked at one of her pointed nails. "I don't know what—"

Lightning lit up the sky.

Thunder cracked so violently that the entire castle shook.

"*The child*, Arbina," the Nitesh spat. "The child in the womb she should not even have."

Draven's heart stopped. "What?"

Lex grabbed Draven's arm.

"How many of your daughters have you given this ability to?" the Nitesh shouted.

Arbina's smile widened, and her eyes flashed in Draven's direction. "Finally. I wondered how many it would take before she found you." Arbina began walking then, her figure dancing over the water's surface as she continued to ignore them.

"*How many, Promregis?!*" the Nitesh shouted again.

"All of them," Arbina said shortly.

"Wait," Draven cut in, stepping up from the shadows. "You're telling me… Aydra is carrying a…" his voice choked on the word "child?" he finally managed. "My child?" His eyes darted between the women in the room, and he felt the blood draining from his face. "But how? How can she be with child? What—"

"Ancient stories tell of a race of beings beyond our shores," the Nitesh began darkly. "A race of savages, power hungry and greedy, the same beings who have arrived on our shores now—"

Draven and Lex exchanged a wide-eyed glance, but the Nitesh continued to speak, and they didn't have a chance to ask her about the words she'd used.

"—The stories say they grew children in their women's bellies over a period of time and birthed them as squalling babies. These children would share the nature of both their combined givers, a man and a woman." The Nitesh turned to Arbina. "I will assume this is where you received such an idea."

Arbina smiled a sly, mischievous smile that sent a chill down Draven's spine. "It is," she answered.

The Nitesh screamed.

Lightning struck the tree.

"*You have meddled with Haerland!*" the Nitesh shouted. "Meddled with the sanctity of this land! What will this child even be?!"

"A child of greatness," Arbina affirmed. "Born of the Sun and Darkness merged as one."

"You do not know what powers this child could hold," growled the Nitesh. "You could unleash something so dangerous onto our kind that it kills every being in this land."

"Or saves it," Draven interjected.

The wind stopped.

The Nitesh turned slowly, staring at him.

Draven's mind raced. He swallowed as he looked between the bewildered eyes before him. "This child... it could be what brings our inner war to an end. It could be the one who brings our races together. Unites our world."

He deliberately moved down the steps, nearly stumbling in his daze, heart beating wildly in his chest.

"Draven—"

He *ran*.

He knocked down three Belwarks on his way through the castle, jumping between and over the Dreamer servants walking the halls until finally, he reached her room.

And when he burst through the doors, his heart swelled at the sight of her sitting up in the chair in the moons light as her sister brushed her hair.

His Queen.

His best friend.

His partner.

His equal in this life.

Mother to his child.

Mother to the child of Sun and Darkness.

70

Aydra's eyes widened at the sight of Draven bursting through her door. The wild look on his face made her insides drain.

"Draven, what—"

He was standing beside her before she could blink, and he reached for her hands. She stood and faced him, unable to make out the flaring happiness in his dilated sage pupils. He kissed her knuckles and then whispered, "Oh, Aydra," before cupping her face and kissing her lips.

She felt her feet lift from the floor, and she pulled back to look at his face as he spun her.

"Draven!" His happiness practically radiated into the room, and she couldn't help the laughter that emitted from her lips. "Draven, what— what are you so happy about?"

He put her down then, still staring at her face as though it was his first time looking upon it.

"Have I told you how much I love you?" he whispered.

"Draven, what is going on," she demanded.

"Arbina has given us a gift," he told her.

A full frown slipped onto her face, thoroughly bewildered by the words she knew couldn't be true.

"That doesn't sound right. Try again."

He chuckled under his breath. "Come sit with me," he said as he took a step back. Her gaze narrowed, but she followed him to sit on the bed nonetheless.

"Draven..."

"A child grows inside you," he said quickly. "Our child."

Glass broke behind them.

A ringing filled her ears.

She blinked, feeling lightheaded, and not because of the pain in her stomach.

"What?" she managed, sure she hadn't heard him right.

"What did you say?" Nyssa managed, leaving the glass broken on the floor as she came to stand beside her sister.

Draven didn't look away from Aydra. "A child of Sun and Darkness. Born of the Promised and the Venari. *Our* child grows in your belly."

Aydra wasn't sure she'd understood what he said.

"What—But how… Our children are born of the Lesser Ones. No Lesser being can conceive—"

The door opened, and the Nitesh walked in, Lex following behind her. Aydra's heartbeat pounded in her ears as the Nitesh crossed the room to her. There were tears in her eyes, but she took Aydra's hands, and she sat down beside her.

Aydra listened to the Nitesh tell them what Draven was on about. She listened to her tell the stories of the ancient beings, of the ones across the seas who could bear children. Her sister sat behind her, and Draven squeezed her hands, that wild happiness still radiating through him.

She wanted to be happy as Draven was.

She wanted to dance with the glee her sister held behind her.

But all she could think about was what her brother and the Council would do when they found out.

Once the Nitesh had finished, Aydra inhaled a deep breath and stood from the bed. "I need to speak with the Nitesh," she told them. "Alone."

Draven, Nyssa, and Lex did not argue. Draven kissed her forehead, and she memorized the look of pure happiness in his features. The door closed behind them a moment later, and Aydra pulled her robe tighter around her.

Aydra stepped up to the window and looked out of it, the shadow of her phoenix passing over the moons.

"So this is how my mother plans to finish me," she whispered. "I will assume you agree?"

She could hear the Nitesh's pause and shift in her weight as she stood from the bed.

A pause long enough that she knew meant the Nitesh agreed.

"Not will I pretend to know how others will take this news," the Nitesh replied softly.

"They will kill me," Aydra whispered. She looked back at the Nitesh over her shoulder, and the gaze the woman gave her confirmed her suspicions. "They won't understand. They'll think it a trick of Duarb. A play to take over Magnice." Aydra paused to swallow what felt of sap sticking to her vocal cords.

"You have to get Draven out of here."

"Not will he leave you." The Nitesh walked around the bed then and stood beside her at the window. "Leave. Both of you. Take refuge in my realm," she begged.

"I'm not running," Aydra managed. "I will not live in fear or bring their treachery to your realm."

"Pride," the Nitesh almost laughed. "You condemn yourself and this child because of *pride*." She started walking in paces in front of the bed, and Aydra hugged her chest tighter, biting back the tears in her eyes.

"Then tell them, you do not," the Nitesh said then. "Stay here. Get care. I will check in."

"My brother will be looking for any reason to harm me now that I have humiliated him. The Council has simply been biding their time since I nearly blinded him," Aydra told her. "If you are traveling back and forth to this castle, he'll know something is wrong." She paused, her weight shifting as she felt the nausea well up inside her once more, and this time not because of the child in her belly.

But then an idea hit her, and for the first time, she breathed with ease as she allowed it to fill her.

"We'll go to the Forest," Aydra said, meeting the Nitesh's eyes. "It's the only way. They won't be suspicious. They'll simply think I've run away with Draven again, abandoned Magnice for good. But we have to leave before the sun rises."

The Nitesh's golden eyes widened, and she seemed to contemplate it a moment. Her gaze darted to the floor, moving back and forth, and then she nodded.

"Yes. Yes, quickly—"

Aydra darted to her dresser and began throwing clothes onto her bed. The Nitesh ran for the door, and she opened it swiftly to urge the others inside. Draven bounded to Aydra's side at once.

"What are we doing?" he asked as he touched her back.

"Help me pack," she said fast. "We have to go to your kingdom. It's the only way. I cannot stay in Magnice and have this child here. They won't understand."

Draven's eyes were narrowed, and she knew he didn't understand the extent of what was happening.

"What do you need me to do?" Nyssa asked her as she took her side.

Aydra turned and grabbed her sister's arm. "I need you to go back to your room. Act as though you know nothing. You did not see Draven and Balandria. They were never here. Lex—" she stepped past Nyssa to Lex "—go with my sister. Protect her and try to keep the noise of my departure to a minimum. I do not know what will happen once we've left. When it is time, I'll send for you all. I do not wish for any of you to have to live here under their thumbs."

Lex nodded, and Aydra hugged her tightly, feeling a lump rise in her throat when she pulled back, and Lex pushed her palms against Aydra's cheeks.

"I'll look after them," Lex whispered.

Aydra gave her a tight-lipped smile. "Thank you."

She hugged her again, breathing in the ash and fire smell of her best friend, before then turning to her sister and giving her a long hug. Nyssa's tears stained her shoulder, and she almost choked on the words she said to her.

"Be strong for me," she whispered, pressing her hands on Nyssa's cheeks. "Listen to Lex. I will send word when it is time. You know I cannot stay here. You know what would happen if they found out."

Nyssa was shaking as she nodded. "I do."

Aydra wrapped her in her arms again, swaying with her sister in her arms as she kissed the top of her head. "Go back to your room. Stay quiet. Take your brother to the cliffs tomorrow and tell him what has happened. Do not tell him within the confines of these walls. There are spies everywhere."

Nyssa and Lex left the room only a few moments later, leaving Aydra to finish packing her things. Draven still stared at her in silence, his mind obviously working out what was happening and why they were going.

"Spit it out, my King," Aydra said as she started buckling her back closed.

"What happens if they find out about our child?" he asked in a low voice.

Aydra stopped moving, but only for a second, and then she ignored his question. "The Nitesh will check in with us. She doesn't know how long it will take for this child to come to term."

457

"You're dodging the question."

Aydra ignored him. "I will send a letter back for my brother once we are safe, explaining that I have left of my own accord, unable to stay a prisoner in this realm any longer."

"Belwarks have already seen me coming in," Draven argued. "They know I am here. I threatened a few on my way to you yesterday."

Her hands dropped, and she glared at him over her shoulder. "Good job."

"What happens if he thinks I have come and kidnapped you in the middle of the night?" Draven asked, stepping up to her side. "What if they come for us?"

"Do you not want me in your kingdom?" she dared to ask.

"I do—" he paused, a great sigh leaving him as he closed his eyes, and his hand pressed to the small of her back. "I want you there more than I want the Dead Moons to rise," he breathed. "I only worry of what could happen when they find out you've left with me after declaring you a prisoner."

"Whatever happens will not be as bad as them finding out I am with child," she argued.

"*What. Will. Happen?*" he growled deliberately.

"I can tell my brother and the Council that I am giving up my crown for good—"

"Aydra, what will happen—"

"—That I am banishing myself to the Forest—"

"Drae—"

"—We can be safe there. With your people—"

"Aydra, tell me!"

"If they find out, we will die," she snapped.

Draven froze on the spot, and she watched as the words moved through him.

A heat rose on her chest and neck, and a nervousness filled her as the still silence encompassed the room.

"If they find out, they'll drive a knife through my stomach and throw us both from the tower. We will be condemned. They will not understand or see this child as we do. As a bridge between our worlds. They will see it as a monster."

"She is correct, Venari," came the Nitesh's words.

"So then we'll fight," he said, taking her hands.

The tears swelled inside her, and Aydra couldn't stop her heartbeat from throbbing so hard in her ears, she thought they might bleed.

"If they find out, we won't be able to fight. We won't be able to run. We have one chance. If they find out about the child, that chance will be gone," she explained. "If they find out, and we escape, my brother and the Council will destroy everything to find us. To destroy us. The peace we just bartered between our lands will cease to exist. The war will turn between Magnice and every other realm instead of the united Echelon against the strangers. Everything we just acquired will have been for nothing."

The words seemed to click in his head then, and she watched every muscle in his body tense, almost to the point of visibly shaking. He reached for her bag on the bed and threw it over his shoulder.

"One chance?" he asked.

"Only this one," she said, heart skipping at the look in his eyes. "There is no other."

"Someone should inform the Chronicles," he muttered as he picked her other bag off the floor.

"Of what?"

"The only time they'll ever hear me utter these words." He paused after swinging her last small bag on his arm, and then he met her eyes. "We're running."

71

The Nitesh followed them out of Aydra's bedroom and through the halls.

Draven's steps were wider than Aydra had ever seen of him. He didn't speak, and she could feel her body tensing with anxiety and the anticipation of Belwarks being around every corner. The adrenaline pulsed through her bones, and she kept one hand on her sword on her belt at all times.

"I will meet you in the Forest," the Nitesh spoke to Aydra as they walked. "I must see my mother. Tell her of what has happened."

"Do you think Haerland will help us?" Aydra asked.

"I will not pretend to know of her reaction. I can only hope she knows the two of you, approves of your mating."

"You make us sound like a pair of wild Wyverdraki, Nitesh," Draven mocked ahead of them.

"What he means to say is we appreciate you," Aydra insisted.

She could see the smirk on Draven's face, so different from his attitude only minutes earlier, and her chest swelled with the sight of him hauling her things through the castle to run away with her for their child.

"Swift in your journey," the Nitesh told them. "You cannot rest."

"We could take the phoenix," Aydra suggested.

The Nitesh froze on the spot. "Take what?"

Draven stopped walking, and Aydra nearly ran into him. He tensed at her side. He didn't turn, but Aydra watched as the vein in his neck flinched.

Aydra frowned between them, unable to focus on just one of their annoyed faces. "The… the phoenix…"

"What sort of phoenix?" the Nitesh hissed deliberately.

"A… black… one…" Aydra said slowly, watching as the Nitesh's eyes bulged. "I'm sorry, am I missing something?"

"You didn't—*Venari, turn and face me!*" the Nitesh demanded.

His eyes meeting the Nitesh's, Draven turned just slightly, but he didn't answer her question. "This isn't the time," Draven growled.

"*Venari!*"

Draven rounded on the Nitesh, his figure towering over her petite one. "I did what I had to do," he said in a low voice. "I don't have time to explain my reasons. She is free. That is all that matters. If we do not hurry, my freeing her will have been for nothing."

Aydra was so confused.

Draven straightened, and he reached for Aydra's hand as he spoke to the Nitesh's glaring figure. "If you're done shouting at me, I'd like to get my family to safety. We can talk about the phoenix once we're safe in my realm. Until then, you can help, or you can leave."

Aydra didn't have time to think about their argument. Draven was already starting down the hall. She met the Nitesh's flared nostrils and blazing eyes over her shoulder as he tugged on her hand, and she followed behind him.

"What's going on?" she whispered to him.

"It's fine. She's being dramatic," Draven muttered.

"I shall show you drama," the Nitesh growled behind them. "Freeing the Sun," she mumbled beneath her breath. "You know—"

Aydra's head spun. "Wait—*what*—"

The sun peeking through the window ceased her words, and her stomach dropped. She gripped tighter to Draven's hand and felt her heartbeat pick up. "Shit," she cursed.

His urgent eyes met hers. "We can make it."

They ran through the remainder of the halls.

They opened the last double doors together and burst down the steps to the courtyard. Aydra started to reach out for the phoenix. She could feel it far away, but it answered her call nonetheless. The recognition of it filled her, and she inhaled sharply.

"She's coming," she managed.

Draven froze at the bottom step. "Balandria—"

His eyes were widened with fear as he looked around them. Aydra's heart dropped to her stomach. They couldn't leave without her.

A shadow passed over the sun.

"Go—" the Nitesh urged them. "I will find your Second. Bring her to you. You two must leave."

The phoenix circled over their heads.

But the noise of armor sounded in Aydra's ears, and she froze.

They appeared from every direction, blades pointed at them. Along the top of the catwalk on the walls, the Belwarks drew arrows. Draven dropped her bags to the floor and pulled his own swords. Back-to-back, the pair faced the horde of Belwarks surrounding them.

Aydra found the face of her brother's Second coming up beside them.

"Is there a reason you've surrounded us as though we are criminals?" she spat at Bard.

"Word of the Venari First and Second inside our walls reached us overnight," Bard said, his attention on Draven.

"I came for the meeting," Draven as though it were obvious.

"And now you're fleeing the kingdom with the Queen under cover of darkness with the Nitesh in tow," Bard said. "Or should I say kidnapping the Queen."

"What can I say? She's a beautiful creature to behold," Draven spat back. "Thought she'd be better off in my hands."

Aydra saw a guard move out of the corner of her eye. But Draven was faster. The pommel of the guard's sword came towards him. Draven shoved his own sword handle into Aydra's open hand behind him. Draven's arm pushed out, and he caught the throat of the guard in his fingers.

The guard's sword clanked on the ground. His gasps for air filled Aydra's ears, but she didn't look away from the stare she shared with Bard.

"He's not kidnapping me," Aydra affirmed. "I am leaving. For good this time."

"You'll have to explain such a desire to your King and the Council. Get their approvals," said Bard.

"My King is right here," she snapped. "He approves— don't you, my love?"

Draven's hand tightened around the guard's throat. "Well, you're a bit annoying, but I wouldn't leave here without you."

She couldn't help the smirk that rose on her twisted lips. If they hadn't been surrounded by Belwarks and trying to flee, she would have kissed him.

"You'll be going nowhere," came a new voice.

The guard Draven had been choking fell to the ground. Aydra

jerked in the direction of the new voice. Of the person standing at the top of the steps in the doorway. The amusement she'd held only a moment earlier vanished, and she felt her fists curl in on themselves.

Fucking—

"Ash," Bard called out. "I did not realize you had arrived."

Ash's gaze stared through Aydra to the point that she shifted uncomfortably beneath it. The sight of the smirk on his lips made her insides grow cold.

"He knows," Aydra uttered under her breath.

Belwarks began to shift as Ash started down the steps, speaking with Bard as he walked. Aydra didn't hear what they said. She reached out for the phoenix and told it to stay where it was, not wishing for it to be slaughtered by the arrows pointed at them.

Nausea crept into her turned stomach. Her chest began to heave, and she felt Draven turn sideways behind her.

"What?" he managed.

"He knows," she breathed, her voice strangled. "He knows. Somehow. He must have heard—" Aydra grabbed the Nitesh's arm. "Who else was with you in the Throne Room?"

"Myself, the Venari, your Second," the Nitesh replied. "There was no one else."

Aydra's eyes met Ash's smug face, and she grabbed Draven's hand. "He was."

Ash stopped just before her, and she felt her nostrils flare as she glared at him. "I should have killed you in the Forest," she hissed just loud enough for him to hear.

"You should have," Ash agreed. He turned and gave Bard an upwards nod. "Cuff them," he demanded. "All three."

Bard nearly balked. "My orders—"

"The Venari is not kidnapping your Queen," Ash cut in. "He is running with her."

"Tell me, *Captain*," Aydra seethed. "Why would we run?" she said, daring him to speak the words.

Ash took one step in her direction, and his hair fell over his eyes. "Because of the cursed Venari monster growing in your belly."

The wind picked up.

"My child is not—"

Ash snapped his finger.

An arrow hissed through the air.

"Draven!"

463

The arrow thunked into Draven's shoulder, and he stumbled off balance.

Aydra heard the crows in her ears. She could hear the grunt beneath Draven's breath, see the curl of his fists as he steadied himself. His eyes blazed up through his hair.

The wind engulfed the courtyard walls into a cyclone.

Belwarks fell off balance as it knocked them every way. Arrows flew everywhere but their targets. Necks cracked as some fell over the side of the wall.

The pommel of a sword hit Draven in the back of the head, and the wind ceased.

Aydra lunged as his knees gave way beneath him. "Wait—" Hands grabbed her arms, and she pulled on their grips. "*Get your hands off me!*" She stomped the foot of the one holding her. Her head launched into the nose of the one in front of her, and she bolted forward again just as two Belwarks picked Draven's unconscious body up to his knees.

"Let him go!"

Belwarks grabbed her forcefully this time, causing her to be picked up off her feet, legs kicking in the air as she was still trying to get to him. The crows were circling, waiting for her orders. She seethed through her gritted teeth.

Kill—

The sight of Ash stepping up in front of Draven with his sword drawn made her orders cease. Ash pulled Draven's head up by his hair, the tip of his blade pointed at Draven's throat. Ash paused and looked back at her.

"Stand down your swarm, or I spill his blood over this yard," Ash warned.

Aydra forced herself to breathe. She nearly choked on her own spit as she glared at the Dreamer before her.

"A right hero you are, Ash," she spat. "Only able to threaten the life of the great Venari King once you've had your lackeys subdue him."

Ash seethed down at her and warned once more, "Stand down."

Aydra stared through him a moment longer, feeling her body shake as she contemplated whether he would actually kill Draven.

She finally released the crows, and they flittered to silence around the courtyard.

"On what grounds do you detain us?" she growled.

Ash pushed his sword back in its sheath, and he shoved Draven

back into the arms of two Belwarks.
   "Treason."

72

They were taken to the Throne Room.

The Council was already there, lined up on either side of the thrones. Movement caught the corner of her eye as they entered, and she looked up to see her youngers, Lex and Corbin at their sides, standing between the throng of Belwark guards above them in the gallery.

Draven was forced to his knees, chains latched around his wrists at the edge of Arbina's pool facing sideways. He was shaking his head as though regaining consciousness when she and the Nitesh were walked to the edge of the pool. He looked up at her through the tangles of his hair, and then she could see his gaze narrow as he realized where they were.

The color disappeared from his face. He struggled against the irons. "Drae—"

"It's too late," she mouthed.

Draven's movements ceased. She could see the fight within him draining just as hers was.

The noise of hobbled steps filled her ears. Aydra's heart dropped as she knew who was coming.

It was the first she'd seen her brother since she'd been labeled a prisoner in her own kingdom.

Bard walked behind Rhaif. He didn't look at her as he passed; his great cloak pulled heavily around his shoulders. And when he sat and finally looked at her, she felt her chin rise higher in the air in defiance of the satisfied arrogance he had plastered on his features.

A long scar streaked across his right eye. The socket was closed, mangled as though it had been melted. A streak of his hair was missing over his right ear.

A shadow passed over the sun.

Aydra's gaze darted over the members staring at her, tightened jaws and glares resting on all their faces.

"What is the meaning of this?" the Nitesh finally hissed.

"Bring forth the witness," said one of the council members.

The noise of light armor came up the steps, and Aydra recognized it without looking back. Ash came into her line of vision then, and she heard Draven yank on his chains.

"Jealous bastard—"

whitish!

The whip met Draven's back. He gasped and his back arched, but he didn't fall.

"Stop!" Aydra shouted as the guard began to wind up again.

Rhaif held up two fingers.

"Don't worry, pet," said Ash as he came to stand in front of Rhaif. "You'll get what's coming to you."

Aydra launched a wad of spit at Ash's face this time. It landed in his eye, and he grimaced as he wiped it away. "To think I ever let you in my bed," she growled.

Ash straightened and pushed his hands behind his back. "You should have never let me out of it," he agreed.

"Enough," said Councilwoman Reid. "Captain, please tell the rest of the Council what you told me."

Ash cleared his throat. "The Queen carries the Venari's child in her womb."

Gasps echoed in the air, mumbles quickly following. Rhaif held up a hand again, and he shifted in his seat.

"How is this possible?" he managed, fist tightening over the chair arm. His gaze flickered to the Nitesh, and he gave her a nod. "Nitesh. Explain."

"He's lying," Aydra blurted out. "I am a Lesser being just as all of you are. Born beneath the very tree behind us. How could I carry a child?"

"Are you calling the Captain a liar?" asked a council member.

Aydra glared at Ash. "Among other things," she muttered. "He is jealous of the relationship I share with the Venari King. He would say anything to see Draven in chains."

"Call Arbina," demanded Ash. "She can affirm my story."

Aydra's heart skipped. The Nitesh's arm grazed her own, and

Aydra felt her breaths shorten as she looked down at her.

"What are you waiting for, Nitesh?" called Councilwoman Reid. "Call her."

"I am already here," came Arbina's voice from the gallery.

Aydra looked up and caught a glimpse of her mother, sitting nonchalantly on the edge of the balcony as though she were a child watching a play. She hopped off the side in an instant, coming to stand by Aydra's side.

Arbina smiled down at Aydra, and Aydra resisted the urge to smash her face into her mother's nose. Arbina reached out for Aydra's hair, but Aydra flinched backward.

"Don't touch me," she hissed.

Arbina appeared confused by her words, but she turned her back on Aydra nonetheless. She shrugged and began to pick at her nails again. "What is the meaning of this?"

"Don't play coy," said Reid. "Is it true?"

"You'll have to be a bit more specific," drawled Arbina.

"The child claimed to be growing inside your daughter's womb," said Councilwoman Ebonrath.

Arbina shrugged. "Yes… it's true," she said slowly.

Murmurs sounded around the room, and Aydra watched Arbina's eyes squint at them. "What? They've all been able to do this," Arbina added.

"If they have all been able to grow a child, then why is she the first to conceive within her womb?" another council member asked.

Aydra met the Nitesh's gaze, and Arbina smiled wickedly down at Draven.

"Because of the being she has mated with," Arbina cooed.

"We should freeze her roots," called out a council member. "Make it so that she cannot attempt this destruction again."

Arbina balked. "What?" She stepped forward to the man, towering over him as thunder rumbled in the distance. "Try and touch my tree. I dare you."

"No," Aydra cut in. "Do not stop our line because of this."

"Why should we not? It is by her doing that this monstrosity lives inside you," said another council member.

"Our child is not a monster," Draven growled.

The guard struck him hard across his cheek. She heard the growl from his throat and knew it was taking everything in him not to encircle the guard with his wind.

"We are not the ones to punish my mother," Rhaif said then. "If Arbina will be punished, it will only be by the Nitesh's doing." His gaze met the Nitesh's. "What say you?"

The Nitesh shifted on her feet. "I must convene with my own mother before I can do anything."

Rhaif's hand waved at her. "Then leave. Come back to us with your answer."

The Nitesh turned to Aydra once more, but Aydra shook her head. "Go," she whispered.

The Nitesh disappeared in a tornado of smoke.

"On the matter of the child," spoke up a council member. "I move for immediate eradication."

Aydra's stomach dropped.

"As do I," agreed another. "This child cannot be allowed to walk this land. It is an abomination."

"A cursed demon inside her womb. We must execute the entirety of her to be sure to rid us of it."

"What— *no*," Draven cut in. "I am the reason she is with child. Take me. Not her."

"Do not worry, Venari. You will be executed as well," said Reid.

"There is no law against it—"

The whip came down on his back again, and this time he was thrust forward to his chest. Aydra lunged at the sight of him in pain because of her, but she was pulled back.

"Draven—"

He pushed up to his hands and visibly shook the pain of it from his mind as he met her eyes.

"All in favor of Queen Aydra's termination," called Councilwoman Reid.

Aydra's attention averted around the room as hands slowly raised. She could feel her body beginning to tremble.

Each council member, one by one, voted for her death.

Until it was only Rhaif left to vote.

Her heartbeat echoed in her ears.

She pulled against the chains around her arms, starting to take a step forward, but stopping upon seeing the Belwarks shift their weight. Teeth chattering, she met Rhaif's gaze.

"Rhaif…" she heard herself whisper.

"She is your sister," Draven managed.

"Brother, *please!*" Nyssa shouted from the gallery. "Rhaif! *Please!*"

Rhaif didn't move. He stared at Aydra in a way that told her he was truly battling with the decision. A tear dropped down his cheek, for one brief moment, she thought he might say no—

"Burn her."

Aydra's heart stopped.

"*NO!*"

Nyssa and Dorian's screams echoed in the room.

The noise of Draven's shouts were distant in her ears. Her body voided of every emotion as breath refused to catch.

She couldn't look away from the stare of debilitating hatred coming at her from her brother now that he'd made his decision.

This was the day she'd told herself would come.

73

Draven didn't see Aydra for the rest of the day.

He was dragged, screaming, from the Throne Room and up into their tower dungeons. The door was slammed behind him as he was thrown inside.

He couldn't stop the tears crawling down his face.

His love. His life. Both being put to death because of their love. Because of a child that had never grown within one of the Lesser being's wombs before.

The sun had just begun to set when he heard footsteps on the stairs, but he didn't know who to expect as it was only one person. He shot to his feet, thinking maybe it was Balandria or Dorian.

"Nitesh?"

The Nitesh pulled her hood off her head and plopped down outside his cell door. "Sit, Venari," she demanded. "Sit!"

Draven eyed her but sat nonetheless.

The Nitesh launched through the bars and grabbed his shirt, lifting him off the floor.

"What—"

"The Sun, Venari?!" she hissed, throwing him backward. "You released the Sun for her?! You know who the noir phoenix is. You know breaking such a curse could start something you cannot finish."

Draven's jaw set. He rubbed his chest where she'd grabbed some of the hair on it, eyes glaring at her through the bars. "And I would do it again. For Aydra."

"My mother did not place such curses lightly," she seethed. "Do you realize what you could have done?"

"It was one ritual," he argued.

"A ritual that if continued to its potential or in the wrong hands could undo every curse my mother has ever placed upon this land."

"Maybe I should have completed it," he snapped.

"It is *not* the time!"

He knew if she'd been able to slap him, she would have.

"It's the Sun, Nitesh," he argued. "It merely allows her to take flight in her creature form. She is still imprisoned within the phoenix. What harm could breaking an Architect free bring onto this land?"

"You do not know such Sun," she uttered. "She will think herself judge, jury, and executioner in this form."

"She deserves freedom," Draven snapped. "As every other being and Architect of Haerland does."

The Nitesh's lips pursed and twisted, her golden eyes blazing through him. He rubbed his neck as he took a deep breath to calm himself, and then he shook his head. "I care not of a fuck about your curses, Nari," he said, using her true name. "I care about Aydra. She deserved to feel such a bond with her mother Sun after what her brother did to her raven."

"This was your intention with the ritual? Not to spite myself or my mother?"

"It was for her," he answered sharply. "Only her."

The Nitesh stared at the ground then as though she were contemplating his words, debating whether to believe him. Draven's breath evened as he watched, and he then pushed a hand through his hair, allowing it to settle off his face.

"You know, one day, someone will finish what I started," he continued, now more calmly than before. "The Red Moons will rise. Every curse on this land will break. The Noctuans will be free. The Architects and the dead will walk these grounds once more." He paused, eyes darting over her quiet figure. "And there is nothing your mother will be able to do about it."

The Nitesh eyed him a long moment before shifting in her seat. She held out her hands through the bars.

"Your hands," she insisted, more calmly than before.

"Why? So you can—" He realized then what she was doing, and his stomach knotted. "Why are you calling him?"

"Cease your ramblings and take my hands."

He contemplated her but obeyed nonetheless.

A sudden gust encircled the cell. Draven closed his eyes. He could smell dirt, but not like the grime and stench dirt of the corners of the cell.

Actual, freshly stirred, dirt. Fresh grass. Pine needles. Dew in the morning.

The scents filled his nostrils and made his chest swell. In his mind, he could see trees all around him. The wind engulfed his body. He could hear the scream of the Aviteth in his ears.

Home.

The chill of the Nitesh's hands left him, and Draven opened his eyes. The Nitesh was gone. But in the shadows, he saw the man he owed his fate and life to.

"Hello, father," Draven managed.

A man taller than he emerged from the shadows. Hair long and darker than the forest dirt. Eyes as green as the forest roof. Tan skin that glowed golden in the light of the torches on the walls. Deep scars plagued the man's buff torso. Three long scratches cut across his face and strong brows. The man scratched the stubble on his jaw and began to fiddle with the open padlock on Draven's cell door.

"You realize this is open?" the man asked in a raspy voice, his brow heightened.

Draven leaned back on the stone wall and exhaled the long breath he'd been holding. "I'm aware."

"And you don't want to run?"

"I will not leave her to die alone."

The man opened the door and stepped inside, where he took a seat on the barrel near the door. He pushed his hands through his hair, and Draven frowned at the sight of his giver in the cell with him so far from home.

"Why are you here, Duarb?" Draven asked.

"Do you love her?" Duarb asked.

Draven rubbed his hands nervously in front of him. "I do."

"And does she love you?"

Draven met Duarb's eyes. "She does."

"Then there's something you should know."

Draven eyed his giver a moment, and he leaned his head back onto the stone. "I'm listening."

Duarb avoided Draven's gaze and stared at the ground, rubbing his neck in a manner that made Draven curious. "Arbina is not who you think she is."

"What do you mean?"

"I mean… the child… it was not a gift to Haerland."

"You're telling me a child of mine is not—"

Duarb held a soft hand up. "Listen to me, my son," he said, finally meeting Draven's eyes. "You heard her say it yourself. Today. In the Throne Room. Remember?"

Draven felt his gaze furrow, and he tried to remember everything Arbina had said. If anything stuck out to him.

And then the sentence hit him.

I wondered how long it would take for you to find him.

He nearly sent so much wind around the tower that it would have crumbled beneath its weight.

"She planned this?"

Duarb stayed silent for a moment, his heel tapping nervously against the stone. "She's planned it since I was forced into my tree," he said softly. "Since our last fight. She's had it out for me. Always telling me she had something that would one day bring me to my knees. And she was right."

Draven could see the water glistening in his eyes.

"She's known what would happen if a child was conceived," Duarb continued. "She knew the people would think it sorcery, an abomination. Unnatural. And she allowed it to happen anyway. But only if her daughter mated with one of mine."

Draven stared at the bars in front of him, feeling the anger swell.

"Arbina has always been the master manipulator. The Infi children I was cursed with… even they cannot touch her level of betrayal to this land. Everything she does is a lie. She dared them to freeze her roots because she wanted to show she could not be frozen. The pool around her roots would simply not allow it—"

"Then how do I burn her?" came the words from Draven's lips.

Duarb stared at Draven for a long moment, and Draven could see the contemplation in his eyes, the knowing sadness bubbling through his being. Duarb stood then and went to the window where only one tiny sliver of the remaining moon shown above the water. He looked back at Draven's sitting figure.

"I think you know."

74

Aydra was barely conscious. She felt arms underneath her as she was carried up more and more stairs. She wasn't sure where she was being taken. But she could hear the beach in her ears, and every time she glimpsed light, it was from the torch.

"Aydra—"

The noise of Draven's voice made her ears perk. She struggled to open her eyes, desperate to see where he was. She heard iron doors, shouting, and then the sound of something being thrown against the wall.

Which she realized was actually her own body.

"—for this. ALL OF YOU!" she heard Draven bellow.

The room spun around her, and it was barely a second before she felt his arms picking her up and then his body behind hers. She groaned as she tried to bring herself out of whatever poisoned tonic they had given her.

"Draven..."

His arms squeezed around her from behind, and he kissed her cheek. "I'm here," he whispered.

Her subconscious slipped, for how long she wasn't sure. The next time she woke, she was still cradled in his arms, and she could hear his soft snores behind her. She forced herself to turn around so that she could see his face.

The sight of it brought tears to her eyes.

His beautiful face. Marred with a purple bruise and long scratch on his cheek from where he'd been hit with the pommel of the sword. His lip cut open, dried blood in his beard. She reached up to his cheek and pressed her lips softly against his.

He stirred, his hands gently pressing against her waist, and he kissed her back. When she opened her eyes, she was met with the glistening sage eyes she swore into memory. A slow tear trickled down his cheek, and she wiped it away.

She didn't know the words to say. Sitting in his arms on their final night together... Condemned for the only true love she'd ever felt. Her death she did not care about. She knew this day would come. She had known since the night she kissed him at the Gathering in front of everyone.

She laid her head in the crook of his neck and felt the next tear hit her hair as he kissed her forehead.

"I watched them write the scroll," she whispered. "He made me watch as he signed the order. The new law."

"What law?" Draven asked.

"That love between the Venari and Promised daughters is now forbidden," she answered solemnly. "Punishment for the discovery of such a bond would be punishable by death on both parties, for if allowed to flower, an abominated creature would grow in her womb, and the safety of Haerland would be in danger. By order of the King and Bedrani Council."

His hand tightened around her. "Abominated creature," he muttered distractedly under his breath. "Our child is not—"

"You'll be tortured in the morning," she cut him off. "And then the people..." Her words stuck in her throat, and he squeezed her arms. "The people will be allowed stone throws. At sunset... what's left of me will burn. They plan to hang you with the rising sun the next morning." She looked up at him.

"Do you still want to run?" he asked.

She swallowed, a tear running down her cheek. "We can't," she managed. "To run now would bring war and terror to all of our lands. We would have to go to the caves, and my brother and the Council would send an army, burning and killing everything in his path to kill us. They would take the mountains, the forest, the reef... All our friends would perish beneath Rhaif's thumb before the true war is upon us. I do not wish to live in fear my entire life, nor do I wish to bring such a war to Haerland when Man is already knocking on our beaches." She paused and looked up at him. "*You* could run. After you are brought back here to the tower at nightfall. You could escape."

He brought her hand to his lips. "There is something I must do tomorrow night. After it is complete, I will meet you at the Edge on my own accord, in my way. I will not allow them the chance to see the light leave my eyes."

"You don't have to do this," she whispered, her heart shattering at what he was suggesting.

"I do," he insisted. "I wish to die with the noise of the Noctuans in my ears, the warmth of the darkness around me. Not in the sun with the people who have betrayed Haerland staring at me. They do not deserve the satisfaction."

Aydra was unable to move her eyes from his. "I love you so much," she managed.

A long sigh exhaled from his lungs, and he leaned his forehead against hers. "I love you."

Her stomach lurched just moments later, and Aydra grimaced at the feeling of her insides evacuating onto the floor outside the bars. Draven rubbed her back and held her once more when she made her way back to the ground. Every now and then, he would rub her stomach, causing a chill to run down her spine, a swell of raw emotion to fill her. And when he leaned down to kiss her belly, she couldn't stop the silent tears rushing over her reddened cheeks.

"You know, we would have gotten to name it," he whispered.

She had to bite back the sobs threatening her. She'd hardly allowed herself to think about the child as he had, as what it would have actually been rather than a punishment from her own giver to end her life. But as her life seemed to be ending anyway, she laid her head against his chest, and she allowed herself to live inside the fantasy Draven spoke of.

"What would you have suggested?" she managed.

He kissed the inside of her palm and then rested them together back on her stomach. "There is a name for the Venari in the old language... one that means 'Hunter of the Sun'... Theron."

"Theron... sounds too formal," she told him.

He huffed amusedly under his breath. "What do you suggest?"

"The name would have to be grand but not audacious or conceited. A child born of us would know no fear. It would live in shadows and become one with our darkness. Shrouded in the blanket of it. It would ride the dragons. Swim with the serpents. A child formidable and gentle all in one. A child that would have saved us from the division our races have so held on to during these last Ages."

"Fallon," Draven suggested abruptly.

Aydra paused. "Fallon..." she repeated, allowing the name to live on her tongue. She gave his hand a squeeze. "I like it," she said, gazing up at him. "What does it mean in the old language?"

"Leader in darkness," he informed her.

Her gaze narrowed, and she felt a frown slip on her lips. "Is that actually true?"

His facade broke, and he chuckled under his breath. "I've no idea."

She allowed the laughter to radiate through her, and she sighed into his shoulder as his lips pressed hard to the top of her head. His lips lingered there a moment, and she felt the wetness of his tear streak her cheek.

"He could have ridden in the sun with the phoenix," he whispered. "Crawled in the grasses with the Rhamocour."

"And if it was a girl?" she asked him.

He pulled back. "That is a petrifying thought."

She almost laughed. "Why?"

"Because a daughter would have killed me slowly, and deliberately, with the anxiety of what she would do next."

She laid her head against his chest again, and she sighed heavily as he began to caress her stomach once more. "You would have loved her nonetheless."

"I already do," came the crack of his voice.

The declaration of his words broke her. The sudden reality of what they were being forced to give up poured from her mind and shattered her insides. Images of a reality she would not have flashed before her eyes. Draven introducing their child to the dragons, the laughter of it ringing in her ears. She could see the smile on his face as he held it and kissed its cheek. And then he would look at her with a happiness never wanted to let go.

She nearly hurled at the overwhelming angst of such a fantasy flooding her mind and drowning her beneath it. But he held her tightly against him and stroked her hair, his own tears coming down his cheeks as he attempted to hold himself together for her.

"I wonder what the Chronicles will say about us," Aydra whispered after a while. "Whether they'll speak of us as villains, as though we fell in love to spite our kind. If they'll say our child was as it should have been —a greatness— or if they'll say it was an abomination."

Draven's hand squeezed hers. "Maybe we should write it for them."

She looked up and met his serious gaze, jaw taut with determination. "How could we do that?"

The noise of footsteps on the stairs leading to the tower disturbed their moment. Aydra's heart jumped in her chest, and she clenched onto his shirt. She heard keys jangling and thought perhaps it was guards coming up. Draven's arms squeezed around her.

But then—

"Dorian."

Dorian appeared in the doorway, followed quickly by Nyssa. Aydra moved from Draven's arms and crawled to the iron doors.

"You know you cannot be seen here," she insisted.

Dorian held up a set of keys as he crossed the space. "Thought we would spring you free." He put the key in the lock, but the sudden grasp of Aydra's hands on his made him stop.

"No," Aydra said softly.

"Do not worry for us any longer, youngers," Draven said from the corner. "Our lives end here. But you two must remain."

Nyssa's eyes were tearing up. "Please. Let us free you—"

"You must be strong," Aydra whispered as she reached out for Nyssa. "The boats will not stop. I do not know how long it will be before Lovi's beaches are swarmed with Man."

Nyssa's hand rested on her cheek. "I will avenge you, my sister. The Council will pay for what they have ordered."

"No," Aydra said shortly. "No. You must focus your energy on the ships."

"You remember what we talked about?" Draven asked Dorian then. "Bring the horn to me tomorrow night. After… " Draven's eyes flickered to Aydra, and she squeezed his hand. "After I am brought back here," Draven managed. "You know the plan, Dorian. You know what is coming. What you must do."

Dorian's hand tightened around his sister's arm.

"Bide your time," Draven continued. "Be patient. Balandria hasn't left yet. Find her and have her come to me at once. Then find Nadir. It is only a matter of time before an armada arrives on his shores. These last boats have been scouting boats. When they don't arrive back at their home across the seas, they will start sending more ships."

"My brother will not allow us to send aid," Aydra interjected.

"They will not be telling him anything," Draven said, meeting her eyes.

Aydra paused, confused by this plan that Dorian apparently already knew of. Draven reached a hand out and cupped her cheek.

"Do you trust me?" he asked.

She blinked back the tears in her eyes and looked between him and her younger brother. The touch of Nyssa's hands wrapping around hers brought breath back to her lungs. As her gaze darted between the pair standing before her, she saw something change in their eyes. Their playful teenage selves were fading, and just there, in the corner of her eyes, she could see them older, matured.

Haerland's saviors.

The true King and Queen.

Finally, she met Draven's eyes again, and she nodded. "More than I trust the sun to rise," she whispered.

"I don't like leaving you," Nyssa interjected. "It should be you two on the High thrones. You two to lead the Echelon. Look at what you achieved at the meeting. Peace. We—"

"This is the only way our people survive," Aydra cut her off. "If we were to run, our entire land would become divided. Rhaif would not stop until we were found, and he would bring war to every corner of Haerland looking for us. We cannot risk that. Not after we just brought our people together. We will not be the cause of the people perishing. We—" she pointed between herself and Draven "—are not the King and Queen to lead you into battle against Man. Nor is Rhaif. You are that King and Queen. You two, and Balandria. You three will unite our kingdoms and finish what we started. Do not let Rhaif take us backward. Your reigns will bring in a new Age. One that knows no division between our races, only peace and camaraderie across the lands. But you must defeat the strangers onshore to do this."

"What if we can't?" Nyssa asked.

"Then the people will wait for the First Sign of the awakening darkness."

"What is the First Sign?"

"An Infinari child."

Dorian and Nyssa exchanged a long look, and Aydra grasped Nyssa's hands in hers.

"Can you do something for me?" she asked Nyssa.

Nyssa nodded. "Anything."

A tear slipped down Aydra's cheek as she pulled the tourmaline ring off her finger, and she set it in Nyssa's hand. "Give this to Lex. Tell her under no circumstance is she to come to this tower. She is to protect you. Follow you. And you will listen to her. Do not treat her as beneath you. She is your equal, the only person you can truly trust to lay their life on the line for you." She felt her jaw shaking as Nyssa curled the ring in her hand. "She is my greatest friend."

"You know she will not listen if I tell her she is not to come to you," Nyssa argued.

"It is an order," Aydra affirmed. "She will respect that."

Nyssa reluctantly nodded. Aydra gave her a tight-lipped smile as she squeezed her hand again. "Exhale the fire, my sister," she whispered. "But don't forget to breathe in the smoke."

Aydra took hold of Dorian's hand in hers too then, and she stared between them.

"I am so proud of you both," she told them. "Be brave for me. For Haerland."

A sob emitted from Nyssa's lips, and she broke into tears in Dorian's arms.

"You have to go," Draven managed. "Find Balandria for me. Send her here. And Prince—have her bring quill and parchment."

Dorian's eyes squinted, but he nodded nonetheless. He nudged his sister in his arms. "We have to go," he whispered.

Nyssa screamed and lunged at the bars again, her hands grabbing hold of Aydra so tightly that Aydra's breath caught in her throat.

"Nyssa, we have to go!"

"*No!*"

It was the tears on Dorian's face when he last looked at her that did her in.

Draven's arms wrapped around Aydra as she felt her heart shredding. Dorian grasped Nyssa around her waist as he pulled her backward. He had to carry her down the steps, her cries cutting through the still night air. Aydra's heart bled as Draven pulled her back against him, and the screams of her sister's pleas echoed in her ears.

It was all Aydra could do to keep her composure as Balandria fought to keep a stern face for her king when she came by. The wind circled the tower as both of them stood on either side of the bars, and she watched a silent tear stretch down Balandria's face.

"I wish you would run," she told him.

Draven gave her a small smile and pressed his hand to her face. "You know better than to think I would."

She huffed under her breath, and she shook her head at him. "I do," she managed.

Draven reached into his shirt then, and he pulled the stone and chain he always wore over his head. "Take it this time," he insisted.

Balandria slowly bowed her head so that he could place it around her neck. Her gaze met his when she lifted her head once more. Draven gave her a proud smile.

"Balandria Windwood. Venari King," he said as he clapped her shoulder. "I couldn't have asked for a better successor."

When Balandria left them, Draven practically fell backward into the hay bales at the corner of the bars. Aydra held his hands as he cried quietly, and after a while, she held him against her chest, staring out at the stars sparkling back at them in the sky. Tears came down her own face as she tried to assure him he'd done his part in being a great king, leading his people out of the shadows they'd rested in for generations.

Her body felt empty and full all at once.

Empty because she knew this was the end, full because of the love she'd felt just within those last few hours. Proud of the people her siblings had become. Proud of Balandria for trying to keep a stern face in front of her king.

It was all she could have asked for on her last night.

The parchment Balandria had brought him was quickly filled with their story. The truth. Not whatever lies the Chronicles would say about them. Their love. Their comfort in darkness. How they'd found each other despite the fear and hatred their givers had so spewed upon their races throughout history.

Upon its completion, Draven stuffed it between two rocks, securing it for whomever he thought would need it in the future.

As he sat back against the wall, he cradled her in his arms, the both of them fighting the drooping of their heavy eyes. They'd not slept the night before, but neither wanted the morning to come any faster than it would already.

"I have to tell you something," Draven whispered after a while.

She sat her chin on his chest and met his gaze. "This isn't like the other times, is it?" she said, almost playfully. "I don't think I can take anymore faints of surprise."

He chuckled under his breath, and he grasped her hand in his, kissing her knuckles. "No, not like the other times," he promised.

"Then tell me."

Draven sighed, and her eyes squinted at his solemn facade, staring at the ground as his mind worked.

"You know what I'm going to do," he whispered as their eyes met.

Her stomach dropped, and she remembered the words he had spoken to her the night of the Infi attack. He toyed with her hands in his a moment, and then he continued.

"I always knew you would never allow me to save you—"

"Draven, you did save me," she interjected.

His brows knitted together, and he squeezed her hand, but he didn't respond.

She reached up and felt his face, her thumb grazing the gash across his cheek. "You saved me from a blinding sunlight which I did not know was killing me. From living out the rest of my days wondering what it would have felt like to know the truth of this world."

"You would have been fine without me," he whispered.

"I know," she managed. "But you made me so happy. So loved. My equal partner, in light and in dark."

His jaw was trembling, and he closed his eyes. "I am taking my own revenge against this kingdom for what they have put you through. All of them. This kingdom, your giver, your brother... they will all burn for what they've done to you and every other queen to have ever sat subdued on that throne. The flames of darkness will envelop the sky. And the Rhamocour's shout will be the last thing they hear before my death."

Aydra's heart skipped. "You're bringing the Noctuans here? To Magnice?"

"The dragons," he answered. "Do you have a problem with that?"

She thought about it a moment, staring at their entwined hands in his lap. "Our crown does not live within a castle. It lives within a people. These walls have betrayed that crown, made it grow greedy and unyielding..." She paused, meeting his eyes. "As long as Nyssa and Dorian are safe, it can crumble to ash and smoke," she finally determined.

He smiled, his forehead leaning against her temple as he hugged his arms around her, knees bent and cradling her in his arms. "There's my Queen."

75

With the rising sun came the clanking of armor.

They'd tried to stay awake as long as they could.

But they couldn't stop sunlight from coming.

"No—no, *wait!*"

The realization of the day hit her chest. She was ripped from his arms by a Belwark. Her heart cried out for him as she reached for the bars. "Draven!"

Draven grappled desperately for her hands through the bars— "Aydra, no, *wait!*"

Their fingertips barely touched before the pommel of the guard's sword struck his face, and he fell onto the dirt with a thud.

"Draven!"

Arms wrapped around her own, and she kicked and screamed, but it was of no use.

Her fingertips burned with the last of his touch on her skin.

Her fight ceased as they dragged her through the castle, her own body heavy between the two Belwarks who carried her. Her dragging feet creased the black runner down the halls. The sun flickered through the windows, and she knew it wasn't clouds hoarding over it. It was the shadows of the crows following them.

She was thrown onto the floor between Arbina's pool and her brother's throne. The Council was lined up around the chairs, each standing with their hands in front of them. She didn't have to look up to know who's black boots were slowly coming toward her.

She glared up at her brother through the tangles of her hair. When he bent down in front of her, she spat the blood from her mouth onto his face.

"Coward," she breathed.

His jaw tensed, and she watched as he wiped his face with the sleeve of her dress.

"I always knew you'd betray the crown," he said in a hushed voice.

"By falling in love with someone that wasn't you?" she dared. "Forgive me for wanting actual love, brother dear."

Rhaif's nostrils flared. He stood and snapped his fingers above her. "Take her to the square."

The ropes scratched her wrists.

She could already hear the murmurs of the people gathering around. She wondered what lies the crown had told about her to have them gathering stones.

This was the same square that she had executed the Infi. The same square that she had protected the people on who would now bring her to the brink of death by a stone throw. This square where she had sworn to her raven that they would have their day.

This would be the day the Chronicles would soon call a reckoning for the people, a mercy enacted by the King himself, to protect their land from the abomination of the child growing in her womb.

Lies.

Her heart shattered upon seeing Draven being dragged up the steps to the platform across from her. He stared at her through his hair.

The Venari King shoved to his knees.

But it was only when she saw the shears being handed to Bard that her heart truly screamed.

"No—no, wait! *DON'T*—"

Bard pulled Draven's hair to a knot on the top of his head, and he cut it crudely.

Aydra screamed. Her knees gave out beneath her as she watched his hair fall to the wood. Draven avoided her eyes, tears streaking his face.

The Venari King ripped of his crown for the second time in his life.

Bard came around and picked up a lock of it, and then he held it high in the air with a great, mocking bellow. The crowd cheered gleefully, their shouts of celebration making Aydra's ears ring.

These were the people that had once loved her.

It amazed her what fear would do to a people.

Perhaps the Infi had infiltrated her streets more than she'd previously thought.

When Bard was done mutilating Draven's hair, he spoke to the crowd, asking for a number of lashes to be given.

Aydra barely heard the words.

She hoped Balandria was not there to witness it.

The people decided on fifteen lashes for Draven. His agony filled the air with each slash and break of the skin on his back, his shirt ripping from his chest.

Bard spoke words that she didn't hear. She couldn't take her eyes off Draven's figure, his stomach lying on the wood as blood poured from his back. She heard the crowd cheer and saw Bard walk down front, his arm wrapping around a child's shoulders as he handed the boy a small rock.

It was the first stone to strike her.

Aydra closed her eyes, trying to shut out the pain of the small rocks that struck her flesh from then on. The sun's warmth shrouded her face. The crows sat on the buildings all around her. Her cheeks stiffened with dried tears.

This was the sun she would die beneath upon its setting.

The stones were nothing to the flames she knew would lick her flesh later.

Aydra didn't remember being moved off the pole. She wasn't in the dungeon. She was alone in the Throne Room, the drip of the water falling over the edge the only noise in her ears.

Tied to Arbina's tree.

Her arms were above her. A rope was strapped around her middle.

And Arbina was sitting on the steps.

A cold wind wrapped through the open columns of the room. A wind warning of the winter that would rise with the Dead Moons that night.

Aydra looked out at the ocean, memorizing her final sunset. Orange streaks littered the sea, blues and purples cascading over the wave-like clouds above them. The teal serenity of the ocean was stark against the pinks. She sighed and leaned her head back against the tree.

Arbina's fingertips touched the water as she gazed down at her own reflection. "You could easily get out of this," Arbina said.

Aydra barely had the strength to speak. "Go away, mother," she managed.

Arbina's head tilted as she laid her hands across her knees. "You would die for him? Even though his death is inevitable?"

"I will die for every Queen to have ever sat subdued on that throne. I die so that my sister does not suffer the fate I was forced to live with. I die to show the true cowardice of this Age." The pain of her body tore through her, but she pushed it out of her mind.

"Tell me, mother," she forced herself to say. "How long have you been whispering thoughts in my brother's ears?"

Arbina stood, her arms wrapping around her as her defiant gaze met Aydra's. "Since you decided to become the kingdom's executioner."

Aydra's heart shattered, and she felt her body begin to tremble. "I should have let them freeze you," she hissed.

A small smile rose on Arbina's lips. "My daughter… you should know freezing would not take to my poisoned waters."

What Draven had told her the night before filled her with strength and made her smile. A quiet chuckle emitted from her lips, and Arbina's weight shifted.

"What?" Arbina asked.

Aydra smiled. "I wish I was going to be here to watch you burn."

Arbina's eyes blazed, but as she opened her mouth to speak, the doors at the back of the room opened, and a throng of Belwarks entered.

Draven was unconsciously dragged between the last two guards' arms.

He was thrown on the ground in front of Rhaif's chair, and his chains were wrapped around the stone legs of it. The guards left him and filed back out the same door. She watched as they came to stand in the gallery above the open room.

Aydra's chest constricted with seeing him again, his hair cut short to his head, the lashings on his back. She struggled against the rope bindings despite herself.

"Draven," Aydra managed. "Draven, can you hear me?"

He stirred just slightly, head moving around on the stone as though he were drunk. His palms pressed to the cold floor. She heard him grunting as he pushed himself up to his knees.

And then she saw the realization of where he was grace his features.

"Aydra—" He yanked on the chains, desperation in his widened eyes. "Aydra, no—"

Tears streaked her face as the doors at the back of the room opened once more.

The Council filed in, followed by her brother.

And then finally her youngers.

With Lex bringing up the end.

Aydra struggled against her bindings at the sight of Nyssa's sobbing face and Lex attempting to hold herself together. "No— *No*, Lex! Get them out of here! Take care of them!" she shouted. "Don't—"

"They will watch their traitorous sister burn with the rest of us," said one of the Council members. "Watch what happens when you betray the crown."

"Enough," Rhaif said, coming around to the front. He paused in front of Draven. "Venari King on his knees, void of the shroud of hair he so-called his crown." Rhaif pushed his hands behind his back, chest puffing out proudly. "I always knew this day would come."

"Coward," Draven spat.

The back of Rhaif's hand seared across Draven's face.

"You will watch her burn, Venari. This is all because of you. This is your fault," Rhaif hissed.

Draven spat the blood from his mouth onto the ground. "Long live my Queen," he breathed.

The veins in Rhaif's neck popped to the surface with the clench of his jaw. He pulled his sword from his belt and struck Draven across the cheek again, making him fall to the ground.

Rhaif handed his sword to Bard with a final huff, and he stepped to the edge of the pool.

"Last words, my sister," he asked of her.

She began to shake at the sight of him standing there. Injured yet proud. Saliva stuck like tree sap in her throat. Her exhausted body crippling with every heavy breath.

She begged her voice to be loud enough so they could all hear her.

"I hope you remember the days we played together," she started shakily, her chest beginning to heave. "I hope you remember all the times we laughed. The times we cried. When we loved each other... I hope those beautiful moments haunt you for the rest of the cursed days you walk this land. I hope the sounds of my *screams* fill your ears when you sleep and that every time you use your fire on another that all you see is my face in the flames. For every time you burned me. For every time you raped me. For every time you told me it was the last. For every promise that you didn't keep. And when the day comes that someone does, finally, end your life, I hope they do it with as little mercy as you showed your loving sister. Your sister who was put to death for simply falling in love with someone who wasn't *you*."

The words seethed from her lips, and she felt her body tremble violently, saliva dripping from her mouth. Rhaif's eye glistened, and she could see the flames of his form rising.

"Burn her," came his final words.

Aydra's entire body limped, and a void filled her.

The Council filed out one by one. The doors closed behind Rhaif. Aydra could see them lining up on the next level above the Throne Room as the Belwarks had done before. Lex wrapped her arms around both Dorian and Nyssa, and then she held up a tightened fist to the sky. Aydra saw the ring on Lex's finger, and Lex gave her a slow nod.

"Aydra—"

Her gaze averted down to Draven's struggling figure. His eyes pleaded with her as he sat up on his knees, struggling once more against the chains. She could see his chest heaving up and down, but he fought, and he looked directly at her as the words came from his lips.

"From once a wind—"

Her heart crumbled, and a lone tear streaked down her cheek.

"And brisk of leaves—"

Her eyes never left his as her shaky voice joined his. She barely got the words out.

There came a night.
So dark it seemed
No more light
The curse it brings
And so the dying moons said to the sun

"Set me free," they both managed to end.

Draven tugged on the chains once more. Desperation in his features but accepting of their ends.

This was it.

Her knees weakened, and as she stared at him, she memorized his beautiful face.

"I'll meet you at the Edge when it's done," he promised. "Nothing less."

The tear stretched the length of her cheek, her heart bleeding in her chest at his words.

"I love you," she whispered.

Draven's head shook just noticeably, and she watched his throat move as he swallowed his tears. "I love you."

Two guards appeared from the back of the room, flaming arrows in their hands. They pulled them back on their bows, and Aydra drew a jagged breath upon seeing the flames soar through the air towards her body.

The pain of the two arrows hit her. Flames licked at her flesh. She screamed, struggling at the anxiety of it engulfing her body. She felt her heartbeat slowly deteriorate in her chest from the one arrow that had hit her high.

Her head fell back against the tree trunk, and she screamed only a few moments longer at the angst of the fire before succumbing to the weight of the Edge.

76

Draven's shouts wailed through the darkening sky with Aydra's own shrieks. His eyes swelled with the tears he couldn't fight. Her screams bled his ears. As though someone had ripped his insides clean from his body and fed them to his own kind. As though the Berdijay was there playing tricks on him.

His only reprieve was that her screams didn't last long.

One of the men's arrows had pierced her high on the chest.

He wasn't sure who the guard was, but he was sure the guard would pay for the mercy he'd shown their Queen.

Draven sat back on his knees and watched in a trance-like state as his love turned to ash in the same pool she'd been born in.

And then he collapsed onto the floor.

His heart was numb, his body limp, when he was picked up off the ground of the Throne Room, and then taken to the tower dungeon once the flames had died.

He was thrown mercilessly into the cage, and the door was locked behind them. He could hear the Belwarks mocking him as they left the room. It was dark outside. He picked himself up to a seated position and curled his legs into his chest. His foot began to tap nervously as he sat in the corner of the cell, allowing Aydra's screams to fill him.

His love.

His Queen.

Dead because she'd carried his child.

Dead because of the fear the people held of his kind.

It was the first time he'd been away from the Forest for the start of the Dead Moons. He longed to hear the comforting cries of the Noctuans. But as the noise of someone's footsteps filled his ears, he knew he wouldn't have to wait long.

"You're late," Draven told Dorian upon his reaching the tower.

Dorian paused on the top step and pulled the horn from around his back along with a pail of water. "Would you like me to go back? I can wait and show up another night."

Draven exhaled an audible breath, watching Dorian cross the room to him. "Thank you," he said as Dorian placed the horn in his hand. "Get your sister and get out of here. Hide below the Belwark Temple and do not come out until sunrise. They will not know the difference between friend and foe."

Dorian nodded. "What will you do?"

Draven stared past him towards the open doorway that led to nothing below, and he clenched the horn in his fist. "Burn it to the ground."

77

The first song he played on his horn was of Samar's.

The water in the pail rippled, the wind encircling him. He watched as Samar's figure assembled itself, first with bone, then with muscle, and finally with flesh. When she took her first step out of the bucket, her eyes opened, and a look he was not accustomed to being greeted with by Samar filled her features.

Tears.

"She is gone, isn't she?" Samar whispered.

Draven's hand clenched around the horn. "Will you help me?" he asked softly.

Samar's velvet touch lingered on his hand, and she nodded. "Anything."

He asked her to turn the water to the waters that ran through the Forest of Darkness. He would need such waters to call on the Wyverdraki and Rhamocour. Samar poured the pail onto the floor, and she crouched down, her hands pressing into the wet stone as she muttered words Draven did not hear.

The water warmed beneath his feet. She stood and once more faced him. "Your hand," she said, holding out her own. He placed his hand in hers, and she drew a deep cut into his palm.

"You are ready," she told him.

Draven's weight shifted. He curled his bleeding hand around the horn, and then he brought it to his lips.

The sound of the Wyverdraki call pulsed through the horn, followed by the great song of the Rhamocour.

And then he waited.

493

Samar sat across from him in the cell as Draven leaned his back against the wall. He wasn't accustomed to her being so quiet, but he knew why. He knew she'd come to love Aydra during her time in the Forest.

All Draven could think about was the promise he'd made her.

It was two hours before he heard the cries of the Wyverdraki echo in the night air. His heart constricted as he was reminded of their song. The tears that stung his eyes, he pushed away.

Samar picked the lock on his door, and it creaked open.

"They await their orders, my King," she said with a bow.

Draven's hand tightened on the horn, and he remembered the bellow Duarb had taught him the night before. His lips pressed to the end of it, blood on his palm, and he closed his eyes as he blew through it.

Fire cut through the sky.

The tower shook, and he felt the Rhamocour wrap herself around it. Her great roar made a chill run down his spine. Purple flames erupted in the air above him. He could feel its heat on his skin, and he closed his eyes.

He blew through the horn again. Shrieks and screams filled his ears from the shops below. He stepped to the edge of the archway and looked out of it to watch the Wyverdraki family's fire burn through the streets.

The Rhamocour curled her head down to him. He closed his eyes and pressed his forehead against her nose, his hand reaching up and stroking her face.

"For her," he whispered.

The beast's apple green eyes blinked deliberately at him, and then she lowered her head. Draven lifted himself to her neck. He pressed the horn to his lips again, and they dove into the darkness.

Draven had never ridden on the back of the Rhamocour before. It was a new sensation, feeling the wind on his scalp and wrapping around his body as the dragon's wings cut into the air. He wondered if this was how Aydra felt when she would ride on the Aenean Orel.

The Rhamocour circled the kingdom. He watched people running in the streets, the same people he'd seen stone his love earlier in the day. A wave of anger pulsed through him that he could not control, and he sent the fire bellow through the horn.

Her body heated beneath him, and purple flames filled the streets.

He had the Rhamocour drop him into the Throne Room after a few more turns around the kingdom.

His feet hit the stone floor. Arbina's tree was blackened where Aydra had burned against it earlier. He brought the horn to his mouth —

"WHAT ARE YOU DOING?"

Arbina's scream echoed off the Throne Room pillars. Draven tightened his fist around the horn, and he glared back at her.

"You're the reason for all this," he seethed. "The reason your children have all betrayed one another. The reason the love of my life had to die on her own brother's orders... all because she loved me. All because you—you decided to take out your hatred for my giver on your own daughters." A tear slipped down his face, and he fought the shake of his body. *"How could you?"*

Arbina's arms wrapped around her chest, and she stared haughtily at him from the middle of her pool. "My daughters have never lived up to their full potentials. They—"

"Never lived up..." Draven scoffed, not believing what she was saying. "You are *jealous* of them. Of their strength. Of their freedom. So you had your sons torture them into thinking they were less than what they were." He turned towards her as the Rhamocour's cry filled the air, and a small smile spread on his lips. "I bet Aydra scared you senseless."

"Aydra should have learned her place."

"What—to sit on the throne as nothing more than a trophy? An accessory? She could have ruled over the entire Echelon."

"Then maybe you should have kept your hands off her."

"I loved her!" he cried out. His knees hit the rock floor at the edge of her pool, and his voice caught in his throat. "I loved her."

His words were barely a breath as the tears filled his eyes again. He could see Aydra's face reflected back to him in the water, her smiling eyes...

As his hand clenched around the horn again and he felt the emptiness of her death pour through him, Arbina's slow laugh consumed his ears, and his body began to shake.

"You poor, *poor*, dear..." she mocked, now coming closer to him.

The Rhamocour circled the room.

"Begging for her life... You look just like your giver before I had Haerland curse him."

His eyes shot up to meet hers. "What?"

Arbina's wicked smile filled her face. "He thought he could get

495

away with what he did to me. With betraying our love for the love of his pitiful night creatures… Imagine my glee when Haerland caught us during an argument and took my side."

Draven slowly stood, his heartbeat pulsing in his ears at what she'd just said. "Everything you've ever gifted your daughters with… the ability to hear creatures, the child she could bear with only a Venari… all because he didn't love you? For revenge? You gave two just so you could use your daughter as a *pawn*?"

She gave him a deliberate once over, chin rising high. "And I will continue to do so until he is nothing more than a shriveled skeleton in the forest."

Draven lunged.

—The phoenix shrouded around his body just as his skin grazed the poisoned waters. He was thrown back onto the stone floor, head hitting the steps.

"*YOU!*" he heard Arbina shout.

The phoenix landed at his feet and straightened, its black flames and smoke enveloping the floor. Draven looked through the haze of his stumble, seeing Arbina's face paled at the sight of the black phoenix in her room.

"Where did she come from? *How—how is she here?!*" Arbina shouted, eyes flickering to Draven but hardly leaving the phoenix. Draven had expected this reaction from Arbina. Of her seeing her mother Sun in her creature form.

The Rhamocour's talons clenched onto the gallery above the Throne Room. The stone crumbled beneath its weight.

Draven stood deliberately to his feet, his hand trembling as he moved beside the phoenix, and the great bird nudged his arm. Draven met her searing amber eyes, and she gave him a slow blink. He took her nudge as a sign of her approving his deed, and his stomach knotted. He gradually brought the horn to his lips once more. Arbina continued to shout and scream, but he ignored her as she nearly stumbled in her own waters.

"*Don't you dare!*"

He bellowed the fire command once more.

Purple and black fire poured onto Arbina's limbs.

Draven stood in the Throne Room and watched the purple and gold Noctuan flames engulf her. He watched Arbina flee and cripple herself into the poisoned waters she so prided her tree with.

He stood at the edge of the room and stared down the side of the sloping cliff, allowing the flames of the Wyverdraki to spread as they poured their fire onto the shops and homes below.

Magnice was burning.

But the noise of feet bolting up the steps startled him. He did not think anyone would venture out into the open of the castle.

So when he turned and found Rhaif standing at the top step, adrenaline surged through his body and made his heart constrict.

His fist clenched at his side. His chest began to heave.

Rhaif's hands turned black, and he lifted his shirt off his head as the lightning streaks of ash climbed up his body. Blue flames erupted on his muscles. Rhaif cracked his neck and crouched low.

"You will scream just as she did… *Hunter*," Rhaif snarled.

A gust of wind wrapped itself around Arbina's tree and blew the flames out.

And then the phoenix landed behind Draven.

He felt its beak nudge his neck, and a chortle emitted from its throat. Draven reached up and gave its great nose a soft pet.

Rhaif's flames flickered as his eye darted between the two. "Fight me like a man, you *coward!* Not with your creatures."

Draven almost laughed as he handed the horn to the phoenix. "Is that what you want?" he asked, slowly stepping towards Rhaif. "To finally have the chance to fight me as you have so wished to do for twenty years now? To finally prove yourself just as good as your sister?"

"Leave my sister out of this."

"If you wanted your sister left out of it, you shouldn't have burned her and my child."

"Your child…" Rhaif's nostrils flared, and he shook his head. "A creature that would have ruined our would."

"Since when have you ever cared about this world?" Draven growled. "You sit on your throne, ignoring the reality of the war on our shores, the troubles of your own people. You know nothing of what your brother and sister have done to secure the safety of your kingdom from—"

"Your kind?" Rhaif spat.

Draven's fist curled in on itself. "The Infi are not—"

"You are no better than them. You brought your curse onto my family, onto my sister. You are the reason she is dead!"

Draven lunged.

Wind whipped around him and blew Rhaif's flames to a minimum as Draven launched into him. He grabbed his legs in his arms, picking him up off the ground and then slamming him into the floor. Rhaif jerked upwards at the break of his back, crying out with a wail rivaling that of the dragons' around the castle. Draven launched himself on top of him, beating Rhaif's face with his bare fists.

He could feel the heat of Rhaif's flames trying to grow again, but the wind ensnared them both, and Rhaif struggled beneath Draven. Rhaif's knee kicked up into Draven's injured back. Draven yelped, his attention averting just enough that Rhaif could get a punch in.

Draven felt the agony sear through his bones. He grasped Rhaif's throat in his hands and picked him up, just to throw his head back into the stone. Once. Twice. Blood trickled on Draven's fingers. His entire body shook as he screamed in Rhaif's face.

And then he pressed his thumb into Rhaif's remaining eye.

The noise of Rhaif's shrieks bounced into the night sky. Blood pooled beneath Draven's finger. He moved his hands to Rhaif's throat and pressed into his trachea.

"Beg, Sun boy," Draven growled. "Beg as you wanted her to."

Rhaif cried out in agony, his flames attempting and failing to come to the surface as the wind whirled around their bodies. Draven could feel Rhaif's pulse beneath his strained fingers, feel as his life drained towards the Edge and his flames begged for air.

But he released Rhaif's neck the moment before he snapped it between his fingers. He watched Rhaif's facade break, his head lolling on the floor slowly, side to side, almost in slow motion. His eye trickled with blood.

"Kill me—take your revenge—" he heard Rhaif say. *"Do it!"*

Draven slowly backed off him as saliva emitted from Rhaif's mouth, as though he were in agony of the thoughts that had just flooded him. Rhaif's face was askew, and he struggled to roll himself up onto his elbow.

"KILL ME!" he begged through the sobs.

Draven stared at the faltering king on the ground, at the tears that couldn't evacuate Rhaif's now absent eyes, instead forcing the angst of his failure to converge itself into the pile of wailing saliva dribbling from his mouth and onto the floor.

"TAKE MY LIFE!"

Draven forced his breath to even, and for a moment, he considered obliging, taking the life that had condemned his love, the one who had blamed Aydra for his mother not loving him…

But the shame on her face the night she'd told him about it all entered his mind.

And his jaw trembled at the weeping man before him.

"That's not what she wanted," Draven forced himself to say.

The phoenix purred beside him, her head sniffing Rhaif's struggling body. She tilted her head to Draven. Draven took the horn from its beak, and the bird shook out a piercing cry that made his ears throb. Cold black flames swarmed the Throne Room.

Draven pressed the horn to his lips again.

The Rhamocour's roaring bellow filled the air.

And fire once more engulfed Arbina's tree.

78

Draven's heart no longer existed.

He ached for the Edge, for this day to be done, to see Aydra's face again.

His feet led him up the steps to the high tower.

Back to the place he knew would take him from this land.

He slowed as he reached the top step, the large archway on the opposite side of the room staring back at him. The window to the Edge.

He took his boots off his feet and allowed his toes to feel the cold stone beneath him. Wind wrapped through the tower, and he stepped to the archway.

Screams. Fire. His dragon kin.

Their wings flapped mercilessly in the air as they splayed the kingdom with their flames.

The tower shook, and the roar of the Rhamocour bellowed through the land as it wrapped itself around the building.

He wished he could tell her goodbye.

"Are you sure about this?" came the voice of Samar at his back.

Draven didn't turn. His fist tightened around the horn, and a great exhale left him.

"I am," he told her. His head tilted down slightly, and he glanced over his shoulder. "Send them home once I am gone."

He could see Samar's head bow slightly. "I will. And the horn?"

Draven stared at it in his hand. "I do not wish for any of my future brothers to have to bear the hurt of losing such an equal. I will take the horn to my death. Perhaps without it in the world, future Venari will not fall as easily as I did."

The wind whipped his body again, and he closed his eyes.

Aydra's smile radiated through his bones, and he felt a tear stretch down his face. His toes curled around the edge of the stone floor, and he pressed the horn to his chest.

"Nothing less," he whispered.

Wind met his falling body.

And the only noise of his death was the splash his body made in Arbina's pool.

The Rhamocour cried out only once more.

79

Magnice was laid to ruins.

The shops and homes of the bottom levels were nearly unrecognizable. Rubble crowded the streets. Some Dreamers and Belwarks had managed to get to safety below the Temple where Lex had forced Nyssa and Dorian to hide.

Two boats arrived in the dark of the morning two days later.

It was Lex and Aydra's old company that met the strangers on the beach and struck them down. Lex spared one for interrogation. Dorian was the first to meet them on the beach.

He slowed his horse upon seeing Lex pointing her sword to the throat of a stranger, men's bodies strewn across the sand.

"Find the King," he instructed Corbin.

Corbin lingered only for a moment and then set off towards the ruins of Magnice again. Dorian hopped down off his horse, his blue cape billowing in the wind from the beach as he strode across the sand to Lex.

"How many?" he asked Lex.

Lex's jaw was taut. "Two boats. Fifty," she replied.

Dorian looked around at the women and men Belwarks, obviously tired from the massacre. "Raid the boats. Then burn them. Make sure there is nothing of value before you set it ablaze," he instructed them.

The guards bowed and set off to do as he asked.

More hooves sounded around them, and Dorian looked up to see Nyssa as she arrived. Her eyes widened between the pair, and she dismounted her steed.

"What's happened? Is it the strangers?" she asked.

"Savages!" the man on his knees dared say.

The pommel of Lex's sword met his nose.

Nyssa balked and grasped Dorian's arm. "Have you asked it about where it came from?" she asked him.

"I haven't," he replied, eyes flickering up the beach where he could see a string of Belwarks coming towards them, a carriage in tow. "Waiting on him."

His glare met Lex's, and as the Belwarks lined up on their horses and the carriage came into view, Dorian had to avert his eyes.

Rhaif's blind and injured figure held on to his Second as he helped him to his feet.

Dorian wasn't sure how Rhaif was alive. But when asked about it, he was told Rhaif had managed to get himself into Arbina's pool and that her waters had at least been able to heal the burns on his body in the time he was able to stay under.

But what it had not healed was his now absent eyes and the limp of where the phoenix had broken him. Nor had it truly healed the appearance of his mangled skin.

Bard stood at Rhaif's limping side, and he straightened Rhaif's crown on his head as he wobbled to Dorian and Nyssa's right.

The stranger's cackle radiated through the still air.

"This... This is your king?" the man mocked.

Rhaif's hand tightened around the staff in his left hand. "Who is this person?"

"Strangers from across the seas," Lex said.

"How many?"

"Two ships. Fifty men," Dorian answered.

"And the others?"

"Dead," Lex said shortly. "Would you like to see their heads? They're still rolling in the surf, I think—Oh wait. You can't, can you?"

"Another remark like that, Second Sun, and I'll have you beheaded," Rhaif warned. He took another step towards the stranger, and Bard took a step sideways, releasing him.

"Who are you?" Rhaif asked the stranger.

The man spat on Rhaif's boots. "Why should I tell you?"

"You are a stranger in my kingdom," Rhaif answered. "If you'd not like to end up like your brethren, you'll bow before me and tell me who you are."

The man's chortle sounded from his lips again. "You are not my king," the man seethed. "My King is Sir Aeron of Mathis, Son of Aderon, High King of the Seven Seas, and ruler of Man. There are a thousand ships with their eyes on this land. It is only a matter of time before your shores are breeched. Your people will perish. We will toss your children from your walls. This kingdom will cripple beneath our weight. You will all be our slaves. You—"

Rhaif snapped his finger.

The cut of a sword sliced through the air.

The stranger's head fell onto the sand and rolled into the surf.

"Lies."

Dorian's eyes widened at the word his brother had just uttered.

Rhaif clenched the staff. "If any of you so much as utters a single word of what was spoken here, I'll make sure you never speak again," he growled. "Tell no one. This stays here."

Nyssa squeezed Dorian's arm as he exchanged a long look with Lex. Lex gave a short nod, and Dorian met his sister's eyes.

This was it.

The moment Aydra and Draven had warned them of.

They would leave.

Tonight.

Appendix

Aydra Ravenspeak's Mark

Mark of the Venari King

Noctuans

A group of cursed creatures, only allowed free roam of Haerland at night during the Dead Moons. The Dead Moons last for fourteen days, and happen every seventy-two days. These are the creatures forced to live beneath such tyranny.

Aberd

- The Aberd is a great marsupial creature. It swings through the canopy of the trees without sound, using its longer-than-body tail for balance and also to help them move at great speed. They have hands similar to ours; long, lanky arms, black fur, yellow slitted pupils, and razor-sharp teeth. Their cackling whoops surround you in an ambush from above, where they will slit your throat from behind before devouring you.

Aviteth

- The Aviteth is the Noctuan brother of the Aenean Orel. A great bird, six feet tall, wingspan twice that size. Its feathers shimmer black as a shadow. There are only three left in this Age, having been killed for sport in the last. Their cry follows the Ulfram's howl. It is so high-pitched and splintering that it causes the eardrum to bleed, therefore giving away your location. There is no way to hide from them. The smell of blood guides them to their prey. It drives their entire being. You are still alive when they begin to shred the flesh from your bones.

Berdijay

      - A shadow giant made of swamp and ash and your worst fears. Twenty feet tall. Eyes red as blood. A giant of rotting melted flesh, burned and braided like hair on his body. He smells of your worst fears and will consume you inside your mind. He speaks in riddles, confusing you and brining the nightmares you didn't know existed to the front of your mind, forcing you to step inside it.

Bullhorn

      - The Bullhorn is the Noctuans' most familiar. He is the only one of his kind. A great beast no less than eight feet tall. He carries a double-headed axe in his elongated sausage fingers, equipped with long pointed nails like daggers. The Bullhorn has the head of the Ulfram, the lengthy tree-limb like grey horns of a bull, and the torso of a man. Its lower body is more like the haunches of the bull, but he stands on his wheel-sized hooves upright. The black thick fur that covers its entire body is thick around its hips, and splayed out as a mane around his head and down his back in a V.

Bygon

      - The Bygon is known by her more familiar names: the shape-shifting siren, the nightingale, and the Dead Moons' composer. Her songs carry through the trees on the wind, causing weak-minded people to fall prey to her lullaby. She carries them into a deep slumber and then devours their blood in spurts, keeping her prey alive as she consumes them. Her form shifts from mist in the air, forming as bone and blood, followed by muscle and then flesh, until she is fully corporeal before you as her true self: skin pale and luminescent as the moon, board-straight black hair, usually appearing wet and silk-like. Her eyes long, lips thin, jaw petite. The chartreuse green of her irises reminds you of moss. But this is not the form she will take you in under her spell. She will shift into a being more desirable to you, and engulf your blood under the cover of that guise.

Noirdiem

      - The Noirdiem are deer-like creatures. Their bodies are

barely corporeal, instead of flesh and muscles on their bones, they are merely iridescent skeletons with horns growing out of the heads of the males. Their bodies glow elegantly against the dark of the forest around them. Different from the other Noctuans, these creatures are at peace with the darkness. They are said to be a sign of welcome from Duarb if they appear to you.

Rhamocour

- The Rhamocour is a great dragon-like beast. U-shaped scales darker than black cover its body, only giving way to the light when fire looms against the iridescence of its scales. A row of ascending thin boney spikes rises gradually out of the back of her neck as she extends her long neck upward. Her great wings span the same length as her body down her long tail. Menacing talons grip the earth, and the horns on her head cut into the sky. She will stare at you with her apple-green eyes as she debates whether you are worth the energy of her kill, or if you are only worth consuming in her purple fire.

Ulfram

- The Ulfram's wolf howl is the first noise after the wind that you'll hear when the Dead Moons rise. The alpha female's song penetrates the darkness, sending chills down your spine. When you meet her, you'll not see the rest of the pack. Five feet tall at the tops of her pointed ears. Black lines, like shadows, lined beneath her eyes and down either side of her nose. She has sharp yellow-green eyes that cut through the shadows. The sheen of her dark silver fur will vibrate in any light you shine at her. The rest of the Ulfram pack is oppositely colored with black fur and silver lines down the sides of their noses.

Wyverdraki

- The Wyverdraki are the smaller cousins of the Rhamocour. These dragon beasts vary in color from brown to emerald to orange and red, some featuring stripes or brindle on their scales. They travel in a pack, hunting down livestock and sharing with each other as a family. Their fire is orange, and they fly over the Forest of Darkness during the Dead Moons cycle, singing their song.

Pronunciations

Names:
  Aydra (Eye-dra)
  Draven (Dray-vin)
  Nyssari (Nis-ar-ee)
  Dorian (Dor-e-an)
  Rhaif (Ray-f)
  Balandria (Bal-an-dre-ah)
  Nadir (Na-deer)

Lesser Ones:
  Arbina (Are-bee-na)
  Duarb (Do-are-b)
  Lovi Piathos (Lo-vee Pee-aye-thos)
  Mons Magnus (Mons Mag-n-us)
  Somniarb Crelib (Some-knee-arb Kree-lib)

Lesser Beings:
  Venari (Vin-are-i)
  Infinari (In-fin-are-i)

Places:
  Haerland (Heir-land)
  Magnice (Mag-nis)
  Dahrkenhill (Dark-en-hill)

Scindo Creek (Shin-doe Creek)
Preymoor (Prey-more)
Bedrani (Bed-ron-ee)
Hills of Bitratus (Hills of Bit-ray-tus)

Creatures:
Noctuans (Noc-too-ans)
Ulfram (Ool-fr-am)
Wyverdraki (Why-ver-dra-cki)
Rhamocour (Ram-o-coor)
Berdijay (Bear-di-jay)
Aenean Orel (A-knee-an O-rel)
Aviteth (Av-i-teth)
Noirdiem (Noir-dee-am)
Bygon (Bye-gone)

Bonus Scene

Thank you for purchasing this exclusive edition of
Dead Moons Rising.

The BONUS scene in this special edition is one filled with *spice*.

You may remember the 'fade to black' scene with Aydra and
Draven in the Forest, when she says,
"Put on the skull, my King."

This is that scene.

Please be aware, this scene is, once more, not intended for persons
under eighteen years of age. This scene is between two consenting
adults and is in no way meant to be a guide to exploring sexual
fantasies or BDSM.
This is simply a smutty escape.

Bonus Scene

The anticipation of their planned night had Aydra unable to do anything more than fantasize about seeing Draven in that damned phoenix skull again. How it fit over his head as though it had been sculpted for him and him alone. The beak point that nearly scratched his chest when he looked down. The black horns that grew out of the top.

Aydra could hardly pick at her food. Flashes of him holding her wearing that thing. Perhaps holding her over the railing in the air or roped to the bed. His hand over her throat or yanking in her hair.

She was almost positive he could have told her to crawl and she'd have done it while he was wearing it.

Laughter around the table launched her out of her fantasy. The cups rattled with someone's feet that had just kicked onto the top. Aydra cleared her throat and laughed out of habit, at least trying to act like she hadn't just been staring at the table and imagining her King's hands over her throat and between her legs…

Draven's darkened gaze caught hers across the table. A slight playfulness danced in his eyes as the right corner of his lips pulled up. He was leaned back in his chair in his usual way—leg thrown over the side, leaning into the corner, tapping his cup on the table. But there was something different about his dangerous aura that night. Different about his usual strong silence as he listened to his family tell jokes and stories.

He was plotting.

Chewing on a broken piece of sugarcane. Eyes wandering so deliberately over her that she had to shift in her seat. It was taking everything in her to keep her composure and stay present.

And Draven knew it.

The smile spread wider over his lips when he locked eyes with her again. Teasing in nature. He adjusted himself in the seat and sat up as one of his friends began talking to him.

She needed a bath.

She was going to come at that table if she sat there another moment.

His eyes followed her as she pushed to her feet, that stupid smirk searing in her mind. She could hardly get up the stairs with how tightly her thighs were clenching together.

As the water filled the tub, she stripped. She didn't even bother to try and heat it.

It wasn't to the rim yet when she climbed inside and sank herself into a comfortable position. Relaxing her head on the lip, eyes closing, knees bending.

The image of Draven standing on that hill with the skull on filled her vision, and she groaned as she pushed her fingers between her legs. Imagining him hovering over her in it, his firm cock in her mouth and choking her. She pressed a finger inside herself and moved against her hand, pretending it was his fingers.

"Dirty girl," came Draven's voice from the door.

Her heart skipped at the sound of his voice.

Her fantasy disappeared as she opened her eyes and rolled her head to the left, but she left her hand between her bent legs. He was leaned against the doorway, hair pushed over to one side and wrapping a long belt around his hand. Pipe hanging out the side of his mouth.

And the skull hanging on his hip.

Her chest caved at the sight of it. Shadows danced over his face with the firelight flickering. She could hear loud noises down below, as though Draven had told them to celebrate louder that night and bring in the drum circle.

"Here, I thought I would have to warm you up with this…"

His lashes lifted, and they locked eyes as she leaned her head around the fabric screen. Smoke filled the air with his exhale. A sweeter smoke than the one they'd been using since she'd been there. A smoke that intoxicated her and made her want more.

His boots echoed on the wood floor as he started towards her. Stalking in nature. He walked around the screen and paused a moment to take her in. She eyed the belt wrapped around his arm, biting her lip out of habit.

His long legs moved straddle over the end of the tub, and he sat down on the lip, leaned over towards her. He extended her the pipe, which she gladly took, as he reached into the water and pulled her foot onto his knee. His fingers dug into her arch as he massaged her.

"Keep touching yourself, my Queen," he rasped.

He was toying with her.

Being gentle and firm all at once. That skull taunted her. He knew exactly what he was doing, and it made her impatient. She inhaled a deep breath

breath on the pipe and kept his gaze as she reached between her legs once more.

"I wonder…" his voice trailed. He pressed hard at the very center below the ball of her foot, and her body reacted in a way she couldn't comprehend.

Aydra paused. "Venari, what are you doing to me?" she asked.

"So *eager*," he drawled. He walked his thumb from the base of her foot up to her toes, one at a time with increasing pressure. Aydra nearly moaned at the sensation of it. How that and the smoke was relaxing her every nerve.

It wasn't just the water making her wet. She dipped a finger inside herself, feeling the slickness of how ready she was, different from the water in the tub, and she circled that around her clit as she watched him.

"Do you remember the one thing you said you'd never do?" he asked as he slowed in the pressure and began feather-like movements against her skin.

She swallowed at the dare in his gaze, and she remembered the night in the castle. "Beg," she breathed, and the thought made her heart rattle.

The right corner of his lips quirked. He set her foot into the water again and reached for the other one. "I cannot wait to hear those words come from your beautiful lips."

Her mouth sagged with the dig of his finger into the other foot, and she pressed harder on her clit, moving her fingers side to side. She stared at the skull as she continued her movements, and he continued to make her limp with the pressure of his fingers.

A groan escaped her that she didn't know was coming, and she leaned her head against the lip of the tub again. Thighs tightening, toes pointing. She began to squirm with the rise of her orgasm.

"*Draven*," she moaned, utterly relaxed in that water. "I'm going to…" her breath hitched, and Draven dug his finger into that spot at the ball of her foot so harshly, she nearly came apart. But she looked up, chest heaving, and a darkness had replaced the tease.

"Not yet," he told her. "I need to hear you beg for that end." The pressure eased on her foot, and he began the slow touches once more. "Slowly, my Queen."

She did as he asked.

She was practically aching to release. She closed her eyes out of habit and relaxed her neck again. Sitting there on that edge. Jaw quivering as she slowly circled herself. Her end was right there.

Begging to let go.

"Draven..." her eyes opened when she picked her head back up, and she forgot how to breathe.

He'd put on the skull mask while she was turned away. A whimper left her, and she swore she saw him smile under that mask.

—He grabbed her legs.

She was pulled straddle onto him so swiftly, she nearly started to fight back out of instinct. Her breath caught. Her hands pushed against his chest, but he grabbed her wrists. And for a moment, they didn't move.

Water dripped from her naked body onto his. Her heart pounded. She wanted to kiss him. To feel his tongue against her own and taste the blood on his lip that she so wanted to bite. He leaned forward, and her eyes fluttered as the skull dragged over her cheek.

"Draven..." she managed.

He nuzzled the cold bone into the crook of her neck in response and pushed her hands around his neck. His fingers trailed over her bare thighs. Slowly. Inch by inch. She arched into his wet shirt and pulled his head closer as those digits wrapped around her ass.

Her hands found the horns atop the skull. Rubbing them as she would have his cock. Relishing the stiff bone beneath her fingertips and palms. His fingers trailed between her ass cheeks, the other hand gripping her flesh and digging his nails into her skin. She groaned at the sensation of his grip, loving the way he touched her. The ache turned to pleasure when he brushed his fingers over her entrance, and she inhaled a sharpened breath.

"Such a dirty girl," he whispered. "Did the thought of this skull and my cock make you this wet at the dinner table?" he asked.

"Yes," she moaned, arching into him. Two fingers delved inside her. Deep enough, her thighs clenched around his waist.

"Do you know what I was thinking about while I watched you sitting there? Denying the need to pleasure yourself as you fantasized about this night?" he asked as he took his fingers out and pushed his thumb inside her.

"No," she grunted, hips moving against his hand.

His thumb slipped, and he pushed the first two fingers inside again. Her cheeks clenched out of instinct as his thumb teased her other entrance. She groaned again when he drove that thumb into her ass, relaxing and sinking into his three-fingered tease.

"I was thinking how sexy you're going to look with your hands tied behind your back from your neck while you choke on my cock."

It was then she realized the belt he'd been wrapping around his arm was no normal belt.

Draven leaned back. His free hand cupped her neck, making her breath slow. Those two digits slipped from inside her. He dragged his touch over her spread ass and spanked her hard enough to make her jump and moan at the same time.

He let go of her neck and moved the skull back off his face. The beak tip hovered over her head and scratched her scalp in the best way, like a single claw dragging over the top of her head. A chill shivered down her spine, and she nearly limped in his arms.

"Kiss me," she begged, needing to feel his mouth on hers.

"Are you ready for the game, my Queen?" he asked, nose brushing her cheek. "Because once I kiss you, all this teasing is over, and you're *mine*."

He grasped her ass and her throat when he said it, and Aydra's chest fell. Her eyes opened, and she met his under the mask. "Fucking kiss me, Draven," she practically pleaded.

He jerked her neck, a smirk rising on his lips. "You sound so good when you beg," he whispered.

His lips slammed into hers, and adrenaline surged her veins. Their usual kisses were passionate. Hungry. But this kiss. This was biting and need. Fighting with desperation. His hands squeezed on her throat and ass, making her squirm and moan into his mouth all at once. She was tired of feeling that shirt on him. She gripped her hands to the fabric of the vee of his tunic and pulled. The stitching resisted. She whimpered against his mouth. Draven's hands moved to hers, and together they ripped.

The noise of his shirt shredding almost caused a smile to rise on her lips. Finally, her breasts arched into his bare chest as she shrugged the shirt to the ground. Arms wrapping fulling around him, she squeezed when she felt him shift.

His hands were back around her ass, and he was standing from the tub. He moved the skull back over his face.

She leaned in and began to kiss his throat, wanting to taste him and make him spiral like she knew her biting his throat would do. She thought he would stop at the bed. Throw her on it and tell her to hold her hands together. But cold air swept over her as they moved onto the deck, and she realized he was carrying her upstairs.

"Not this bed?" she asked.

He shoved her back against the wall. Hands pinned over her head. Her head slammed into the wood.

In full view of his people down below.

Someone whistled.

"Would you rather I fuck you right here so my people can watch instead of using their imaginations to go with your screams?" he growled, the skull brushing her cheek. "Or perhaps you'd like me to bind your wrists and throat now. Let you give them a show on these steps. I doubt they've ever seen a Sun Queen on her knees."

Tempting.

She nearly said yes.

"They can watch as you fuck me over the railing upstairs," she said in his ear.

The moment the words left her lips, he pulled them off the wall and threw her over his shoulder. Her bare ass was exposed high in the air to the entire Venari race as he paraded her up the rest of the stairs like his favorite trophy. A few people cat-called from down below, and Aydra flipped them off.

He threw her onto the bed.

She quickly pushed her hair off her face. Him. Standing over her naked body. Chest still glistening with the remaining water from the bath. She swallowed at the sight of the moons' light reflecting off the ivory bone skull.

His head tilted sideways, and her clit began to ache.

Draven pulled his knife from his pocket. She held her breath as he leaned down onto the mattress over her, hands pressing into the bed on either side. She leaned back as he hovered, and then she felt the blanket move from beneath her.

Rip from beneath her.

He'd sheared a piece of fabric from it, and he let it brush over her cheek when he straightened again.

"Turn around," he told her. "On your knees."

The last thing she wanted to do was take her eyes off him in that skull, but she obeyed the quiet order nonetheless.

The fabric brushed against her throat, making her shudder. For a moment, her back arched and she grasped her own breasts. She denied herself from touching her throbbing clit and instead rubbed her thighs together as she sat on her knees. Allowing herself that friction only.

She realized then that he was tying her hair up.

He gathered her thick hair in one hand and pulled it to the top of her head before moving the fabric around it. And not just a ponytail. He wrapped her hair into a bun much like the one he usually wore.

"This is much easier to tie with two hands," he muttered, breaking his Venari facade.

She resisted the urge to laugh.

He heard her snort, and his hand gripped the back of her neck, making her nearly giddy. She wondered if he was smiling under that skull despite his dominance over her.

His hand moved around her throat, and he tipped her chin back, thumb brushing her lip. She couldn't help herself from running the tip of her tongue along the pad.

She didn't see him take the restraint off his arm, not realizing what was happening until she felt the leather against her throat.

Oh.

Chills ran over her flesh. She sank into the sensation of it as he pulled it taut around her. A cold ring touched her skin at the nape of her neck, and she felt another piece of leather drape down her spine.

"Hands behind your back," he said in her ear.

She adjusted herself and did as she was told. The leather was soft against her skin. Much smoother than she was used to leather belts being. As though it were made for pleasure and pleasure alone. The buckles hooked, and when she moved her hands, it tugged on her neck.

The fantasies she'd thought about exploring with him were coming to life, and it made her chest swell.

"Stand up," he whispered in her ear.

He tugged on the strap against her back as she stood and backed into him. Flush against his chest, she couldn't resist moving her restrained hands over his hardened cock through the fabric.

He didn't stop her. Instead, his hand moved around her, and she watched as he showed off the dagger in his palm. A short, jagged blade that looked like it would tear flesh apart, not just slice through it. There was ivory embedded within the blade, almost like the bone had merged with the iron. The handle had a slight bend in it. Black, smooth leather-wrapped around the hilt with a silver circular pommel.

"Do you like this?" he asked her.

She swallowed, wondering if he was planning on using that blade on her skin or something else. "Yes," she breathed.

"That's good," he said. The ivory skull pressed to her cheek as he sank his head against hers. She closed her eyes and sighed into it, her heart skipping.

"Because you're going to fuck it while you choke on my cock."

Aydra's knees buckled.

Draven caught her and whirled her around. "Stay still."

He moved two steps back from her, tossing the knife up and down in his hand, and then he threw it into the wood floor. Aydra squeezed her thighs as she felt herself drip. He bent down, pushing it further into the floor, securing it, and when he was satisfied, he straightened up to cross the space to her again. He was straining through his pants, and she wanted him in her any way she could have him.

"Draven…" she pleaded, arching her back as he stilled before her. "Please."

His hand cupped against her cheek softly.

"I love hearing you say that." His thumb dragged over her lip again as he tugged her forward. "Kneel, my Queen," he instructed.

She realized what he meant by her fucking that dagger then.

She sank to her knees one by one. Spreading her legs wide. The end of the dagger tickled her entrance, cold and hard. Her breath stilled, and Draven began to remove his pants.

Her thighs tightened as she hovered over that blade. She couldn't stop herself from moving her dripping clit slowly along the pommel. The chilled iron made her chest heave, her eyes flutter. She wanted her release. Right there on the precipice. Threatening to topple over and rock her to her core. And as he removed his pants, she began to salivate.

Completely bare Draven—all except for that fucking skull— stood over her. Cock hard as he stroked it deliberately in his hand. She started to lean forward, wanting to lick the moisture off his tip, but he caught her by the neck, and he knelt in front of her.

"Spit," he said as he held out his hand.

She gathered the saliva in her mouth and didn't lose her gaze with him as she did what he told her to. He reached between her bent legs and moved that saliva over the dagger's pommel, thumb grazing over her clit. She flinched when he put pressure on her, and she swore she heard him chuckle when she groaned.

"Sink onto that knife, my Queen," he whispered. "But don't move until you've my cock in your mouth."

She did.

She had to adjust her knees as she sank onto it. The bend of the handle moved inside her until it hit that point in her that made her weak. She was careful not to push all the way, having to use her straining thighs to hold herself from being cut.

He straightened over her and pulsed those fingers around his cock again. "There's my Queen."

Aydra kept his stare as she leaned forward, and she finally tasted him. The saltiness made her moan, and she resisted the urge to go for another lick.

He slowed his movements, pinching his cock, and he whispered, "Are you ready for me?"

"Yes," she breathed.

The back of his knuckles tickled her cheek. "Open your mouth."

Her lips parted, and she groaned when he finally let her take him.

With every stroke he moved in her mouth, she moved on that knife. Rocking her hips over it and relishing the ridges of the leather inside her. Her arms bound behind her left her solely at his mercy. He thrust slowly into her at first, allowing her to tongue the underside of his cock and suck hard when he drew back. He cursed as both his hands curled behind her neck.

"Arch your back," he whispered. "Just like that. Let me see your ass move on my dagger."

It was a show, and she was already reaching again.

He guided her head, pushing her further and further on his length until she gagged, and he held her in place. Drool dripped down her mouth. She was about to explode from the pleasure of that dagger hitting her spot. Her arms strained as she whimpered, the noise vibrating in her throat. Her hips began to grind quicker, her release on edge.

"Are you coming on that knife?" he asked her.

She pulled back, sucking on his tip, and she muttered, "Mmhmm," around his length. Draven cursed the sky again and thrust deeper into her mouth. Aydra's entire body began to shake. Her thighs were on the verge of giving out. But she didn't stop. She was there. *There*. That curve hit her just right. She closed her eyes as he continued to thrust in her mouth. Her heart was about to explode.

"Come on my dagger, my Queen," he told her. "Shatter over my dagger like you're going to shatter on my cock."

His words sent her over the edge.

She fell apart over that knife.

Spilled and quivered around it. Cried out and shook. Draven thrust hard down her throat, to the point she began to choke.

"Such a dirty girl," he whispered as he wiped away the drool on her chin. He moved from inside her mouth, and Aydra straightened slowly, the knife slipping out of her and nearly causing her to collapse. But Draven caught her.

He picked her up like she was nothing, and suddenly her legs were wrapped around his waist. She gripped her thighs tight to him, and he lifted the skull back off his face.

He was sweating, face red, and a wicked delight in his eyes. Just seeing his face made her chest flutter. He leaned forward, kissed her hard, and her muscles seemed to come alive again.

"Did you like that?" he whispered.

"Yes," she breathed.

"Do you want more?" he asked as he tugged on her bottom lip with his teeth.

"*Fuck yes.*"

Draven looked like he might grin, but he pushed the skull back down and smacked her ass hard. She trusted him completely as he drifted them to the edge of the roof to the railing. He sat her ass on it, and before she could say anything, he flipped her around.

Her lower stomach laid across the wood. She could see the entire forest below, including all his people. Her feet didn't hit the floor, but the tips of her toes brushed the lumber. She started to kick, but he grasped the leather strap along her spine and tugged. Her neck jerked back.

"I've got you," he promised, fingers trailing along her ass. "Stand on my foot and bend your other leg up on the railing. That's it."

She'd never been more exposed in her life. But there was a thrill to it that she craved.

His length brushed her entrance, and Aydra groaned at the tease.

When he filled her, they both cursed. He gripped that leather strap and tugged, making it tighten around her throat.

And then the Venari King fucked her like the stories.

Thrusting hard against her hips to the point she couldn't feel her ass. Gripping on the leather and making her breath shorten. She cried out in strangled breaths, cursing and screaming his name. Vision blurring and stars behind her eyes. Every hit of his cock inside her made her muscles weak. Already so sensitive from her first release, she was ready to fall apart after mere seconds of his torture. She tried to hold herself. To clench every muscle in her body. This pleasure was too good to stop. Every gasp of her breath made her head spin.

It was almost painful holding onto that release. Tears pricked the corners of her eyes.

"Draven…" she pleaded. "Fuck, Draven— I can't—"

"Come for me, Aydra," he consoled her.

The orgasm ricocheted through her. She lost her balance, and for a moment, the world spun. Bright lights prickled her darkened vision. The next thing she knew, her feet were back on the ground. She sank against Draven's chest as she heard him unhooking something. The leather around her neck loosened, and he moved that ring.

He clasped the restraints on her front, the leather strap between her breasts, and her arms were restrained before her. Once she was back in her leathers, he picked her up by her waist and sat her on the railing.

"Are you ready to fly?" he asked.

Aydra's heart dropped. "What—*Draven!*"

He'd shoved her torso back and grasped onto her thighs at the same time. His cock slammed into her as gravity tried to pull her down. But she was safe in his hands, and Aydra allowed herself to limp in that darkness. To let her back bend into the weightlessness, only her thighs clenching around his waist as he laid into her.

A rush of cold sweat brushed over her forehead. She was lightheaded from the entire ordeal. But this… she loved this. One slip and she would have somersaulted into a free fall, cracked her neck on the ground, and never seen sunlight again.

But she knew Draven had her. Knew he wouldn't let her go any more than she would have let him go on the Orel that day. She swore she heard him laugh, and when she finally looked back up, reality swooped back over her.

Draven grabbed the leather strap and pulled her back up. Still inside her, he moved them from the railing and carried her to the bed, where he laid her down. She trembled beneath him as he reached for the top of his headboard. Her hips picked up, and he started moving inside her once more. Every stroke was deeper than the last. Using that headboard as leverage to bury himself in her. Her head threw back as she groaned loudly, high-pitched gasps with his every stroke. He was hitting that spot again, his pelvis rocking against her clit.

The headboard snapped in half.

He threw it over his shoulder as though it hadn't been some great wooden piece and was merely her panties. He straightened over her and grabbed her thighs, picking her up slightly until her ass hit his own thighs, and he slammed into her again.

Oh, *there*.

Eyes rolling, her back arched. She needed to grab something. She needed to extend those muscles as her third orgasm started to rush to the surface. She thought she might just keep convulsing with this one. Unsure if she would be able to ever stop spilling over him.

She wanted to grip those sheets.

Her body began to squirm as she begged for anything to hold onto besides her own fingers. She thought she might break them. She was trembling, nearly crying, with the need.

And then his thumb pressed to her clit.

She wanted to murder him.

"Fuck—Draven, *please*," she begged, moving her hips against him. "Please." She nearly screamed as he fucked her quicker. Bruising her backside and leaving hand prints on her thighs.

She couldn't breathe. Whimpering and nearly drooling. Dammit, she needed this release. His finger moved fast over her clit. Her legs kicked, toes pointed and straining. Her back arched up off the bed. She cried out his name again, and he asked if she was ready to come.

"Yes," she pleaded. "Yes. Come with me, Draven. Come with me."

Her words were hardly coherent. But Draven cursed, and as she felt herself reach her own edge, Draven groaned louder than she'd ever heard him. It sent her spiraling. She convulsed and released her orgasm over him just as he released inside her.

And it kept coming.

She continued to flinch and jerk even after he moved from inside her. He pushed the skull off and laid it on the pillow by her head. She finally managed to open her eyes and see him, and the sight of it mad her heart flee.

Sweat dripped down his nose and landed on her stomach. He was spent, but he didn't stop to recover. Chest rising and falling with the deep breaths he was taking, he reached to her hands. She couldn't move as he took the restraints off. He even had to lift her head to take the one from her neck. And when they were off, he paused over her.

She eyed the triumphant smirk on his lips.

"What?" she asked.

He reached for one of her hands and kissed her knuckles. "I do love hearing you beg."

Aydra grabbed the other pillow and smacked him with it. Her body ached with the movement, and she regretted the action instantly.

"You really shouldn't move," he bantered after dodging the throw. "You might come again."

And she knew he was mocking her. But all she could manage this time was to flip him off.

Without another word, he tugged her up into a sitting position and kissed her gently, smiling against his lips. She sighed into it, hands pressing against his cheeks.

It continued to baffle her that this was the same man she'd hated and distrusted for so long.

When she pulled back, she searched his beautiful face for a moment before feeling his hands move under her.

He swooped her up into his arms and stood off the bed, and she nuzzled into him.

"Where are you taking me?" she managed.

His lips brushed her forehead. "Fur blankets, a bath, and food."

"Such a *romantic*, Venari," she teased as she closed her eyes.

His deep chuckle vibrated against her, and as she looked up, his nose nudged hers. "Only for you."

Acknowledgements

It was ten years ago that I started this journey into Haerland.

Ten years ago that I started writing and drawing out maps, writing letters to myself from my characters to imprint the backstory into my mind. This was not the initial story I wrote. This was supposed to be a background story, one I knew the outline of and its impacts on Haerland's future, but never one that I ever intended on publishing. I wasn't sure how their story would be taken in its true form as it was always a darker story than the initial story I wrote exploring this world.

But here we are.

Draven and Aydra have always been the backbone story of this world. Their story was always 'where it all started'. To finally get the chance to delve into this space and get to know them has been a journey I never expected. I never expected... *them*. These two characters that would change my life. I never expected how much both of them, and especially Aydra, would influence me as a person. Jumping head first into this self-publishing world was not something I ever anticipated myself doing. And yet, here I am. Running with her into the fire. Burning kingdoms like we always said we would.

I have to thank (as crazy as this sounds) booktok for helping me realize we were now in a time when stories like this would be accepted and sought after. That stories with women like Aydra would be fully embraced. That dark fantasy and grey characters were a thing we wanted more of. I don't know when exactly this changed, or when we finally as (especially female) writers decided we were going to take back adult fantasy and push it further than it's ever been pushed. But I am grateful for whomever started it. Thank you.

From the beginning of this journey, I had the support of my family. Most especially from my sister, who was the only person who understood when I would say 'my characters aren't talking to me' or 'my characters are making me crazy'. I still feel crazy saying it sometimes, but she always understood, and I cannot express how grateful I am for that push to get these stories out of my head. To my sister, all of these books are for you. I hope you know how much I appreciate and love you.

For the rest of my family, I cannot thank them enough for their unwavering support through this entire process and really through my whole life. Even with every mistake and crazy decision I've ever made, they've always been there supporting me. I love you guys and I know I would not be where I am today without that constant support and backbone.

To Zach, thank you for being there and giving me the time and space to figure this all out. I know how much of a journey this last year has been for both of us, and I appreciate your support when I just decided I was going to do this and you didn't question it. I love you and I am excited to be taking this journey with you.

Something else I didn't expect at the beginning of this process was the amount of support I would receive as an indie author from the fantasy community. I did not expect the amount of beta readers I would receive from a single booktok video. I did not expect the amount of people wanting to read this story from a single quote. I think I just didn't expect any of this.

So to my beta readers, thank you for taking that plunge with me into a world you had no knowledge of before hand except for photos, quotes, and an inspo board. Thank you for all of your feedback and gracious comments. You all truly helped me see I had a story worth getting out there. I don't know how I will ever repay all of you for helping me out, but I am so grateful for each and every one of you.

To my ARC readers and everyone who has supported me from day one that I started my marketing on TikTok, thank you! I don't know how I was lucky enough to find a group of like-minded people willing to take a chance on this, but here we are! Everyone who read an ARC and reviewed, did cosplays, helped me out in any way, you all are rockstars and thank you so so so much! For all those on booktok who duet'ed my videos, constantly commented and shared, making sure the word got out and helped me, thank you! I don't know that I would be publishing had you all not been so fantastic.

To Leighann, you were the first person to fangirl over my story and I have not forgotten how much support you've given me from the beginning. I hope to one day return that support when you finish and publish your book.

To Kay… KAY! I still remember our initial conversations where I just decided to throw you a beta copy of DMR because you loved the chapters with Draven, even though you weren't sure if you would be able to beta read it. I didn't care. You liked Draven, so I, of course, was like here—take him! I cannot thank you enough for how much you've helped me these last few months. With everything. Really. I'm pretty sure I would have released on the wrong day with a terrible cover had you not been there to tell me to reconsider. Or completely flopped when it came to Insta marketing. Your help with this has been invaluable. I appreciate you so so much, and I hope you know that. One day, you'll be bossing me around, telling me deadlines, and helping me keep my head on straight, and hopefully I'll be able to repay this debt! Thank you.

To everyone I missed-- friends, readers, and everyone in between... Everyone who took a chance on me with knowing nothing more about this book than the aesthetic boards and a few quotes. I am eternally in your debt. I appreciate you all so much.

Thank you for helping me burn the kingdom.

Go out and channel your inner Aydra.

We'll meet back here when the Red Moons Rise.

9 780578 307770